# Cityscape

## A Novel

Andrew Noles

Cover Photograph by Kelly Gordon

For all the people who've made up my cityscape over the years… there are way too many to name, but please know that you have all played a part in my story and I couldn't have done this without you.

# CITYSCAPE

# NIGHTLIFE

*Tyler*

He stands on the other side of the room looking away, his white shirt sticking out from the colors around him. For Tyler Welik, it feels like time stops. Though they are surrounded by people, he can't take his eyes off of him. Everything, from the brick walls to the music that fills the room, sets the stage for this one perfect moment.

Tyler calls for him, but no sound comes out. His words drown in a sea of conversation, every whisper growing to a shout as it runs across the ceiling. He tries to yell again before walking toward the boy, but his feet drag.

A foreign noise, a blaring note, suddenly tears through the mass of people, but no one seems to notice. The crowd thickens as the boy starts to walk away. More people crowd Tyler's line of vision as the noise, a song, pierces his ears, but again no one else pays it any attention. He calls out, his voice straining over the chaos, but the boy is gone.

Tyler wakes up with a jolt, the sunlight streaming through the windows of his loft a reminder that he once again forgot to close the curtains when he got home. His phone rings again and he reaches for it, Jade's smiling face on the screen. He'd been having that dream about Pete again.

*Why is she calling me at... oh crap, it's already noon?* he thinks, glancing towards the clock on the dresser. Clearing his throat, he holds the phone to his face.

"Hello?"

"Took you long enough."

"Hey."

"I woke you up, didn't I?"

"Yeah, but it's cool, I needed to get up," Tyler mumbles. "I have to be at work in a few hours anyway."

"Yeah… I go in at four."

"Me too. Do you know if Chelle's working today?"

"I don't think so. Why?"

"Oh, I wanted to ask her about something," says Tyler, with a yawn. "I'll just shoot her a text later."

"Okay," Jade says. "Sorry we didn't get to meet up, by the way. Last night didn't turn… well, things didn't go quite as I'd planned."

"I heard you were in some kind of trouble," Tyler says, yawning again as he looks around the room, noticing the black masquerade mask casually tossed onto a pile of clothes. His eyes land on a napkin he left on his dresser, a phone number carefully written on it in blue ink. He smiles to himself. "That sucks you missed Underland though. That place was pretty wild."

"So I've heard."

"I guess I'll just have to go again and take you with me next time…"

"I'm in."

"So wait, what went down last night?"

* * *

*Jade*

Twenty six hours before she wakes up Tyler with a phone call, it's Friday morning and Jade Verrit flops down on her couch, her cell phone on speaker. She should have started getting ready for work ten minutes ago, but she's been placed on hold again. The jazz pouring out of her phone is doing little to save her quickly souring mood. Pulling her light brown hair behind her ear, she starts to massage her temples. She stares at the pile of papers and envelopes on the couch next to her, a faraway look in her eyes. Losing patience with the bank, she ends the call and pulls the cluttered coffee table closer to her, opening her laptop.

She signs onto her neighbor's internet and logs into her bank account only to find that the situation is as bad as she had been afraid of. She has yet to pay the rent from last week and with bills due for her cell phone and car repairs, as well as a student loan payment due to be taken out on Monday, she doesn't have enough to cover

2

everything. Her next paycheck won't be deposited until Thursday.

*Good luck getting your monthly $110 from an account with twenty bucks in it,* she thinks bitterly. Sometimes, she wished she had been able to stay in school, if only to avoid having to repay the loans.

"All these damn bills," she says aloud. Putting her fingers on the bridge of her nose, she closes her eyes in an attempt to stop the stress headache she feels forming behind them. She swore it wouldn't happen again, but here she is, slowly descending into a pit of money woes. If only her phone hadn't been stolen or maybe if her brakes didn't need to be replaced, she wouldn't have dipped so dangerously low with her finances.

*Can't change any of it now,* she thinks, fighting back tears. She sighs deeply, coming to terms with the idea she's been trying to talk herself out of all morning.

She reaches for the end table, pulling a stack of photos out of the drawer. Flipping through them, she finds the one she's looking for. The photo shows Jade, a little over a year ago, sitting on the lap of a man who looks to be years older than he actually is. He has a faint smile, his eyes glazed over; she holds a beer. She turns the picture over and finds what she's looking for – a phone number scribbled in ink. The man's name is Mike Aubold, a name Jade could never forget, even if she could never remember his number. And Mike is not someone she wants to keep in her cell phone.

It's the last thing she wants to admit, but she needs his help.

* * *

"Oh, c'mon, Chelle – it's just for tonight!"

"Absolutely not! You and I both know what an awful idea this is!" says Chelle Mastens, Jade's best friend and co-worker. The two waitresses are in the kitchen at Caramaya's Bar and Grille, discussing the phone call Jade had made earlier in the day. "Why don't you ask Tyler? You know he could spot you some ca-"

"No, Chelle," interrupts Jade. "I'm not asking any of you to bail me out of this. I got into this mess; I'm going to get out. This is going to tide me over until next week's payday. And I've only got two more payments left on my brakes. Once that's paid off, I can start saving up money again. It's just been a little tight lately is all."

Chelle sighs.

"Order's up, Jade," says Kevin Mackenzie, one of the line cooks.

"Thanks Mack," Jade replies, loading three plates of food onto a tray. "Tonight will put enough in my account to cover for Monday and this month's rent. And the phone bill. I'll have to be a few days late on the car payment, but it'll work out with next pay period."

On her way to the front of the house, Jade stops and looks over her shoulder.

"It's no big deal," she says. "It's just like running an errand."

She walks through the doors, leaving Chelle standing in the kitchen with Mack.

"She's a big girl, Chelle."

"You don't know what Mike's capable of…"

"She'll be fine."

"I guess," says Chelle, conceding to Mack's point. "But to make sure, we're going with her."

\* \* \*

Later in her shift, Jade sits in a booth rolling silverware by herself. She has gone over the conversation from earlier today again and again in her head.

"Well, well well…" is how Mike had answered the phone, making Jade cringe. She tried as quickly as she could to explain her predicament to him. True to form, he didn't care too much for the story. Mike Aubold is a busy man, especially when it comes to his business.

"Alright, Jade," he'd said. "I can help you out. Give me this afternoon to… collect a few things and I'll be in touch."

"Thanks, Mike," she'd said quietly. There was an uncomfortable silence.

"I think about you sometimes."

*Click.*

That was almost six hours ago and she has not heard from him yet.

*Will he come through? What if he doesn't?* she sat there thinking. *I'll figure something out but damn, this was going to take care of everything… Chelle's not happy I called him and neither is Tyler, but their situations are different. Not better, exactly, but different.*

Jade finishes a set of silverware and looks around the restaurant. Tyler is pouring a drink, Chelle is delivering a tray of waters to a table.

*He has my number now, why hasn't he called? Or texted? Seriously, how long does it take to send a text?* Lost in her thoughts, Jade mindlessly rolls set after set of silverware into red napkins.

"Mind if I join you?"

She looks up, snapping out of the scenarios flying in her head.

"Hello, Mike," she says. "Sit down."

"It's good to see you, Jade," he says, sliding across the table from her. His cropped hair is darker than she remembers, the lines on his face a little deeper. His leather jacket creaks as he folds his arms on the table. "I'm glad you know you can come to me."

She doesn't say anything.

"How's your arm?"

"It healed a long time ago. Good as new."

"Well that's good... So! Desperate times, huh?" He leans back in the booth, folding his arms again. His carefree attitude sets Jade on edge. "I mean, they must be if you had to call me."

"Something like that... did you think about it?"

"I did. And I've got a good one for you. Let me tell you, honey, your timing is perfect. Tonight's one of my biggest jobs of the fall and it's all yours."

"What do I have to do?"

"Just deliver some party favors."

Jade knows that the 'party favors' are likely to get her arrested should she be caught. But, as Mike had said, these were desperate times.

"What kinds of 'party favors'?"

"Just a few things of the herbal and pharmaceutical variety."

"Where?"

"Out in the 'burbs..."

"When?"

"Christ, Jade," he blurts out, his mood suddenly darkening as he pounds his fists on the table. "I didn't know we were playing twenty-fucking-questions! What time do you get off?"

"Sorry," she says quickly, looking around to see if anyone noticed Mike's outburst. "Supposed to be ten, probably earlier if we stay slow."

"Good," he says evenly. "Shoot me a text when you're about to get off and we'll meet up. I'm not letting my merchandise sit around this place."

"Yeah, that's probably a good idea. So, how much were yo-"

"Five hundred and fifty," he says bluntly. "You get this done for me, I give you five hundred and fifty dollars."

"I thought the number we discussed was a little higher than that?" she asks.

"You get this done, you get five fifty," he repeats with a dangerous grin. "You get this done *well*, and maybe with some extra work, there could be a bonus in it for you."

She tries to hide her disgust as he winks at her.

"Alright Jade, I'm out of here. Hit me up when you're off." He stands and straightens his jacket, running his fingers through his hair. Before he walks away he looks down at her from where he stands.

"You look good, by the way."

She looks at him with a forced smile.

"Thank you."

\* \* \*

Across the restaurant, Chelle stops at the bar. Tyler stands behind the counter drying a tray of glasses, his blonde hair pulled into a short ponytail.

"Did you see who Jade's with?" she asks.

"Sure did," he says, rolling his eyes.

"I can't believe she'd go back to him, after everything he did."

Tyler finishes drying a tumbler and puts it on the shelf.

"I know," he says. "But you know Jade as well as I do. She's going to take care of herself in her own way."

"I know, but someone's gotta make sure she doesn't get herself killed in the process." She pauses. "Mack and I are going with her."

"Does she know that?"

"Not yet," says Chelle, looking back toward the bar. "But she'll get over it soon enough."

"See, Chel? You've got things figured out," says Tyler. "Now, what's up for tonight?"

"Oh!" she says. "Is everyone still going to Underland?"

"A club that used to be a railway station and I get to wear the black light makeup I bought today? Is that even a question?"

"This place has *you* written all over it," Chelle says, smiling. "Simon sounded like he didn't want to go, but I talked him into it. Phin and Carrie are still coming, right?"

"Last I talked to Phin, yeah, he was planning on it."

"Awesome – so while I'm out making sure Jade doesn't get herself killed, you two go put in some face time with your parents and then we can all meet downtown!"

"Sounds like a plan," says Tyler.

"Oh, and Simon's still bringing his hot friend, you know, the one I was telling you about?"

"You guys are too good to me," Tyler says with a grin.

Chelle looks back towards Jade, who is once again by herself rolling silverware. She catches a glimpse of Mike walking out of the restaurant.

"Alright," says Chelle. "Time to go back to work. I'll stop by later."

\* \* \*

Two hours later when Jade gets cut, she whips out her phone and texts Mike.

"*I'll be out in 15.*"

As she's pulling on her coat, Chelle walks up behind her.

"We're coming with you," she says. "Mack and I, I mean."

"No you're not," says Jade.

"Yes we are, Jade, and you're not going to stop us. We're your friends. We care about you. If you won't let us help you, at least let us be there... for moral support."

Jade sighs.

"Fine. But wait for me out back. I've got to get it from him first."

"He didn't leave it with you?"

"C'mon, Chel – you know him better than that."

"And you know better than this."

"Spare me the lecture, okay? I can still leave you here."

"Alright," says Chelle. "I just don't want you to get hurt."

"I appreciate that, really I do. But I'm a big girl and I got myself into a mess that I'm going to get myself out of." Jade's phone vibrates. "This is him. If you two are really tagging along, be out back in fifteen minutes."

\* \* \*

As she walks through the front doors of Caramaya's Bar and Grille, Jade immediately sees Mike's beat-up car.

*He's got more money than God, but he still drives that piece of shit?* she thinks, approaching his passenger door, which squeaks as she gets in.

"Want a smoke?" he asks, playing with a cigarette between his fingers.

"No thanks," she mumbles.

"Suit yourself," he says, a cloud of smoke escaping past his lips. "How was work?"

"It was alright," she says. "Slow."

They sit in silence for a moment.

"So what the fuck, Jade?"

"Huh?"

"What the fuck? I don't hear from you for forever then you call me up out of the blue asking for a job?"

"I told you - "

"I don't give a shit about your sob story." She looks at him, feeling the tension in the car rise. "What's your angle?"

Mike starts breathing faster.

"My what?"

Mike snaps and pounds his fists on the steering wheel.

"Your angle, Jade?! What is it?!"

"Mike, I-I," she says. "I don't know w-wha – "

"Are you working for the cops? Are you fucking wired right now?!" He reaches for her throat and stops himself when she lets out a scream. He takes a deep breath and runs his fingers through his hair.

"Don't you *ever* fucking try that again," Jade says, an edge of menace in her voice. "And no, I'm not working with the cops and I'm sure as hell not fucking wired. I needed your help. And if that's too much to ask, then I'm done here." She reaches for the door handle.

With one last inhale, Mike tosses his cigarette out of the window.

"Wait."

"What?"

"I'm sorry. I just gotta look out for myself, you know baby?"

"Don't call me baby."

"Fair enough," he says. "Here." He hands her a small brown paper bag and a note with an address scribbled on it. "It's a nice little stash, a few pills, some weed. Nothing huge, just some rich fucker trying to liven up his party. You drop this off, get the money and bring it back to my place. We'll call it a night."

"Fine," she says, taking the bag and stuffing it in her purse, thinking that the address looks vaguely familiar. "I'll let you know when I'm on my way back."

Jade tosses her hair as she steps out of the car.

Mike stops her before she walks away.

"I meant what I said earlier... you look good."

* * *

Ten minutes later, Jade pulls her car around to the back of Caramaya's so Chelle and Mack can get in.

"How'd it go?" Chelle asks.

"There's not much to talk about, Chel. I got in, got the stuff and got out. Now we just drop it off, get the cash and take it back. Then I need a drink." Mack nods in agreement.

"Here," says Jade, handing Mack the address. "My battery's low, will you put this in your phone? Tell me where I'm going."

As Mack enters the address, Chelle sees the look on Jade's face.

"Why is your face red?"

"I'm nervous, okay?"

"Did he do something to you?"

"What? No, of course not."

"What happened in that ca – "

"Leave it alone, Chelle," Jade yells. "I took care of it."

"What, does he have to break your arm again before you realize how dangerous he can be?"

"He didn't break my arm."

"That's not how I remember it," Chelle says quietly.

"My arm broke when we were in an accident. It was raining and he lost control of the car."

"I know that's the story, Jade, but – "

"Uhh, excuse me ladies," interrupts Mack. "Are you sure this is the right address?"

"Yeah, why?" asks Jade.

"Um, well, this says we're heading out to Bay Ridge."

"What?" asks Chelle, clearly surprised.

"Yeah, he said it was some rich guy," says Jade. "Let's head out."

\* \* \*

Chelle and Mack make idle talk about work as Jade drives toward Bay Ridge, one of the more affluent suburbs of the city. They talk about who is hooking up with whom, how bad their manager is at being a manager, and how some lady was hitting on Tyler tonight. Jade hears none of this, thinking only about the car accident that left her with a broken arm last year.

It was a rainy night in August; Mike was a little buzzed and they had both been smoking. This was before he had people working for him; he had to run a delivery himself. They found themselves on the wrong side of the East Bridge and before they knew what was happening, gunfire erupted around them. Jade had never been more terrified in her life.

As they sped away, Mike lost control of the car and slammed into the median. Miraculously, neither of them was seriously hurt, aside from Jade's injuries. When the cops came, she feigned ignorance as Mike told them that they were out for a drive and got turned around in the rain, and that was how they wound up in the middle of the gunfight. They were transported to St. Sebastian's Hospital and that was that. The crash was officially reported as an accident, a product of the rain and a panicked driver attempting to stay out of the range of fire. No charges, no trouble.

But Jade's friends knew what had really gone on that night. They had watched her spirit crumble away bit by bit for as long as she had been with Mike. And even though that night was the beginning of the end for their relationship, the greater damage was already done. From that night on, people began to worry about Jade. They would constantly ask if she was okay, if she needed help. Her brother, Luke, stopped calling just to talk. No one trusted her anymore.

"Jade!" yells Chelle.

"What, oh sorry," she says. "I was just thinking."

"Well, I'm not trying to be whatever, but what's wrong with your car?"

"Huh?"

"Yeah," says Mack from the backseat. "Your dashboard is going dim."

"And I don't want to freak you out, but your speedometer is at zero," says Chelle, slightly panicked. "And we're still driving."

Jade looks from Chelle in the passenger seat to the road to her flickering dashboard.

"Fuck."

* * *

Jade is able to pull off the highway and into a gas station before her car completely dies. The three friends sit in the car trying to decide what to do.

"Do you want me to call Tyler?" asks Mack.

"No," says Jade, trying to stay calm. "He's getting ready for that thing at his parents' house."

"Don't they still live in Bay Ridge?" asks Chelle. "He's probably on his way out here right now."

"Don't call Tyler," says Jade.

"I'll call Simon," says Chelle.

"And make him drive all the way out here?" asks Jade. "No. Don't do that."

"Well what do you want us to do?" asks Chelle.

Jade notices the bus stop at the gas station.

"Tell you what," she says. "Why don't you two grab a bus and get on with your night." Chelle starts to protest, but Jade stops her.

"This is my mess, Chel. You two have done enough and look — we're out in Bay Ridge, when was the last time this area was on the news for a crime worse than insider trading? I'll be fine."

Chelle looks at Mack. He nods.

"Alright, Jade," he says. "Call us if anything comes up, okay?"

"You got it. I'm gonna call for a jump and I'll get this business taken care of and I'll meet up with you guys in a few hours." She gestures toward a bus that is approaching the station.

"Alright, but please be careful," says Chelle.

"I'll be fine," says Jade.

Chelle and Mack get out of the car and walk to the bus stop.

"I don't like this," says Chelle as she swipes her transit card. Chelle and Mack board the bus and take their seats; the doors close and the bus drives away.

Back in the parking lot, Jade gets out and opens the hood of her car. She gets out her phone to call for help and as she dials, the battery dies.

"Perfect," she says, her lower lip quivering. She tries very hard not to cry as she exhales. She sits on the curb and buries her face in her hands.

"What am I going to do?" she whispers slowly to herself. People walk by, they look but no one offers help.

"What am I going to do?" she asks again.

A handsome guy in his mid-20s walks out of the gas station and sees Jade.

"Excuse me," he says. "Do you need some help?"

She looks up at him, tears in her eyes.

He smiles at her.

"Hi," he says. "I'm Bobby."

* * *

*Bobby*

When he was 16, a family friend described Bobby Glachome as being magnetically enigmatic, an idea he continues to perpetuate even now in his mid-20's. The co-founder of a relatively small but exceptionally lucrative multi-media company, he finds himself living in a style rarely afforded to his contemporaries. He has never taken his good fortunes for granted, however, an attribute that those who knew him before his success find particularly endearing.

An hour before Jade Verrit flops down on her couch across town, Bobby finds himself walking on autopilot toward the event space on Peridot between 11th and 12th where his company will be hosting the launch of a new project, a web series. He is absentmindedly sipping his beverage of choice from Café et Gâteries (large hazelnut mocha with an extra shot, easy on the foam), his eyes shielded from the other pedestrians by mirrored sunglasses.

While stopped at a crosswalk, he notices a shop that has opened across the corner called Midway Costume Supply.

*A costume shop,* he thinks. Taking a gulp of his coffee, he has an idea. *They don't need me there just yet. I'm gonna check this place out.*

Walking into the store, Bobby is greeted by a perky teenager who looks up from her phone with a smile. Her handwritten nametag reads 'Lexie'.

"Welcome to Midway Costume Supply!" she says.

"Hello," he says casually, tucking his sunglasses into the inside pocket of his leather jacket. He heads for the aisles filled with accessories and props. As he's looking at the price of some police shades, two blonde guys walk by, one with spiked hair and the other with his hair pulled into a short ponytail.

*They have the same nose,* Bobby thinks. *I bet they're brothers.*

"How long do we have to stay tonight?" he hears the one with the spiked hair ask. "I promised Carrie we'd be there by eleven."

"Seriously, Phin, we're just putting in an appearance then we're getting the hell out," says the other.

"Well you know how they get with these stupid parties. It's like we're still little kids to them or something. I mean, it's bad enough they're making Cody go."

"Cody lives there," says the blonde one, looking at masquerade masks. He looks at the price tag and approves with a nod. "And I think he's off school today, too. He said something about helping them get ready when I talked to him the other day. I don't know why you're making such a big deal out of the Halloween Ball this yea-"

"Freeze, bitch," says Phin, picking up a plastic rifle and aiming it at his brother who starts to laugh but then rolls his eyes.

"Seriously, if you didn't want my help, why am I here?"

"You're no fun," says Phin, putting the gun down. The two wander out of the aisle as Bobby smiles to himself.

*Yup, they're brothers,* he thinks. He picks up a fake pistol but puts it back on its peg hanger after looking at the price. *Sometimes I wish I wasn't an only child.*

After looking around, Bobby decides to purchase the cheap aviators, along with a cop hat and badge set that comes with a baton as well.

*You never know when things like this could come in handy,* he thinks.

He stands in line behind the brothers from earlier as they check out. It looks like the one settled on a cowboy costume while the other is just getting a neon colored makeup palette.

*Interesting choices,* thinks Bobby. *I wonder what happened to the mask.*

"Next," says Lexie.

Bobby steps up to the counter.

"Did you find everything alright?"

"I did," he says. "Thank you." They finish the transaction and Bobby steps out into the sunshine. For a moment he considers going back in and attempting to recruit Lexie to model for his company, but then decides that she is probably still in high school.

*She would have made a great addition to the roster,* he thinks. His train of thought shifts when he notices he has several texts asking why he's not on site yet.

He hails a cab to get over to Peridot quicker.

\* \* \*

After a successful event, the first thing on Bobby's mind is stopping for a fountain soda and taquitos on the way to the after party at a house in the suburbs. It is this fleeting thought that leads him to the same gas station where Jade Verrit's car has broken down. Walking out of the gas station, he sees her sitting hunched on the curb, her face in her hands. Always chivalrous, he approaches her.

"Excuse me," he asks. "Do you need some help?"

She looks up at him, tears in her eyes. He smiles at her.

"Hi," he says. "I'm Bobby."

"Jade," she says with a sniffle. "And I swear I'm not helpless, I just... I don't know what to do."

He sits down next to her.

"Well, let's start with the car. I can't help but notice your hood's up... what's going on?"

"I don't even know," she says. "I'm still paying off the new brakes and the damn thing just broke down. I was driving out here with two of my friends and it started acting up and the speedometer was at zero and we were still moving and I didn't know what to do so I got off the highway and came here but then it just *died* and I didn't want to ruin their night so I sent them back."

She pauses to take a breath.

"And then my phone died, too."

"Jesus, you're having a Friday," Bobby says.

"You could say that." Jade wipes her eyes and tries to smile.

"Lucky for you, I'm here," Bobby says with a grin.

"And who are you, my guardian angel? Because right now, I think I'd be better off with a mechanic."

"I'm no angel," Bobby says, laughing. "But I do know a thing or two about cars. And my uncle's a mechanic." Bobby jumps up to take a look at the motor.

"Go ahead and get back in the driver's seat," he says. "I want to try something."

Over the next half hour, Bobby tests out a few things with Jade's car and eventually gets it running again with a jump. He closes the hood, brushing off his hands.

"You want my honest opinion?" he asks.

"That depends on how much it's going to cost me."

"Sounds like it's your alternator," says Bobby. "You'll need to have it replaced."

"Great," says Jade, sighing. "Just what I need."

Bobby looks at her, a plan coming together in his mind.

"You know, I could call my uncle for you?" he says. "We could have him take a look at your car and if it needs to stay there, I can take you wherever you were heading. I'm sure he'd cut you a deal better than anywhere else if it needs work."

Jade hesitates.

"Seriously, are you my guardian angel?"

Bobby laughs.

"I told you, I'm no angel. But I'm not gonna leave you now. You just needed a little help and I'm happy to offer it."

Jade Verrit can be an especially stubborn young woman, but she is not so headstrong as to ignore when a helping hand she desperately needs is being extended.

"You sure about this?"

"Definitely!"

"Alright," she says. "I'll follow you there."

* * *

Jade follows Bobby to his Uncle Rudy's body shop. Uncle Rudy meets them there and gives Jade's car a quick inspection. After talking with him, Jade feels comfortable leaving her car there to have the repairs made. She cannot believe how quickly her luck turned around after meeting Bobby; now if only she could get her phone charged to call Chelle.

That's when Jade remembers she still has an errand to run.

"Bay Ridge?" Bobby asks when Jade tells him the address.

"Yeah," she says. "I just have to drop something off. Then I can catch a bus back to the — "

"You don't have to catch a bus anywhere," he says. "I'll take you wherever you want to go."

"Alright then."

Bobby enters the address into his GPS.

"Calculating," says the computerized female voice.

"Thank you, Carol," says Bobby. "I call her 'Carol'."

Jade laughs.

"Doesn't everyone name their GPS?"

"I wouldn't know," Jade says, immediately realizing how rude the remark sounded. She furrows her brow, hoping he didn't take it that way.

"Yeah," says Bobby as the two start driving. They ride in silence for a few minutes. Though Bobby and Jade feel relatively comfortable around each other, especially for having just met, there is still a feeling of awkwardness between them. Bobby turns on the radio to break the silence, but quickly regrets the decision when there is nothing playing except commercials and a report about a fire at the Southside Pier. He turns the radio off.

They ride in silence for a few more minutes and then both decide to talk at the same time.

"So what do you – "

"What else was – "

They laugh awkwardly.

"You go first," he says.

"I was just gonna ask what else you were up to tonight, other than, you know, being my knight in shining armor."

"This was it, really," he says. "I had an event earlier, that's what I do – I help run special events for a multi-media company, and I was just heading home for the night. Felt like a taquito and boom – there you were."

"Wow," she responds. "I would have felt bad if I'd ruined your plans for tonight." She pauses. "I hate this."

"Hate what?"

"This helplessness. I mean, I know I'm not *completely* helpless, but it's like, it's all I can do to stay afloat, you know? You get hit with this, that, this again and there's no time to regroup. How do other people do it? I mean, I know it's sink or swim but how can you swim when everything comes at once and won't stop…"

"…you get thrown a life vest." Bobby glances at Jade and grins. She smiles back as they exit the highway in Bay Ridge.

"Nice houses," Bobby says a few minutes later as they turn into a neighborhood.

"Yeah," says Jade. "I just have to drop something off at a party."

"Okay," says Bobby. "So tell me about your friends, the two you sent back."

"Chelle and Mack?" asks Jade. "They're great, I mean, they're there for me, you know? We all work at Caramaya's Bar and Grille downtown. Chelle and I are servers and Mack works in the kitchen. He's really chill, just kinda goes with the flow. Everyone loves him. Sometimes Chelle can be overbearing, but I know she means well." She pauses. "She's probably called my phone about a hundred times by now."

"Do you want me to get you a charger?"

"What? Oh, no – you don't have to do that! You've done so much for me already!"

"Well let me know, I'm sure I can drum something up."

Jade smiles at him.

"So you work in special events?"

"Yeah, I – " Bobby's answer is interrupted by Carol the GPS, who informs them that they are arriving at their destination on the right.

When Jade sees the house, her heartbeat increases and she feels dizzy.

"This is it?" she asks, trying to keep her voice even.

"Yup, looks like," says Bobby. "Everything alright?"

Jade suddenly realizes why the address sounded familiar. She had only been here once before and while the address may have slipped from her memory, a house like this is not easily forgotten.

Bobby parks in front of the house where Tyler and Phin Welik's parents live.

* * *

Twenty minutes later, Jade is sitting in Bobby's front seat listening to the radio as she tries to decide what to do. She had come up with a story on the spot about how she'd seen her ex's car in the driveway and asked Bobby to circle the block a few times. She stares out of the window, lost in her own thoughts.

"So what's up with this guy?" he finally asks, breaking the silence.

"Huh?" replies Jade, snapping out of her daze. "He, uhh... he's trouble."

"And that's his house?"

"Yeah... no, sorry, I guess he's just there. Shit. I need to call Chelle."

"Here, use my phone."

Bobby grabs his cell phone out of the cup holder and offers it to

Jade.

"This is going to sound ridiculous, but I don't actually know her number by heart," she says, motioning for Bobby to put his phone down.

"Hey, happens to me all the time," he says, trying to be understanding. Bobby realizes something more is going on that Jade is not telling him about, and he doesn't fully believe it has to do with a bad ex.

"I could go in with you?" he offers.

"No, that's okay…" Jade trails off. "I guess let's go back, I just gotta drop this stuff off."

"You got it."

"I'm sorry, Bobby. I know you were just trying to help me out, I didn't mean to put you in a situation like this, I – "

Jade doesn't get a chance to finish her sentence. At that exact moment, the cop that had been following them for some time decides to put on his lights and pull them over.

*Shit,* Bobby thinks. *What's the speed limit out here? Was I even speeding?*

The only thought in Jade's head revolves around the drugs in her purse.

Bobby turns down the radio and rolls down his window as the cop walks up alongside his car.

"Good evening, officer," he says.

"You folks in a hurry?"

"Not exactly."

"I watched you blow three stop signs in the last few minutes, pal."

"I did?" Bobby asks, genuinely surprised. "I'm sorry about that, officer. We're not from around here."

"Then what are you doing out here?"

"We were just heading to a party and got lost."

"License and registration, please," the cop says. "And I want to see her ID, too." Jade turns to look toward the officer, the beam from his flashlight shining into the car. She reaches down for her purse and dips her hand in, her fingers brushing the bag of drugs as she feels for her wallet. She smiles nervously.

"Come on, Jade, where's your ID?" asks Bobby.

"J-just a second," she says, her fingers finally finding her wallet. She's worried she's taking too long. She pulls it out, leaving her purse on the floor, hoping the cop didn't hear the crinkle of the paper bag. She opens her wallet and slides out her driver's license with trembling fingers.

"Here you go."

The cop takes their information and walks back to his car.

"What was that about?" asks Bobby, his face illuminated by the spotlight from the police car behind them. He rolls up the window.

"I just get nervous around cops." They sit in silence. Jade tries to subtly sniff the air to see if she can smell the weed in her purse.

*Is she sniffing my car?* Bobby thinks. *I didn't think it smelled that bad in here...* He tries to hide an incredulous look from her in an attempt to give her the benefit of the doubt. Bobby turns on the radio, hoping for music but only hearing commercials. He quickly turns it off. After another minute, the silence has become unbearable.

"Is something wrong?" asks Bobby. "I mean, I know tonight's been kind of crazy all around, but... are you okay?"

"Yeah, I'm fine."

*No, you're clearly not.*

"You've been acting different since we drove by that house. Do you not want to go to your party? I can take you anywhere else, you know. I don't mind, really."

"It's not that, Bobby."

"Is it the ex? Because I'm not gonna start anything with him. I mean, hell, you and I just met. I don't even have to go in! I will if you want me to, but-"

"No," she says, a faint smile sneaking across her mouth.

*Who is this girl?* he thinks. *What is her story? I know there's more going on here than a party or an ex-boyfriend... after this jerk lets us go, I'm gonna find out. I want to make sure she's alright. She seems nice enough, a little high strung, but I can handle that. She's gorgeous and such a pretty girl shouldn't have so much on her mind... definitely girlfriend material... Wait, what am I thinking? I just met this girl tonight! I –*

Jade opens her mouth to say something when the cop walks back to the car and knocks on the window.

"I'm letting you two off with a warning," he says, handing Bobby their ID's. "Just do me a favor and obey the road signs, okay?"

"Alright, sir," says Bobby. "Thank you."

The cop walks back to his car; Bobby drives off.

"That was close, huh?" he says to Jade.

"Yeah," she says nervously, looking out the window.

They ride in silence until Bobby slows to a stop at a red light. He turns to face Jade.

"Do you wanna tell me what's in your purse?" he asks.

Jade snaps her head around to face him.

"We've come this far," he says. "I'm not gonna leave you now."

* * *

*Phin*

"Freeze, bitch," says Phin Welik, aiming a plastic rifle at his brother, Tyler. The two are at Midway Costume Supply in search of last minute costume ideas for their parents' annual Halloween Ball tonight.

"Seriously, if you didn't want my help, why am I here?" asks Tyler. Out of the corner of his eye, he notices someone else standing in the aisle with them looking at costume props. He rolls his eyes at his brother.

"You're no fun," says Phin, putting the gun down. He looks at a few of the other props on the shelves in front of him and then notices that Tyler has wandered into another aisle.

"Hey, what about this?" Phin calls after him, grabbing a sword off the shelf.

"Jesus, Phin, what's with you and the weapons?"

"What?" he asks in a tone of phony innocence. "Ever since we were kids, you always said I needed to accessorize!"

"Oh, shut up," Tyler says, playfully. Phin sets the sword down and the brothers continue shopping. They walk into an aisle containing mostly masks and wigs.

"Going the masquerade route again, huh?"

"You could say that," says Tyler. "I already have a mask though."

"So what are we doing here? I thought I was the one who needed a costume."

"Give me a sec, you never know what you'll find." Tyler takes an ornate masquerade mask off its display peg. The mask is brown with gold trim, a gold leaf design painted across the left eye.

"Alright, I'm gonna move on," says Phin. "Catch up when you're done drooling over these masks." Phin walks on, eyeing an assortment of costumes in bags.

*I can't believe we still have to go to this thing,* he thinks. *And that I have to get a damn costume. I wonder what Carrie's doing? She's lucky she doesn't get off work til later... just in time to meet up – that worked out real nice.* Phin is absentmindedly running his hands over the various costumes stuffed into bags on the shelf, passing on Airman, Firefighter and Ghoul before settling on Cowboy.

"This will work," he says aloud.

"You're going as a cowboy?" asks Tyler, walking up from behind.

19

"Why not? It's a classic."

"I can get behind that."

"Where's the mask?"

"I liked that one, but I'm still gonna go with the one I got from that shop in Old Town, the new one. It matches my cape."

"You're ridiculous. What's that?" asks Phin, gesturing to the makeup palette in Tyler's hand as they walk toward the counter.

"Black light make up," he answers. "For tonight at Underland? You guys are still coming, right?"

"Oh yeah," Phin says. "Carrie's gonna meet us there. Is Chelle still bringing that guy?"

"Yeah, and Jade's coming. Maybe Mack too," says Tyler, putting the makeup on the counter. "Jade's friend Tara was maybe going to come, too, but she has to work.."

"Gotcha," says Phin.

The guy who was looking at costume props earlier gets in line behind them as the girl behind the counter, Lexie, starts to ring up their purchases.

"Awesome," says Phin, swiping his credit card. "You know I love a good party... just not the one our parents throw every Halloween."

\* \* \*

As he is adjusting his cowboy hat later that evening in his parents' dining room, Phin hears the clank of his mother's shoes in the hall, announcing her approach.

*Thank God they're not big on carpet,* he thinks, remembering a few times her arrival was preceded by the noise of her shoes on the marble floor, allowing him time to avoid being caught in a variety of compromising situations.

"Phin, darling, where's your brother?" asks Meredith Welik, waltzing into the room, her flapper dress and the feather attached to her headband dancing with movement. She is careful not to spill the drink that sloshes back and forth in her martini glass.

"I told you he'll be here after work," says Phin, pinning on a sheriff badge.

"Oh right," she says with a laugh. "Is Carrie coming?"

"Negative, she won't be off work til way late."

"Oh that's a shame," she says, sipping her drink. "I like that girl."

"Me too, that's why we're together," he says turning to his mother. "At least I hope it is... How do I look?"

"Everyone better watch out tonight," she says with a laugh. "There's a new sheriff in town!"

Phin rolls his eyes.

"Come on, Phinny, there are people I want you to meet."

\* \* \*

An hour later, Phin is relieved when he sees an ornate black cape swooping through the crowded room toward him, his brother Tyler hiding behind a black masquerade mask.

"Sheriff," Tyler says, with a nod.

"Phantom."

"I'm not a phantom!"

"Coulda fooled me – and half the room. They all keep asking for you."

"Didn't I tell Mom and Dad I'd be late?"

"Come on, you know how they are."

"True. Where's Cody?"

"Sir Lancelot? Last I saw him, he was in the kitchen with his little friends from school."

"Oh, nice. Hey, have you noticed this year's party seems a little… I don't know, it doesn't feel the same as before. Something's off."

"Yeah," says Phin. "It's boring. I want to leave."

"Come on," says Tyler, with a sigh. "Let's grab some food."

On their way to the kitchen, Phin starts to notice what Tyler is talking about. Whereas in years past there was a constant murmur of chatter with boisterous outbreaks of laughter, tonight the conversations are more subdued. The costumes, the music, even the atmosphere – it all feels forced.

*Is the annual Welik Halloween Ball a dying tradition?* thinks Phin. For as long as both Phin and Tyler can remember, their parents held a massive party each year around Halloween for their father's clients and business contacts. It was the one time each year all of these people would get together and mingle, unwind. The Welik Halloween Ball had become somewhat of a legend in various social circles throughout the city, but tonight, the spark that had for so many years invaded Phin's home and been the cause of great annoyance was nowhere to be found.

Tom Welik, their father, is staring out the kitchen window as Phin and Tyler walk in. Their younger brother, Cody, is perched at the island in the center of the kitchen, talking with a few of his friends.

"Everything okay, Dad?" asks Tyler.

"Hmm? Oh, Tyler. Glad you made it."

"Yeah," he says. "I told you and Mom both that I had to work tonight but I'd be over after."

"That's right, that's right…"

"Hey Dad, what's up with everyone tonight?" asks Phin.

"What do you mean?"

"I don't know, the ball just seems off this year."

"Well, hopefully more guests will arrive later," Tom says slowly. "One in particular. And I think I may take your mother's suggestion and bring back the acrobats in the backyard next year. Everyone loves a good show, don't they?"

Phin shoots a confused look over to Tyler who is eating off of a plate of hors d'oeuvres. Tyler rolls his eyes.

"Okay… hey I think we're gonna head out soon."

"Alright, sounds good. Make sure you tell your mother you're leaving. You two have a good time tonight, give my best to Carrie."

Phin nods.

"And Tyler, look after you brother," he says, looking back from the window.

* * *

An hour later, Phin and Tyler are walking downtown, the brisk autumn air causing Tyler's cape to swirl around his ankles. Tyler left the masquerade mask in his car, painting designs on both him and Phin's faces to prepare for the black light party at Underland.

"So what was that about at Mom and Dad's?" asks Tyler.

"I have no idea. Honestly, I didn't notice anything until you pointed it out, but once you did, I couldn't ignore how awful this year's party felt! Do you think something is wrong with Dad's business?"

"I don't think so, there were a ton of people back there. Maybe they just weren't drunk enough yet, I don't know."

Phin's phone lights up as it receives a text.

"Oh, it's Carrie! She's there already."

"We're only a block away. I should text Chelle and see where they're at."

"Who's that guy she's seeing? I never remember his name."

"She's still with Simon and he's bringing a co-worker of his named Alan."

"And what do we know about this Alan?"

"He's cute. And single. Not much more to say, there."

"You gonna try to get with him?"

"Hell, I don't know… maybe."

"What's Pete up to these days?"

Tyler snaps his head around to face his brother.

"Let's not talk about Pete."

"Oh, hey!" says Phin, suddenly. "We're here!"

The two join the crowd standing outside of Underland and look for any familiar faces. Underland had made quite a splash in the social scene earlier in the month when it had opened. Not many new clubs could boast that they were located in an abandoned railway station, a selling point that rocketed Underland to the top of the social scene. There was no club quite like it anywhere else.

"Phin!"

The brothers turn around to see Carrie Candelario emerge from the crowd, streaks of pale pink running through her platinum blonde hair, her slinky pink dress shimmering in the light emanating from the club.

"Hey baby," says Phin, pulling her into a quick kiss and holding her afterward.

"Hi Tyler! The black light makeup looks great!" she says.

"Thanks," he replies. "I just did it in the car, actually. Loving this look, by the way! Did you do the pink yourself?"

"I did!" she says, nestled behind Phin's left arm. "Do you really like it?"

"You look amazing!"

Tyler's phone vibrates.

"Looks like Chelle and the guys are already inside," he says.

"Let's go!" says Phin.

\* \* \*

As he walks down the staircase entrance to Underland, a path of neon rabbits painted on the walls leading the way, Phin feels his level of excitement rising. He has only seen photos of the recently opened club and if the entrance is any indication, he is in for a wild time. The further the three descend, the louder the music gets and the more the lights flash until finally they are standing on a balcony overlooking a massive dance floor with waves of people pulsating with the bass, all lit with black lights. There is a bar on the terrace and two more downstairs on either side of the dance floor. Exit signs glow throughout the complex.

"This is awesome!" Phin yells to no one in particular. Carrie can feel his excitement and smiles. Tyler leads them down another staircase, this one made of glass blocks that change colors with the beat. Waiting at the bottom are Chelle and her boyfriend, Simon Dawes, and his co-worker Alan.

"Chelle!" yells Tyler.

"Hey, boo!" she screams back, wrapping her arms around him. "You know Simon and this is Alan."

Alan smiles at Tyler. Simon looks bored.

"Nice to meet you!"

"Have you guys been here before?" Alan shouts over the music.

"No," answers Tyler. "But this place is amazing!" He looks around and notices the DJ's overlooking the crowd.

"Lead the way!" Tyler says, winking at Carrie and turning to follow Alan.

"So what are we waiting for?" asks Phin. "Let's dance!"

* * *

A little while later, a sweaty Tyler pulls Chelle aside to take a shot.

"So what happened with Jade?" he asks, standing at the bar.

Chelle rolls her eyes.

"That girl… well her car broke down and she sent me and Mack back to the city, said she'd let us know when she got home. I called her a few times but her phone's off. I'm guessing it's dead."

"Do you think?"

"Probably, knowing her luck lately… I don't want to hound her, you know, I just want to make sure she's okay."

"I know, especially knowing she was talking to Mike earlier today."

The bartender walks over with their lemon drops.

"To bad decisions!" shouts Chelle.

"To bad decisions with cute boys!" yells Tyler. They clink their glasses, tap them on the bar and take the shots.

One of the bar top dancers walks by, hears this and laughs. Chelle winks at her.

"I told you Alan was cute!"

"I know, I know," says Tyler, the two of them walking back to the dance floor. "Hey, where's Simon?"

"Being boring somewhere."

"What?"

"What? Nothing." Chelle winks at Tyler. "Let's find your brother!"

Tyler and Chelle move toward the dance floor and find Phin dancing with Carrie and Alan.

"Where's Simon?" Chelle yells out.

"He ran to grab a beer I think," answers Phin.

The tempo of the song starts to shift; a new song starts. Fog billows out of several strategically placed smoke machines. Carrie spins to face Phin. She smiles as he pulls her in for a kiss. Lights flash around them in time with the beat. Tyler and Alan move close, facing each other. Lasers cut through the fog, moving around the room. Alan places his hand on the small of Tyler's back. They smile.

Chelle checks her phone and looks around for Simon. She still hasn't heard from Jade. Simon finally returns with a beer in hand and she smiles weakly. When the song ends, two cannons at each end of the room shower the dance floor with confetti.

*What a night,* thinks Phin.

* * *

Later, Carrie and Alan run off to one of the bars for a secret shot while Simon and Chelle are still dancing. After a trip to the men's room, Tyler and Phin join the pair at the bar.

"I could probably get you on at the store," Alan says to Carrie.

"That would be awesome!" she yells, sipping a vodka tonic.

"I'll see what I can do," Alan says to her and then faces Tyler and Phin. "Now it's my turn. I'll be back!" He heads off in the direction of the bathrooms.

As Tyler orders another beer, Carrie gestures for Phin to come closer.

"I think they'd be really cute together!" she says into his ear. "Tyler and Alan."

Phin nods in agreement, taking a drink of his beer.

"At least get his mind off of Pete for a while," says Carrie.

Phin shoots her a look and jerks his head toward his brother. Luckily, the music completely drowns out their conversation and Tyler cannot hear a word.

Chelle walks up, digging through her purse.

"You guys, I have to go," she says. "I just got a text from Jade, she's in some kind of trouble and I have to pick her up. I don't know where Simon is, just tell him there was an emergency. He came with Alan so he'll be fine." She hugs Carrie and Phin goodbye.

"You better not leave here without Alan's number," she says into Tyler's ear after giving him a kiss on the cheek. He digs in his pocket a moment and pulls out a napkin with a number written on it in blue ink, grinning ear to ear.

"I love it!" she yells, walking away. Not long after that, Alan returns to the bar with Simon in tow.

"Alright you guys," yells Phin. "Grab your drinks and let's get back out there!"

\* \* \*

*Chelle*

The bus makes its way toward the gas station. Chelle looks at Mack. He nods. It's the last thing she wants to do, but if Chelle Mastens knows anything about Jade Verrit, it's how far she can push Jade before she shuts down, and Chelle's already gone well past what she thought tonight's limit would be.

*Probably because Mike's involved,* she thinks.

"Alright, Jade," Mack says. "Call us if anything comes up, okay?"

"You got it. I'm gonna call for a jump and I'll get this business taken care of and I'll meet up with you guys in a few hours." She gestures toward a bus that is approaching the station.

"Alright, but please be careful," says Chelle.

"I'll be fine," says Jade.

Chelle and Mack get out of the car and walk to the bus stop. The two get in line behind three other people waiting for the bus.

"Are we doing the right thing, Mack?"

"I think Jade has a good handle on what she's doing," he says as the bus comes to a halt and its doors open with a *whoosh*.

"I just don't know why she won't let us help her, you know?"

"It's a pride thing, Chelle... I thought you of all people would understand."

Chelle snaps her head to face him.

"Hey now," she says.

"I'm just saying... have a little faith in her, is all."

Chelle's phone starts to ring and she pulls it out, silencing it once she sees that Simon is calling. She and Mack board the bus.

"I don't like this," says Chelle as she swipes her Metro card. Chelle and Mack board the bus and take their seats; the doors close and the bus drives away.

"I know you don't like this," says Mack, obviously growing bored with the conversation. "You've been saying it all night."

"No, not that. I don't like being this person, Mack. I don't like being 'The Worrying Friend'. I just want to be the friend, you know? I'm not her mother."

"No one's asking you to be," he says slowly.

"No, I know they're not. But if she's not going to look after herself, someone has to. Isn't that what a good friend would do?"

"Maybe... but an even better friend would just be there to catch her when she falls. *If* she falls. Who knows? This thing tonight could work out just fine for her."

"Yeah."

"Let her do her thing tonight."

"You're right... I need to stop."

"You don't want to push her away, Chel."

The two sit in silence for a few minutes as the blurry city passes by through the bus windows, illuminated by the street lights and surrounding vehicles.

Chelle pulls out her phone and skims a text from Simon telling her to call him when she can before typing a new message to Jade.

*"You're a badass!"*

She hits send, puts her phone away and looks at Mack.

"You sure you don't want to come to Underland with us?"

"Nah, that's alright," he says. "I'm beat after today. And I have an early shift tomorrow, so I'm probably gonna pass out early. You guys have fun though!"

\* \* \*

"Hey babe," Simon answers his phone.

"Hey," she says, walking into her apartment.

"Me and Alan are ready whenever you are – I'm thinking we're just gonna take a cab, is that cool?"

"Yeah, that's fine – I'm just now getting home. I had to run an errand with Jade and Mack."

"Oh," says Simon. "Are they coming?"

"No, well, Mack's not. Jade's gonna meet us later," says Chelle. "It's kind of a long story. I'm gonna go get ready, it shouldn't take that long."

"Okay, sounds good."

There is silence on the line.

*Four months in and we're already running out of things to talk about,* thinks Chelle. *Lame.*

"Well hey, I'm gonna go get ready," she says.

"Alright, cool. Give me a call when you're leaving."

"Will do," she says. "Talk to you then."

They hang up. Chelle runs through an abridged version of her getting-ready-to-go-out routine, slipping into one of her favorite dresses and touching up her makeup. She runs her fingers through her hair and grabs her keys, checking her phone for any messages from Jade. There is nothing.

*"Leaving now"* she texts Simon.

\* \* \*

As she walks toward the entrance to Underland, Chelle gets a text from Simon.

*"Meet us inside, we're grabbing drinks"*

"I guess it was too much to assume he'd wait to go in with me," Chelle says aloud. She rolls her eyes and continues walking.

*This is getting old,* she thinks. *I should have just stayed with Jade.*

Chelle arrives at Underland and gets in line to go in. With a grin and a wink, she slips past the bouncer and follows the fluorescent rabbits painted on the wall, descending into the club. Feeling the music pulse around her the further she goes, she cannot help but give in to the rush of adrenaline that entering the club brings. The stresses of the day – Jade, work, Simon – they all melt away as the walls around her seemingly come to life.

*Just what I needed,* she thinks. *Put Jade out of your mind – she'll let you know if she needs your help. Get yourself a drink and have a good time!*

She finds Simon and Alan standing near the bar on the balcony overlooking the dance floor, each monitoring the crowd with a drink in hand. Alan catches her eye first and waves her over. She walks over to them both.

"Hey babe," Simon yells. He makes no attempt at a hug or kiss, instead opting to take a swig of his beer bottle. Chelle smiles back. "Have you heard from your friends?"

"No, not yet."

"This is Alan."

"Hi," she says, shaking his hand. "Nice to finally meet you!"

"Likewise," he says with a smile.

Chelle orders a drink.

"Let's go downstairs!" she yells to Simon and Alan. They nod in agreement. After she pays for her drink, they head down a flight of glass block steps to the dance floor. Finding a slight open space, the three maneuver toward it and start dancing.

*Tyler's gonna like him,* she thinks, watching Alan dance. She feels her phone vibrate and pulls it out.

"They're outside," she yells to the boys. "Come on!" She leads them to the base of the glass block staircase. After waiting a few minutes, Tyler comes walking down the stairs, followed by Phin and Carrie.

"Chelle!" he yells.

"Hey, boo!" she screams back, running toward him and jumping into a hug. "You know Simon and this is Alan."

Alan smiles at Tyler. Chelle sees this and smiles to herself.

"Nice to meet you!"

"Have you guys been here before?" Alan shouts over the music.

"No, but this place is amazing!" answers Tyler. He looks around and notices the DJ's overlooking the crowd.

"Lead the way!" Tyler says. He winks at Carrie and turns to follow Alan.

\* \* \*

Later, as she is reapplying lip gloss in the bathroom, Chelle gets a text from Jade. She looks down to read it.

*"Hey – call me when you can… there was trouble, nothing major, I'll explain later… anyway I can get a ride?"*

"Fuck," she says, looking back up at herself in the mirror. She throws her lip gloss in her purse and rushes out of the bathroom. She finds Tyler, Phin and Carrie at the bar on the balcony. She walks up to them, searching for her keys in her purse.

"You guys, I have to go," she says. "I just got a text from Jade, she's in some kind of trouble and I have to pick her up. I don't know where Simon is, just tell him there was an emergency. He came with Alan so he'll be fine." She gives Carrie and Phin each a hug goodbye.

"You better not leave here without Alan's number," she says into Tyler's ear after giving him a kiss on the cheek. He digs in his pocket a moment and pulls out a napkin with a number scrawled on it, grinning ear to ear.

"I love it!" she yells, blowing kisses to her friends as she turns to walk away. She ascends the stairs and soon finds herself street level, walking briskly to the lot where she parked her car and dialing Jade.

On the third ring, she answers.

"Hey, Chel."

"Jade! Oh my God, are you okay? What's going on?!"

"Hey, I'm okay – my car's just in a shop and I need you to come get me."

"Where am I heading?"

"I'm still out in Bay Ridge."

"Are you okay?"

"Yeah, I'm fine – you're not gonna believe what happened though."

"What are you talking about?"

"Can we talk about it when you pick me up? I didn't get to charge my phone all the way."

"Okay," says Chelle, slightly annoyed that Jade won't give her the full story right now. "I'll be there as soon as I can."

"Can you come back to that gas station?"

"Sure," Chelle says. "I'll call you when I'm close."

\* \* \*

Chelle races out to the gas station in Bay Ridge where she left Jade hours before. She finds her sitting outside, sipping on a frozen drink. She pulls up to the curb.

"Going my way?" Chelle asks.

"I believe I am," says Jade, with a smile. She hops up and gets in the car.

"Where am I going?" Chelle asks.

Jade hesitates.

"Mike's," she finally says.

"What?"

"Yeah," says Jade. "I didn't go through with it. I still have his stuff, we need to take it back."

"Are you serious? He's gonna be so pissed!"

"He'll get over it."

"What about the money?"

"That's taken care of."

"What?"

"I know, the whole story's crazy," says Jade. "Let's go though, I want to get this shit out of my purse."

"Well look at you!" says Chelle, noticing a distinct change in her friend. "Why the sudden change of heart?" Chelle pulls toward the gas station exit.

"I might have met someone," she says.

"All the way out here?"

"Dude, Chelle, you don't even know," she says. "Make a left out of here and we'll talk on the way."

\* \* \*

"What the fuck, Jade?!" screams Mike. He is standing opposite Jade and Chelle in the dingy entryway to his apartment.

"I told you, Mike," says Jade. "I appreciate that you tried to help me, but this isn't me anymore. I can't do it."

Jade pushes the bag of weed and pills toward him.

"Take your crap back, I don't need this shit anymore." The light in the hallway flickers, casting shadows on the peeling wallpaper.

"You bitch," he says through gritted teeth. "That was one of my biggest sells of the year and you fucked it up!"

"Did I? I mean, really. You're the one who gave it to me."

Mike lets out an aggressive, angry grunt.

"You fucking bitch."

"Fuck you, Mike."

Chelle looks nervously between the two. "The hell did you just say?"

"I said fuck you. I realized tonight I don't need you anymore."

*Oh my God,* thinks Chelle. *He's going to kill us.*

Mike looks at her through squinted eyes. His fists are clenched.

"That's right," says Jade. "I don't need you. I should have stayed the fuck away from you since the beginning. You all but ruined my life and do you know how hard I've had to work to piece things back together? And then today, I come to you for help and you show up at my work acting like a dick and you try to threaten me? Never again. This is it – we're fucking through. And if you ever come near me again, I will fucking ruin you. I will personally see to it that you rot in a goddamn jail cell."

*Damn, Jade!* thinks Chelle.

Jade turns to leave.

"C'mon, Chelle."

Mike stands in the doorway of his apartment, mouth slightly hanging open. And as Jade walks out of Mike's building for what she knows to be the final time, she looks at Chelle and winks.

"For what it's worth, you were right, Chel," she says. "Calling Mike was a really, really bad idea."

"Well, yeah," says Chelle. "I figured you'd see that eventually."

"And I'm sorry I had to put you through all of this."

"Hey, I'm still here."

"Thank you."

Jade hugs Chelle and looks at her phone.

"Hot damn it's late," she says.

"Yeah, I've been running on empty for a while now."

"Sugar's?" asks Jade. "My treat."

Chelle considers for a moment.

"I'll drive," she says with a smile.

* * *

After they order their food from the counter at Sugar's 24 Hour Diner, Chelle pours some cream into her coffee cup and turns to Jade.

"So his name's Bobby?"

"Bobby Glachome. Ring any bells?"

"None, sorry."

"He's really hot and actually seems pretty genuine."

"What's that like?" Chelle jokes.

Jade laughs.

"It's so crazy, Chel – things like this don't happen every day, you know?"

"I can't believe that cop let you guys off with a warning."

"Oh, I was freaking out the entire time! I had all that shit in my purse and I mean, yeah, I really didn't want to get caught but as we were sitting there I realized I really, really didn't want Bobby to get in trouble because of me."

"Yeah, guilty by association."

"Right! Here he was being a nice guy and then *bam*, the girl he went out of his way to help winds up having a stash of drugs on her and he winds up in jail? I would have felt terrible."

Their waitress, an older woman whose nametag reads 'Shirl', walks over and places two plates of food in front of them.

"You gals need anything else?" she asks, her raspy voice echoing off the walls.

"No, I think we're good," says Chelle. "Thank you."

"I'll be back to check on ya." Shirl says, turning to walk toward the register where the only other people in the diner, a young couple on a first date, are waiting to pay.

"So what happened after the cop let you guys go?" asks Chelle.

"Well, we pulled away and by this point I was like shaking, I was so freaked out. And so he asks me what's going on and before I can stop myself I just spill everything. Like, I mean, everything."

Chelle nods, dipping her toast into her freshly broken egg yolk.

"And he was so amazing with it. I showed him the bag and he was really calm and just said that if I would let him, he'd be happy to help me and all he asked for in return was to see me again."

Chelle coughs on her toast.

"I know! Who knew guys like that were even around anymore?" Jade takes a drink of her black coffee.

"Preach... you know Tyler got a number tonight, too?"

"Oh, yeah?"

"Yeah, Simon's friend Alan."

"And how do we feel about Alan?" asks Jade before taking a bite of her eggs.

"He's nice enough, I just ... I don't know."

"The connection with Simon?"

"Yeah," says Chelle. She sighs. "I don't know how much longer we're gonna last, Jade."

"Yeah?"

"Yeah... I think we're just growing apart. And, I mean, it's not that he's a bad guy and we had a good run, it's just... I don't think it's working out."

"You don't seem happy, Chelle," says Jade. "And not that I'm in any position to be psychoanalyzing anyone, but I've noticed this change in you lately. It's like you worry so much about other people so that you don't have to worry about yourself. Does that make sense?"

"That makes a lot of sense actually," says Chelle. The two sit quietly as they finish their food. Eventually, Shirl brings their check over and Jade lays down a twenty dollar bill.

"I told you this was on me," she says.

"You sure?"

"C'mon, Chel, it's the least I can do."

"Thank you," Chelle says, smiling.

"What a night," says Jade as they are walking out of Sugar's.

"You're telling me," says Chelle. "Alright, let's go. With any luck, we can get back to my place before the sun comes up." She unlocks her car and they both get in.

"I was gonna ask if I could just crash with you," says Jade. "I'll head home tomorrow before I have to be at work."

"Of course," says Chelle. "And I can take you out to get your car whenever it's done, just let me know."

She starts her car and pulls out of the parking spot.

"Thanks," says Jade. "I'm wiped out."

* * *

*Mack*

"Have a good night, Mack," says Chelle as they head their separate ways from the bus stop. She heads to the lot to get her car while he makes his way to the railway station. He plugs in his headphones for the trek home as Jade is across town praying her car makes it to the shop for repairs.

After getting off at his stop, he decides to grab a few slices of pizza to take back to his place for dinner while Jade sits in Bobby's car hoping the cop doesn't find the bag of drugs in her purse. Walking into his apartment, he grabs a beer and sits on the couch, turning on the TV.

"Let's see what's on tonight," he says to himself, as Phin and Carrie are kissing outside of Underland.

Later, as Tyler is dancing with Alan and Simon is getting another drink, Mack is engrossed in the first person shooter game that he

33

bought last week. He stops to pee as Jade is giving Mike a verbal lashing the likes of which he has never seen. And by the time Chelle and Jade walk into Sugar's, Mack is in a deep sleep, this wild Friday night, no more or less extraordinary than any other, the furthest thing from his mind.

# PROM

The song starts.

The students in attendance at Central High's prom continue dancing, adjusting to the tempo of the new song. A glance around the room shows a group of relatively common teenagers, each with a wealth of extraordinary potential. Each is unique, living in a moment in time that will live in their minds for years to come, though they will age and this moment will become one of a countless collection of memories. Each memory of this one moment will take on a meaning as unique as the person it belongs to.

But in this moment, they are dancing at prom and none of that matters. They sway almost instinctively, some with more skill than others, dance moves flowing into the next with ease, smiles and laughter flashing from one face to the next, lighting up the room. Though few words are spoken, another world entirely lies just beneath their carefully assembled exteriors. The things racing through their heads, from thoughts and feelings to dreams and nightmares, all of their hopes and fears... the silence is deafening.

But this is a good song, and, again, in this moment, nothing else matters.

Garrett Harmon and Holly Rogers are dancing together in the middle of the crowd. Ten minutes ago, they were named Prom King and Queen to the surprise of no one. In the almost two years they have been together, they have become Central High's power couple; their victory tonight was a foregone conclusion even before they were nominated for Prom Court. Garrett's arms are wrapped around Holly's waist, while her hands rest on his shoulders. They spin around slowly.

Holly is going away to a state school that is three hours away in the fall; she is leaving town at the end of July. Garrett plans to attend a community college while working full time. He is not leaving town and he is worried about losing Holly. He would never reveal it to anyone, but she was the first girl he had sex with. He didn't want to just give his virginity away to anyone, but he didn't want to graduate with it either. Garrett would hear the other guys talking in the locker room about their various conquests and while he didn't exactly want to *be* one of those guys, he did want to experience what they were talking about for himself.

Holly had had plenty of experience in various bedrooms before Garrett came along. At first, she found him a little attractive, if somewhat awkward. But there was something charming about him she couldn't get out of her head, and if it didn't work out, well, this was only high school.

*You don't just take home the first pair of shoes you try on at the store and wear them for the rest of your life,* she would think to herself. *Boys are no different.*

Lately, Garrett has felt himself drifting away from Holly. He's sure it has to do with her impending departure for college and his own insecurities about what to do after she's gone. They've discussed maintaining a long distance relationship, but the discussions have been sporadic, no definite plans are in place.

Truth be told, Holly had given her relationship with Garrett a four month maximum when they first started dating during sophomore year. And now, here they are, dancing together at senior prom, the Prom King and his Queen.

"Hey you two!" shouts Dawn Bailey, approaching them on the dance floor. "Pose for a picture?" She is the editor of the yearbook and she treats her camera like a child, rarely leaving home without it.

"Sure!" answers Garrett. He leans close to Holly. They smile as Dawn snaps a photo and bounds away into the crowd.

The music surrounds them.

"I love you," Garrett says into Holly's ear. She hesitates and forces a smile. Holly and Garrett have been growing distant lately. She never knows what to say; he feels uncomfortable even holding her hand in public. Neither can pinpoint exactly what has changed in their relationship.

Garrett doesn't know it, but Holly is two months pregnant with his child. She has told only one person about her pregnancy – her half-brother, Tim Foster. Their parents had married last summer and while the living situation was rocky at first, now they got along as if they had grown up together. She hasn't told Garrett; she is afraid of his response.

Despite her initial indifference toward a relationship with Garrett, Holly has come to find that she does care very deeply about him. But now, with her pregnancy and school and college and graduation looming, Holly finds herself retreating more and more into her own head, trying to make sense of the cards life has dealt her at only eighteen years old.

"I love you, too, baby," she says, moving her hands down his arms to rest her head on his shoulder. She'll tell him.

Soon.

There are two DJ's in the DJ booth. One is named Mike and the other is Philip. While Philip is handsome and looks young for his age, the lines on Mike's face cause him to look years older than he actually is. Neither DJ particularly cares for the other, but work is work and they were both scheduled for this prom.

A group of senior girls come up to the table and are talking to Mike. They are all blonde and have dresses cut low enough to tempt even the most chaste of their classmates. In the pocket of his leather jacket, Mike has one remaining bag of cocaine that he hopes to sell tonight.

*These girls strike me as willing customers,* he thinks. *Probably more in the market for some dick than blow, though...*

"What'd you say your name was, sweetheart?" he asks one of them.

"Heather," she says, giggling. "Heather Matthews."

Heather Matthews is wearing a slinky, midnight blue dress adorned with rhinestones. Her hair is pulled into an up-do, her makeup as flawless as the spray tan she skipped lunch for a week to afford.

Heather doesn't know it yet, but she will be the third girl Mike has sex with this week. And while Mike is busy soliciting new business, Philip is paying more attention to the job at hand.

*I hope we get out of here on time tonight,* he thinks, watching the audio levels bounce up and down. He quietly mouths along to the words, trying to learn the song as best as he can. Another senior, Jazmine Lloyd, leans seductively over the DJ booth in an attempt to get

Philip's attention.

*Barking up the wrong tree, boobah,* he thinks, smiling weakly at her. *Nice contour on the cheeks though.* She asks him to play a song he knows they don't have permission from the school district to play, but lies and says he'll find it. An English teacher, Mr. Luke Verrit, walks by and tells the girls to let the DJ's do their job.

Mike sees Mr. Verrit and does a double take.

*I know his sister,* he thinks. *Jade Verrit... now there's a name I haven't thought of in a while. Not since October... And he has no idea I am who I am.*

Philip looks at Mike.

"What?"

"Worry about yourself, Phil."

"Whatever."

Erik Winters is making his way through the crowd. He's known by most of his classmates as "Stoner Erik". Coming down from an earlier high, he grips the bag of cocaine in his pocket he bought from the DJ with the short hair. Looking around, he sees faces blending into each other, not completely sure of his surroundings. Finally, he remembers he is at prom and he needs to find his friend, T.J.

"Stoner Erik!" someone yells.

He spins around but can see no one he recognizes.

*Damnit,* he thinks. *Where the fuck is T.J.?*

He moves through the crowd, trying to find a familiar face, being greeted only by strangers. All he can hear is the hum of the music blaring in the room. People give him weird looks. The room is spinning. He shuts his eyes to try and make it slow down, but it doesn't work.

*I need to find a bathroom,* he thinks.

Erik finally manages to find T.J., who is talking to a girl named Janelle. He remembers Janelle from middle school, but has hardly noticed her throughout their high school years, at least that he can remember right now.

"Jesus, Erik, what happened to you?!" yells T.J. Trovato, one of Erik's only friends. "You're drenched in sweat!"

Erik has trouble formulating words, his mouth feels like it's full of sand.

"B-b-bathroom," he finally stammers.

"It's that way, dude," says T.J., pointing toward one of the walls. "Do you need me to come with you?"

"No," says Erik, slowly. "I-I'm fine." He smiles, thinking of the bag in his pocket, its powdery contents and the high that he's about to grant himself. He stumbles away from T.J. and Janelle, walking with jerky movements and swiping a straw out of a glass on a table without even looking down as he passes.

Erik doesn't like being called "Stoner Erik". He doesn't like the way people look at him, the way his friends and teachers glance with apathy at another lost cause or the way his parents ignore him to cover their disappointment. He walks into the bathroom and stares at himself in the mirror, his hair matted down and a sweat stain spreading across his chest.

*I'm only seventeen,* he thinks. *What am I doing?*

Erik wants to change, he really does. But then his body cramps with pain, his addictions gripping him from the inside out, threatening what feels like a thousand years of torment if he even dares to go too long without a fix. He wants to go to school next year, to make something of himself. Erik wants to prove everyone wrong.

But he can't. At least, not tonight.

*Just one more time,* he thinks to himself, pulling out the plastic bag. He looks around to find that he is alone. Stumbling into an empty stall and sitting on the toilet, he pours the contents of the bag onto the back of his trembling hand and inhales the cocaine sharply through the straw. The white powder flies into his nostril, the drug quickly taking effect.

His tense body starts to relax and his arms fall to his side.

*There it is,* he thinks.

Dana Peterson is dancing with her boyfriend, Tim Foster. They have been together since winter break. Dana is a talented pitcher on the varsity softball team; Tim plays soccer in the fall. They had always noticed each other in the hallways at school, but never really talked until a party at Hunter Jamison's house around Thanksgiving.

They found that they had a lot in common that night. They both liked the same kind of music and had an affinity for classic cars. Tim's family is well off; he drives a little sports car that is always clean, while Dana earned her pickup by working various odd jobs, and it is usually messy. They were, of course, both huge sports fanatics and it was no surprise to any of their friends that their first date was at a hockey game downtown.

Dana is dancing with Tim, but she has someone else on her mind.

Lexie din Tei walks by the DJ booth and looks at the DJ named Philip.

*I wonder if he took a date to his prom,* she thinks to herself, trying not to sound so bitter in her own mind. She smiles at him faintly. He smiles gently back, nodding a slight acknowledgement to the fact that neither of them are straight. Lexie continues on and sits down at a table near the back of the room. Sadly, she is alone. She looks to the dance floor and sees the rest of her friends dancing.

*They'll never know how easy they had it,* she thinks. Lexie din Tei has had a difficult time recently, facing the hurdles of finding herself while preparing to leave behind the only stable thing in her life — theater. She's the kind of girl who never quite fit in in her early years, only finding a group of friends when she joined Central High's drama program. The other thespians, they were more than friends; they were a family. She performed in her final show, a self-directed one act, three weeks ago and already feels its absence in her life. Beyond theater, the only other activity Lexie din Tei had participated in was a season on the junior varsity softball team her sophomore year.

That's where she first met Dana Peterson.

Lexie sees Dana dancing with Tim.

*I wonder if she's happy,* she thinks. *I hope she is. Despite everything that's happened, I hope, at the very least, that she's happy.* She thinks of the time she had spent working with Dana at Midway Costume Supply back in October. They had worked so many hours together, just the two of them, getting to know each other. They hung out several nights a week, talking about everything they could think of, becoming closer and closer. Dana was one of the few people Lexie allowed to call her by her full name.

"We're kindred spirits, Alexa," Dana had said. For once in Lexie's life, things were starting to make sense. They shared their first kiss one night after closing the store, the connection between them a palpable force.

Lexie loved feeling Dana's smile in her kisses.

But as quickly as it happened, whatever they had had ended just as fast. Halloween came and went, the store closed and Dana moved on. She started taking longer and longer to return Lexie's texts until the replies ceased altogether; she avoided Lexie in the halls at school.

*What did I do wrong?* Lexie thought constantly. *Would it have been so awful to be with me, just the two of us?* She finally came face to face with Dana again at a hockey game, and later found out she was on her first date with Tim Foster. Despite the fact that Tim was in the stands waiting for Dana to return, the two girls had shared one last kiss that was as beautiful to Lexie as it was painful.

Though they rarely spoke since, neither was ever far from the other's mind. And now, here they are, seniors at prom; Dana with a boyfriend, Lexie by herself.

*One dance*, thinks Lexie. *All I want is one dance*. She stands and walks to the bathroom.

Across the way, Dana Peterson watches Lexie din Tei walk to the bathroom by herself. Her heart breaks a little and she rests her head on Tim's shoulder.

Dana blinks away tears as she realizes the mistake she's made.

Cody Welik is standing with a group of his friends among the tables that remain in the ballroom where prom is being held. He has his arms wrapped around two of them, Colleen Bauer, who is technically his date, and Annika Heighesser, who is technically dating Evan Gallagher.

When he transferred to Central from Knightfield Prep at the start of sophomore year, Evan Gallagher was one of the first friends that Cody Welik had made. And though they maintained a casual friendship, things changed when they met Annika, an exchange student who would be joining them for their senior year. Both boys had started to develop feelings for her, each unbeknownst to the other.

The first time Cody had brought Annika around had been at his parents' annual Halloween Ball; she had hit it off well enough with everyone, even if he didn't introduce her to his brothers. Cody, who had for so long closed himself off to the idea of a relationship, had finally decided he was going to ask Annika out on an actual date over winter break. He was crushed, however, when he found out on the last day of finals that Evan had taken Annika to a movie the night before and asked her to be his girlfriend.

She had, of course, said yes.

Despite the initial sting of heartbreak, Cody had maintained his friendship with Annika and the two continued to grow closer. Eventually, though, Annika was spending as much time with Cody as she was Evan. She got to know Cody's friends, his family and even went shopping with his mother.

But for some reason unknown to Cody, she refused to break things off with Evan. He didn't understand it, but decided to go with it.

When the time came to find a date for prom, he had asked his friend, Colleen, knowing that if he had gone with his gut and asked Annika, she would have had to turn him down.

Evan is currently dancing in a circle with a few of his football teammates. He has forgotten all about Annika for the moment. He will take her home later in his truck before heading to a hotel party. This summer, she will be going back to Europe; she and Evan will eventually lose touch. She will, however, talk to Cody on a regular basis, even if their relationship never moves beyond friendship.

Annika and Cody were both nominated for prom court. It was a surprise to them both. In a perfect world, they would have been named Prom King and Queen. As it played out, however, neither was even elected to court. Cody didn't care about it as much as Annika did – she really wanted to be on prom court, if only to say she had had the complete high school experience. Cody would have only wanted to be king with Annika by his side.

So now, here they are, dancing in the shadows away from the dance floor. Colleen joins them. After meeting her through Cody, Colleen was quick to become friends with Annika, even though she goes to West High. Annika turns to Cody and starts to sing along with the song. Colleen snaps a photo of the two.

Annika puts her arms around Cody as Colleen takes another picture. Paul St. John is sitting at the table and rolls his eyes behind his thick glasses. He is very observant and quickly figured out the dynamic that has developed between Cody, Annika and Evan. Paul is friends with both boys, and refuses to take a side.

Cody feels the full force of Paul's judgmental eye roll. He smirks in response. Cody turns to face the dance floor, pulling his two dates in close.

*It's not like we're doing anything that's so wrong,* he thinks.

Leonard MacClayton doesn't know how, but every year he winds up having to chaperone prom. Leonard, or Mr. Mac as he is known around school, is standing on the side of the dance floor, watching his students enjoy themselves. He sees many familiar faces. They all look so happy, so grown.

Every year around this time, he can't fight the feelings of nostalgia that creep in day after day. His students, many of whom he has taught since their days as gawky freshmen, are about to move into the next phase of their lives. Though no one ever truly finishes growing up, Leonard always enjoys watching his students at prom, enjoying one last celebration before they set out into the real world, young adults who no longer need his instruction. And, of course, a crop of new students are waiting to take their place in three short months, a new class of awkward freshmen ready to embark on the journey called high school.

But Leonard MacClayton won't be there to see these new students.

After forty one years of teaching in Central High's social studies department (and six times being named Teacher of the Year), Leonard has finally decided to retire. He's thinking of tonight as a swan song for his career, though few, if any, of the students realize it. One last time to dress up with his colleagues, one last time to reflect on just how much his students have grown over the last four years.

One last prom to end his career as an educator.

Luke Verrit, a young English teacher, walks up to Leonard. Leonard had been Luke's mentor two years ago when he had first been hired at Central High.

"How're you holding up?" he asks.

"Hanging in there," Leonard replies. "Only about an hour to go."

"Yeah," says Luke, nodding. "Have you seen Kim?"

Kim McKee is a science teacher who started at Central High this year. Luke had noticed her right away at the start of the year staff orientation. Marlene Chapman, who works in the audio visual office and has always thought of herself as a sort of matchmaker, had set the two up on their first date in the fall and they made their relationship official on Valentine's Day.

Though they tried to keep the status of their relationship as private as possible, the good news had spread through the entire school before the end of the next week.

"Last I saw her, she was out by the ice sculpture."

"Oh, thanks! How's your night going?"

"Not too bad," says Leonard. "Just kind of taking it all in."

"Oh yeah!" says Luke. "The last prom, huh?"

"Indeed, it is," says Leonard. "You know, it's funny… when I first started having to chaperone prom, I must admit, I was pretty annoyed – having to give up a Saturday night and all. But then, I don't know, as the years went by, I found it to be something I looked forward to. Not just for myself, but for the kids… as a rite of passage."

"That's understandable," says Luke. The two men stand side-by-side for a moment, watching the crowd of dancing students, making sure everyone is staying relatively behaved, the older man set to complete his career as a teacher, the younger man just beginning.

Kim McKee walks up behind them.

"There you two are!" she yells over the music. "I've been looking for you both."

"Oh?" says Leonard. Luke moves to stand next to his girlfriend.

"I found someone out in the lobby you might like to say hello to," she says.

Just then, an older woman walks through the doors to the grand ballroom. She is dressed in a deep purple gown with a matching shawl, her white hair curled. Leonard's mouth falls open before breaking into a grin.

"Marilyn!" he yells. Leonard MacClayton had married Marilyn Reiss forty five years ago when they were in their mid-20's after being high school sweethearts. Being a couple that lived a modest lifestyle, they'd recently thrown a small party for their sapphire anniversary.

"Hello, my love," she says, walking up to him slowly. Luke looks at Kim and winks, Kim smiles back.

"You look beautiful," Leonard says. "But then, you always do. What are you doing here? I thought you were staying home tonight?"

"These two thought it would be a fun surprise," she says, gesturing toward Luke and Kim. "And what can I say, I love to dance."

"Thank you both, so much," he says, turning to face the other two.

"No, Leonard," says Luke. "Thank you for everything you've done for me over the past few years. Now take her out there, the lady wants to dance!"

"Oh! Well, in that case," says Leonard, bowing toward Marilyn. "May I have this dance, madam?"

"Forever and always," says Marilyn, taking his outstretched hand. Leonard leads her to the side of the dance floor and the two embrace, dancing together at one last prom as they did so many years ago when they themselves were seniors in high school. On the side of the room, Kim slips her hand inside of Luke's.

"We did good, Mr. Verrit," she says.

"Well," he says, with a grin. "We did well."

"Whatever," she says, as they quickly kiss and look back toward the dance floor.

Lexie din Tei comes running toward the two.

"Mr. Verrit, Miss McKee," she says. "I think something's wrong."

Hunter Jamison is in a group with a bunch of his football teammates. They are all dancing to the music, having a great time. Most of them are buzzed.

"Hey dude," yells Evan Gallagher. "Did you see Miss McKee?"

"Hell yeah – she's looking hot tonight!" replies Hunter.

At times, Hunter can blend in very well with this crowd, but other times the differences between them can be striking. While most of the team spends their weekends smoking, drinking and getting off through one party after another, Hunter tends to show up, have a few laughs and head home early. During his four years at Central High, he's only thrown one party. Most of his friends are heading for community college, but Hunter found out he had been awarded a football scholarship to a state school three months ago.

And what sets Hunter apart from the group tonight is that he will be going home after prom, he will not be attending the hotel party his friends have planned.

A few years ago, Hunter had an uncle who was killed by a drunk driver and has been uncomfortable around alcohol ever since. Avoiding it in high school, however, is not so easy. Tonight alone, he has had opportunities to drink while taking photos before prom, in the limo on the way to prom and twenty minutes ago in the bathroom, to name a few.

After prom ends, the limo the group rented will take them back to the hotel where they will be staying for the night. Hunter will be convinced to at least socialize with his friends for a little while before heading home, but will drink only soda.

Hunter is a good kid, a star athlete going to a top school with a scholarship, well-liked by his peers. His mother is proud.

Hunter will leave his friends at the hotel and on his way home, at approximately 1:15 A.M., his car will be struck by another, spinning around twice before hitting a tree and shattering two windows.

But Hunter will not die.

He will be taken to the hospital, and in a few days, will be released. Aside from lacerations on his face and torso, the only major injury Hunter will sustain is his leg. His right leg will be broken in several places, but will be fine to walk on in a month or two. And with physical therapy, he might be ready to play football again by the fall.

Two days after the accident, Hunter will learn that the driver of the car who hit him died in the accident. After the collision, she flew through her windshield and landed in a ditch on the side of the road. He will also learn the identity of the person who saved his life.

Across the dance floor, Mandy Seton smiles at him. She really likes Hunter, but he seems so far away tonight, like he's distracted by something. She's supposed to be going to the hotel party after prom, but she doesn't really want to. She decides to make a brief appearance before heading home. Mandy, like Hunter, has not been drinking at all tonight.

Mandy Seton will leave the hotel shortly after Hunter, taking the same road. She will pull out her cell phone to try and call Hunter to make sure he is okay after seeming so distracted all night. His phone will ring and he will not pick up. On her third attempt at calling Hunter, Mandy will see the accident on the side of the road, stop and call 9-1-1.

Hunter will tell everyone how Mandy saved his life.

Hunter smiles back at Mandy. He has always liked her and for a moment, he considers the possibility of asking her on a date. But for now, he's dancing with his friends and she's dancing with hers.

Janelle Lloyd and her twin sister, Jazmine, are nothing alike. Jazmine likes to go out, party and have a good time with her friends from the step team. Janelle, on the other hand, is content to sit at home on a Saturday night, playing video games or reading a book. Jazmine actually had to convince Janelle to come to prom, as she had no intention of coming.

Now that she's here, though, Janelle is glad she came. As soon as she walked in, she turned heads. Janelle and Jazmine Lloyd are identical twins, but they have such radically different styles, few people realize they are identical. Janelle is typically content to stay in Jazmine's shadow.

But not tonight.

Tonight, Janelle is getting as much attention as her sister and is finding that it isn't all that scary – she's finding she likes it. Shortly after dinner, T.J. Trovato came up to her and asked to dance.

"Go for it!" mouthed Jazmine to her sister.

"Okay, sure," said Janelle. Janelle and T.J. danced until Erik Winters came stumbling up to them a few minutes ago. Erik and T.J. were friends, and for a time in middle school, Janelle had had a crush on Erik. But when they started high school, he fell in with the druggie kids and now she rarely thinks of him.

As Erik stumbles away, T.J. resolves to finish the song with Janelle then go check on his friend. T.J. looks at Janelle and smiles, he's always thought she was pretty but tonight she is stunning.

"Are you having a good time?" he asks.

"I am," she says. "Would you believe I almost didn't come tonight?"

"Really?" he asks. "I'm glad you did."

They smile and the song continues.

"What's going on over there?" Janelle suddenly asks.

T.J. looks to the side of the room and sees Lexie din Tei running toward Mr. Verrit and Miss McKee. She points to the men's restroom and suddenly T.J. feels as though someone punched him in the stomach.

He knows something is wrong with Erik.

"A-are you okay?" asks Janelle.

"I'll be right back," he says, leaving her. He rushes to the side of the room and goes with Mr. Verrit into the men's restroom.

Jazmine comes up on the arm of Blake Pines.

"Janie, what was that all about?"

"I don't know, Jaz," says Janelle. She turns to her sister and smiles. "It was fun though!"

"Get it, girl! Is he coming back?"

"I think so," says Janelle. "How's your back?"

Jazmine has been having increasingly frequent bouts of back pain lately. She figures it's probably related to overdoing it at step team practices.

"It's good tonight," she says. "Don't worry about me, sis!"

"Alright," says Janelle. "I'm gonna go check on T.J."

Jazmine and Blake continue dancing as Janelle walks toward Miss McKee, who is talking with Lexie.

"…and that's when I heard the crash," says Lexie.

"Is everything okay?" asks Janelle.

"It's alright, Janelle. Mr. Verrit's checking things out," says Miss McKee. At that moment, T.J. comes running out of the bathroom and heads for the lobby.

Mr. Hirsch, an assistant administrator, stands in front of Max Noire, who is sitting on a chair in the lobby outside of the ballroom. Max is known as much for his spiky black hair as he is for being a troubled student with a penchant for bad behavior, most notably kleptomania.

"Really, Max?" he asks, sighing angrily.

Max stares at him defiantly, his expression blank. Several students came to Mr. Hirsch about twenty minutes ago, claiming that they had seen Max lifting various electronic devices from other students and slipping them into the liner of his jacket.

"I have to report this, you know."

T.J. arrives in the lobby and runs up to Mr. Hirsch.

"Mr. Hirsch," he says, panting. "Something's wrong in the men's room. We need to call 9-1-1!"

"You stay here," says Marvin, glaring at Max, gesturing for another teacher to come keep an eye on him.

Janelle enters the lobby and approaches T.J. After Mr. Hirsch runs off, Janelle asks T.J. what's going on and he tells her that Erik is passed out in the bathroom, a small bag with bits of what looks like cocaine on the floor next to him. In about fifteen minutes, the paramedics will arrive and Erik Winters will leave his senior prom on a gurney.

Everyone will know the story by Monday.

Tonight, however, T.J. will be shaken. One of his closest friends could have died and he almost let it happen. He and Janelle will go for a walk on the terrace outside of the ballroom and he will let his guard down with her. He will tell her the things he has kept inside for so long, about Erik and other aspects of his life. She will listen and react appropriately.

And when he moves in to kiss her, she will not stop him.

As the song nears its conclusion, everyone continues to dance. The worries in their minds, the problems they'll face in the future, none of it comes into play in this moment, this four minute microcosm of life for the students and faculty at Central High. This moment will lead to the next and before long, prom will be nothing but a memory of a night that held infinite possibilities and played a part in the stories of countless lives, a memory to be held for years to come.

But right now, all that matters is this song, this dance, this moment in time. Garrett smiles at Holly; Cody laughs with Annika and Colleen. The DJ named Mike writes his number on a piece of paper he gives to Heather while Dana looks around for Lexie. Hunter smiles at Mandy; Janelle takes T.J.'s hand into her own. In the bathroom, Mr. Verrit checks Erik's pulse as Miss McKee grabs Mr. and Mrs. MacClayton from the dance floor. Students laugh, photos are taken, memories are created.

And when the song ends, the next one starts.

# COMING HOME

Brannon Saether steps off of the M83 bus, his satchel and suitcase in tow. Having landed at the airport an hour ago without any set plans, he decided to take the first bus that pulled up to the terminal for arrivals, get into the city and find his way from there. It's been years since he's been here, but it feels like he just left yesterday.

The roar of an engine fills the air as the bus pulls away from the stop, leaving Brannon alone on this day in early November, the sun shining and the trees bare. He pulls a ball cap out of his bag and puts it on his buzzed head.

"It's good to be back," he says to himself.

* * *

The Southside Pier was one of those places that no parents wanted their kids to go without supervision, so naturally, kids snuck off to The Pier as often as they could. The Pier hit the apex of its life in the mid-70's, with crowds wandering in and out from the beach to ride the various rides or play the games on the boardwalk. Though it never quite reached the level of international fame as similar attractions, the Southside Pier drew a modest crowd through most of the '80's. The owners were eventually forced into bankruptcy by 1989.

The Southside Pier sat in various stages of decay over the next several years, though it continued to draw crowds of a different sort. Gone were the families on vacation, the locals taking a day off work to spend at the beach. In their place, an assortment of drug dealers and vandals alongside groups of kids who made a game of exploring a living monument to the past, a relic of days gone by, never to be reclaimed. The rides, including a small Ferris wheel and a collection of bumper cars, and the midway games were overrun by foliage and graffiti.

The Southside Pier was the perfect place for Brannon and his friends to spend one of their first nights of summer.

* * *

The first person Brannon runs into from his group of childhood friends is Genevieve Delphe. He has been back in town for about a week and staying with a friend of his brother's while searching for both an apartment and a job. He takes an afternoon off and finds himself wandering the cobblestone streets of Old Town bundled in his coat and scarf.

He sits at a table on an empty sidewalk terrace, sipping a small mocha as he watches the crowds walk past. He'd intended to get a larger drink, but had used one of his last dollars to tip a street performer and must have dropped the rest of his pocket change somewhere in Old Town.

*I can't believe it's been so long since I've been here,* he thinks. His father had received a promotion in his company years ago and had uprooted the entire family. His brother, Aaron, was the only one to stay behind, as he was already in college at the time. Though he has not been in the city in over a decade, he already feels right at home.

As he sits lost in thought, he starts to feel as though he is being watched. Turning around, he spots a girl in a black and white checkered coat and beret, her short, dark hair falling just below her chin. When he faces her, she slowly pulls off her black rimmed glasses.

"No way," she says, walking toward him grinning. "Brannon?"

He stands.

"Hello, Genevieve," he says, smiling. He puts his arms out and they hug for what feels like minutes, leaves rustling around their feet.

"It's so good to see you!" she says.

"You too," he responds. They sit down at the table, the tree branch overhead swaying in the autumn breeze.

"How long have you been in town?" Genevieve asks, putting her glasses back on.

"About a week."

"Oh, wow! Have you called any of the old crew yet?"

"Not yet, I was trying to get a few things lined up first."

"Sounds like a good plan," she says. "How long are you here for?"

"Indefinitely, I guess."

She nods.

"I graduated a couple months back, traveled a bit and then, I don't know, figured I'd come back here, see what I left behind, see where I could pick up." He pauses. "So what are you up to these days?"

"Well, I'm working at the winery down here," she says. "And I have a few projects in the works. I just rented a studio space, so I'm excited to get into that." Brannon remembers how talented an artist Genevieve was when they were kids. While the rest of the group was struggling with color wheels, she had sketched a self-portrait out of charcoal that had looked so lifelike, Brannon remembers thinking she had cheated on her project and brought in a photograph.

"That's awesome!" he says. "I'd love to come by sometime."

"Sure, that'd be great – here, let me give you my number." She takes his phone and enters in her information.

"So do you still talk to any of the old group?"

"Yeah."

"Do you guys get together a lot?"

"Not really," she says. "I probably see Yorick the most. He works down here, too. You might run into him sometime. Tyler and Chelle work together and I don't think I've seen Kate but maybe once or twice in the past year."

"Gotcha," says Brannon. "Do you ever get down to the Pier anymore?"

"The Southside Pier?"

"Yeah."

"I haven't been there in years, but Brannon, didn't you hear?"

His puzzled look answers her questions.

"It burnt down about a month ago."

"What?"

"Yeah, the entire thing went up in flames."

"Wow… that's crazy!"

Genevieve looks at her phone.

"Oh crap," she says. "I need to get back to work."

"Oh gosh, sorry!" apologizes Brannon.

"Nah, it won't be a big deal," says Genevieve. She stands and puts her glasses back on.

"It was good to see you, Gen," he says.

"You too, Brannon! Let me know if you need any help with anything, okay? Hopefully I'll get to see you again soon!" He stands and gives her a hug goodbye.

After Genevieve has walked away, Brannon sits and thinks about the conversation he just had, the friends he left behind and the destruction of the Southside Pier, the one place he felt held so many memories of the formative years he'd spent in the city.

*I can't believe it's gone,* he thinks.

He sits at the table, sipping on the mocha that has cooled considerably. His thoughts turn back to his friends.

*I meant to keep in touch,* he thinks. *It just didn't happen.*

He finishes his drink.

*I need to find them,* he thinks.

\* \* \*

Brannon pedaled faster and faster on his bicycle, making his way to the Southside Pier. He and his friends had decided that spending a night together on the Pier would be the perfect kickoff to what was sure to be the perfect summer. They were teenagers now; the world was at their fingertips.

*I want to get there to see the sunset,* he thought, his backpack swaying behind him. He had packed a few essentials for the night, including a small pillow and a blanket, as well as some snacks to share with the group.

Finally nearing the Pier, he looked around to make sure no one was watching him. He and his friends had decided they would hide their bikes under a tangle of tree branches to keep random people passing by from realizing there was a group of kids sleeping overnight on the Pier.

*Not kids,* he thought. *Teens.*

There was only one other bike chained to the fence under the tree when he arrived, its pink frame telling him that Kate Farrell was already here. He saw where she had carved her initials; he was quick to put his next to hers. Yorick had suggested they each do this as a way to initiate the night. Brannon chained his bike next to Kate's and walked out onto the Pier. He looked around but didn't see her.

*I thought we were all going to meet at the bumper cars,* he thought. Finally, he noticed a small figure with bright red hair sitting on a bench toward the end of the Pier looking out over the water. He wanted to yell for her, but knew that it was best not to as it was still daylight and didn't want this epic night to be over before it even began.

"Hey Kate," he said when he finally made it out to where she was sitting. Her backpack sat on the wooden boards next to her feet.

"Brannon!" she said, excitedly. He sat down next to her.

"Is anyone else here yet?" he asked.

"Nope, just me," she said. "And I haven't seen anyone else, so I think we're good so far! I can't wait 'til everyone gets here."

"Me, too. Are you hungry?"

"Not really," she said. "I ate before I left."

"What did you tell your parents?"

"That I was going to Chelle's."

"Yeah, I told mine I was going to Yorick's."

"Do you think they'll check?"

"Nah, I doubt it."

They sat in silence for another few minutes, the water crashing below and the sounds of birds in the distance. The sun cast an orange glow over the entire pier until it dipped below the horizon and night began to fall.

"Let's go see if the others are here," Brannon said.

"Alright."

Walking down the pier back toward shore, Kate hopped over a few boards that looked weaker than the rest. They looked at the various games and attractions.

"I bet this place was awesome when it was open," she said.

"Oh, I'm sure," said Brannon. "I would have loved coming out here." He looked at a skee ball game that was covered in vines and had a hole in its ramp. Like all the arcade games around it, its paint was chipped to the point where the point values for the holes were almost unreadable.

When they arrived at the bumper cars, the rest of their friends were there. Tyler and Yorick were leaning on a bumper car; Genevieve and Chelle were chatting about the boys in their class. Dusk was setting in.

"Where were you two?" asked Genevieve, pulling off her purple glasses as Brannon and Kate walked toward the group.

"We got here early and wanted to watch the sunset," said Brannon.

Genevieve raised her eyebrow at Brannon.

"Did anyone see you guys?" Kate asked.

"No," answered Tyler. "I kept an eye out."

"I had to dive into that stupid bush because a car drove by," said Yorick.

"Are you okay?" asked Kate.

"Yeah, I'm fine."

"Well that's good."

"You guys, I'm so excited!" called Chelle from where she was standing.

"Me, too," said Kate.

"So, what do you guys want to do first?" asked Brannon.

\* \* \*

Utilizing various platforms of social media, it doesn't take Brannon long to track down the rest of his group of childhood friends. Within three days, he has connected with both Tyler and Chelle; he has yet to hear from Yorick or Kate.

*Maybe they don't get online much?* thinks Brannon, staring at his phone as he thinks about the situation. He sits alone on a stool at a table for four in Murphy's Pub, swirling the last gulp of a pint of beer in the bottom of his glass. Lights from the street above stream through the short windows that line the top of the walls as people on the street hurry past.

Brannon checks the time and looks around. Tyler had written him back almost immediately and the two had agreed to meet here to catch up. He thinks back to when he and Tyler were kids, classmates in middle school complaining about their brothers. Tyler and Brannon each have two brothers, although Tyler is the oldest and Brannon is the youngest.

As he's finishing his beer, the door to the pub opens and a familiar face walks in. Tyler Welik has a long scarf wrapped several times around his neck for warmth; his hair is tucked behind his ears.

Brannon stands to greet his old friend.

"Tyler!" he calls.

Tyler looks around and sees Brannon. He walks over, smiling, and gives his friend a big hug.

"It's so good to see you!" he says.

"You too, man," says Brannon. "Let's go get a drink!"

They head to the bar and order a pitcher.

"How've you been?" asks Brannon.

"Good, good," says Tyler. "Just keeping busy with this and that…"

"Awesome."

"How about you?"

"Oh, same," says Brannon. "Just trying to get back into the swing of things, you know, looking for a job and all that."

The bartender returns with their pitcher and they walk to the table.

"So what brings you back?" asks Tyler.

"You know, I've been getting that a lot lately," says Brannon. "You'd think I'd have a better answer by now."

Tyler laughs.

"For real though, I don't know – I mean, my whole family pretty much moved away but I always felt like this was my home. I went through school, fucked around here and there and then one day it just kind of came to me that I wanted to come back."

Tyler takes a drink.

"That makes sense," he says. "Where are you staying?"

"I'm still looking for a place. I'm at a friend of Caleb's until I find somewhere more permanent."

"Hey, I think there might be a few openings in my building!"

"Oh?"

"Yeah, it's an old foundry they rehabbed into loft spaces."

"That's awesome!"

"Yeah and relatively cheap, too. I'll look into it for you."

"Dude, thanks," says Brannon. He takes a drink of his beer. "So what are you up to these days?"

"Not a whole lot, really... I work with Chelle, we work at Caramaya's, you remember that place?"

"Yeah."

"I finished school, I'm just kind of seeing where life takes me right now."

"I definitely understand that," Brannon says slowly. He takes a drink. "You seeing anyone?"

Tyler snorts.

"That's complicated."

"Oh?"

"Well, you know I'm gay, right?"

"Come on, Ty, I grew up with you," says Brannon.

"Just wanted to be clear," says Tyler, laughing as he takes another drink. "Pretty much everyone knew before I did."

"Was it hard? Coming out, I mean?"

"That's the thing," says Tyler. "I never really had a big 'coming out' moment... I was always just myself, just, I don't know... more open, I guess."

"That's good, though, isn't it?"

"Oh yeah," says Tyler. "I've had it pretty easy compared to other people I've known."

Brannon picks up his glass and finishes the beer inside.

"So what's so complicated?" asks Brannon.

Tyler smirks.

"Well, I met this guy like a month ago… his name's Alan. He works in retail with Chelle's ex. Anyway, we hit it off really well at first, started hanging out a lot."

Brannon nods as he pours more beer into his glass.

"I mean, like, four or five nights a week, you know? So then out of the blue, he just stops talking to me for two weeks, no explanation."

"That's weird."

Tyler refills his glass.

"I know! So then he randomly starts texting me like nothing's wrong, like it hasn't been two weeks since I last heard from him but instead of texting back and forth like we did, it'll take hours for him to get back to me, and then it'll just be one word, maybe two if I'm lucky. And it wouldn't be such a big deal if I didn't know that he's capable of more regular communication, you know?"

"Are you sure you're not reading too much into it?"

"I don't know, man, but it's driving me crazy," admits Tyler. "I mean, is it me? Is it something I did?"

"I doubt that," says Brannon. "The guy sounds like an ass."

Tyler smiles.

"I feel so crazy for even worrying about it," says Tyler. "I mean there's a ton of other people out there, you know?"

"I hear you, there," says Brannon. "Is he the first guy you've gone with?"

"Oh, no," says Tyler, laughing. "I didn't imprint on him or anything… there's been a few. There was only one other serious one, though. Pete. We went to school together."

"What's the story with that one?"

"Pete was… well, I guess you could say he was my first love," says Tyler.

"Say no more," says Brannon, looking down into his glass. "I know all too well how deep that hook can go."

"The sad part is we weren't even really together that long."

"Really? What happened?"

"I screwed it up," says Tyler. "Looking back, I don't think I was really ready for a relationship at that point, so I started to push him away."

"I'm sure it wasn't all your fault."

"Nah, probably not, but I wasn't very nice to him toward the end," says Tyler. "I've been trying to make it right ever since."

"Do you guys talk?"

"Yeah, but not often," says Tyler. "I've written him a few letters to try and clear the air, but I don't know…" His voice trails off as he stares into the glass, his right index finger running the rim.

Brannon takes a drink.

"Jesus, I didn't mean to turn this into a free therapy session!" Tyler says, looking up.

Brannon laughs.

"It's all good," he says. "I'm enjoying this! I mean, not the part where you have to deal with asshole gay dudes, but you know, hearing what you've been up to."

Tyler finishes the beer in his glass.

"So you said you work with Chelle? How's she doing?"

"She's good," says Tyler, the tone of his voice lightening considerably. "She said you reached out to her, too."

"Yeah, I was able to find everyone online. Haven't heard from Yorick or Kate, though."

"Well, Yorick's probably busy with his magic shows in Old Town."

"Wait… what?"

"Oh, yeah," says Tyler. "He's a street performer sometimes."

"That's wild!"

"And I know Chelle wants to get together with you."

"I can't wait to catch up with her, too!"

"Yeah, just give her a call."

Tyler empties the remaining beer in the pitcher into his and Brannon's glasses.

"I will," says Brannon. "Hey, Kate hasn't said anything, has she?"

"No," answers Tyler. "I haven't talked to her in a few months."

"Is she okay?"

"Yeah, she's just busy a lot of the time. She kind of pulled away from the group after you left. We still saw her but not as often. You know how that goes, though, sometimes friends just grow apart."

Brannon thinks for a moment. He holds up his glass.

"To growing back together," he says.

"To old friends," says Tyler, grinning.

They clink their glasses and take a drink.

\* \* \*

It didn't take the group long to decide that they wanted to set up for the night before doing anything else. Having been to the Pier a handful of times, they knew there was an old office that was mostly intact behind the arcade that would be the ideal place for them to sleep. It was set deep enough in the arcade to be away from the boardwalk and had a door that could be locked.

"This is perfect!" said Kate, rolling out her sleeping bag.

"I know, and we can keep the window open so we can hear the water, too," said Chelle as she pulled a stack of magazines out of her backpack. The others murmured in agreement as they, too, unpacked their bags, transforming the forlorn office into cozy, overnight accommodations. Aside from the window, part of the ceiling had broken away, providing a view of the night sky.

Once their sleeping space was set up, the group decided to go out into the arcade to find any games that could still be played. Luckily, there were several skee ball machines that were still functional, even though they had to keep score themselves, as well as a pool table that was only missing a few balls and had one stick to share between them. Yorick and Brannon had brought snacks and drinks to share with the group.

After the boys had finished a game of pool, Yorick ran back to the office and came back with a glass bottle.

"What's that?" asked Chelle.

"Beer," said Yorick. "I grabbed this before I left my house. I didn't know if anyone would want any."

"I've never had beer," said Chelle.

"Me neither," said Kate.

"Well, I think this is a good starter beer," said Yorick, with an added air of maturity. "My dad likes to drink some sometimes and I figured he wouldn't notice if one was missing."

"I've always wondered what beer tasted like," said Brannon.

"Well, here," said Yorick, "I mean, we *are* teenagers now." With a slight struggle, he twisted the cap off and handed the bottle to Brannon, who raised it to his lips. He took a small drink and swished it around in his mouth, swallowing a moment later.

He wrinkled his nose.

"I don't know if I liked that."

"Let me try," said Tyler. Taking the bottle, he took a drink, swallowing almost right away as a shudder ran through his body.

"Ew," he said. Genevieve was the next to try, followed by Yorick and then Chelle, who actually spit hers out.

"That's nasty!" she said. "How do people drink that stuff?"

Yorick took another drink.

"It's not as bad the second time. You want some, Kate?"

"No thanks," she said over her shoulder as she rolled a skee ball, landing in a hoop that would have given her forty points if the game's electronics still worked.

"Alright," said Yorick, passing the bottle to Brannon.

"You're right," he said. "It's not so bad the second time. Still, I'm glad we brought soda." They passed the beer around, taking sips and swigs, as the played their next game of pool.

Soon after, it was too dark to see in the arcade anymore so they made their way back to the office where they were set up to stay the night.

\* \* \*

The crowd in Old Town dissipates as the magic show in the square comes to an end until only one spectator remains, sitting quietly as the magician packs up his props. Finally, he stands and walks over to his old friend. It is a cloudy Tuesday afternoon, the air is cold as winter approaches.

"Hello, Yorick," says Brannon. "That was a hell of a show."

"Thanks," says Yorick, turning to look at him. "It was probably one of my last for the season. I heard you were back in town."

"Yeah, just kind of seeing where life takes me, I guess," says Brannon. He can hear the aggression in Yorick's voice. There is an awkward silence as a tourist walks by and drops a dollar into Yorick's collection bucket.

"So how are you?" asks Brannon.

"Fine."

Yorick grabs his bucket and starts counting the day's haul. Brannon puts his hands in his pockets and shifts around nervously.

"You okay?"

"Yup," comes Yorick's quick answer.

"Okay," says Brannon, not fully believing him. "I just, I don't know – I'm sorry if I caught you at a bad time."

Yorick looks up to the face of his old friend.

"Why are you doing this, Brannon?"

"Doing what?"

"This… Coming back to town, trying to get *the gang* back together. What's the point? We're not little kids anymore."

"Whoa," says Brannon, put off by Yorick's response.

"You left, we moved on. We grew up without you."

59

"That's harsh, man."

Yorick finishes packing his things and turns to walk away but stops to face Brannon again.

"Do you know what your leaving did to her?" he asks.

"I should go."

"No, I'm serious. Do you know how hard it was for me to stand by and watch her feel so sad and know, deep down, that no matter what I did, I couldn't make her feel better? That I wasn't the one she was thinking about whenever she'd stare off into space?"

"I didn't choose to leave, Yorick."

"No, but you didn't choose to keep in touch either."

"Okay, obviously I made a mistake coming here today. But this city is my home as much as it is yours and I don't know what your problem is, but I'm back and I'm here to make a life for myself. And I would have liked you to have been a part of that, but for whatever reason, I've pissed you off and I'm sorry, for whatever that was." He pauses. "But that was a long time ago and you need to get over it."

Yorick stares him in the face for several seconds before turning around and walking away. Brannon watches him walk down the street and round a corner, disappearing from sight.

*Well that didn't go as well as I would have liked,* he thinks.

Later that night, Brannon's phone rings with a number he doesn't recognize coming through. He hesitantly answers the phone.

"Hello?"

"Hey," says the person on the other end. "It's Yorick."

"Hey."

"So, listen," Yorick says. "I'm sorry about earlier. I was being an ass and you didn't deserve that."

"Okay."

"It's just… it was hard for me, you know? I missed you a lot, but once you were gone, things between me and Kate started changing, the way I felt about her, I mean. It took a long time but I finally worked up the nuts to ask her out and she turned me down. She said we were too good of friends, but I knew the real reason why."

Brannon is quiet.

"The real reason was you."

Brannon stares at his feet, not saying anything into his phone.

"And I get it, it wasn't your fault. But she missed the hell out of you and all I wanted was to make her feel better, to be the guy she thought about before going to sleep at night. But that spot was already taken by you, even though you were a thousand miles away.

And that's a little tough to stomach at fifteen… it tends to stick with you for a little while."

"I'm sorry," Brannon says quietly.

"You shouldn't be sorry," says Yorick. "You didn't do it; it's just the way it all played out." Yorick breaths a sigh of relief, having finally said the things he's held inside for so many years.

"Do you still talk to her?" asks Brannon.

"Sometimes."

"Yeah, I haven't heard from her since I've been back. I'm starting to wonder if I will at all, especially now."

"I don't know, man," he says. "All you can do is try."

"You're right."

"So, let's try this whole catching up thing again," Yorick says. "Would you wanna grab a beer sometime? Tonight, even, if you're free?"

Brannon remembers the first time they drank together, how neither of them had cared for the taste of beer.

"Sure," says Brannon. "That would be nice. I can meet you somewhere in about an hour?"

"Awesome," says Yorick. "I know just the place. I'll text you the address."

"Okay, cool."

"You know, sometimes Chelle and I still laugh about how she spit out that beer that night we stayed on the Pier."

"I was just thinking about that night!" says Brannon, smiling.

"Those were good times."

"Yeah," agrees Brannon.

"Well then, let's pick up where we left off," Yorick says.

\* \* \*

An hour later, having filled up on snacks and stories, the group decided they wanted to go out and explore the Southside Pier further. They made their way out of the office they were calling home for the night and out onto the Pier's boardwalk. The moon cast an ethereal glow over the entire Pier as the water idly lapped below. While they did not need flashlights on the boardwalk, each was glad to have one in hand to explore the areas that the moonlight couldn't reach.

Further down the Pier, the group split in half, with Tyler, Chelle and Genevieve going to explore another arcade while Brannon, Kate and Yorick stopped to look around the entrance of the old Ferris wheel. Most of the cars, enclosed cages that could seat up to four adults comfortably, had been removed when the Pier closed for safety reasons.

"Do you guys wanna try it out?" asked Brannon.

"It probably doesn't work anymore," said Yorick.

"And I don't know that I'd want to ride it if it did," said Kate.

"Well we wouldn't ride it, you guys," said Brannon.

"Come on," said Kate. "Let's check it out."

The group made their way through the queue to the loading dock, where a few cars remained attached to the structure, while others were scattered about an empty patio space.

"I dare you to get in one," Yorick said to Brannon, aiming his flashlight toward a car still connected to the wheel, particles of dust dancing in the beam of light.

"Get in one of those?" he asked. "No problem." Strutting fearlessly up the stairs to the nearest car, he opened the door and stepped in. The door creaked behind him as it closed on a hinge.

"See? This isn't so bad!" Brannon jumped to illustrate his point, unaware that doing so would cause the car to rock.

"Brannon!" screamed Kate, as the cage groaned on its rusty hinges. "Get out of there!"

Steadying himself in the cage, Brannon moved quickly to get out, opening the door and jumping back onto the platform.

"See?" he said. "Perfectly fine."

The Ferris wheel car continued to sway back and forth, finally coming to a halt.

"That could have been bad," said Kate. "What if it fell?"

"But it didn't," said Yorick.

Just then, a piercing scream tore through the Southside Pier. The three friends looked at each other, frozen.

*Oh my God, have we been caught?* thought Brannon. *Are the others okay? What's going on?*

"That was Chelle," Brannon finally said.

Instantly, they took off for the boardwalk. Racing down the Pier, they called for their friends, not worrying about who might hear them.

"We're over here!" they heard Tyler yell.

Genevieve and Chelle were close by, visibly shaken.

"What happened?" asked Brannon. "Are you guys alright?"

Kate rushed over to the two girls and attempted to comfort them, giving each a big hug. The wind had started to pick up and the water below was rolling more aggressively with each wave. Dead leaves rustled in the corners of the Pier.

"It'll be okay, you guys," she said.

"We were just in the arcade over there," said Tyler, panting as he nodded his head to the darkened entryway behind him. Brannon could just make out a row of old arcade machines and small, mechanical rocket ship.

"It's a lot like the other one, just with different games and stuff," he continued. "It's really dark back in there though, so we had to use our flashlights to look around."

"Why did you scream?" Yorick asked Chelle.

"T-there's something in there," said Chelle, stumbling over her words.

"I saw it, too," said Genevieve, her eyes wide behind her glasses.

"What is it?" asked Brannon, a little afraid of what he was about to hear. Tyler looked from Chelle to Genevieve before answering his friend. He seemed to be choosing his words carefully.

"We found a dead body."

\* \* \*

"Hey stranger," says Chelle, walking to Brannon's table. Her apron is messy and her hair is pulled back. It is late in the evening at Caramaya's Bar and Grille; the tables have already had their condiments collected.

"Chelle!" Brannon says, standing to give her a hug.

"I was wondering when you'd get here," she says, with a smile. After two failed attempts at getting together, Chelle invited Brannon to meet her for a late dinner at Sugar's 24 Hour Diner. She told him to meet her at work and they'd go from there.

"I got a little turned around on Canal."

"That happens," she says. "I hear things didn't go so well with Yorick."

"At first," says Brannon. "But I get where he was coming from. Hard to believe that was almost three weeks ago."

"What's hard to believe is how busy my schedule gets around the holidays," Chelle says with a laugh.

"I hear that," says Brannon. "Yorick and I are good now, though."

"That's great," says Chelle. "I've got a couple of things to finish up, do you want anything while you wait?"

"No, I'm good," he says.

"Okay," she says. "I'll be back in a few."

While he is alone, Brannon thinks back over the past few weeks and how quickly things have changed. He landed a job as a bank teller and would be moving into one of the vacant lofts in Tyler's building by the end of the week. Christmas was coming and he had decided to spend the holiday in the city.

*If only I could get a hold of Kate,* he thinks. Despite messages and invitations to connect online, Brannon has not heard a word from Kate in the month and a half he has been back. Truthfully, he is starting to worry that he will not be able to repair the damage that his long absence inflicted on their relationship.

"You ready?" asks Chelle as she walks up. She slips her coat on.

"Yeah, let's go," says Brannon, standing. The two walk out the front door and into the still air of the winter night.

"Glad I brought my hat," says Brannon, tipping his cap toward Chelle.

"I'm glad I brought my everything… and that Sugar's isn't too far from here."

Brannon laughs.

"Sure didn't miss this cold," he says. The two don't talk much as they hurry toward Sugar's Diner, only commenting on the weather and the various places they pass by. They are grateful to walk into the heat of the diner, finally able to shed their coats. They take seats at the counter and notice that it has started to snow outside, the flurries drifting through the streetlight beams.

"It's so pretty when it snows," says Chelle.

"Yeah," says Brannon, with a smile. "So what's good here?"

"Oh, this is one of my favorite places," says Chelle. "If you're in the mood for breakfast, you have to try the Sugar's Special. Their burgers are really good, too."

Brannon looks over the menu. When their waitress, an older woman whose nametag reads 'Shirl' walks over, he decides to take Chelle's advice and orders a Sugar's Special with a small coffee; Chelle orders a club sandwich. When they are alone again, Brannon turns to Chelle.

"So what are you up to these days? How are you doing?"

"I'm doing well," she says, taking a drink of soda. "I broke up with my boyfriend last month so I'm getting back into the dating scene."

"Oh, I'm sorry to hear that," says Brannon.

"Don't be," she says. "It wasn't working out. It's best for both of us."

"Oh, well, congratulations then?"

Chelle laughs.

"How about you?" she asks. "I was glad to hear that you were back in town."

"Yeah," he says. "I'm doing alright. Kind of just packed up and came back, didn't really have anything concrete set down, you know? Just a few ideas about this and that."

"That's brave."

"I guess," he says.

"Tyler tells me you're moving into his building?"

"Oh yeah," he says. "That's a really nice place. I'm glad he told me about it."

"Well, you know Tyler," says Chelle. "Always helping his friends."

"He told me about Alan."

"Really?" asks Chelle, raising an eyebrow. She takes another drink of soda. "Did you meet him?"

"No," says Brannon.

"You're not missing much," says Chelle. "What did you think?"

"Well, I guess we always knew Tyler was gay."

"No, well yeah we did, but not about that – what did you think about the Alan story?"

"I don't know," says Brannon. "Tyler's a good looking guy. I don't know why he's so hung up on this one in particular."

Chelle claps her hands together.

"Thank you!" she says.

"What?"

"I've been saying that for weeks!"

"Really?" Brannon takes a sip of his coffee.

"Yes, oh my God, Alan's awful. I don't know how to approach Tyler about it," says Chelle. "Besides, he works with my ex and I don't know, it's just kind of weird to still stay in the same social circle, you know?"

"He'll have to make the decision on his own," says Brannon, thinking about the decisions he's had to make on his own through the years.

"I guess."

"Hey, I wanted to ask you about something," Brannon says.

"What's up?"

"Have you heard from Kate?"

"What do you mean?"

"Since I've been back."

"Why?"

"Because I haven't. Everyone else reached out in one way or another except her."

"I talked to her a little bit."

"Is she mad at me?"

"Not exactly," says Chelle. "It's just... I don't know, weird for her, you know?"

"Why?"

"I'm just gonna say this," says Chelle. "You were her first love, Brannon. And then you were gone and she thought it was over and done with but now you're back and that brought up a whole bunch of emotions she hasn't had to deal with in a long time."

"Well, I didn't mean to put her out," Brannon says.

"Don't take it the wrong way," Chelle says quickly. "It's just gonna take her some time."

Shirl walks over with their plates of food. She sets them down with additional napkins, refills their drinks and walks away.

"You're right," says Brannon.

The two sit and eat in an awkward silence for a few moments until Brannon has an idea.

"Hey, what are you doing next Friday night?"

"Nothing that I know of, what's up?"

"I'll be moving into my new place and, well, do you think you or anyone else of the old crew would want to come over and help me put up some decorations? It's almost Christmas, after all."

"Oh, sure!" says Chelle, excited at the prospect of getting everyone together. "I think that would be really nice."

Brannon smiles.

"I'll send out a text and see who else can make it," he says. When he grabs his phone, he notices that he has a notification that came through about ten minutes ago.

Kate Farrell has accepted his request to connect online.

* * *

"A dead body?" asked Brannon, unsure if he had heard Tyler correctly.

"Yeah, a dead body," Tyler said. "A corpse."

Chelle and Genevieve shivered at the memory.

"What do we do?" Kate asked Brannon.

"Well, I guess we should call someone," he said.

"The police?" asked Yorick. "And what do we tell them when they ask why we're all out here?"

"He has a point," said Tyler.

"We could pretend you guys never saw it?" suggested Yorick.

"I'm never going to forget that," said Genevieve, her voice trembling. She took her glasses off to clean the lenses on her shirt.

"Oh no!" screamed Chelle.

"What's wrong?" asked Kate.

"My watch," she wailed, clutching her wrist. "I lost my watch and my grandma got it for me for my birthday!"

Kate looked toward Brannon.

"Is it in there?" he asked.

"It's gotta be," said Chelle, choking back tears. "I checked the time before we went in and now it's gone!" Kate gave Chelle a reassuring shoulder rub.

"We'll get it," she said.

"I'm not going in there," spat Yorick.

"I'll go in," said Brannon.

"I'll go with him," said Tyler, his flashlight in hand.

"Be careful," said Kate. The rest of the group moved away to wait in the shadows while Brannon and Tyler went on the mission to rescue Chelle's watch.

As the two boys made their way through the abandoned arcade, Brannon could not stop the chills that ran through his body.

"W-Where all did you guys go in here?" he asked Tyler.

"All over the place," he replied. "We didn't split up though. It's too creepy." Their flashlights shone through a mess of cobwebs. The floorboards beneath them creaked, the water beneath the floorboards crashed against the support beams over and over, a perpetual wave of noise that kept both boys on edge.

They heard a squeak.

"What was that?" asked Tyler.

"I'm sure it was nothing," said Brannon, his heart starting to beat faster.

"Yeah," said Tyler. "N-Nothing. We'll go with that."

They continued to move around the arcade until they came to a particularly dark aisle. Brannon swore he could smell something rotten mixing with the smells of the water and old boards.

"This is it," said Tyler. "This is where it is."

They had not yet found Chelle's watch and neither boy wanted to return empty handed to their friend. Despite his best attempts to stop it, Tyler's hands were shaking.

"I'm scared, Brannon."

"Don't be," he said, the words practically catching in his throat.

He breathed slowly and deeply, trying to keep from feeling light headed. They both swept their flashlights down to the floor, running along the various machines in the hope that they'd find Chelle's watch. Brannon lead his light further and further away from himself.

When the beam landed on a pair of cold, dead eyes, he screamed. "Oh shit!"

Tyler screamed and turned around. As Brannon swung his flashlight around to follow his friend, he noticed something.

"Tyler, wait!"

"What?!"

"L-look at this," he said, his voice still shaking. As he had turned around, the flashlight had illuminated the rest of the body the face was attached to, and while there *was* a lifeless body lying on the floor, this particular form had never held any life to begin with. Tyler and Brannon were looking at an old fortune teller game that had fallen over, or perhaps been pushed, and the fortune teller inside, a gypsy woman swathed in jewels and a purple scarf, had fallen out and onto the floor.

As they swung their flashlights around to get a better look at the scene, Brannon spotted Chelle's watch on the floor, a short distance from the fortune teller.

Tyler laughed first and Brannon started soon after he picked up the watch. They giggled all the way out of the arcade and back out to the boardwalk.

"Here you go," said Brannon, handing Chelle her watch.

"Thank you," she said.

"What's so funny?" asked Yorick.

"You guys have to come with us," said Tyler.

"Go back in there?" asked Genevieve, sounding almost offended at the suggestion.

"Trust me," said Tyler. "You don't have anything to be afraid of."

"He's right," Brannon said. "It's not what you think."

"Well, I trust you guys," said Kate. "So let's go see what this was all about."

* * *

Hours after his dinner with Chelle, Brannon sends out invites to his old friends for the housewarming party. He has gathered from most of the group that they haven't all been together in a while and thinks it would be fun for everyone to see each other. The replies came soon after.

Chelle, of course, said yes. Tyler said that he might have plans with Alan, but he'd let Brannon know. Yorick and Genevieve had both said yes, as well.

Kate didn't reply.

On Friday night, Brannon has gotten most of his things unpacked and is, for the most part, settled into his loft. He spent the afternoon shopping for decorations and a Christmas tree that everyone could help assemble. Stopping by the corner store on his way home, he even grabbed a bottle of eggnog for them all to drink.

*This will be fun,* he thinks. *Like old times.* His stereo is quietly playing Christmas music and it is once again flurrying outside. His friends arrive soon after, each bringing a small house warming gift as well as drinks to share as the night progresses. Even Tyler shows up later in the evening, telling the group that his night with Alan had ended early. And though he smiles and laughs more in this night than he has in a long time, Brannon cannot help but feel the absence of Kate Farrell cutting deep into his heart.

After everyone leaves, he sits on his couch and looks out his large, industrial window as the snow swirls in the night sky. He swishes what's left of his whiskey and soda in the bottom of a tumbler.

*Where is she?* he thinks. He takes a sip and feels the alcohol warm his throat.

Across the room, a notification pops up on his computer screen.

*What's that?* he thinks, finishing his drink. He walks over to investigate, sitting down at his desk before opening the internet browser. His mouth hangs slightly open as he strokes the stubble on his cheeks.

The message is from Kate.

She wants to talk.

* * *

After a few more hours of exploring the Southside Pier, the group of friends decided they wanted to get back to the office and get to sleep. The time was nearing 2:30 A.M. and each was getting tired.

Brannon and Kate, however, decided to stay out a little while longer. They were in a pair, they'd said, so they could look after each other. No one had any objections. A little while later, they found themselves laying on two benches, side by side, staring into the night sky. The moon shone brightly, surrounded by stars.

"This was fun," said Brannon.

"Yeah," said Kate. "It was. I'm surprised no one caught us."

ANDREW NOLES

Brannon laughed.

"Me too, actually," he said. "Hey, can I ask you something?"

"Sure," Kate said, slowly. "What's up?"

Brannon sat up on his bench.

"Earlier when I was in that Ferris wheel car, why did you freak out so bad?"

"I didn't want you to get hurt."

"Yeah, but I was okay."

"I know, Brannon," Kate said, sitting up so she could look at him. "I just didn't want anything to happen to you. That would make me really sad."

She smiled at him.

"Thanks," he said. He stretched his arms out and looked around. "We'd better start heading back."

Brannon and Kate walked back toward the old office where the rest of their friends were sleeping.

"Hey," he said, stopping her. "What do you say to one more game of skee ball?"

She smiled.

"Sure."

They made their way into one of the arcades and picked two machines side by side they could play at, moonlight streaming through a hole in the roof.

Brannon's first three tosses landed in the ring worth ten points. Kate had landed two in the twenty point rings and one in the thirty.

"I'm gonna catch up to you," he said a grin.

"I doubt that," she said, giggling.

They continued to toss their skee balls, keeping mental note of their points as it had been years since the machine had actually been powered up.

On her last toss, Kate's ball landed in the ring worth forty points. Brannon had one ball left to throw.

"I'm still gonna win," he said.

"Prove it," said Kate.

Brannon stepped up to the machine and rolled his last ball up the ramp and toward the rings. It shot into the air and landed in the ring worth fifty points, putting Brannon ahead of Kate by ten points.

"Yes!" he said, jumping up and down.

"Alright, alright," she said. "You win."

He smiled at her.

"Good game," he said, extending his hand.

"Yeah, yeah," she said with feigned apathy.

She shook his hand.

"We should get back," said Brannon.

They heard a noise, a faint creaking.

"Wait, did you hear that?" she asked.

"Yeah," he said.

The noise was growing louder.

"It almost sounds like – "

The creaking became cracking and years of neglect and decay with Brannon's jumping acting as a catalyst caused part of the floor in the arcade to crumble, falling at least twenty feet into the crashing water below.

Kate snapped her head around to look at Brannon just as the floor gave way.

"Brannon!" she screamed, but it was too late.

He looked at her with terror in his eyes as he fell through the floor, unable to even scream for help.

* * *

The snow crunches under the wheels of the cab as it slowly makes its way down 8th Street, windshield wipers batting flakes away as quickly as they can. Brannon sits in the back seat, staring out of the window, lost in his thoughts. It is Christmas Eve and he cannot believe he is on his way to meet Kate.

"Over here," says Brannon, snapping out of his daze. The driver pulls over to the curb in front of St. Kevin's Cathedral. Brannon hands him a fifty dollar bill.

"Keep the change," he says. "Merry Christmas."

"You too, buddy!" says the enthusiastic driver.

Brannon gets out of the cab, smoothing his pea coat as he looks to the top of the main steeple, momentarily breathless at the sheer beauty of this moment: the architecture, the snow, the girl waiting for him inside.

*This is happening*, he thinks. He takes a deep breath and walks toward the entrance. Pulling the heavy door open, he quickly ducks in and brushes away the snow that has collected on his coat.

After Kate had written him online, he wasn't sure how to proceed. He had run countless scenarios through his head for how this would play out, coming face to face with the girl he left behind so long ago.

He follows the signs to one of the balconies, hoping to have a better view of the pews below. Kate had told him that she would be attending Christmas Eve mass at 10:30 P.M. with her family and that she could stay afterward if he would like to meet her there. It was the first time she had offered to meet in person and he was not going to let this opportunity pass him by.

He walks to the front of the balcony and surveys the quiet cathedral. He sees people scattered throughout, some kneeling, some sitting, most deep in thoughtful prayer. He looks to the statues making up the Nativity at the base of the altar, hand sculpted, hand painted figures flanked by evergreen branches and strands of white lights.

"It's beautiful, isn't it?"

Time all but stops.

Brannon can feel his heart beating in his chest, faster and faster; his breath catches in his throat. Slowly, he turns around. And there, after all those years, she sits.

Kate Farrell.

"Hi," he says, a smile on his face. He walks over and sits down next to her.

"Hello."

"It is," he says. "It's beautiful."

*And so are you*, he thinks. Her red hair falls in loose curls around the shawl that drapes her shoulders.

"I've always loved coming here on Christmas Eve. It's a nice escape before the craziness that starts tomorrow."

"I know what you mean."

They sit in silence and watch the people below as they move about St. Kevin's Cathedral. A little girl is curled up in a pew next to her parents while an altar boy clears away the remnants of the mass that just ended. An old woman with glasses on a beaded chain lights a candle and drops a few coins into a jar; their clanking echoes throughout the church.

"It's nice to see you," she says.

"It's great to see you too, Kate."

She turns to face him.

"I'm not going to dance around this, Brannon."

He knows what is coming next.

"Why did you come back?"

"Well, I finished school and – "

"I know that's what you told the others," she interrupts. "But really, why did you come back?"

He starts to speak, but stops, contemplating how best to say what has been on his mind for so, so long.

"For you," he finally says. "I came back for you."

She faces forward and slides her hand over his.

"I'm glad you did."

"You know it wasn't my fault, right?" he asks. "I didn't want to go away. But there was no way I could have stayed, I wasn't even old enough."

"I know that now," she says. "But I'd be lying if I told you I understood it then. That it was easy for me to watch you just go away. And this isn't somewhere I'd want to be caught lying."

Brannon smiles.

"I'm sorry it took me so long to write you back," she says. "It's just that, well, I worked so hard to put away all of the things I felt for you. I mean, to be honest, I didn't know if I'd ever see you again. And then all of a sudden, here you were, back in town and ready to pick things up and I wasn't sure what I wanted to do."

"Well, what do you want?"

"Let's take this slow," she responds. "I want to see where things go."

He turns his palm upward so that their fingers intertwine. Kate scoots closer to him and rests her head on his shoulder. The years between them melt away, until it feels as though just last night, the two were exploring the Southside Pier.

"It's getting late," Brannon says.

"Yeah," agrees Kate. "I should get home."

"Me, too."

"What are you doing tomorrow?"

"Tomorrow? Oh, I don't know. I don't have any plans really."

"You should come over."

"Yeah?"

"Yeah," she says.

"I'd like that."

She smiles at him.

"Let's go," she says.

They stand and leave the balcony, their footsteps echoing throughout the cathedral. The midnight bells begin to ring as they step out into the snowy night.

"Merry Christmas, Kate," Brannon says.

"Merry Christmas."

And there, in the first few moments of Christmas, as snow falls around them on the steps of St. Kevin's Cathedral, Brannon pulls

Kate close and gives her the kiss each has dreamed about for so many years.

* * *

"Oh my God, Brannon!" screamed Kate, unable to move. She wanted to run to where Brannon had fallen through the floor to see if he was okay and help him back up, but she was terrified that the floor would continue to break away and she, too, would fall through.

She didn't know what she would do if he had gone all the way to the water, as there was no way he could have survived such a fall. The seconds she stood there felt like days.

She started to cry.

"Brannon?" she called softly.

The waves crashed below.

An owl hooted.

Somewhere in the distance, church bells rang.

Kate shut her eyes tight, not wanting to believe what she just saw.

"Kate!"

Her eyes snapped open.

"Brannon?!"

"I'm okay!" he yelled. "I'm just a few feet down, I'm standing on a support beam that seems like it's pretty steady. I just need help getting back up!"

"Is it safe for me to come over there?"

"I don't know," he called. "Is there anything around you that you can use to pull me back up?"

She used her flashlight to look around the arcade, finally seeing an old mop resting near a strength tester.

"I'll be right back!" she yelled. She ran to the game and grabbed the mop, stepping lightly for fear of falling through the floor.

"I'm back and I have a mop," she said when she returned.

"Okay, that'll work!" said Brannon. "Can you lay it over the hole?"

"Yeah, but how close do I need to get?"

"Only get as close as you have to," he said.

Taking a deep breath, Kate approached the hole Brannon had fallen through. When she was a few feet away, she dropped to her knees and pushed the mop on the floor toward it until it cut across the gap in the floor like a tiny bridge.

"Will that work?" she asked.

"I'll give it a try!" Brannon yelled back. She sat there on her knees, trying to keep her flashlight steady over the hole so Brannon could see where to grab.

She gasped when she first saw his hand reaching up to grab the mop handle and was relieved to watch him steady his grip as the other hand came up. She watched him work his way to the side of the hole, hand over hand as though he was on the monkey bars at the school playground.

"How're you doing?" she asked.

"I'm getting there," he said.

She watched his hands move to the side of the hole and feel around, making sure it would support his weight when he tried to lift himself up.

"Is it safe?" she called.

"I think so," he said. "I'm about to jump up."

Kate held her breath.

She watched as Brannon lifted himself up, cautiously grabbing the floor. When they heard the sickeningly familiar sound of old wood creaking, she lunged forward, grabbing his hand in hers as he jumped forward.

The two rolled away to safety as another small piece of the floor broke away and fell to the water below. They stayed on their backs, staring at the ceiling.

"You okay?" she asked.

"You saved my life, Kate," he said.

"I-I-I... I guess I did," she said.

"Thank you."

"You're welcome," she said, realizing that they were still holding hands. They stayed silent as the events of the last few minutes played on a loop in their minds.

"Do you think the office is safe for us to be sleeping in?" Kate asked.

"Oh, I think that's fine," Brannon said. "It's closer to the shore and it's not as high up there. Besides, it didn't take much for that floor to break and we've been in that office all night."

Kate sat up and looked down at Brannon.

"I'm glad you're okay."

"Me, too."

"I don't know what would have happened if..."

"I know," said Brannon, sitting up. "It was scary."

They looked into each other's eyes, their faces drawn toward each other.

"We should probably get back," said Kate, snapping out of the moment.

"Yeah," Brannon said. "We should."

"Do you think we should tell them what happened?"

"We could, but I wouldn't want to scare them."

"Good call," she said.

Ten minutes later, Brannon and Kate walked back into the room where their friends were fast asleep in their sleeping bags. A few hours after that, the group woke up to a room bathed in sunlight. They rolled their sleeping bags and collected their things. They walked together down the pier to where they had locked their bikes. Laughing about the stories of the night before, they parted ways and set plans to get together that afternoon at a festival in Old Town.

Two months after the night on the Southside Pier with his friends, Brannon's father received the news that he'd been promoted at work and would be transferred. By the time school started again, Brannon was gone and would not return to the city until many years had passed.

\* \* \*

On the afternoon of New Year's Eve, Brannon and Kate sit in a cab on their way to what remains of the Southside Pier. The day after Christmas, Brannon had written the entire group, reminding them of a night that most had all but forgotten. He found it fitting, in a way, to bring everyone to the pier, the place where they had felt so alive as children, to ring in the new year.

*Who knows what this year will bring,* he thinks, looking at Kate.

She smiles back.

"What?" she asks.

"Nothing," says Brannon. "Sometimes, it just... I don't know. It feels surreal, to be here with you, in this cab. Going back to the pier."

"Well, believe it," she says, leaning over to give him a kiss.

The cab driver lets them out in a parking lot and drives away. Most of the snow from the Christmas snowstorm has melted, though piles remain here and there throughout the lot. A short distance away, Tyler and Chelle sit in Tyler's car, listening to music as they wait for the rest of the group. Genevieve and Yorick pull up as Tyler and Chelle are getting out of the car to greet Brannon and Kate.

Everyone is excited to see each other and they fondly recall their adventure on the pier as they make their way down to what remains of the entrance.

"You guys, look at this," says Genevieve.

"What is it?" asks Yorick.

"I'm pretty sure this is the tree we hid our bikes under," she says. "See – look! There's our initials!"

There, in the bark of the tree, were six sets of initials, carved so many years ago at the beginning of their adventure on the Southside Pier.

"I still can't believe we didn't get caught," says Chelle.

Tyler and Yorick nod in agreement.

The six friends stand and look out toward the water, over the burnt ruins of the Southside Pier.

"Hey guys," says Yorick. "I have something for us." He pulls a beer for each of them out of his bag.

"Oh my God!" says Chelle. "I promise I won't spit this one out!"

"Times sure have changed, huh?" Genevieve asks, laughing.

"Well at least we're of age now," says Yorick, smiling as he passes the bottles around. "Let's have a toast."

"A toast to a new year," says Genevieve.

"To the Southside Pier," says Tyler.

"To not getting caught that night we stayed here," says Yorick.

"To the memories," says Chelle.

"To old friends," says Kate.

"To new beginnings," says Brannon.

Each raises their bottles and takes a drink.

Genevieve starts to laugh.

"Do you guys remember that 'dead body'?" she asks.

"Oh, come on!" says Chelle. "That fortune teller was damn creepy!"

"No, what's creepy is that we took her back to that office with us," says Tyler.

Brannon smiles.

"Do you guys think any of that stuff survived the fire?"

"Nah," says Tyler. "I'd doubt it."

Over the next hour, the six friends wander the beach that used to be home to the Southside Pier. They share stories of how their lives have changed over the years and reminisce about the days of their youth.

Stepping away from the group, Brannon and Kate look toward their friends.

"Isn't it crazy?" she asks.

"What?"

"This," she says. "This whole thing, the Pier is burnt down but we're all here, back together like we're kids again."

"I don't know," he says. "I kinda like it."

"Me, too," she says, leaning in for a kiss.

Brannon puts his arm around her shoulder and looks at his childhood friends, now a group of young adults. In an hour, the group will part ways and get ready for their various New Year's Eve plans, though they will get together more often now that they have reconnected. Brannon and Kate will spend the rest of the day together and ring in the New Year quietly in his loft.

What the future holds, he can't be sure, but in this moment, surrounded by the friends he considers family near the charred remains of a place they all hold so dear, Brannon realizes that for the first time in years, he feels as though he is where he's supposed to be.

Brannon smiles at the thought.

"Come on," he says to Kate. "Let's catch up with the others."

# UNTITLED 'LONELY MODEL' PROJECT

*Thursday*

The lines on the paper stare him in the face, silently challenging his ability to write, his creativity, the passion he's fostered since childhood that he's finally decided to act on. Simon Dawes unleashes an exasperated sigh and leans back in the folding chair, covering his face with his hands. He can feel the minutes of his break at work slowly ticking away, leaving him, once again, creatively unfulfilled with an empty page of notebook paper.

*What am I doing wrong?* he thinks. *This used to come to me so easily when I was a kid.* He scribbles a few lines on the paper then rips it from its spiral and crumples it into a ball.

"This is pointless," he says.

The door to the management office opens and Simon's general manager, Ivy Risidik, walks out. Ivy had personally hired Simon to work at The Cinderhösen Clothing Company some time ago and relies more on him than most of his co-workers.

"Oh, hey there," she says.

"Hey."

"How much longer are you on break?"

"About five more minutes," says Simon, glancing at the clock on the wall.

She walks over and sits down next to him at the break table.

"Everything okay?" he asks.

She hesitates.

"I just got off the phone with Pietro De Luca."

"De Luca… how do I know that name?"

"He's the personal assistant to Cinnamon von Cinderhösen."

"Wait, as in…"

"…the owner and CEO of The Cinderhösen Clothing Company," she finishes.

"So, the big boss."

"Yeah," says Ivy. "The big, big boss."

"What did he have to say?"

"She's coming here," says Ivy. "Cinderhösen will be here for a visit in one week."

"Oh, shit!"

"My sentiments exactly."

"Did we do something wrong?"

"Nope," says Ivy. "She just likes to visit a certain number of stores each year and ours finally came up."

"Just in time for the holiday season, too."

"Yeah, her timing couldn't have been worse," says Ivy. "And I was hoping her store visits were just stories the higher-ups made up to scare general managers… damn it!"

"We'll be okay. It's just a visit."

"Simon, this is the woman that threw an entire wall of jeans on the floor because they weren't folded to her liking during one of these 'routine' visits last year."

"So she's particular?"

"She once broke a mannequin in half because of its placement."

"Very particular."

"I'm calling a leadership staff meeting for tomorrow," says Ivy. "I know it's your day off, but could you stay for a few hours afterward to start getting stuff together?"

"Sure."

"You're awesome," she says. She looks at her watch. "I'm gonna run outside for a cigarette real quick, get back out on the floor and tell Kirby he's next in the break rotation."

"Okay," says Simon.

Ivy stands and walks back to the management office.

"Hey Ivy?" calls Simon.

"Yeah?"

"It's just a visit," he says. "Don't freak out."

"Thanks, Simon," she replies. "I'll try not to."

\* \* \*

*Friday*

"Alright everyone, let's get started," says Ivy, addressing the seven people on her leadership team scattered about the back room of The C³. "I know this meeting was short notice so first of all I want to thank all of you for coming. And a special thank you to those of you who *aren't* hung over… Dominic."

Dominic Thorton raises his head from the table, a pair of wayfarers hiding his bloodshot eyes.

"Why do you have to single me out?" he asks. He lifts his sunglasses and raises an eyebrow at his general manager, a smirk on his face.

"Not today, Domino," Ivy says with a sigh.

"Well why aren't any of the sales kids here?" he asks.

"We have six days to get this place in perfect condition for Cinnamon von Cinderhösen's visit, I needed to talk to you guys alone first," says Ivy. "Try not to screw around too much?"

"Alright, fine," Dominic says, folding his arms on the table.

"We can do this, you guys," says Ivy. "It's just gonna take some extra teamwork." She looks around the room, mentally running through the roster, from her assistant managers, Alan Brodecker and Jacinda Hall, to her two shift leads, Simon Dawes and Kirby Cochrane, and her three sales specialists, Imani Tahan, Dominic Thorton and Carrie Candelario, who started last week.

"Clearly we have our work cut out for us," Dominic says under his breath.

Ivy rolls her eyes.

"Well, you're not wrong," she says. "Here's how I want this to go – obviously, we'll be open throughout the next week leading up to this visit, so I need everyone on their A-game with sales. Help the sales associates every way you can. If our numbers aren't there when Cinderhösen gets here, the rest of our work doesn't mean a thing. This goes for all of you: Lead by example.

"I need all of you selling as much as you can. Everyone who walks through that door is greeted and no one leaves without an upsale – they're buying jeans? They need a belt. They're buying a top? They need a coordinating scarf. Wardrobing… Got it?"

The group murmurs in acknowledgement.

"And push the credit apps, okay? We're falling behind for the month," she continues. "Moving on, Simon and Kirby, you're both in charge of overall presentation. Kirby, I want you to focus on the sales floor. Everything is folded and hung up in its correct place.

We're evicting the dust bunnies; every surface is dusted and polished. We'll all be pitching in with this, even the associates if we need them."

Kirby looks to the three sales specialists, wondering how much work he can pawn off on them before getting in trouble.

"Simon, I need you to work your magic with the display windows. As you know, each store decides what goes in them and you're my main man for this."

"You got it," says Simon, smiling.

"Alan and Jacinda, you'll be helping me with the million things that are bound to go wrong between now and this visit."

They nod their heads.

"I want to take today to hammer out a plan and get a few things squared away and then I'm not as worried about the weekend, we just need to stay on top of things," says Ivy. "Because of the visit, we're getting a drop shipment on Monday and I want to bust all that stuff out as quickly as we can. Alright, we have about a half hour until the mall opens. Alan, will you go count the drawers for me? We need to get the tills up. If no one has any questions, I'm gonna run and get a coffee."

No one says anything.

"Very good," says Ivy. "Meeting adjourned."

Everyone stands and heads toward the sales floor.

"Hey Simon," calls Dominic.

"What's up?" he asks.

"Aren't you off today?"

"Yeah, but Ivy asked if I'd come in and start getting things ready for this visit. Are you gonna stick around, too?"

"Nah, fuck that," says Dominic. "I'm going home and going to bed."

Simon rolls his eyes.

"I'll see you tomorrow."

* * *

Later that morning, Kirby is standing behind the register while Simon is emptying a box of rolled boxerbriefs into a display bin near the counter. Kirby loosens his belt while Simon arranges the packs of underwear into neat rows.

"Getting a little tight?" Simon asks. "I'll give you first dibs on the belt box if you wanna get one from here."

Kirby shoots him a dirty look.

"Very funny, ass," he says. "I've just been going on a lot of dinner dates lately... Not that you'd know a lot about that."

Simon shoots a hurt look toward Kirby.

"Sorry," says Kirby, shifting in his too-tight shirt. "I need to start going on dates to the gym or something."

"You could always go by yourself?"

"Please," says Kirby, rolling his eyes. "Why do anything like that when you can get someone else to pay for it and *maybe* get some play while you're at it?"

Simon raises an eyebrow as a woman walks in wearing a floppy hat.

"Good morning," Simon says.

"Let us know if you need help finding anything, okay?" says Kirby.

"Okay, thanks," she says, hurrying away.

Kirby turns to face Simon.

"Do you think we did something wrong?" he asks.

"With that lady?" responds Simon.

"No, I don't care about her," says Kirby. "I mean this visit."

"No, Ivy said that Cinderhösen makes visits like this all the time."

"Yeah, I know, but, you know... what are the odds?"

Simon looks at him, confused.

"Look, I'm just saying, when the bigwigs come to town, it never ends well. Assholes are clenched, tensions run high... heads roll."

"Come on, Kirby," says Simon, rolling his eyes. "Don't you think you're being a little dramatic?"

Kirby shrugs.

"I'm just being cautious," he says, walking over to stand by Simon. "These people don't care about little workers like us."

Simon finishes filling the underwear display, takes a deep breath and crinkles his nose.

"What's that smell?"

"Oh!" says Kirby. "That's my new cologne, don't you like it?"

"You smell like an old gigolo."

"Oh, fuck you, Simon."

"I'm just giving you shit!" Simon says, laughing.

"Yeah, whatever," says Kirby. "First you call me fat, then you say I smell bad... and it was a gift from the new boy, for your information."

"Oh? Did he give it to you at one of the dinner dates?"

"That was a different guy," says Kirby.

"Is this the guy from the shoe sto – "

"That didn't work out," Kirby says quickly. "You know that new guy that works at the perfume store?"

"The little blonde one?"

"My little perfume store twink," Kirby says, smiling. "I don't usually go for guys like him, but what can I say? I like his smile."

"What's his name?"

"Nice try, Simon, but I actually remember this one. His name's Benni," Kirby says proudly. "He spells it with an 'i.'"

"Of course he does," Simon says, shaking his head. "How do you keep it all straight?"

"You just go with it," says Kirby. "And you trust that someday things are gonna work out."

The woman in the floppy hat walks up holding a blazer.

"Great choice!" says Kirby, turning his attention to the customer. "You know we have the best necklace to pair with that, right?" He slides out from behind the counter and whisks her away to look at the jewelry racks.

*He's always so good at wardrobing,* thinks Simon as he picks up the empty box and heads to check the progress on a task he assigned to a few of the sales associates.

* * *

Around 3:30 that afternoon, Carrie Candelario comes in for her closing shift with her boyfriend, Phin Welik, walking behind her.

"Hey Simon," she calls.

"Oh, hey!" he replies, continuing to fold a stack of jeans. Phin stays on the floor while Carrie goes to the back to clock in. He glances through a rack of dress shirts and walks over to Simon.

"Hey man," Phin says. "How's it going?"

Simon looks up and smiles.

"I'm good, how are you?"

"Not bad," Phin responds. "Haven't seen you in a while!"

"Yeah, I know," Simon says awkwardly. "Working in a mall does that, especially at this time of the year."

"Gotcha," says Phin. "So how've you been?"

"Can't complain. I'm sure Carrie told you we've got a big visit coming up."

"Yeah, she said the woman this place is named after is coming in?"

"That's right," says Simon. "Everyone's kind of freaking out."

"I know Carrie's worried since she's still the new girl."

"Eh, I don't think she'll be the new girl for long," says Simon. "I know they're still looking for another sales associate or two, maybe some holiday help. Plus, Alan's the one who technically got her in here and he practically runs this place, so she'll be fine."

"Is he here today?"

"Alan? No, well, he was here for our meeting this morning but then he took off. Jacie had the day shift and Ivy's coming back to close."

"Gotcha."

Carrie walks out.

"Hey, Simon," she says. "Jacinda's in the back, she asked me to see if you could go back there for a few minutes before she pulls Kirby's drawer."

"Oh, sure."

"Hey, it was great to see you," Phin says, holding out his hand.

Simon clumsily shakes it.

"And I was sorry to hear about you and Chelle."

"Thanks," Simon says with a forced smile and gritted teeth. He quickly turns and walks toward the back, ignoring the sound of Carrie hitting Phin in the arm and the hushed *"What?!"* that follows.

\* \* \*

By 4:10 P.M., Simon is standing at the counter in the coffee shop talking with his friend, the barista Ravi Suthyan.

"Grande mocha with a shot of vanilla, easy on the foam?" asks Ravi.

"You got it, man," Simon replies.

"I didn't expect to see you today," says Ravi, ringing up Simon's drink.

"Yeah, well, that's what happens when your company's CEO decides to pop in for a visit with only one week to get ready." He hands Ravi his credit card.

"One week?!" he blurts out. "That's insane! At least you had some warning though, it could have been worse."

"True," says Simon. In a sequence of quick movements, Ravi grabs a steaming pitcher and pours the milk in, tosses in a thermometer and puts it under the steam wand.

"So hey, man, I've been meaning to ask you," says Ravi. "You been down by the toy store lately?"

"Not really, no. Why?"

"Well you know I've been seeing Alontay that works there, yeah?" Ravi grabs a grande cup from the dispenser below the counter.

"Oh, I didn't know that," says Simon. "Good for you."

"Yeah, I heard through the grapevine that she'd been scoping me out for a bit, so I went down there one night just to say hi and give her my number, right? So we start talking and decide to go to that diner, Sugar's, to talk more after our shifts. The next thing I know, it's 4:00 A.M. and I'm picking up the check!"

"I knew chivalry wasn't dead."

Ravi pours two freshly brewed shots of espresso into the cup.

"But yeah, that was our first date a few Fridays ago," he says. "So last night, we're hanging out and she tells me about this girl that works with her named Hannah."

"Okay."

"So Hannah's kind of new, you might have seen her walking around, little blonde chick, big smile?"

Simon shakes his head as Ravi squirts two pumps of vanilla syrup into his drink.

"You'd probably know her if you saw her," Ravi says. "But what I'm getting at is that apparently she's got her eye on a certain employee at The C³." He pours the steamed milk into Simon's drink.

"If it's Kirby or Alan, I can guarantee you neither one is remotely interested."

"No shit," says Ravi, mixing the mocha together. "I'm talking about you!"

"What?"

"Yeah, man! And I mean, you're both single," he says. "Why not? You two can meet up here, it's a neutral place and what's better than a coffee shop hook up, eh? Am I right?" He puts a lid on the drink and sets it on the counter.

"Dude, come on, it hasn't even been a month," Simon says, rolling his eyes as he picks up his drink. "This is real life, Ravi, not some show on TV."

"This isn't real life," says Ravi. "This is the mall. We could probably have our *own* show on TV. You gotta get back on the horse, man!"

Simon raises an eyebrow.

"Okay, not my best metaphor," Ravi admits. "But you know what I mean!"

Simon takes a drink of his mocha.

"Thanks, but no thanks."

"You should think about it."

"I'll let you know."

"Good!" says Ravi. "You gonna be in tomorrow?"

"Tomorrow and every day until this visit's over."

"Ouch."

"Tell me about it."

* * *

*Saturday*

A little before noon, Simon is walking into the mall.

*Thank God I'm working a mid today,* he thinks, fighting his way through the traffic in the mall. *Saturdays are supposed to be busy, but this is ridiculous!*

"Simon!" calls Ivy when she sees him walking in. Simon is momentarily overwhelmed by the amount of people in the store.

"Hey Ivy," he says slowly.

"We've been slammed all morning," says Ivy. "I've got Carrie and Imani on registers right now and all the sales kids I could afford on the floor. I need you to take over for Carrie for a while so she can go on break. Alan and Dominic should be here in a little bit and when they get here, I want you to start planning out what to do with these windows!" She gestures toward the front of the store and the displays that have been there for the past month.

"Sounds good," Simon says.

"Awesome, go get clocked in."

The first part of his shift is a blur of transactions and rejected credit applications with a few returns sprinkled in to keep the day interesting. Ivy eventually pulls Imani and puts Carrie back on the register. Finally, Alan arrives for his closing shift and takes over Simon's post, allowing him time to start working on the window displays for the visit. Typically, Ivy just has him change what the mannequins are wearing and move them around. He knows, though, that with Cinnamon von Cinderhösen coming, he needs to do something more.

He sits at the break table, tapping his pen on a blank legal pad.

*Where do I even start?* he thinks. He makes a column for each of the eight mannequins in the windows and sits back.

"Now what?" he says aloud. Usually, he just takes in suggestions for what to put on the mannequins and gets them back out in a shift, but this time it's different. Ivy is counting on him, his co-workers are counting on him. Cinnamon von Cinderhösen herself is counting on him, even if she doesn't know it yet.

He thinks about Chelle and the night they broke up.

"I can't do this anymore, Simon," she had said. They were

standing outside of El Scorcho after an exceptionally awkward night of karaoke.

"Do what?"

"This. You and me. Us."

He was silent. He had a feeling this was coming.

"I'm done."

He looked to the ground.

"Are you going to say anything?"

He swallowed and looked at her.

"I'm sorry."

"That's it? That's all you've got?"

"I'm sorry it didn't work out," he said. "I'm sorry I didn't want to sing tonight and I'm sorry I couldn't be the boyfriend you wanted me to be."

Chelle shook her head as she stepped to the curb.

"It's not just about the singing," she said, raising her hand. Within seconds, a cab had pulled over and she opened the door.

"Good bye, Simon," she said as she got into the cab.

Chelle closed the door and looked away as the cab drove off, leaving Simon alone on the dark sidewalk. He had always figured things weren't going to last with Chelle, but that didn't ease the pain of the moment, nor did it stop him from thinking about it frequently in the following weeks.

"Earth to Simon," says Dominic.

Simon snaps his head around, not realizing that Dominic had walked in while he was lost in his memory.

"What are you working on?" asks Dominic.

"Oh, uh, the windows for the visit."

"I see..."

Dominic puts his bag in his locker and closes it.

"Yeah, exciting stuff."

Dominic and Simon both nod awkwardly.

"Hey, man, are you okay?" asks Dominic, adjusting his name tag.

"Yeah, yeah, I'm fine," says Simon. "Just a little nervous about this visit is all."

"Oh," says Dominic. "I wouldn't sweat that. She'll come, she'll criticize, she'll leave. I've been through corporate visits in retail before, they're all the same."

"Yeah," says Simon, only half paying attention.

"Alright, well, I'd better get out there before Ivy shits herself."

"Will you tell her I'm gonna go on break?"

"You got it, bro."

* * *

On his breaks, Simon enjoys walking laps around the mall, stretching his legs a bit and visiting the friends he's made during the time he's worked there. He walks past Bezel & Crown, a small watch shop to see if his friend, Charlie, is working. Charlie has owned his own watch repair business for years; he quickly took Simon under his wing after the two met at a meeting of the mall tenants that Ivy had asked Simon to accompany her to. Since then, Simon has enjoyed stopping in for regular chats with Charlie, if only for the advice the older man frequently offers.

Today, however, Charlie has a line of customers waiting to speak with him, so Simon walks on and ducks into one of the employee access halls to bypass most of the mall traffic on his way back to work.

He walks down the hallway toward The C³, his steps echoing off the concrete floor and the exposed drywall. He hears a door close ahead of him, followed by two giggles.

*What the hell is that?* he thinks. He walks past one of the posters that security had put up over the summer.

"IF YOU SEE SOMETHING, SAY SOMETHING!" it says in bold, capitalized letters above the number for security.

*Not that they'll get here anytime today,* thinks Simon. He slows his pace so that his steps don't echo as loudly. He continues down the hallway toward the noise. The giggling has stopped and been replaced by something else, he isn't sure what.

*Was that a grunt?* he thinks. *Damnit, I don't want to witness anything…*

Simon pulls out his cell phone and pulls up the number for Mall Security, his finger nearing the call button. Unsure of what he is about to walk into, he reaches the end of the hallway and turns left toward the corridor that will put him out closest to The C³.

"Oh for fuck's sake!" he yells.

There stands Kirby, his mouth locked onto the mouth of the thin blonde boy from the perfume store. They stop kissing and Kirby looks toward his co-worker.

"Oh, hey Simon."

"What are you doing here? You're off today."

"I came to pick up my check."

"We have direct deposit."

"Oh my God, you're right!" Kirby says, snapping his fingers. "Well, it's a good thing I was here, Benni got lost in the hallway and I had to show him the way out."

"I'll bet you did."

"Hey, now," says Kirby, his hand still on Benni's waist. "Shouldn't you be getting back to work?" Kirby asks slowly, raising an eyebrow and jerking his head toward the exit.

"Uh, yeah," says Simon. "I most definitely should."

"Good. I'll see you tomorrow!" Kirby grabs Benni's hand and the two walk past Simon in the direction he just came from. Shaking his head, Simon walks toward the exit of the employee hallway when he hears the two start to giggle again, followed by the obnoxious sound of making out.

He rolls his eyes.

\* \* \*

By 6:30 P.M., the hordes of shoppers have thinned out a little and the people from the opening shift have been gone for over an hour. Simon and Alan are folding shirts on the floor while Dominic handles the register with one of the sales associates. When Alan's phone vibrates, Simon clears his throat.

"I thought we were supposed to leave those in our lockers?"

"And I thought *I* was the manager on duty," says Alan. "It's just a text anyway." He looks down, trying to hide his phone between a few shirts as he checks it. He looks up, shaking his head as a slight smirk spreads across his face.

"That's an interesting reaction."

"It was Tyler."

"Oh," says Simon. "I didn't realize you two were still talking."

"Well, yeah," says Alan.

"How's it going with him?"

"We talk every now and then."

"Oh."

"Yeah, we had plans to go out the other night, but something came up."

*Why didn't Alan tell me that before now?* thinks Simon. *Is it that awkward to talk to me?*

They continue to fold clothes in silence.

"I'm sorry, I just didn't know if it would be uncomfortable for you," says Alan.

"What?"

"I mean, me and Tyler, whatever we are, talking about it around you. I know you and Chelle worked together to set us up and I didn't know if it would be weird to talk about since…"

"…since Chelle and I broke up."

"Well, *yeah*," says Alan.

"Don't worry about that. I'm happy for you guys," Simon says with a forced smile.

"Hold it, poodle," says Alan. "Don't go planning my gay wedding just yet."

"Oh?"

"He's a nice guy and all, I just don't know if I'm looking for a relationship right now like he is."

"Oh."

"And besides, you and Chelle did good with this one, but who's to say someone better won't come along?" says Alan, winking.

Simon shrugs his shoulders.

*That's one way of looking at it,* he thinks.

"He's a good kisser, at least," says Alan.

"I didn't really need to know that."

"Hey, you're the one that brought it up."

Simon rolls his eyes.

"Anyway, you're about ready to get out of here," says Alan, slipping his phone back into his pocket without replying to the text.

"Already? Wow," Simon says. "It feels like I just got here."

"Well lucky you," says Alan. "You get to do it all over again tomorrow."

"Lucky me," says Simon.

\* \* \*

*Sunday*

On Sundays, the mall is open from 11:00 A.M. until 6:00 P.M. Simon walks into the mall thirty five minutes before it opens. Jacinda and Imani are opening with him, and will be replaced later in the day by Alan, Kirby and Dominic, with an assortment of the sales kids coming in through the day. Simon agreed to work open to close today to help get ready for the visit; Ivy tasked him specifically with cleaning up the backroom and making progress with the display windows.

While Jacinda and Imani get ready to open the store, Simon is in the back, cleaning up the scattered remnant of last week's shipment. He is breaking down boxes and stacking them on a flat dolly that is parked in the hallway just outside the store's backdoor.

*What am I going to do with those windows?* he thinks as he slides his box cutter into the strip of tape that runs along the outside of the bottom of the box. Setting his box cutter on a shelf, he holds the box up and attempts to kick it open.

*Oh, come on!* he thinks when some of the tape sticks and the box doesn't break down right away. He kicks it twice, snapping the tape from one of the bottom flaps, finally able to flatten the box. He tosses it onto the pile and methodically picks up the next one. The walkie talkie clipped to his waist beeps.

"Hey, Simon?" calls Jacinda.

"Yeah?" he replies, wiping away the sweat that has formed at his hairline. He looks at his phone and is surprised to see that the mall has been open for almost an hour.

"Hey, we're pretty slammed," she says. "Can you come out here for a bit?"

He looks around at the mound of boxes that have yet to be broken down as well as the stack in the hall behind the store.

"Sure. I'll be right there."

He closes the backdoor, locks it and walks toward the sales floor. Just before leaving the backroom, he is hit by a wave of dizziness, having to lean against the wall for support.

*Oh shit,* he thinks, closing his eyes. *What is going on?* He takes a deep breath and exhales slowly. His stomach rumbles.

*I probably should have eaten breakfast, especially since I skipped dinner last night...* his thoughts trail off as he tries to think of the last time he ate a decent meal.

*Yesterday morning? No, Friday night. No wait, I was working on that stupid window plan... Lunch on Friday? I went and saw Ravi at the café, that counts doesn't it? No, I guess not... damn, how have I not eaten a full meal since Friday? What is this job doing to me?* Breathing slowly, the dizziness subsides and Simon is able to steady himself.

*I'll make sure to have a good lunch today,* he decides, stepping out onto the sales floor.

\* \* \*

A half hour later, Simon is stuck behind the register with Imani while Jacinda and three sales associates attempt to help as many customers on the floor as they can.

"Dude," says Imani. "We are so understaffed for today."

"I know," agrees Simon.

"I mean, what, is it get a bunch of free shit day and no one told us?"

Simon laughs, calling up another customer.

"Hey, how are you?" he asks, receiving no reply other than a cold, bewildered stare from the woman on the other side of the counter.

"Did you find everything okay today?"

"I'm in a hurry," she spits out.

*Oh, fuck you*, thinks Simon, rushing to finish the transaction as quickly as he can.

"That'll be $47.82," he says, with a forced smile.

The store phone starts to ring. Simon gives the crabby woman her bag and looks out to the sales floor. Jacinda is with a customer and has another waiting. The phone rings again. He looks over at Imani and realizes she is working through a return; she gives him an apologetic look. The phone continues to ring.

"I'll be right with you," says Simon to the next customer in line, who rolls his eyes in response. Simon picks up the phone.

"All jeans are on sale at The C³! This is Simon, how may I help you?" he answers, making sure to give the corporate-mandated greeting.

"Yeah, good afternoon," says the voice on the other end. "This is Officer Briggs with mall security, how are you today?"

"Busy," says Simon.

"Alright, well I'm calling because we see on the security cameras that you have a large pile of broken down boxes behind your store."

"Okay."

"Yeah, we're gonna need you to move those right away."

"Are you serious?"

"Very. This is part of your tenant agreement with the mall and poses a fire hazard. You'll need to get that cleaned up immediately or your store could be subject to a fine."

"Okay, hang on," says Simon, his anger rising. "Let me ask you something. A month ago, I literally watched a girl grab a scarf and put it in her purse. My company procedures don't allow me to approach her so I called you guys to come down here. It took you a half hour to get to my store and by the time you got here, that girl and our scarf were both long gone. We have boxes sitting back there for what, like twenty minutes? And you're on the phone telling us we have to move them right this second?"

"I'm just doing my job, sir."

"Well, so am I," says Simon. "Or at least I'm trying to."

"You need to move those boxes."

"Tell you what," says Simon. "You come down here and man this register and I'll be happy to get rid of the damn boxes."

He slams the phone down and realizes Imani is staring at him.

"You okay?" she asks.

"Fucking ridiculous," says Simon, shaking his head. "I'll fill you in later."

He takes a deep breath and calls the next customer up to check out.

\* \* \*

By 2:00 P.M., Alan, Kirby and Dominic have clocked in, allowing Jacinda and Imani time to take breaks while Simon finally takes care of the rest of the boxes behind the store. As he is wheeling the dolly back into the store, he looks at the nearest security camera sticking out of the ceiling.

"This one's for you, Briggs," he says aloud, flipping it off. He steps into the backroom of his store and closes the door. Jacinda is at the break table.

"Hey there," she says.

"Hi."

"Hey, I know this morning was rough," she says. "I just wanted to thank you."

"Oh, no problem."

"I texted Ivy, we're gonna look at the upcoming schedules, probably gonna be adding a few people on weekends now that we're heading into the holidays."

"Yeah, that's probably a good idea."

"By the way, I heard about your call with Briggs."

"Oh, jeez," says Simon, sitting down next to her.

"Don't sweat it," Jacinda says. "Imani told me what he called about and that was way out of line, especially with how busy we were."

"Are we getting fined?"

Jacinda laughs.

"That was an idle threat," she says. "Briggs has no way of doing that, he'd have to submit to the management office and Ivy goes drinking with Joe in the management office at least two nights a week."

"Really?"

"Oh yeah, this is the mall. Everybody knows everybody else." She pauses. "And all of their business."

"I guess you're right."

"Hey, it's your break time," she says. "Get out of here for a while."

\* \* \*

Walking back to The C³ from the food court, Simon sees that

94

Charlie is working on a watch; Bezel & Crown is empty. He decides to stop in.

"What's up, Charlie?" he asks. The old man looks up and pulls his glasses onto the top of his head.

"Just living the dream!"

"I hear that," says Simon, laughing. "You been busy today?"

"Earlier today, yes," he says. "We're definitely heading into the holidays."

"Yeah, we were slammed. What are you working on?"

"Oh, just replacing a battery. What's up?"

"Not a whole lot, really, we just have this visit coming up."

"Oh, really?" he asks, genuinely interested.

"Yeah, our CEO is coming. Cinnamon von Cinderhösen? Maybe you've heard of her... anyway, she visits a few stores each month and I guess our time was finally up."

"Well that's kind of exciting, isn't it?"

"It's more nerve-wracking than anything."

"Oh no!"

"Yeah, we just have a lot to do before she comes."

"What does Ivy have you working on?"

"She's got me doing the windows as my own personal project."

"That's a good thing, though, isn't it? That she trusts you enough to take care of that? I mean, that's a big part of the store, it's what draws people in."

"I guess that's one way of looking at it," Simon answers, his voice trailing off. "I've just been so overwhelmed lately. I realized this morning I hadn't eaten a decent meal in like three days."

"That's not a good thing, Sport."

"I know."

"Is it just the visit that's overwhelming you?" asks Charlie. "What about Chelle?"

"We broke up, remember?"

"Oh, I know, you told me. But how are you feeling about it?"

"I'm alright. Things just didn't work out."

"Okay," says Charlie.

"It's just... I don't know. I really liked her and I wanted it to work out, it just... wasn't. And I didn't know how to salvage the relationship." He pauses. "People have been treating me differently since the breakup."

"How do you mean?"

"It's like they're treating me with kid's gloves, like I'm sick or something. I mean, it's bad enough that I feel like a failure."

"You're not a failure, Sport," Charlie says. "And maybe they're treating you a little differently because they're just worried about you?"

"Well they don't need to be," says Simon. "I'm fine."

"Of course you are," says Charlie. "They probably just want to be sure."

"Yeah, maybe you're right."

Charlie smiles at his young friend as the grandfather clock in the corner starts to chime.

"Oh crap," says Simon. "I'd better get back."

"Okay, Sport," says Charlie. "Stop by this week if you get a chance, alright?"

"I'll see what I can do," Simon says. "See you around!"

* * *

Fifteen minutes before the mall closes for the day, Simon and Dominic are folding the jean wall. Kirby is folding a stack of t-shirts behind the register and Alan is in back counting down one of the drawers.

"Hey, can I ask you something?" Dominic asks Simon.

"Sure, what's up?"

"So you're pretty good friends with that guy at the coffee shop, aren't you?"

"Ravi? Yeah, we're cool."

"Do you think he could do something for me?"

"Like what?"

"Um, uh…" stalls Dominic.

*Uh oh,* thinks Simon.

"Aw, hell," says Dominic. "Do you think either of you could give my number to the girl that works there?"

"The one with the nose ring?" He finishes folding a pair of jeans and grabs another.

"No, the other one – Roni."

Simon raises an eyebrow.

"Oh come on, don't look at me like that! You gotta admit she's hot." Dominic puts his stack of jeans in their place on the wall.

"Well, yeah," says Simon.

"Then what is it? Oh shit, is she seeing someone already?"

"Not that I know of." Simon grabs another pair of jeans to fold.

"Come on, man."

"You should walk down there and give it to her yourself," says

Simon. "It would mean more."

"I would but I just get so nervous around chicks!"

"I have a hard time believing that. Though it might help if you didn't call them 'chicks'."

"Duh, Simon, I wasn't born yesterday." Dominic finishes folding another pair of jeans and puts them in their spot on the shelf.

"Good, then you're old enough to put on your big boy pants and go talk to her!" Simon says.

"I don't know man, it's just not my style."

Simon rolls his eyes.

"Hey guys," says Alan through the ear pieces connected to their walkie talkies. "If there's no customers left in here, go ahead and pull the gate."

"You got it," comes Kirby's reply.

"Alright," says Dominic. "I'm gonna go clean up what's left in the dressing rooms. Aren't you out of here?"

"Yeah, I was open to close today."

"Cool," says Dominic. "I'll see you later man and hey, let me know if you talk to Ravi about Roni, okay?"

"You got it."

As he is packing his bag to head home, Simon replays his conversation with Dominic in his head.

*Not his style?* he thinks. *Not his style to what, just go talk to someone? Well it's not my style to play Cupid.* He stops what he's doing.

*Style, style,* he thinks. *My style versus Dominic's style... and what about Alan's style? Jacie? And Imani or Carrie?*

He snaps his fingers as an idea for the window display finally starts to take shape.

* * *

*Monday*

Having stayed up late the night before trying to write but eventually giving up and surfing the internet, Simon fully expected to show up to work on Monday, the day of the special drop shipment, feeling worn out and dreading work. Walking into the mall, however, he is pleasantly surprised to find that his excitement for the project has replaced the exhaustion he had expected to feel.

*I can't wait to get started on that window!* he thinks, the energy drink he slammed in the parking lot for good measure coursing through his veins.

"Hey Carrie," he calls as he enters the store.

"Good morning," she replies. "I didn't know you were in today."

"Yeah, I'm just here for a few hours to get some work done on the displays."

"Oh, cool," she says as she unpacks a box of polo shirts.

"Who all else is here?"

"Jacinda's working her way through another pallet; Kirby and a few of the sales kids are finishing the recovery that was left over from last night."

"Oh," says Simon. "I feel like we should really get to know them better."

"I've gotten to talk to a few of them," says Carrie. "They're good kids. It's been so chaotic lately though... I figure getting to know them better will have to wait until after the holidays."

"Yeah," says Simon. "Where's Ivy?"

"She's in the back. I think she's sorting stuff."

"Is there a lot of shipment left?"

"Not really, we got through most of it already," says Carrie. "I think our big holiday load is coming in next week, though."

"Perfect."

Carrie finishes unpacking the box.

"How are the windows coming?"

"Good, good," says Simon. "I'm gonna clock in and get started."

"Okay, I'll see you around."

\* \* \*

Walking into the backroom, Simon immediately notices the mounds of boxes in the receiving area that he had worked so hard to clean yesterday and is annoyed.

*The least they could do is break them down,* he thinks. He clocks in and pulls out the notes he had made yesterday before going home on the various mannequins and who would be wearing what. He sits down at the break table and starts to sketch out the display.

Jumping off from the idea Dominic had given him about style, Simon had decided to model each of the mannequins in the display window after one of his co-workers on the leadership team. The store had just enough mannequins to make the idea work. He had been thinking a lot about what pieces they had in stock that would fit the personas of each of his co-workers.

As he looks over his notes, he suddenly hears a noise, the sound of something falling. He stops and looks around.

"Hello?" he calls. "Ivy?"

There is no reply. He starts to walk toward the receiving area when he hears another noise, this time the sound of giggling.

Simon furrows his brow in confusion. Looking around, he notices that the store's back door is slightly ajar and his pulse quickens.

"What's going on?" he asks aloud. After a few seconds with no reply, he goes to grab one of the walkie talkies and call one of his co-workers that is out on the floor..

As he picks up the walkie talkie, he hears the click of a door handle followed quickly by the sound of someone shushing someone else. He spins around to see Ivy, her hair disheveled, creeping out of the management office. A paunchy man stands behind her adjusting his pants. A guilty grin quickly spreads across the man's face.

"Simon!" she says warmly. The man sneaks past her and stands in the middle of the back room.

"What's going on?" Simon asks, even though he knows the answer.

"You're early."

"You asked me to come in today to work on the window displays," he says.

"I did," she says, nodding her head. "Hey, have you ever met Joe from mall management?"

"Hi there," the man says, waving sheepishly.

"Joe and I were discussing some new marketing programs coming up for the store in the mall! Table tents in the food court and such."

Joe nods enthusiastically.

"That's great," says Simon.

"Right," says Ivy. "Anyway, I'm going to see him out and you'd better get to work! I can't wait to see what you've got cooked up for those windows!" She winks at him and scoots Joe out the back door.

Simon shakes his head.

* * *

"Is everybody fucking everybody in this mall?!"

"Pretty much," says Jacinda. "I told you, Simon – this is the mall, it's like, this weird cesspool of sin and debauchery... and discounts."

Jacinda is sitting at the break table drinking an orange juice while Simon dresses a mannequin in her likeness. He didn't want to tell everyone what he had seen earlier in the morning, but he knew that he could trust Jacinda and wanted to get her take on the situation.

"But I mean, why is this all coming to a head this week?" He pauses. "No pun intended," he adds with a grimace.

"It's a high stress period, bud," she says. "This visit has everyone here on edge and the holidays have the rest of the mall stressed out. It's basically mating season out there."

Simon looks at her, his eyebrows raised.

"Don't look at me like that!" she says. "I'm happily taken."

*Must be nice,* thinks Simon. Though he tries to hide it, Jacinda can read the reaction on his face.

"Oh, shit, Simon," she says. "I didn't mean it like that."

"No, I know." He drapes a teal scarf around the mannequin's neck, letting it fall over the shoulders.

"You're gonna pull through, you know."

"Yeah."

"I'm serious! You're a great guy. You're really nice and good looking… hell, if I was unhappily taken, I'd consider banging you back here… right… now," she says with added dramatics as she runs her hands down her body before dissolving into laughter.

"Stop," he says, rolling his eyes.

"For real though, don't let the others get to you. They're all just doing what they need to do to get by. There's gotta be some way you find an outlet for all this stress?"

"I've been trying to write again."

"There you go!"

"I've just been so distracted with everything going on, it's not so easy," says Simon.

"I get that, really I do. Especially working here – it starts off as a part time job, a way to pay the bills and the next thing you know you're having nightmares about this place and rambling on and on about it to your friends."

"You, too, huh?"

"Happens to all of us," Jacinda says, finishing her juice. "Just don't forget to take some time for yourself, okay? Now if you'll excuse me, I have to go put the management desk back together." She stands and tosses her bottle into the trashcan.

"Hey," she says, noticing the mannequin Simon has been dressing. "She's looking really good!"

Simon smiles.

"I'm glad you think so," he says. "She's inspired by you."

* * *

*Tuesday*

By Tuesday evening, Simon wonders if he should set up a cot in the backroom and start having his mail delivered to The $C^3$. He stands at the register, flipping through the store's winter catalogue trying to decide which pieces his co-workers would be most apt to wear. Earlier in the day, Ivy had helped him put up a simple tree that the mannequins, once clothed, would all be helping to decorate.

"I love it!" she had said when Simon explained the concept to her.

"Each one represents someone here and we're all working together."

"That's fantastic! I love it!"

Simon felt a great rush of pride knowing that his idea, which he had worried so much about, was not only well received by his boss, but praised as well.

"I'll get it together as soon as I can!" he assured her. The mannequins for Jacinda, Imani, Alan and Dominic had all come together quickly and, after today, Ivy, Kirby and Carrie would be complete as well.

*That just leaves one, lonely model, all on his own,* thinks Simon, thumbing through the catalogue pages. He had kept an eye out for something to put on the mannequin he was basing on himself, but so far nothing had jumped out at him. He circles a top that he'll use on the mannequin of Carrie as the store's phone rings.

"All jeans are on sale at The C³. This is Simon, how may I help you?"

"Hello Simon," says the person on the other end. Simon immediately notices the caller's British accent. "My name is Pietro De Luca, I'm calling from the office of Cinnamon von Cinderhösen?"

*Holy shit,* thinks Simon, his heart beating faster.

"Yes, Mr. De Luca, hi! How are you?" he says.

"Please, call me Pietro, and I'm doing quite well, thank you."

"Great. What can I do for you?"

"Well, as you know, Ms. von Cinderhösen will be visiting your store in two days. We're actually going to be visiting several stores on this trip and I'm finalizing our travel itinerary. I just need to make sure a few things are in place before we arrive. Who is your manager on duty?"

"That would be Alan Brodecker, but I believe he's stepped out for a few minutes. Is there anything I can help you with?"

"Certainly," says Pietro. "As I'm sure you've heard, Ms. Von Cinderhösen can be quite particular on her visits. She holds her stores to the same standard company wide and expects them to be nothing less than fabulous. That said, I'm sure your store will be quite exceptional."

"Thank you."

"Of course. While I have you on the phone, I also wanted to confirm that your store has a wireless internet connection. Ms. Von Cinderhösen will be working on the road and must have a reliable connection."

"Oh, yeah," says Simon. "The mall we're in has free wi-fi so that won't be a problem."

"Excellent," says Pietro. "I'll be adding a line to your store's budget to stock the refrigerator for Ms. von Cinderhosen's visit as well. Your store manager... Ivy is her name?"

"Yes."

"Ivy will be receiving an e-mail at the general manager's e-mail address with the particulars on this."

"Okay, I'll let her know."

"Thank you, Simon. Do you have any questions at this time?"

"Not that I can think of," says Simon. "I've been working on a new window display for your visit that I'm pretty excited about."

"Oh, really?" asks Pietro, intrigued. "That's good to hear... a lot of stores focus solely on one facet of these visits, be it their numbers or store cleanliness. They often forget to include the display window, the cover by which our book is judged, if you will. I'm quite excited to see what you've done."

"Well thank you."

"Not a problem. If there's nothing else, I have a few more stores to call that we will be visiting. If you could please give those notes to Ivy, I will follow up with her via e-mail."

"You got it."

"Excellent," says Pietro. "Well then, Simon, I will see you on Thursday."

"Have a great day."

"You as well."

Simon hangs up the phone.

*I just talked to Pietro De Luca,* thinks Simon. *He's going to tell Cinnamon von Cinderhösen about my window display. And they're going to be here in two days.*

Simon stares blankly for a moment before speaking.

"Holy shit."

\* \* \*

An hour later, Simon and Alan are steaming a selection of button-down shirts that arrived yesterday and still had creases from shipping.

"So how's your special project coming?" asks Alan.

"The window? It's good, it's coming along."

"I see that you and Ivy put up that tree earlier today."

"Yeah."

"And I hear you're modeling the mannequins after each of us."

Simon smiles sheepishly.

"I think it's a great idea," says Alan. "So long as you don't fuck up the one that's based on me."

Simon laughs.

"No," he says. "Yours came together pretty quickly."

"So who's the one you're having trouble with?"

"Huh?"

"The one that's still naked in the back room."

"Oh, the lonely model? That's me."

"Awkward."

Simon rolls his eyes.

After steaming a few more shirts, Alan looks toward the front of the store as Tyler Welik walks in carrying a bag from the book store.

"Oh, shit," Alan says quietly.

Simon looks up to see Tyler walking toward them.

"Hey," says Tyler. "Haven't seen you in a while."

"Hi, yeah," Alan says. "I've been busy."

"Hello, Simon," Tyler says evenly.

"Oh, that's right," says Alan. "I almost forgot that you know the lonely model."

"Hi," says Simon, his cheeks turning red.

*Is this seriously happening right now?* he thinks.

"You mind if I take a quick break? I've been here since noon," Simon says.

"Sure, go ahead. Imani's in the back, I'll call her if I need anything."

"Okay," says Simon. "It was good to see you, Tyler."

"You, too."

\* \* \*

"So let me get this straight," says Charlie. "He's your ex-girlfriend's gay best friend who is now dating one of your managers?"

"Pretty much," says Simon. "Although I don't know if they're actually together or what... Alan's been pretty vague about that." He's perched on a stool in Bezel & Crown, having decided to spend most of his break decompressing over the last few days with Charlie.

"Sounds complicated, Sport."

"You don't know the half of it," he says, shaking his head.

"How's your window project coming along?"

"Oh, it's coming together pretty well," says Simon. "I about have everyone else's mannequins finished and Ivy is helping me arrange them all in the front tomorrow."

"I'll have to stop by and see it before the big visit!"

"Oh, yeah," says Simon. "I still have to figure out what to put on my doppelgänger."

"You didn't do yours first?"

"No, I found it easier to start with the others and one lead to the next and now I'm the only one left." He laughs a little. "I've started referring to him as my lonely model."

"You have to make time for yourself, Sport."

"I know, I know," says Simon. "Jacie was telling me the same thing earlier."

"She sounds like a smart girl," says Charlie. "When was the last day you had off?"

"It was, uhh…" Simon's voice trails off.

"See what I mean?" asks Charlie. "You have to think about it."

"I was supposed to be off on Friday."

"But you had to work."

"Well, yeah," says Simon. "We have a lot to do for this visit."

"How's your writing coming?"

"What do you mean?"

"You used to come in here telling me all about the untitled stories you were working on, plotting out. I loved hearing about those, but you haven't mentioned them hardly at all over the last few months."

"I've just been so busy with work projects," says Simon. "I haven't had much time to devote to anything else."

"Are you sure it's just work?"

"What do you mean?"

"Well, forgive an old man for being too bold, but I'm worried about you, Sport. I'm worried you're burying yourself in your work to avoid processing your breakup with Chelle."

Simon is silent.

"And I'm sorry if I'm out of line for saying so, but you two were only together for what, a few months? I never even got to meet her. Don't let yourself get so hung up on one person for so long.

"I see so much of myself in you and I don't want to see you miss out on life." He pauses. "We all go through rough patches, but the true test of character is how you pick yourself back up and move forward, or so I've always thought."

Simon can feel a lump rising in his throat as he blinks away tears, the emotions he has worked so hard to contain threatening to unleash their pent up fury.

"You don't have to say anything," says Charlie gently. "I just had a few things I wanted you to think about."

"Thank you for that," Simon says quietly.

"Don't mention it." Charlie looks at a clock. "Alright, I'm gonna close up shop early tonight. A few of the neighbors and I are getting together to play cards."

"That sounds fun," says Simon. "I'd better get back to work anyway."

"You'll be alright, Sport. It'll all make sense someday… and even if it doesn't, at least you'll have had a hell of a time."

"Thank you, Charlie."

"Just promise me you'll take some time for yourself after this Cinderhösen woman's visit, you've earned it."

"I will," says Simon, smiling. Charlie sees Simon out through the front of Bezel & Crown before pulling the gate for the night.

"And good luck with your untitled lonely model project," he calls through the gate.

On his way back to The C³, Simon reflects on his visit with Charlie. Though it had hurt to hear such harsh truths from the older man, he knows that Charlie was right. Without even realizing it, he had been burying himself in his work in an attempt to prove to others that his breakup with Chelle had not fazed him.

*And where did that get me?* he thinks. He sighs.

*Two days,* he thinks. *This visit will be over in two days and then things are going to start changing.*

He passes Hannah from the toy store and when she smiles at him, he smiles back.

\* \* \*

*Wednesday*

"Good morning, Ivy," calls Simon, entering the back room on Wednesday morning. He had had to drag himself out of bed, realizing that today would mark his twelfth day of working in a row.

"Hmm? Oh," says Ivy, sitting at her desk. "Morning."

Simon puts his things in his locker and walks over to the door of the management office.

"Getting excited for tomorrow?"

"Not really," says Ivy. She shuffles a few papers around on the desk. "I got an e-mail from Pietro De Luca with a bunch of things to have ready for when Cinderhösen gets here, reports and stuff like that. Oh, and he sent a list of suggested snacks."

"Are you kidding?" Simon asks with a laugh.

"No," says Ivy. "And I have no idea where to get half of this shit."

Just then, an unfamiliar noise wafts through the vents in the backroom. Having spent so many hours in The C³, both have grown accustomed to the regular noises they hear in the mall on a daily basis and this was nothing they'd ever heard before.

"What is that?" asks Simon.

"I have no idea," says Ivy. "But I can I tell you that whatever it is, I don't have time to deal with it today."

"It sounds like… is that a car that won't start?"

"It sounds like a fucking banshee."

The door to the backroom opens and Kirby storms in, hysterically crying. Ivy jumps up and rushes to him with Simon by her side.

"Oh my God!" she says. "Did someone die? Are you okay?!"

"N-n-no," Kirby says through sobs.

"What's going on?" asks Simon.

"It's B-B-Benni," says Kirby, weeping.

"Who?" Ivy mouths to Simon.

"Perfume store twink," he whispers in response.

Ivy nods sympathetically.

"One of my friends s-s-saw him at Underland last night and he was making out with some other g-g-guy!" Kirby's lower lip trembles as he dissolves into another wail. Ivy puts her arm around him.

"I'm sorry to hear that, sweetheart," she says to him. He buries his face in her shoulder, sniffling, as she looks to Simon for assistance.

"Yeah, man, it's his loss," says Simon. "And, you know, were you *really* going to end up with a guy you referred to as 'perfume store twink'?"

Kirby smiles meekly.

"Come on, Kirb," says Ivy. "It'll be okay. Go get yourself cleaned up and focus on getting through today." She pulls a five dollar bill out of her pocket. "Something from the coffee shop, my treat?"

Kirby sniffs.

"Thanks Ivy," says Kirby, taking the five. He wipes his eyes and takes a deep breath. "Do you guys want anything? I'm going back on my diet, so I'm just gonna get something small."

Ivy and Simon politely decline.

"Okay, I'll be back," says Kirby, his voice low. He walks out of the backroom and once the door is closed, Ivy looks to Simon.

"Alright, be real with me," she says. "What the hell was that?"

"I don't even know," says Simon with a sigh.

"Were they even together?"

"I don't think so? And that's the first I've heard about a diet."

"Probably something that little fucker from the perfume place said to him. I think he looks fine, maybe a little cheeky, but who doesn't want a man with some meat on his bones? He looks so much better than that blonde skeleton he was trying to get with."

Simon shakes his head.

"Oh, Christ," says Ivy. "Look, I love the kid and I hope he's alright but I also hope he gets his shit together today – this visit is happening tomorrow and we need everybody on top of their game."

"He'll have a lot to focus on to pass the time," Simon says, thinking of the many things he's focused on over the last few weeks to pass the time for himself. "I'm sure he'll be fine."

\* \* \*

*I'm glad I was never like that after Chelle and I split,* thinks Simon as he walks to the coffee shop later that morning. When Kirby returned, he was in much better spirits and told Simon and Ivy how he'd resolved to not focus on Benni, instead redirecting his energy toward having a productive day and getting the store in the best condition it could be in for the visit.

Ivy was elated while Simon was sure that Kirby had taken a few hits from the glass piece in his car before coming back from his coffee run.

"What up, Simon," says Ravi as Simon approaches the counter.

"Not a whole lot, how about you?"

"Same old, same old… Hey, I had a visit from a co-worker of yours earlier today. Kirby? Is he doing alright?"

"Yeah, sorry about that; Ivy sent him down here. I'm sure he'll be fine."

"That's good."

Simon nods.

"Besides, I thought everyone knew about that Benni guy and the creepy shoe store manager."

"The creepy shoe store manager?"

"Yeah, one of the girls in the shoe store told me Benni was waiting for them the other night when they were walking out and left with the manager... ach, what is his name..."

"You never cease to amaze me, Ravi."

"What can I say? People love to talk to baristas. We're like bartenders for the caffeine starved... except we don't make shit in tips."

"Speaking of, I'll take my usual."

"You got it, bro." Ravi grabs a steaming pitcher and pours in some milk.

"Hey, I've been meaning to ask you, what was that girl's name? The one at the toy store?"

"Hannah?" Ravi asks, looking up from the steam pitcher. "I thought you weren't interested?"

"Well, I've been doing some thinking, I guess, and I figure, hey, it can't hurt to talk to her, right?"

"Well, well, well... look who finally decided to get back in the game!"

"Don't say anything, okay?"

Ravi grins.

"It was her smile, wasn't it? I told you she's gorgeous!"

"Well, yeah, but – hey wait, how did you know I saw her the other day?" Simon asks over the sound of the steam wand.

"What do I always say, dude? This is the mall. And she likes hot chocolate with a little bit of raspberry in the mornings." Ravi mixes Simon's drink together.

"So she's talked to you about me?" he asks.

"I've played matchmaker between you two long enough, Simon. Go talk to her!" He puts a lid on the cup and sets it on the counter.

"I think I just might," says Simon with a smile.

"Let me know how it goes."

"You got it," says Simon, dropping three dollars into Ravi's tip jar. "I'll see you around, Ravi."

\* \* \*

Simon walks into the toy store, sipping his mocha. He doesn't see Hannah behind the counter or in any of the first few aisles. Just when he is about to give up and head back to The C³, he sees her from behind, stocking a shelf with action figures.

"Excuse me," he says, walking up to her.

"Yes?" she says, turning around. "Oh, hello!"

"Hi," says Simon, his nerves starting to jitter. "I've seen you around the mall and I wanted to come and introduce myself. I'm Simon." He extends his free hand.

"It's nice to meet you, Simon," she says, shaking his hand. "I'm Hannah."

"I don't mean to bother you while you're working, I just wanted to know if you'd want to hang out sometime," he blurts out, adrenaline rushing through his body.

A grin spreads across Hannah's face.

"That would be great," she says. She pulls a card from her pocket and writes her phone number on it with the pen she has stuck behind her ear.

"Awesome," says Simon, taking the card.

"I'd better get back to work before my manager comes over," she says.

"Oh, yeah, sorry," says Simon.

"It's no trouble," says Hannah. "Text me sometime, okay?"

"Sure," says Simon, smiling. "You got it."

"Awesome," she says. "I'll see you soon!"

"Yeah, see ya." Simon turns and walks out of the store.

*I'd almost forgotten what that feels like,* Simon thinks as he walks back to his store. *I like it.*

Before he goes back into work, he stops to look at the progress on his window project. He has arranged the mannequins so that they all seem to be doing something while showcasing the clothes he'd put on each one.

*I gotta get that lonely model taken care of,* he thinks.

\* \* \*

*Thursday*

"How did you sleep last night?" asks Simon.

"Uh, is 'not at all' an option?" replies Ivy. They are standing in the back room of The C³ with Jacinda and Imani making sure that everything has been tidied up. Cinnamon von Cinderhösen is due to arrive any minute.

"Remember, it's just a visit," says Jacinda.

"I know," says Ivy, straightening the scarf she's wearing with her black dress.

The door to the back room opens and Alan walks in.

"Hey, you guys?" he says. "They're here."

\* \* \*

"Darling, it's fabulous," Cinnamon von Cinderhösen says through a thick, European accent. She stands near the front of the store wearing a large fur coat over a slinky purple dress, impossibly high stilettos and large sunglasses. A sleek hat with a feather sticking

109

out is perched atop her head.

*She sounds bored,* thinks Simon.

"Thank you," Ivy says quietly. She shifts uncomfortably in front of Cinnamon von Cinderhösen, next to Pietro De Luca. Jacinda, Alan and Simon stand nearby, while Dominic and Imani work the cash registers and a team of sales associates handle the customers on the floor.

"Truthfully, Ivy, your store looks fantastic," she says, the bangles on her wrist jingling as she taps furiously on her phone. "Obviously, you have a great team here and are setting the bar very high for the other stores I'm going to visit on this trip."

"Really?"

"Yes, darling, now, if you'll please walk with me to the backroom, I have a conference call I need to get on with purchasing."

"Sure, right this way," says Ivy. The two start to walk toward the back room.

"One last thing," says Cinnamon, stopping. "Who did the window display?"

"Simon was in charge of it," says Ivy.

"Ah, Mr. Dawes," says Cinnamon, turning to Simon. "I hear you spoke briefly with Pietro a few days ago."

"I did, yeah," says Simon, nodding.

"I like your display, but I have one question."

"Okay?"

"Pietro tells me that each mannequin is modeled after an employee in your store, which is a concept I appreciate very much. But, if I may ask, why is one of them wearing a bathrobe to the party?"

Simon clears his throat, his palms starting to sweat. He can feel every pair of eyes in the room on him.

"Well, as I was getting the window together, I found myself having trouble defining... well, myself, actually," he says. "Everyone else's mannequins came together pretty quickly, but I just couldn't pinpoint what I wanted my own representation to be."

Cinnamon von Cinderhösen glances at her diamond encrusted watch.

"That's when it hit me that I can't be the only person who feels that way. And I thought about how I could be anything right now, how any of us could be anything. I dressed the last mannequin in a bathrobe to kind of represent that. He hasn't defined himself yet, he's the customer who is coming in here who might not know who he is or who she wants to be, or even what he's coming in to buy, but they'll be able to find themselves at The C³."

A moment of silence passes over the group as Cinnamon glances from Simon's face to the window up front, slowly taking in Simon's explanation of the window display.

"And it uses a piece that rarely gets used in the displ–"

"I like it," Cinnamon says, turning around to continue on with Ivy, her heels clicking as she walks away.

Simon feels a great weight lifted off of his shoulders. His co-workers disperse into the store as Pietro De Luca walks over.

"That's it?" asks Simon.

"That's all it needs to be," Pietro says. "Very well done, Simon. That's one of the best responses she's had to a display in a while."

Pietro smiles.

"Thank you," he says, shaking Pietro's hand.

"Of course," he says. "I'd better get back to Ms. von Cinderhösen. I'll be sure to catch you before we leave." Pietro walks off, leaving Simon alone in the entryway.

*Has it only been a week since we found out they were coming?* thinks Simon. *It felt like an eternity.* He looks toward the front of the store at his display and smiles.

*I did it,* he thinks, running his fingers through his hair. *Thank God I'm off tomorrow.*

\* \* \*

*Friday*

Around 10:30 A.M. on Friday, Simon rolls over in bed and starts to wake up. This is the first day in almost two weeks that he has woken up on his own without an alarm and without anything to do for the day. He spends the next half hour lying in bed, relishing the thought of an entire day ahead of him that is all to himself.

He gets out of bed and pours himself a bowl of cereal, eating at his table with mail scattered across it.

*I'll take care of all of that today,* he thinks. After breakfast, he moves to the couch and picks up the book he has been reading off of the coffee table. As he begins to read, his phone rings.

"Really?" he says aloud. He picks up the phone and sees that someone on the store is on the other end.

"Hello?" he says.

"Hey Simon, it's Ivy."

"Hey there."

"I wanted to thank you again for everything you did leading up to the visit. Cinderhösen really liked our window display and said that our store was impeccably clean. She was also very impressed with our credit apps, particularly the numbers you've been bringing in."

"Oh, awesome!"

"Yeah, she asked me to share that with you."

"Thanks," says Simon.

"Hey, while I've got you on the phone, is there any chance you'd want to come in today for some extra hours? I know it's your first day off in a while..."

"Fourteen days, actually."

"Really? Wow, I didn't realize it'd been that many."

"Yeah," says Simon. "Thanks for the offer, but I'm gonna have to decline... I have plans already."

"Alright, no problem. Thanks again for all your hard work and I'll see you this weekend!"

"You got it," says Simon. "Bye, Ivy."

He hangs up the phone.

*Sorry, Ivy,* he thinks. *Today is a day for myself.*

Later that afternoon, Simon goes to the park by his apartment. It is an unseasonably warm day and he intends to take full advantage of it. Sitting on a bench, he pulls out his notebook and a pen, having decided to write about the past few days as a way to get back into writing.

Before he begins, though, he has an idea. He feels around in his bag for his phone and pulls it out.

"*Hey there*" he types in a text.

He thinks of Chelle and their failed relationship and how, for the first time since their breakup, he's not blaming himself or feeling like a failure.

"*If you're free, would you wanna do something today?*" he types, finishing the message.

Simon sends the text to Hannah, excited at the possibility of what could develop between them. They'd been texting back and forth steadily since Wednesday night, hanging out in person seemed to be inevitable. He smiles at the thought.

Simon puts his phone down and picks up his notebook and pen, and when he starts to write, the words flow onto the page.

# GARDEN PARK

*Graham*

"I guess this is it," says Graham Kelly, getting out of his jeep and looking toward the Plaza at Garden Park. The gray building has six floors, none of which display any bit of character with the notable exception of a few windows on the third floor that boast bright pink curtains.

*Maybe someone my age lives there,* he thinks, taking note of the floor.

"Home, sweet home," he says, his breath visible in the wintry air.

He closes the driver's side door and walks to grab his backpack from the passenger seat; it is January and the snow on the ground crunches under Graham's boots. Tossing his bag over his shoulder, he walks toward the building entrance, two weathered lion statues flanking the entrance path.

"Vintage," he says aloud. "Too cool." He ascends the steps and pulls open the front door, kicking the snow off of his boots in the heated lobby. He looks around at his new home taking in as much as he can, from the flickering light fixtures to the musty smell that clogs his nostrils. Having read about the building online, Graham knows that the Plaza at Garden Park was once a luxury hotel, so named for the district it was built in.

Many years ago, Garden Park was the social epicenter of the city. Buildings and business sprang up, property values skyrocketed and excess was a way of life. Unfortunately, it would not last. Like all good things, Garden Park's prime came to an end, leaving in its place

113

block after city block of abandoned buildings and the people who were either too worn out or too poor to follow the money to other parts of town.

Garden Park was not a complete loss, however. The Garden Park Historical Society was established in the mid-80's to preserve what was left of this once booming district. Much of the area was added to a registry of historical places and a great renaissance began with several restoration projects. Though a developer had renovated the Plaza at Garden Park into an apartment building, most of the remaining projects sat unfinished without the flow of money required to fund them. Still, the revitalization of Garden Park drew a variety of people to the district, including the tenants of the Plaza at Garden Park.

Garden Park was just the place Graham Kelly was looking to stay as he transferred to the university downtown to finish his undergraduate studies.

"You're late," comes a stern voice, echoing off the pale green tiles in the lobby. Graham looks up and sees that it belongs to a man standing by one of the couches scattered about; he is irritably tapping his shoe on the floor. Graham is taken aback by the man's tone and how out of place he looks, this man with his crisply pressed suit in a room with peeling wallpaper.

"I'm sorry," says Graham. "The roads are still kinda bad from that snowstorm you guys had."

"I made it here on time," he says. "Victor Cain, Jr."

"Graham Kelly," he says, his extended hand granted a brisk handshake from the cold landlord.

*I'd say 'Nice to meet you', but I'd be lying,* he thinks. *This guy is as much of a jerk in person as he was in his e-mails.*

"Come with me."

They walk past what Graham assumes used to be a front desk toward a set of elevators. An old, brass mailbox sticks out of the wall next to the elevators. As the car descends the elevator shaft, Graham watches the arrow above the door make its way past the other numbers, finally resting when it points to the number 1. The doors open and Mr. Cain pulls aside the gate behind them.

*It's like I went back in time,* Graham thinks as he steps into the elevator. Mr. Cain pulls the gate closed and pushes the button for the fourth floor.

"Make sure you close the gate," he says as the car starts to rise. "Otherwise you won't be going anywhere. And this old thing dies from time to time, just so you know. There's two different sets of stairs that run the whole building if that happens."

"Good to know," says Graham. "What floor do you live on?"

"Me? Live here?!" asks Mr. Cain, finally showing a hint of emotion. "That's funny kid, real funny." They rise through the building in an awkward silence until the elevator finally comes to a halt.

"Here we go," says Mr. Cain. Graham follows him out of the elevator and down the hall, stopping in front of Apartment 4C. Mr. Cain pulls out a set of keys and flips through them, finally picking one and inserting it into the lock on the door. He opens the door and they enter the apartment.

"Well, this is it," says Mr. Cain, flicking on a light.

Graham looks around the living room and feels lucky that he had found an apartment that had come with furnishings. He sets his bag down on the couch.

"No parties, no pets. I'll be around the first of the month for rent. Rent is due when I'm here, no exceptions, and I accept checks only. No rent, no apartment. Here you go," he recites, handing over the key from his key ring to Graham. He turns around to walk out of the apartment, barely pausing to say, "Have a nice day."

"Hey, thanks!" calls Graham, hoping that his simple expression of gratitude annoys Mr. Cain even further.

*What an asshole,* he thinks.

Graham takes the next fifteen minutes to explore his new apartment while it is empty before he brings up his boxes. The living room is connected to the kitchen, separated only by a half wall. A small hallway extends from the living room with doors leading to a bedroom, a bathroom and a closet with just enough space for him to step in. He finds a thermostat and turns the temperature up, hearing the radiator near the window kick on.

"Home, sweet home," he says again. "I'd better get unpacked."

\* \* \*

Two weeks later, Graham sits in his apartment reviewing for his first accounting exam. The television is on even though he is not paying it much attention; outside, snow flurries in the night.

*Why did I ever think this was a good idea?* he thinks, growing increasingly frustrated as he pores over his notes.

Suddenly there is a knock at the door.

*Who could that be?* he thinks, looking from his notes to the door. In his time at the Plaza at Garden Park, Graham has only seen a few of the other tenants in the building. And it wasn't like he'd made any friends at school yet, especially any that would trek out to the Plaza at Garden Park on a winter's night like this. He walks to the door and looks through the peep hole, unable to see anything distinct other than a flourish of purple.

"Hello?" he says, opening the door with caution. Standing in the hallway is a frail looking old woman in a purple sequined caftan and matching beret. With her bright pink lips pulled into a wide grin, Graham momentarily wonders if she is some kind of exotic, tropical animal who got lost and wound up in the city.

"Hi there, Mr. Kelly," says the woman. "I'm your neighbor from the floor below and I'm here to introduce myself. Forgive my rudeness in taking so long to come by, it's just been a difficult winter."

"Oh, hello," says Graham, momentarily caught off guard that this woman knows his name.

"Eulalia Dorothy-Jane Belle," she says with pointed enunciation, extending a delicate hand. "But you can call me Eula."

"Pleasure to meet you," Graham says, shaking her hand carefully. "You can call me Graham."

"Oh, I know your name, dearest! Felix told me all about you." Graham wonders how much Felix Jackson had told Eula about him. Graham had run into Felix a few times in the hallway since they lived on the same floor and could frequently hear swing music from inside his apartment whenever he passed Felix's door.

"Would you like to come in?" asks Graham.

"Oh, you're so kind!" says Eula, stepping into Graham's apartment.

"Have a seat," says Graham. "Sorry about the mess, I wasn't expecting company. Would you like something to drink?"

"You wouldn't happen to have any tea, would you?"

"I can brew a cup real quick, if you'd like."

"That would be lovely!" exclaims Eula, sitting down. Graham walks into the kitchen and gets a cup out of the cabinet. Filling it with water, he puts it in the microwave and sets it to heat up.

"You just moved to the city, yes?" asks Eula.

"I did," says Graham. "I transferred here to finish my Bachelors."

"That's great," says Eula. "I've always been a supporter of furthering education."

"Oh, nice," says Graham.

"You're studying business?" she asks, looking over the books scattered on the coffee table.

"Sure am," says Graham. "I'm working my way through an accounting class that's..."

"Kicking your ass?" Eula finishes bluntly.

Graham laughs.

"Yeah, you could say that."

"Well, if I'm not mistaken, it's still early in the semester, isn't it? You'll get the hang of it, I'm sure – you seem like a bright young man."

"Thank you," says Graham. The microwave beeps and Graham goes to grab the cup of water. He puts a tea bag and a spoon in the cup and walks it out to Eula.

"I hope you don't mind chamomile," he says. "It's all I had."

"My favorite!" Eula says with a big smile. "Thank you."

"You're welcome."

"I won't stay long, Graham," she says, stirring her tea with the spoon. "I wanted to come by though and at least introduce myself. I've lived in this building for years and I like to think of myself as the unofficial welcoming committee."

Graham smiles.

"Welcome to the Plaza," she says, taking a sip of the tea. "Ahh, this is perfect for such a cold winter's night! How are you finding life here so far?"

"Not bad," says Graham. "It's an easy commute to the downtown campus."

"Do you know anyone else in town?"

"Not really," says Graham. "I'm getting to know a few of my classmates, but I'm a transfer and most of them have been in the program together for the past two years so it's not as easy making friends."

"Well, you've got at least one," says Eula, finishing another sip of her tea.

"Yeah, unless you want to count Mr. Cain, too."

"Oh," says Eula, setting her cup down. "I assume you're talking about our irascible landlord, Victor, Jr.?"

"The one and only," says Graham.

*Note to self: look up 'irascible',* he thinks.

"If there's one thing you should know about Mr. Cain, it's that he can be a cold man, but he is not cold hearted... at least as far as I can tell. Victor is nothing more than the product of his upbringing." She pauses to take another sip of her tea, holding the mug in her hands afterward for warmth. "Everyone has a history, Graham, a path that led them to this moment or that. And if you keep that in mind, you'll find you may have more in common with those around you than you think."

Graham thinks about Eula's words as she takes another sip.

"That's part of what brings me here this evening, I must admit," she says.

*Huh?* thinks Graham as Eula produces a book seemingly out of thin air.

"This is a book all about the Plaza at Garden Park," she says. "It is a written history of the building; those who are in it and those who came before. I thought you might like to learn a little bit more about where you're living now."

"Oh," says Graham, carefully taking the book from her. "Thank you."

"Take your time with it! I'm in no rush to get it back. Bring it down to me whenever you're finished."

"This is awesome," mutters Graham, browsing pages of old photos and news clippings. "Did you put this together?"

"I sure did! With some help of course." Eula finishes her cup of tea.

"Thank you for sharing this with me," he says. "I'll be sure to get it back to you."

"Like I said, dear, take your time." She pauses. "Well, it's getting late, and I don't want to keep you from your studies!"

"Oh, they're not going anywhere," Graham says with a laugh.

Eula stands and Graham walks her to the door.

"It was a pleasure to meet you, Mr. Kelly," she says. "Be sure to stop by sometime, I'm just a floor down in Apartment 3B."

When he hears Eula say that she is a floor below, something occurs to him.

"Ms. Belle?" he asks.

"Eula," she corrects him.

"Eula," he says. "You said you know everyone in the building?"

"Just about, why?"

"Well, when I first arrived, the only part of the building that really stuck out was a set of windows on the third floor with bright pink curtains," says Graham. "I didn't know if you knew who those belonged to."

"Those are mine, dear," she says proudly. "I sewed them myself!"

"Oh, nice," says Graham, hoping his disappointment that the

apartment with the curtains doesn't belong to someone his age isn't showing too much on his face.

"I'll see you soon," says Eula. "Have a good night and enjoy that book!"

"You, too!" When he closes the door, Graham sits on his couch and mentally replays the visit he'd just been paid.

*What a bizarre old woman,* he thinks. *Really nice, though, and I guess I'm not surprised those curtains were hers.* He looks from his pile of notes to the book Eula left with him.

"Back to work, I guess," he says with a sigh.

\* \* \*

Three weeks later, after scoring a solid B on his second accounting exam, Graham has a free evening and decides to pay Eula a visit and return the scrapbook she left for him. He takes the stairs from the fourth floor of the Plaza at Garden Park to the third and knocks on the door of Apartment 3B. After a few moments, the door flies open.

"Graham!" exclaims Eula. "What a lovely surprise! Come in, come in!"

"Nice to see you again," says Graham, stepping inside. "I just thought I'd drop this book off with you."

"Oh, lovely! You will come in for a visit, won't you?"

"Sure," says Graham.

Graham immediately notices that Eula's apartment is bigger than his and follows her to a sitting room, where an older, heavyset woman is seated on a couch with music playing from a record player. Eula sets the book down as the other woman pulls her glasses down from where they were perched on her head, a beaded chain connected to both ends getting caught on her ear. Graham recognizes her as a neighbor, but does not know her name.

"Oh, hello," he says.

"Graham Kelly, meet Bea Olloman," introduces Eula.

"Nice to meet you," says Graham, holding out his hand.

"Likewise," says Bea. "You live on the same floor as Felix."

"Mr. Jackson? Oh yeah," says Graham.

"Well, it is lovely to finally meet you! Eula said such nice things about you after her visit."

"Oh, hush you," says Eula.

"What? You did," says Bea. "And for what it's worth, I'm glad someone like you moved into the Plaza, Graham – we could use some more eye candy around here!"

Graham blushes and runs his fingers through his hair.

"My friend, Bea," says Eula. "Born without an ounce of shame."

"Says the old lady in the lime green muumuu," says Bea, with a laugh. She picks up the glass of wine in front of her and takes a drink. "Do you drink, Graham?"

"Occasionally," he says.

"You want a glass?" asks Eula.

"Oh, no thank you," says Graham.

"So what brings you to our humble Plaza?" asks Bea.

"I'm staying here while I'm finishing up my degree."

"How nice," says Bea. "I wasn't kidding about having some more eye candy around these parts, you know. I'm on the board for The Garden Park Historical Society and we've been hoping for quite some time that the area would catch on with you hip, young folks. We even ran a small marketing campaign."

"How did it do?" asked Graham.

"Moderately well, I suppose you could say," says Bea. "Brought in a few new businesses, but nothing large scale, I'm afraid."

"Give it time, Bea," says Eula, sipping her tea. "You're always in such a rush over these things – I'm telling you, in time, the crowds will come back to Garden Park."

"I hope you're right, Eula," says Bea. The clock on Eula's mantle starts to chime and Bea sits upright. "Oh! Is that the time? I must be getting back home, my little ones will be getting hungry."

"Little ones?" Graham asks.

"I have four cats that are like my children," says Bea. "Unless Mr. Cain is around in which case, I hate cats – deathly allergic!"

Graham smiles as Bea and Eula dissolve into a fit of giggles.

"Yes, it is getting late," says Eula. "I'm about ready to turn in for the night."

"Are you feeling alright?" asks Bea quickly.

"Oh, I'm fine," answers Eula. "Just worn out from the day."

"Accompany an old lady home?" Bea asks Graham.

"Sure," he answers. They stand and follow Eula to her front door.

"Thank you both for coming to see me," she says. "You will come again soon, won't you?"

Graham nods.

"Oh, Eula, you know I can't stay away," says Bea. "You're my oldest friend and you make me feel so much younger for it!"

The two women laugh.

"Good night to you both," says Eula, still grinning.

Graham rides the elevator one floor down to drop Bea off at her apartment. After bidding him good night, she turns around.

"You know, Graham, I give tours at an old house in Garden Park a few times a week, Claythorn Manor? Have you heard of it?"

Graham shakes his head.

"Ah, well, they say it's haunted. I thought it might pique your interest... It's steeped in so much of the city's history, I really think you'd enjoy it. You and your friends should come by sometime."

"Oh, I don't really have any friends here," he says, looking down.

"No?" asks Bea. "Well, as Eula's always telling me, give it time. You're a charming young man and I'm sure you'll have more friends than you know what to do with soon enough!"

\* \* \*

The next morning, Graham locks the door to his apartment as he leaves for school. Stepping into the elevator, he thinks about the night before and the hospitality his neighbors have shown him so far.

*Everyone's so nice here,* he thinks. *I really lucked out... now, if only I could make a few friends to like, go out with sometime then I'd be set.*

As much as he loves the Plaza at Garden Park, Graham has started to wonder if he might have an easier time socializing if he were closer to campus, to downtown and the heart of the city. The elevator door slides open and Felix Jackson is standing there, waiting to enter.

"What's up, young buck?" Felix chirps without a moment's hesitation.

"Good morning, Mr. Jackson," says Graham, still a little groggy. "Just heading to school."

"Boom! There it is!"

Graham smiles, having grown accustomed to Felix's animated style of speaking. After he steps out of the elevator, Felix steps in.

"Oh, Graham, I gotta tell ya bud..."

"What's up?"

"I, uhh... run a little side business in the basement of the Plaza a few nights here and there."

Graham raises an eyebrow.

"Nothin' sinister, bro! Just a little place for friends to get together – some music, some spirits, some dancin'," Felix says, miming a few dance moves. "We're open for business at 9:00 o'clock tonight. You should come by!"

"Oh, that sounds like fun," says Graham. "Where is it?"

"The basement," replies Felix. "Now, don't go taking the elevator down there, sometimes it gets stuck. Just go down the stairs and to the left in the corridor. One o' us is usually sitting in the hall taking donations to keep the party rolling. A few bucks'll do for you, if you can spare it."

"Awesome," says Graham. "I'll be sure to stop by."

"Very good," says Felix. "I'll see you tonight then!"

"See you later, Mr. Jackson," says Graham, turning to leave. Felix pulls the gate to the elevator closed and stops.

"Oh! Lord in Heaven, I almost forgot," he says. "Tonight's password is 'Six Cherry Cola'. You'll need it to get in."

"A password?" asks Graham.

"Just a little something we cooked up," says Felix with a laugh.

"Got it," says Graham.

"Very good," calls Felix as the door closes. "I'll see you tonight, young buck!"

\* \* \*

That night, Graham walks down the stairs of the Plaza at Garden Park. He has not gone out since moving to town and is very excited about having a few drinks, even if it's just with a few of his neighbors.

*Who knows,* he thinks. *Maybe this is some big, secret hotspot?*

From the lobby, he can hear swing music faintly emanating from somewhere deep inside the Plaza at Garden Park, the lively beats seemingly bringing the old building to life. There is a sign board near the stairs that lead to the basement with an arrow.

*Here goes nothing,* thinks Graham as he heads down. At the bottom, he goes left through the corridor and sees a man sitting on a stool in front of a door.

"Hey there," Graham says.

"Good evening," says the man. "Can I help you?"

"I, uhh… I was wondering if there was anywhere around here I could get a 'Six Cherry Cola'?" Graham takes a deep breath.

The man says nothing.

*Oh shit,* thinks Graham. *I did something wrong!*

The man's face breaks into a smile.

"Come on in, lil man!" he says. "Are you the new guy Felix told me about?"

"Yeah," says Graham. "I moved in back in January."

"Well, we're glad to have ya! Go on in!"

"What about a donation?"

"Eh, first time for a new resident's on me," says the man with a smile.

"Thank you!"

"Don't sweat it, pal!"

The man opens the door and ushers Graham through a set of heavy, red curtains. Walking through, Graham feels like he's been transported several decades into the past. Blue lights illuminate the brick walls behind an old bar with an art deco motif running throughout. A band plays in front of a dance floor where a few couples are practicing their swing dancing moves. Various seating areas are sprinkled throughout the venue.

*This is amazing*, Graham thinks. *Who knew this was down here?*

Suddenly he feels a clap on the shoulder.

"Graham!" shouts Felix. "So glad to see you down here! Make yourself at home, young buck!"

"Thank you, Mr. Jackson!"

"Stop with this 'Mr. Jackson' bullcrap – call me Felix!"

"Alright, Felix," he says.

"Get yourself a drink, Graham, and enjoy the show!" Felix waltzes away, tipping his hat to a woman he recognizes and blowing a kiss to another. Graham walks to the bar and orders a drink. He turns around to watch the couples on the dance floor.

He slowly notices the girl he is standing next to is watching the dancers. He looks at her and smiles.

She sees him and smiles back.

"Don't you swing dance?" she asks.

"Not really," says Graham.

"I bet you'd be good at it," she says.

"You think?"

"Only one way to find out."

"Are you asking me to dance?"

She laughs.

"It was worth a shot," she says with a smile. "What's your name?"

"I'm Graham." The bartender walks over with Graham's drink.

"Is this your first time here?"

"Yeah," he answers. "Yours?"

"I've been here once before," she says. "You see those two guys out there on the dance floor?" Graham looks and notices two men dancing together among the other couples.

"Oh, yeah," says Graham. "Are they together?"

"That's a whole other can of worms," she says, rolling her eyes.

"Anyway, the one with the long hair is my friend Tyler and the guy he's with is Alan. He brought me and Tyler here a few weeks ago to check the place out. There wasn't really anything else going on tonight so we figured we'd come back for round two."

"Nice," says Graham.

"What's your story?"

"Oh, I, uhh, I actually live in this building."

"Really?"

"Yeah, I just moved to town a few weeks ago."

"And you moved to Garden Park?"

"Yeah, well, I'm here finishing my degree and the office for transfer students said that Garden Park had some really affordable apartments and wasn't too far of a commute for class."

"Oh," she says. "That's cool. How do you like it?"

"It's not so bad, actually. This place has a lot of character."

She nods, taking a sip of her drink. They watch the dancers for a few moments; Graham can tell what a fun time the girl's friends are having.

"So, hey," says Graham. "How about that dance?"

"You actually wanna go out there?"

"Sure, why not," he says.

"I was only half serious when I asked you."

"Oh, come on... let's give it a try!"

She raises an eyebrow, looking from the dance floor to his face.

"Okay," she says, laughing a little.

"I didn't get your name," says Graham.

"Chelle," she says. "Chelle Mastens."

"Great to meet you," says Graham, smiling. "Come on, let's go!"

Graham takes Chelle by the hand and leads her to the dance floor.

\* \* \*

*Felix*

*Well look at him go,* thinks Felix as he watches his young neighbor, Graham Kelly, attempt to swing dance with one of the girls who was standing by the bar.

*I know Alontay would have a ball if I could ever get her here!*

Felix is at the front of the dance floor, playing the trumpet with the band. Looking around the room, he cannot help but smile. Seeing everyone here, from the dancers moving across the floor to the people chatting in the shadows, raises a great swell of pride for this place, a hidden speakeasy to call his own and share with those around him.

*Hard to believe it was only a pipedream just a short while ago,* he thinks.

True, he worried occasionally about not having the proper permits in place but all of that he could sort out soon enough.

Graham and the girl swoop by, picking up the rhythm of the music. They are both laughing and having a great time.

*It's good to see him with someone,* thinks Felix. He remembers the day that Graham moved into the Plaza at Garden Park, a cold day in January. He knew something unusual was happening that morning when he looked out his window and saw the building owner pulling into the lot.

*Mr. Cain?* he thought. *What on the green Earth is he doing here? It's not the first of the month again already, is it?* He watched Victor Cain, Jr., get out of his car and look toward the Plaza at Garden Park, a sneer on his face.

*There's just somethin' I don't like about that man,* thought Felix, an idea formulating in his mind.

Pulling himself away from the window, Felix grabbed a book that was sitting on his coffee table and slipped into a pair of house shoes before hurrying out of his apartment. Taking the stairs two at a time, he reached the lobby just as Mr. Cain was walking in. He quickly jumped onto one of the couches that was facing away from the door, laying down so as not to be seen.

He opened the book with no intention to read and listened carefully. He could hear Mr. Cain's shoes echoing off the floor as he walked closer.

*Aw shit,* thought Felix. *I hope he doesn't catch me.*

Exhaling irritably, Mr. Cain sat down on the couch that backed up to the one Felix was on, taking care to breathe slowly. Felix almost jumped when Mr. Cain's phone started to ring.

"Hello? No, I'm already here," said Mr. Cain. "I'm showing a new tenant his apartment today, if he ever decides to show up." There was a pause. "I know, I can't believe it either – who would want to move into this old dump?"

*Hey!* thought Felix, sharply.

"I know, I can't believe of all the properties, *this* was the one my father wanted me to start with." In the pause that followed, Felix could hear the sound of someone talking on the other end. "It's alright, though. I don't know if this place will be a burden much longer."

*A burden? Much longer? The hell is he talking about?* thought Felix, scrunching his face.

"Yeah... I might have a buyer."

*A buyer?!* Felix clapped his book to his chest in shock.

"Hello?" said Mr. Cain as he turned his head sharply.

Felix froze.

Mr. Cain slowly stood up.

"No," he said slowly. "I just heard a noise. This building always creeps me out. Hey, let me let you go, I think the kid is here. Alright, I'll call you later... mmhmm. Ciao."

He put his phone in his pocket and sighed. Felix could tell the door to the lobby had opened by the rush of cold air from outside. Mr. Cain was tapping his foot on the floor.

"You're late," he said sternly. Felix stayed put until Mr. Cain and the new tenant boarded the elevator, sitting up slowly once he heard the doors close.

"I have to talk to Eula," he said aloud.

And now, less than two months later, here is the new tenant, a bright young man, having a great time. The song ends and Felix takes a bow before stepping aside as the band starts a new song. He approaches a woman perched on a stool at the bar as she sets down an empty tumbler and pulls out a cigarette.

"You know you can't do that in here, Claire," Felix says.

Claire Tenyson of Apartment 6B looks at Felix and raises an eyebrow. She pulls the cigarette from her lips, flashing him a curt smile in the process.

"You caught me," she says.

"How you break those rules upstairs is your own business, but down here I gotta make sure we don't do anything that'll – "

"Yeah, yeah, I get it. You don't want Cain to find out." She catches the attention of the bartender and gestures for another drink.

She sighs.

"I'll be a good girl, Felix."

He smiles, tipping his hat.

"Thank you, *chère.*"

\* \* \*

Later that week, Felix is watching a game show in his apartment when his cell phone starts to ring. He jumps up to grab it.

"Oh! Alontay!" he says excitedly, putting the phone to his face. "Hey baby, how you doin'?"

The phone continues to ring.

"Oh, damnit anyhow," he says, realizing he hadn't slid the answer bar all the way across.

"Goddamn smart phone."

"Well, hello to you, Granddad," comes the reply.

"Oh, hey baby!" says Felix. "You know me and this damn phone, it kills me so."

"It's not even top of the line," Alontay says.

"Oh, mercy," Felix says, always happy to hear from his granddaughter Alontay. She graduated high school two years ago; Felix doesn't see her as much as he used to when she was younger and he'd watch her a few times a week.

"What are you up to?"

"Not a whole lot on the docket today, *chére*. How's school going?"

"It's good, I'm going full time this semester, so it's keeping me busy."

"Very good, very good… And how's work?"

"Well, I'm still at the mall."

"A job's a job!"

"Yeah," she says. "Hey, you wanna have dinner tonight?"

"Oh, sure, baby! You wanna go somewhere? I can come pick you up."

"Actually, how about I just pick some food up and come over."

"Even better!" says Felix. "Come on over whenever you like!"

"Awesome," says Alontay. "Hey, Granddad? Is it alright if I bring a friend with me, too?"

"Of course, baby girl! Any friend of yours is always welcome in my home."

"Great!" she says. "I'll see you around six."

"I cannot wait. Granddad loves you!"

"Love you, too," she says before hanging up the phone. Felix sets it down and looks back at the TV.

*That girl is up to something,* he thinks.

* * *

A little after 6:00 P.M. that night, Felix hears a knock at his door. Having spent the afternoon tidying his apartment, he walks to the door prepared to host a gala event.

"Granddad!" says Alontay when he opens the door.

"Hey, baby girl!" says Felix, pulling her into a tight hug and kissing the top of her head. Behind Alontay stands a boy with dark hair and tan skin holding two bags of food they picked up on the way.

"And who is this young fellow?" asks Felix.

"Granddad, meet Ravi."

"I'd shake your hand, sir, but..." Ravi trails off, gesturing at the bags of food.

"Of course!" says Felix. "Come in, set those bags down!"

The three of them walk into the apartment and Ravi sets the grocery bags on the counter in Felix's kitchen.

"I thought it would be fun to cook a quick dinner together," Alontay tells Felix. "Like we did when I was little."

"I would like that very much!"

Over the next hour, Felix cooks with his granddaughter, delighted at spending the evening with her and her friend. They listen to music and laugh; Alontay fills her grandfather in on what's been going on in her life lately and he gets to know Ravi. After dinner, Ravi excuses himself to the bathroom and leaves Alontay alone at the table with her grandfather.

"That was really good," she says.

"It was," says Felix. "Probably the best I ever made!"

She smiles.

"So what brings you here tonight, Alontay? Really."

She takes a deep breath.

"Well," she says, slowly. "I wanted you to meet Ravi."

"He's a polite young man."

"Yeah..."

"And you two make a great couple. Good lookin', too!"

"W-what?"

"Come on, *chére*, it's obvious you came here tonight to introduce me to your boyfriend!"

She laughs.

"And nothing's wrong with it," says Felix.

"You're not upset?"

"Why would I be upset?"

"Because he's not black."

When Alontay says this, Felix feels a sting in his heart. He immediately thinks back to a long ago time of his life, years before he met Alontay's late grandmother. He remembers his first love and the summer they spent together, he a black musician, she a white singer. They had seen each other around town on various club stages, sharing only fleeting glances until Felix worked up the courage to talk to her. She was easy to talk to and one topic of conversation lead into the next until the club was closing for the night.

They continued to see each other at clubs across the city, enjoying their time together. Unfortunately, it was a different world then and they knew that the feelings that developed between them that summer would never be accepted by anyone in either of the lives. He was being pulled in one direction and she in another until eventually he had to let her go.

Felix had loved Alontay's grandmother with all his heart, but letting go of the golden haired singer was one of his life's only regrets.

"What does that matter, baby? He could be Indian or Asian or even a girl and I wouldn't give two damns so long as you were happy. Does he treat you right?"

"Oh yeah," she says. "It's just, I don't know, some people have had an issue with him and I being together."

"What? Who?!"

"Some people at school."

"Alontay Jackson," says Felix. "Baby girl, don't you ever let the opinions of others get in the way of your happiness. If they have a problem with it, that's just it – their problem. Friends that make you feel bad about yourself and your happiness don't sound like any friends I'd want to have around in *my* life… would you agree? Do an old man a favor and agree."

Alontay nods her head, laughing at her grandfather's way of approaching the situation.

"They're just being stupid, I guess."

"That's right, baby, they are. If that boy treats you right and makes you happy, there isn't much more else you can ask for, *chére*."

Alontay smiles.

"You don't have anything to be afraid of from me," says Felix. "Although, you know, you should really bring him to the speakeasy sometime!"

"I'll have to do that," says Alontay.

Ravi reenters the room.

"There's the man of the hour!" exclaims Felix.

Ravi smiles nervously as he sits down. Alontay looks from her grandfather to her boyfriend, nodding slightly to let Ravi know her grandfather knows about their relationship.

"And just so's you know, I figured that's why you two were here tonight."

"Really?" asks Ravi.

"Mmhmm… and you're both welcome here any time! Now, on to the most important question of the night," says Felix.

Ravi looks to Alontay, confused.

"You all ready for some dessert?"

\* \* \*

*Bea*

"Please, please, please," Bea whispers, staring at the closet door in her apartment. "He'll be around any minute, please don't make any noise." It is the first of the month before Graham Kelly moved into the building and Bea has hidden her four cats in the space, nestled between a few blankets to keep them comfortable

The Plaza at Garden Park has a very strict policy against pets, but Bea just can't live without her little darlings, even though she knows her landlord detests animals.

*Tap, tap, tap,* come three quick knocks on the door. Bea takes a deep breath.

"First of the month," comes the gruff voice of Victor Cain, Jr.

Bea shoots one final look at the closet door, mentally pleading for silence, before opening the door.

"Oh, hello, Mr. Cain," she says pleasantly.

"Mrs. Olloman."

"Here you go!" she says, handing him an envelope with a flourish.

"Thank you," he says dryly. He turns to leave, but stops suddenly as she is closing the door. He looks back at her and sniffs the air.

*There's no way he can smell them,* she thinks, trying to breathe normally. *I sprayed enough air freshener to asphyxiate a rhinoceros!*

"What's that smell?"

"Oh, that's the scent of rose petals, dear. Isn't it lovely?" she answers without missing a beat.

"It's... strong," he says. "See you next month."

"Have a great day!" she calls down the hall, watching Mr. Cain get onto the elevator. After he is gone, she closes and locks her door and scurries to the closet, opening the door. Her cats (Buttons, Bubbles, Mittens, and Mama Cass) mew happily upon seeing her.

"Oh, my little darlings, we did it! We kept you hidden for another month!" she says, beaming. "I do believe this calls for treats all around!"

\* \* \*

The next week, Bea works on a needlepoint in Eula's apartment as a tea kettle begins to whistle. Eula walks to the kitchen to pull it off of the stove. The television is on in the background as the two women watch their afternoon game shows.

"Well, look at that," calls Eula.

"Hmm?" Bea responds, looking up.

"It's starting to snow." Eula gestures toward her windows where, just beyond the neon pink curtains, the gray skies have unleashed a flurry of snowflakes.

"How pretty!"

"Snow at this time of year is so magical," says Eula, setting down the tray with a kettle and two cups. She pauses for a moment of reflection and turns to her friend. "Two spoons of sugar?"

"Oh, thank you, dear," says Bea. Eula serves her friend a cup of tea before preparing her own. They sit and watch the game show until it goes to commercial, at which point Eula turns off the television.

"Are you alright?" asks Bea.

"I need to talk to you about something."

Bea sets down her needlepoint and leans forward.

"Eula, is everything okay?"

Eula takes a deep breath and sets down her tea cup.

"I'm afraid not, dear."

Bea takes Eula's hands in her own, her breath shortening.

"It's back," Eula says.

"Oh, Eula!" responds Bea.

"I'm going in for more tests next week, but I don't think the prognosis looks good this time."

Bea's lower lip starts to quiver.

"Now, now, please don't be too upset."

"How can I not be?" asks Bea, choking back tears. "Y-you're, you might b-be…"

"I might, that's true. It's going to happen to all of us eventually, one way or another. But for now I'm here and we're enjoying this lovely afternoon." She pauses. "I didn't mean to make you so upset, Bea, I just… I just had to tell someone."

Bea grips Eula's hand and gives her a strong smile.

"Well, I will be there with you the whole way," she says.

"Thank you, my friend," Eula says delicately. "More tea?"

"Sure," says Bea, sitting back and picking up her needlepoint. Eula turns the television back on and the rest of the afternoon goes well enough, though the news Eula shared sits in the back of Bea's mind, never far from her thoughts.

* * *

A week later, Bea is spending the afternoon watching Margot Pershing, a ten-year-old girl who lives with her family on the sixth floor of the Plaza at Garden Park. Margot is tall for her age and very intelligent; she enjoys writing stories and has twin brothers, Henry and Harry, who are three years younger than she is. Her parents, John and Meg, are starting to trust Margot to stay alone by herself in their apartment, but today they are planning on being out for most of the day with the boys and asked Bea if she could stay with her.

Bea was happy to oblige. She quite enjoys the Pershing children, even if the twins can be a bit much to handle at times.

"I have a surprise for you today, Margot," Bea says shortly after Margot's parents drop her off. Margot is sitting on the couch petting Mama Cass while Buttons rubs against her legs; Mittens stares at her from across the room and Bubbles is asleep under the coffee table.

"What is it?" she asks, looking up excitedly.

"I thought it would be fun to go shopping! I made sure it was okay with your parents first, and they didn't mind. Does that sound like something you'd want to do?"

"Yeah!"

"Miss Eula is going to come with us, is that alright?"

"Of course," says Margot. "I love Miss Eula!"

Two hours and several stores later, Bea and Eula each have one of Margot's hands as they walk into a second hand store.

"One last stop before heading home," says Bea as they walk in.

"What kind of store is this?" asks Margot, confused.

"Well, dear, it's like a garage sale store," answers Eula.

"Oh, cool," says Margot. "What kind of stuff do they sell here?"

"Pretty much anything you can think of," says Bea. They spend the next twenty minutes wandering the aisles of the store before an old typewriter catches Margot's eye.

"Whoa," she says upon seeing it.

"Do you like that, dear?" asks Eula.

"I've never seen a typewriter in person before!"

"Really?"

"No," says Margot. "I like writing stories on our computer but I've always wanted to see what it would be like to write on an actual typewriter!"

"Let me see this," says Eula, taking a look at the tag on the typewriter. "Would you like me to buy this for you?"

Margot's mouth drops open.

"Really?!"

Bea walks up.

"And what did you two find?"

"A real life typewriter!" says Margot.

"Oh, really," says Bea. "How interesting."

"It's only fifteen dollars," says Eula. "And I think someone has earned a little treat for being so well behaved during our shopping trip today."

Margot lets out an excited squeak.

"Thank you, Miss Eula, thank you!"

Margot picks up the typewriter and the three walk to the front of the store. As she pays for the typewriter, Bea notices that Eula is steadying herself on the counter.

"You okay?" she asks.

"I'm fine," says Eula. "Just a little tired, is all… we've had a long day."

"That we have," says Bea. "Let's head home."

Later that day, Margot is typing on her new typewriter while Bea looks out the window drinking a cup of hot cocoa. She can't help but think about how tired Eula looked toward the end of their shopping excursion.

*I really hope she's going to be okay,* she thinks.

\* \* \*

Bea Olloman does not think of herself as a particularly religious woman, despite being raised in a Christian household. As a board member on The Garden Park Historical Society, she even gives tours a few times a week of a supposedly haunted mansion, the very idea of which would have made her Sunday school teachers shudder.

However, two weeks after the afternoon in Eula's apartment, Bea finds herself sitting in St. Kevin's Cathedral on Christmas Eve, lost in thought. Behind her, the heavy doors open and a young man walks in, brushing the snow off of his coat. Bea turns around at the noise of the door closing and watches him walk up to one of the balconies.

*Six months to a year,* she thinks, turning back around. *Six months to a year… a year can be a long time… or no time at all.*

Two days ago, Eula had shared her prognosis with Bea on the condition that the news would not ruin Bea's holiday.

"After all, I'm not letting it ruin mine!" Eula had said.

Bea smiles, thinking of her dear friend's spunkiness, her courage. She takes a deep breath and grabs her coat. She walks to one of the alcoves on the side of the altar with a statue of the Virgin Mary, rows of candles beneath her. She lights a candle and drops a few coins into the collection jar, their clanking echoes throughout the church.

*Please help her,* she thinks. *Be with her.*

Bea pulls on her coat and turns to leave.

*And if all she has left is a year, then please help me make it the best one she's ever had.* Bea stands for a moment looking at the statue then walks silently out of the cathedral into the snowy night.

\* \* \*

*Margot, Henry and Harry*

Margot Pershing lies on her stomach in the grass outside of the Plaza at Garden Park, pecking away on the typewriter that her neighbor, Eula, had bought for her last December. Margot recently celebrated her eleventh birthday, receiving the stack of writing books that sit next to her typewriter.

It is a hot day in July and thunderheads loom in the distance. Margot is watching her brothers, Henry and Harry, while their parents are at work. The boys had been begging her to go outside all day and she finally relented, despite the threat of storms from the weather report on the radio.

She looks up from the keys of her typewriter to check on her brothers, watching them chase each other around the old swing set on the side of their building. Satisfied that they have not hurt each other or run away, she continues typing.

"Is she looking?" asks Harry.

"No, she's typing again," answers Henry. "Come on." The boys sneak away from the swing set around to the front of the Plaza at Garden Park.

"Do you think we'll get them to do anything today?" asks Henry.

"I hope so!"

For as long as they could remember, the Pershing twins had believed that the lions outside of the Plaza at Garden Park were alive. Henry swore that the one on the left had talked to him once; Harry wholeheartedly believed that he saw the one on the right wink at him last summer. Every chance they got, they would go visit the lions out front to see if they could provoke any further signs of life.

"Hi lions!" says Harry happily as they approach the entrance walkway.

"You guys having a good day?" asks Henry.

The twins stare at the lions, eagerly waiting for any indication that they had heard their words.

"They're not doing anything," whispers Henry after a few moments.

"Shh," says Harry. "Give them a minute, they're made of stone."

The warm summer breeze weaves through both boys. They hear

the sound of a car driving by and cicadas in the field next to their building. The marble lions do not move or make any noise.

"Crap," says Harry.

Henry turns his head sharply.

"Did you hear that?" he asks.

"Hear what?"

"Someone's coming," he says, a mischievous grin spreading across his face. Harry furrows his brow, trying to listen, finally hearing the sound of footsteps that Henry heard a moment ago.

"You thinkin' what I'm thinkin'?" he asks.

Henry nods in agreement and each boy hurries to hide behind one of the pedestals the lions are perched upon.

Vera Sugarbaker is a particularly anxious woman who owns a shop in Old Town and lives alone on the fifth floor. She fumbles with a set of keys as she quickly approaches the entrance to the Plaza. She is struggling to hold two paper bags of groceries in one arm and walking quickly, her sandals flipping and flopping with each step.

Henry smiles at his brother and unleashes a low moan as Vera approaches.

"Hello?" she asks.

Harry replies with the sound of raspy breathing.

"Who's there?" asks Vera, sounding much more concerned. She looks around nervously as the boys stifle their giggles.

"You ready?" Henry mouths to his brother, who nods in agreement.

"Three…" mouths Harry.

"…two…"

"BOO!" shout both boys, jumping out from behind the pedestals.

"Ahh!" Vera screams. She throws her hands up in surprise, knocking her glasses askew and tossing her keys into the air; she drops the grocery bags, which rip as they hit the pavement.

"Ahh!" the boys scream, realizing who they have scared. Though they have never really interacted with Vera Sugarbaker, they know that she is the only tenant on her floor and believe she is a witch. The boys run away as quickly as they can to the side of the building to get away from her.

"Do you think she saw us?" asks Henry, panting as he leans against the side of the building.

"I hope not, I really hope not."

"She'll put a spell on us!"

"I know!" says Harry, panicked.

Suddenly, Margot storms up to them carrying her typewriter, her other arm full of books.

"Where have you two been?" she asks sternly.

"We were, uh…"

"…we were out front looking at the lions."

"Yeah, and then we started a game of tag."

"But we're bored now, so we want to go back inside."

Margot rolls her eyes.

"Alright, let's go." She goes to walk toward the front of the building.

"Wait!" yells Harry.

"What?"

"Why are we going this way?"

"Because we're closer to the front of the building than the back? Honestly, I don't know what's up with you two today," says Margot.

Henry and Harry exchange nervous glances, but when they get to the front of the Plaza at Garden Park, they are relieved to see that Vera Sugarbaker is nowhere to be seen.

As they walk into the building, a passing cloud moves away from the sun, the reflection of which causes a glimmer in the eye of the lion on the right. The shadow from the cloud makes the face of the one on the left look as though its mouth is grinning as a low rumble of thunder can be heard from far away.

\* \* \*

That evening, the phone in the Pershing's apartment rings. Margot hops up from reading in the recliner and grabs it, leaving her brothers on the floor playing a video game. Grabbing the phone, she sees that her mother is calling. The clouds from before have moved over the sun and into the city, casting an eerie darkness over the Plaza at Garden Park.

"Hi, Mom!" she says.

"Hey, sweetheart," says Meg Pershing. "How has your day been?"

"It's been good! I made the boys sandwiches and then I took them outside and they played out by the swing set." Thinking about it, Margot realizes how quiet the boys have been since coming in from outside.

"Good, good. What are you guys doing now?"

"The boys are playing a video game and I'm just reading."

"Oh, nice," she says. "Hey listen, sweetie, I have to stay late at work tonight and your dad has that meeting, so we're going to need you to watch the boys for longer than we thought, is that okay with you?"

"Oh, sure," says Margot. "That's fine."

"Thank you, angel."

"What should we do for dinner?"

"I think there's some ravioli in the pantry or you can see what's in the freezer."

"Okay, I will."

"And make sure the boys get showered after dinner, okay?"

"Sure thing."

"Call me if you need anything, okay?"

"Okay, mom."

On the other end of the line, Meg Pershing smiles.

"Thank you for being such a great helper," she says. "I love you!"

"Love you too, mom! Bye," says Margot, hanging up the phone.

"Who was that?" calls Harry from the living room.

"Mom," answers Margot, walking back in and jumping onto the recliner. "Her and dad are gonna be late so we're on our own for dinner. What do you guys want me to make?"

"Do we have any corn dogs?" asks Henry.

"I want chicken strips!" says Harry.

Margot sighs as neither of her brothers looks away from their video game.

"I'll go see what we have in the kitchen." Margot sets her book down and walks to the kitchen, trying to think of a way to appease both of her brothers.

The phone rings again and this time she sees that her father is calling.

"Hi, Dad," she says. "Mom just called, I know you're both going to be late."

"I'm sorry about that, sweet pea," says John Pershing. "We'll be home as quick as we can!"

"I know," says Margot. "It's fine."

"Hey, listen, I wanted to let you know that we might have some severe weather moving into the area in a little while. Will you guys be okay?"

"Yeah, Dad, we'll be fine. We're inside and I'll keep the boys away from the windows."

"That's my girl! What are you making for dinner?"

"I don't know yet, I'm figuring that out."

"Well, if the boys behave, look behind the cereals in the pantry.

There should be some cookies back there they can have as a treat."

"I think they found those already, but I'll check."

"Alright, I'm going to head into my meeting. Keep an eye on the weather and if it gets bad, go to Miss Eula's, okay? I talked with Miss Bea earlier and she's going to be there this evening."

"Okay, Dad."

"I'll see you when I get home!"

"Bye," says Margot, hanging up. She walks into the kitchen and looks through the refrigerator. Through the window, she sees the trees dancing outside in the wind that has picked up and the lightning that has started to flash over the city.

* * *

An hour later, the boys are watching a movie on TV while Margot cleans up the dishes from dinner. Giving in to both of her brothers' requests, she had made a plate of corn dogs and a few chicken strips as well as a side of macaroni and cheese for them all to share. It started to drizzle outside while they were eating and as Margot stands drying a plate, she sees the rain coming down harder.

"Hey, Margot?" calls Harry.

"Yeah?"

"What's that noise?"

"It's just the rain outside."

"Is it going to storm?" asks Henry.

"Probably," Margot answers. "But we'll be okay, we're inside."

Lightning flashes outside, followed quickly by a clap of thunder. Margot puts the plate in the drying rack, grabs a flashlight and goes into the living room with her brothers. Each is curled on opposite ends of the couch underneath the blankets their grandmother had made for them the previous Christmas.

"You guys okay?" asks Margot, sitting on the recliner.

Henry murmurs an acknowledgment while Harry nods.

Another flash of lightning streaks across the sky and the thunder that follows rumbles so hard it shakes the walls.

"Margot…" says Henry, getting upset. The rain outside pounds against the windows as the wind howls.

"I wish Mom and Dad were home!" says Harry.

"We're okay, guys," assures Margot, though she is starting to become concerned. The storm outside sounds unlike anything she has really heard before, with the lightning flashing almost constantly and the roar of the wind.

"Hey, do you guys want some ice cre – "

138

A bolt of lightning comes down seemingly right outside their kitchen window and is immediately followed by a crack that causes all three of the Pershing children to cover their ears. In an instant, all of the power in the Plaza at Garden Park goes out.

"It's the witch!" screams Harry.

"She's coming to get us!" screams Henry, bursting into tears.

Margot turns on the flashlight, adding a steady light source to the constant flashing from the lightning outside.

"The witch? What are you guys talking about?"

"The witch downstairs," says Henry.

"We scared her today," says Harry.

"We didn't mean to make her drop her groceries!"

"But we did and now she's made this storm outside – "

"– and she's coming to get us!" finishes Harry.

Margot goes over to the couch and sits down.

"I don't know what you two are talking about, but would you feel better if we went down to Miss Eula's?"

"Yes!" they both scream.

"Alright," says Margot. "Bring your blankets and we'll go down there."

\* \* \*

*I didn't expect the halls to be this dark,* Margot thinks as she leads her brothers down the dark corridor. Though they walk this hallway every day going into and out of their home, they've never experienced it quite like this. The lightning outside continues to flash, illuminating the space around the Pershing children just enough for their imaginations to get the best of them.

"What was that?!" screams Henry.

"I saw something!" screams Harry.

Margot swings her flashlight around wildly, trying to ease their fears and keep her own at bay.

"Boys, there is nothing to be afraid of out here," she says firmly. "Now let's go!"

Another crash of thunder sends both boys nearly into hysterics.

"Here," says Margot. "Henry, take the flashlight. And each of you grab one of my hands. We're gonna walk down there together."

"Okay," says Henry, grabbing the flashlight.

"Since the power's out, we're gonna have to take the stairs," says Margot. She leads her brothers down the hall and goes through the door into the stairwell. Walking slowly, they descend step by step, finally reaching the third floor.

"See you guys, this wasn't so bad," says Margot. They walk through the door and into the third floor hallway. After a few steps, they start to hear a new noise coming from outside, as though rocks are being thrown at the Plaza.

"W-what's that?" asks Harry, nervously.

"I don't know," says Margot. "It sounds like…"

*CRASH!*

A window at the end of the hallways shatters from the hail that is pelting it from the outside. The wind whips the rain into the building and all three of the Pershing children scream. Henry drops the flashlight and they are plunged into darkness.

*What am I going to do? What am I going to do?* thinks Margot, her mind racing.

A door opens in the hallways and the flicker of a candle illuminates the space.

"Hello? Who's out here?" comes a soft voice.

"Miss Eula!" yells Margot, a quiver in her voice. "It's us! We're down here and our flashlight broke!"

"Oh, children! Come toward the candle!"

The Pershing siblings walk quickly toward Eula and by the time they reach her door, several of the other adults in the building are also standing there holding candles. Margot notices that Eula is balancing herself on a cane.

*Has she always had that?* she thinks.

"Are you dears alright?" asks Bea.

"I was just gettin' ready to come check on you three," says Felix.

"We're okay," says Margot, panting. "I think the boys are a little scared, though."

"Can we wait here until our Mommy and Daddy come home?" asks Henry.

"Of course you can!" says Eula. "Come in, come in!" She ushers the children in while Felix and another neighbor, Charlie Patterson, run down to the broken window to inspect the damage.

A few minutes later, the three Pershing children are sitting in the back room of Eula's apartment with an old record player. A vanilla candle burns in a jar nearby, the flame casting a warm glow about the room. It continues to storm outside, though the weather has started to calm down.

"I'm gonna leave you three in here with these records," says Eula. "We're having an important meeting out there but I want you three to come out and get Miss Bea or myself if you need anything, alright?"

"Okay," says Margot. "Miss Eula?"

"Yes, dear?"

"I like your cane," says Margot, gesturing toward Eula's cane that has been painted pink and covered in jewels.

"Thank you, precious," she says.

"Thank you for letting us stay," says Margot.

"Of course, dear ones, of course! We are like family here in the Plaza!" She turns and leaves the room, leaving the door only slightly cracked.

Margot and her brothers burrow under several blankets and they listen to old records that Eula has, including two that have companion storybooks. Every now and then, Margot catches little snippets of what the adults are saying beyond the door.

"They say the bridge might be out..."

"...half of the city is without power..."

"...so brave coming down here on their own."

"Who's at the door?"

"Oh, I'm so glad you came!"

"...come in, come in..."

"Would he really sell?"

"Where would that leave us?"

"I can get the window fixed in the morning..."

"He mustn't know..."

Margot isn't sure what the adults are talking about, but she can tell it is very important from how urgently they talk. As the sounds of the storm give way to a steady rain and the occasional rumble of thunder, Henry and Harry both fall asleep under the warm blankets. Soon, Margot, too, finds herself feeling increasingly drowsy until she can no longer keep her eyes open and falls asleep.

* * *

"Up you get," says John Pershing, lifting Harry onto his right shoulder. He then picks up Henry and holds him in his other arm.

"Margot," says Meg Pershing. "Wake up, sweetie. Mom and Dad are here to take you home."

Margot sleepily rolls over, rubbing her eyes. She sits right up when she sees her parents and instantly notices that the lights are back on.

"Mom! Dad!" she says. She wraps her arms around her mother's neck, giving her a tight hug.

"It's good to see you, too, sweetheart," says Meg. "I hear you three had quite an adventure tonight."

"We're so sorry we had to leave you alone," says John. "We both tried to get here as quickly as we could but the traffic was so bad all over the city because of the storm."

Margot smiles.

"Let's head upstairs," says Meg. She leads Margot by the hand after her father and brothers. Eula sits in her living room with another woman.

"Good night, Eula," says John. "And thank you again for taking them in."

"Oh, it was no trouble, John," says Eula. "I'm glad I could help!"

The Pershing family walks out the door, but before they are all out the door, Margot pulls away from her mother.

"I forgot something!" she says. She runs over to where Eula is sitting and gives her a big hug.

"Thank you," she says.

"Oh, dear one," says Eula. "You're very welcome."

Margot turns to leave when she notices the other woman sitting with Eula. She doesn't know her name, but suddenly realizes that this is the woman that lives on the fifth floor, the woman her brothers were so scared of.

"H-hello," the woman says.

"Hi," says Margot.

"Margot, have you met Miss Vera? She lives on the fifth floor."

"No," says Margot. "It's nice to meet you."

"And you, too, Margot."

"Have a good night," Margot says, smiling and turning to leave. Suddenly, she turns around.

"Miss Vera," she begins. "I think my brothers may have scared you earlier today and I'm sorry about that. I should have been keeping a better eye on them when we were outside. They would apologize themselves, but they're sleeping now…"

"Oh, d-don't even worry about that," says Vera. "But I do very much appreciate the sentiment. Have a g-good night, dear."

Margot smiles at the two women and runs to catch up with her family.

\* \* \*

*Claire*

"There isn't a glory hole in town that man hasn't pulled a splinter out of his member from," Claire Tenyson says bitterly, exhaling a cloud of cigarette smoke. "Did you know that?"

"You might have mentioned it once or twice," says Eula.

It is a week before the storm hits the city and both women are sitting on a bench outside of the Uptown Mall. A bus pulls away with an advertisement for a local newscast on its side, the smiling face of meteorologist Rex Benford taunting Claire as it disappears into a cloud of exhaust. Claire takes another drag on her cigarette.

"That asshole can bang anything that holds still long enough," she says before exhaling. "But I decide to speak up about the absurd inequality of pay between myself and the cadre of men I work with, not *for*, but with, and I'm suddenly a troublemaker."

Eula nods sympathetically.

"Did you know his name's not even Rex? It's fucking Martin," Claire says, getting one last inhale off of her cigarette before hitting the filter. "It's fucked up." She drops her cigarette and stamps it out with one of her black pumps.

"Let's go inside for some retail therapy, dear," says Eula.

Claire smiles.

"I'm sorry, Eula," she says. "I didn't mean to bring all of that up."

"Oh, it's quite alright. You don't get to be my age without being screwed over a time or two." She smiles. "Better out than in!"

The automatic doors whoosh open and the two women feel a blast of cool air as they enter the mall, finally finding relief from the summer heat.

*She's walking slowly today,* thinks Claire.

"Do you want to get a scooter or anything?" she asks.

"Maybe later," answers Eula. "Right now, these old bones need to do some walking!" She shakes her hips and snaps, her bracelets clattering with the movement. Looking at her old friend, Claire can't help but laugh.

*She really has no fucks left to give,* thinks Claire, taking in Eula's choice of wardrobe for the day. Eula is known for her eccentric style, but today's leopard print skirt and denim vest ensemble complete with bedazzled cane seems to be even more out there than usual.

*Who is this old bird?* Claire had thought upon first meeting Eula. She had recently lost her job at the TV station; her financial situation had forced her out of her penthouse downtown and into a modest apartment in the Plaza at Garden Park. Claire had holed herself up in her apartment for weeks before Eula came to visit, bringing a pint of ice cream and, more importantly, a listening ear free of judgment.

It took time, but eventually Claire Tenyson found a kindred spirit in Eula Belle.

"There's two of my girls!" greets Charlie Patterson as Claire and Eula walk into Bezel & Crown, the shop he has owned for many years. Charlie lives in Apartment 2A, on the same floor as Bea Olloman.

"I told you I'd come by for a visit sometime soon!" says Eula.

Claire smiles.

"Business good today?" asks Eula.

"I'm doing alright," answers Charlie. "I've got a few jobs I'm working on."

"Very nice," says Eula.

"What brings you ladies out to the mall?"

"Just thought I'd do some walking," says Eula.

"And it's too hot to stay outside for too long," adds Claire.

Charlie nods approvingly.

"Well, sir, we won't keep you," says Eula.

"Eula, my dear," says Charlie, taking her hand. "It is always a pleasure."

Eula takes her hand away with a wink.

"You ladies have a nice afternoon," he says.

"You, too."

Claire smiles and walks with Eula out of the store.

*I like that old guy,* she thinks. *I just never have too much to say to him… we don't really have anything in common at all.*

"You up for a treat?" she asks once they're back out in the mall.

"Lead the way!" Claire and Eula walk side-by-side to the coffee shop. Claire notices the grimace in Eula's face that she tries to hide with each step. After what feels like a half an hour, they arrive in the café.

"Those scones look fantastic!" Eula says.

"Tell you what," says Claire. "You sit here and I'll go get you one."

"That would be lovely," says Eula, slowly lowering herself onto a chair.

"I'll be right back," says Claire. She looks over the bake case and gets in line. She catches the eye of the woman in front of her, who immediately recognizes her and averts her gaze.

*That's right, bitch,* she thinks. *I'm the mouthy TV reporter. Get over it.*

Claire sighs and looks around, seeing the Customer Service desk outside of the café. As she is giving her order to the girl behind the counter, she has an idea.

"Can you box those up for me?" she asks.

"Sure," answers the girl, whose nametag reads 'Roni'. She wraps Eula's scone and Claire's double fudge brownie in separate containers as Claire sneaks out to the desk.

A few minutes later, Eula is surprised to hear a quick *beep, beep* as Claire speeds back into the coffee shop on a motor scooter.

"Thought we could have a little extra fun today," says Claire with a grin. She stands and hands Eula her scone. "What do you think?"

Eula looks at the chair for a few moments, long enough that Claire starts to worry that she may have overstepped her bounds by renting the scooter.

"I think you're gonna have to walk pretty fast to keep up with this old broad!"

\* \* \*

The next day, Claire knocks on Eula's door just before 10:00 AM. Moments later, Eula flings the door open.

"Good morning, my fair Claire!"

"Hello," says Claire, trying not to laugh.

"Come on in!"

"So what are we going to do today?" Claire asks, walking in.

"I'm afraid I'm still a little worn out from yesterday's trip to the mall," admits Eula. "If you could be so kind as to run to the grocery store for me, that would be lovely. And I have some dry cleaning I'd like you to drop off."

"Of course," says Claire.

"Thank you, dear."

Twenty minutes later, Claire Tenyson is driving away from the Plaza at Garden Park, her face hidden behind large dark sunglasses. Her window is down as she smokes a cigarette and an open, half-eaten chocolate bar is on the passenger seat. Eula had given her a bag of dresses to take to the dry cleaner, every single one of them colorful and sequined past the point of audacity.

She feels a little foolish dropping them off and wants to explain to the clerk that they're not her dresses, that they belong to the old woman she works for a few days each week, the only person in this city who'd given her anything close to a second chance.

*So what,* she thinks suddenly. She looks down at her plain, black skirt and white top and thinks about the clothes she's leaving with the cleaner. *So what if they think I wear stuff like this? Who cares if she has clothes that look like this or, hell, are even gaudier? Maybe I should be taking a page out of Eula's book.*

Later, she pushes a cart down the aisle of a grocery store. She looks from the list Eula has given her to the shelves she passes.

*She looked so frail yesterday,* thinks Claire. *I guess it could be any time now... no, no don't think about that, Claire. Think about... making sure you get the right brand of pasta. You know she's particular... You'll have plenty of time to think about that later.*

* * *

Later that afternoon, Claire sits in Eula's apartment sipping on a glass of wine.

"And they didn't give you any trouble at the cleaners?"

"Nope," says Claire. "None at all."

She swirls her wine around.

"Are you alright, dear?"

Claire looks up, surprised by the question.

"What? Oh, I'm fine."

"No, I don't think you are."

Claire smiles even though she feels a lump rise in her throat.

"I'm scared, Eula."

"Of what?"

Claire pauses, carefully choosing her words before saying them.

"Of what's to come," she finally says.

"For you?"

"No, well, a little. But mostly for you."

"Oh, dear," says Eula. "I made peace with things long ago."

"How? How do you do it? How are you still one of the brightest lights I've ever had in my life and you have every reason to curl up and hate the world."

"Curling up and hating the world won't fix anything, least of all my health."

Claire nods.

"I figure... I'd better make the most of the time I have left. I'd better make this as great of a world as I can *while* I can, you know?"

Claire looks at her and starts to cry.

"I figure I'd better live while I'm living."

Claire smiles.

"What are you really worried about?"

Claire tries to smile, though her lower lip is trembling.

"You're the only person who took any kind of chance on me after... after I lost everything. I just..." her voice cracks. "I just don't want to lose you."

"Oh, Claire," says Eula. "I'm not going anywhere for a while yet.

And when I do, I'll never be far from your memories."

Claire sniffs and takes a sip of wine.

"And believe me, if I can figure out a way, I'm going to haunt the hell out of you and Bea and the rest of our family in the Plaza!"

"I'm sorry," she says, laughing as she wipes away her tears. "I didn't mean to be such a downer today. I'm just anxious, I guess."

"I understand. Believe me, I do."

Both women sit in silence for a few moments.

"Claire," Eula says. "I have a project for you."

"Oh?"

"Yes," she says. "I'm going to tell you a story and I want you to write it all down. And when I'm gone, I want you to share it with the world."

"Alright," says Claire slowly, opening a chocolate bar. "What's the story?"

Eula smiles.

"In a city like this, everyone has a story to tell," she says. "This one just happens to be mine."

\* \* \*

*Charlie*

One week after the storm, Charlie Patterson perches on a stool in Bezel & Crown. He is removing links from a watch that a walk-in customer dropped off earlier in the day. Carefully peering over his glasses, he pops the pins out of the links and onto a velvet cloth. He lays the watch down and removes two links.

He leans back, stretching his shoulders, before continuing to put the pins back in and reconnect the watch band. Once he is finished, he places the extra links and pin into a small pouch and puts everything back into the watch's case.

"Hey, Charlie!"

Charlie looks up to see his neighbor, Graham Kelly.

"Oh, hello, Graham," he says. "What brings you in?"

"Well, I thought I'd come by and see the famous shop! Also, I'm taking my girlfriend out for our six month anniversary this weekend and I thought it'd be nice to get her a little gift. She's had the same watch since she was a little girl and it's about on its last leg, so it seems like as good a time as any."

"Very good," says Charlie. "I've got a good number of watches over here that are for sale." He leads Graham to a display case. Graham immediately sees one that he knows Chelle will love.

"How much is that one?" he asks.

Charlie takes it out of the case and looks at the tag.

"Well, what do you know?" he asks. "With your Plaza Neighbor Discount, it's the same as at cost!"

"Charlie, come on," says Graham. "I'll pay the full price, I don't mind."

"Ah," says Charlie. "I'll have none of that! Just buy me a drink at Felix's speakeasy sometime."

Graham laughs.

"Alright, you've got yourself a deal!"

\* \* \*

About an hour later, the man who owns the watch Charlie was working on before Graham's visit returns to the shop. He is talking loudly into his cell phone.

"Yeah, I just have to pick up my watch and I'll be on my way … alright, I'll see you there. Be good." He hangs up.

"Hello there."

"How'd it go?"

"It went fine," says Charlie, pulling the man's watch box from beneath his counter. He opens it up and lays the watch out on the counter. The man picks it up and slips it on, clasping it into place.

"What do you think?" he asks Charlie. "Is it still too loose?"

Charlie leans forward and looks at the watch on the man's wrist.

"No," he says. "Any tighter and wearing it for long periods of time would become painful. Does it have a lot of give?"

The man twists his wrist around and the watch moves very little.

"No, not that much."

"Very good."

"How much do I owe you?"

"Just a couple of links out? Twenty bucks."

"Sounds good to me," says the man, reaching into his jacket for a wallet.

"If I may ask, how long have you had that watch? It's very nice."

"Oh," says the man. "My old man gave me this a few years back after I flipped my first property."

"Excuse me?"

"That's what I do," says the man. "I buy old real estate, rehab it and sell, making quite a bit of profit in the process."

He hands the man a credit card.

"I bet that keeps you busy," says Charlie, swiping the card.

"Yeah," says the man. "Keeps me out of trouble."

Charlie prints out a receipt and asks the man to sign.

"I'm glad I came across your shop," he says, signing the slip. "This watch has been loose ever since I got it; I never thought to have a few links taken out."

He shakes his hand again, amazed at how well the watch stays in place.

"It looks good," says Charlie.

"I'm just excited I can wear it to dinner tonight."

"Oh… a business dinner?"

"Nah, just a pre-celebration dinner with the girlfriend."

"That's exciting," says Charlie. "What's the occasion?"

"I put a bid on a new property to flip," he says. "And this could be the one that sends me to the next tax bracket."

"That much for a house?" asks Charlie.

"Not just a house," says the man. "This is some dump out in Garden Park."

Charlie's heart skips a beat.

"Garden Park?" he asks, surprised.

"Yeah, I know, I thought the same thing when I came across the property. But this place is a gold mine, man. It's this old hotel… there's some tenants but I've handled people like that before."

"You don't say," Charlie says, absentmindedly.

"Yeah," says the man. "Well hey, I'd better get going. Thanks for fixing my watch!"

"Sure thing," says Charlie. "Have a great night."

The man leaves and Charlie falls back onto his stool. After he has had a few minutes to think, he picks up the phone and calls Eula.

"We have a problem," he says when she answers.

\* \* \*

Later that night, Charlie sits in Eula's apartment with Bea Olloman. The tank resting near Eula's feet makes a *psst* sound every time it pumps oxygen through the piece of plastic that rests beneath her nostrils. She'd received her nasal cannula from her doctor's office the day before.

"Do you think he'll kick us all out?" asks Bea, visibly shaken.

"I don't know," says Charlie. "He seemed like a very 'bottom line' kind of guy. I don't think he'd lose any sleep over putting out a group of residents. And he said he's dealt with people like us before."

Bea sits wringing her hands.

"What's worse is I don't know if Cain would even come in here and tell us what was going on. He'd be the type to find some loophole in our agreements and screw us over in the end," says

Charlie.

"What are we going to do?" Bea asks sadly.

Eula sits on the couch, lost in thought. She picks up her tea cup and takes a drink.

"I have an idea, but – "

Eula is interrupted by a quick knocking on her door.

"Now who could that be?" she asks. "Charlie, could you get the door?"

"Sure," he says, standing up.

Charlie opens the door to find Felix Jackson standing on the other side.

"Felix?" he asks.

He walks in past Charlie, shaking and upset.

"Felix!" says Eula, getting to her feet. "What's wrong?"

He enters the apartment and Charlie closes the door behind him. Felix walks over to Eula and gives her a hug and a kiss on each cheek before sitting down with her on the couch.

"I just had a visit from Mr. Cain," he says, his voice trembling. "He knows about the speakeasy and he's shuttin' it down."

Eula takes Felix's hand in her own.

"He can't!" says Bea.

"He can, *chére*," says Felix. "And he did. Turns out all that paperwork I figured we wouldn't need so long as no one really found out about our lil speakeasy really *does* matter. Cain said he won't go to the city so long as we shut down immediately."

"Goddamnit," spits Charlie, beating a fist into his palm. "We're losing everything."

Felix looks toward him.

"Whaddya mean, Chuck?"

Bea looks at Felix, her eyes wide.

"Cain's selling the building," he says. "To someone who's going to flip the property and when the value goes up – "

"We'll all be out on the street!" Bea shouts, borderline hysterical.

"What?!" bellows Felix. "He can't do that!"

"I think he can," Bea says.

"This is… I can't believe this is happening," says Felix.

Eula clears her throat.

"Friends," she begins. "I'm afraid I underestimated Victor, Jr. But we knew this day would be coming, or at least, we had some kind of idea – we talked about it at great length just last week, remember?"

Charlie, Bea and Felix nod, remembering their meeting on the night of the storm.

"I'm not going to lose faith," says Eula. "And neither should any of you."

"But, Eula – " begins Charlie.

"We're not going anywhere," says Eula firmly. "And Felix? Get that speakeasy ready to open next week for business as usual, my love."

Eula tightens her grip on Felix's hand; Bea's mouth hangs open and Charlie raises an eyebrow at the sudden change in Eula's demeanor.

"I have some phone calls to make," she says.

\* \* \*

*Eula*

Five days later, Eula goes upstairs to see Felix. She walks slowly with one hand gripping the handle on her cane, while the other holds a file of paperwork. She knocks on Felix's door and a few moments later he answers.

"Hello, beautiful," he says warmly.

"Hey, yourself," she says. "Can I come in?"

"Of course," Felix says, ushering her into his apartment. He walks with her to the couch, where she sits and lays the file of paperwork on the coffee table.

"We have a lot of work to do, Felix."

He kneels down and starts looking through the papers.

"What's all this?"

"I pulled some strings and called in a few favors downtown," says Eula.

 Felix snaps his head around to look at Eula.

"You mean…"

"The Plaza Speakeasy opens tomorrow night for business."

"How?"

"Technically, it's be classified as a fundraising space for The Garden Park Historical Society. In that folder, you have an occupancy permit as well as a temporary liquor license.

"From there, I've laid the ground work that will allow you to stay in business so long as you choose. Everything is in order so Mr. Cain won't have any reason to try and come after you again."

Felix's mouth hangs open.

"I dunno what to say."

"You don't have to say anything," Eula says slowly.

In that moment, a lifetime of memories flashes through both

Felix and Eula's minds until each rests on a summer they had spent together long ago, he a black musician, she a white singer.

"I'm sorry," she says.

"No, no," says Felix. "I'm the one who should be sorry."

"It was a different time then, you know."

"I know," he says. He sits down next to her on the couch, gingerly touching her pale blonde hair.

"I never stopped loving you, you know," she says. "Every man I met over the years, I secretly compared to you."

"Letting you go has haunted me all these years," says Felix. "And, I loved my dear wife with all my heart, but part of me always belonged to you."

Eula smiles.

"Why didn't you say anything when you moved into the Plaza?" she asks.

"Like I said, that was a different time back then. A whole other life, practically. I couldn't believe that you and I had even been able to reconnect, I wasn't about to spoil anything between us."

"I understand," she says.

"And besides, seeing you all these years, *chére*, well... it made me happy. Knowing that you had done alright for yourself and I had done the same and after all that time, you and I were still able to reconnect and be a part of each other's lives."

Felix puts his arm around Eula as she scoots closer to him. She rests her head on him, feeling his heart beat through his chest.

"I think I'm ready to go," she says.

"Back downstairs? But you just got here," he says.

"No," she answers gently. "Not just to my apartment."

"Oh," says Felix, looking around the room in an attempt to stop his eyes from tearing up. "But, Eula..."

"All that time we were apart, Felix, and then all the time we've lived here together. I'm a part of your story just as much as you are of mine. You know my passing won't change that, don't you?"

"Of course," he says.

"There is, however, one last thing I want to do," she says.

"What's that?"

"I'm coming out of retirement."

"How do you mean?"

"Tomorrow night, The Plaza Speakeasy will play host to the final show of Eula Belle – and I need you to help spread the word."

"Of course," says Felix.

"I had quite a following for a while, you know," she says with a grin. "You may want to make sure you're stocked up on liquor."

"You got it."

"And have the band ready to go at eight o'clock?"

"Anything for you."

"Excellent," she says. She looks around Felix's apartment, glancing at the photos on the wall. She thinks briefly of the life they could have had together, had they only been born a few decades later.

*But this is the life I've lead,* she thinks. *And I'm damn proud of it.*

"I'd like to sit here with you awhile, if you don't mind."

Felix leans back on the couch and Eula rests her head on his shoulder, their fingers delicately intertwined.

\* \* \*

The next night, Eula goes downstairs to the lobby of the Plaza at Garden Park with assistance from Claire and Bea. Felix stands in the lobby, marveling at the parade of cars in the parking lot.

"Hot damn!" he says. "We've never had this many people before!"

"I told you I had quite a following," Eula says, smiling. After she left Felix's apartment, he had called his granddaughter, Alontay, and enlisted her help with spreading the word that not only was The Plaza Speakeasy going to be officially open for business, but that world renowned singer, Eula Belle, would be coming out of retirement for one night only.

Various social media outlets had picked up the news and word spread like wildfire. People across the city cleared their schedules for the chance to hear a local legend, whom few had forgotten about, perform one last time.

And after decades of staying out of the public eye, Eula Belle finds herself sitting in a makeshift dressing room preparing to go on stage one final time. The lights on the mirror catch the sequins on her deep blue dress as she touches up her makeup. She bounces some of the curls in her hair and, for a moment, she sees herself in her early twenties, her skin a little tighter, her hair a little more vibrant, preparing to go on stage.

Felix opens the door and sticks his head into the room.

"It's about five 'til eight," he says. "You about ready to go on?"

Eula looks at him in the mirror, seeing him as he was that summer so long ago.

She spins around in her chair to face him.

"It's show time!"

* * *

The Plaza Speakeasy erupts into applause when Felix introduces Eula and the sound only grows louder when she takes the stage. She looks into the crowd and is humbled to recognize so many faces amongst the packed room. She walks over and picks up the microphone.

"Hello, everyone!" she says.

The crowd bursts into cheers again.

"It's so good to see so many friends here tonight!" She pauses, allowing the crowd to quiet down again. "Now, I'm sure many of you have heard that tonight, for one night only, I'm here to entertain all of you beautiful people!

"For those of you that may not know who I am, allow me to introduce myself! My name is Eulalia Belle, but you can all call me Eula. You probably heard some of my music all while you were growing up and you didn't even realize it. I sang for many, many years in venues all over the world and I've written music for some of the most legendary icons in the music industry.

"Some time ago, I opted to quietly retire, hoping that the legacy of my music would live on as I explored other interests. Now, if all of you being here tonight is any indication, I'd say my music did that and then some!

"Before we get to the show, I do have a few people I'd like to call your attention to. First of all, none of this would be possible without the fantastic Mr. Felix Jackson. Felix? Where are you at, love?"

Felix waves from the side of the stage

"Let's hear it for Felix, everybody!" Again, Eula pauses as the audience claps their hands.

"Bea, are you here?" Eula looks out into the crowd, using her hand to shield her eyes from the lights. Bea stands next to three drag queens at the bar, waving to Eula.

"Ahh, there you are! My dear friend, Bea Olloman, ladies and gentlemen. Now, I'd be willing to bet many of you had to schlep out here to Garden Park from somewhere else in our beautiful city, am I right?

"Well, Bea over there is a board member of The Garden Park Historical Society and the proceeds from tonight's show will go to benefit their fine organization. If I may, Garden Park holds a special place in my heart. This was where I first learned to sing, where I found my passion in life." She pauses. "I fell in love in Garden Park.

"It broke my heart to watch such a rich part of our city start to fade away, but The Garden Park Historical Society is doing its part to bring the shine back to a place I hold so dear. They are truly a wonderful group and I hope that you all will stay involved long after tonight's show."

She smiles at the audience.

*I have missed this,* she thinks. *I love it... standing in front of so many people, the anticipation for a show... Thank God I got to do this one last time...*

"Alright! I swear to you all, this old bat hasn't lost her marbles completely," she says, laughing. The audience laughs with her. "So, before I ramble this night away, how about we get the show going?"

Again, the audience cheers and Eula starts to sing her first song.

"You're really her friend, doll?!" the drag queen next to Bea asks. She is tall with big, red hair and intricately detailed makeup.

"I am," says Bea. "Eula and I have known each other for years!"

"Oh my God, honey, I'm so jealous!" says the queen.

"What's your name?" asks Bea.

"Diamond St. Delicious," she answers. "You've no idea, honey, I've *idolized* Eula for so many years... She's a legend! I had no idea she still lived here!"

"She did a great job staying out of the public eye," says Bea.

"Seriously, I used to dance around my room as a kid listening to her music and singing along. Should come as no surprise coming from someone as fabulous as me," says the drag queen. Bea laughs with her.

"Oh, you *are* fabulous!" she shouts. "And Eula would love to hear that, you should come talk to her later!"

Diamond St. Delicious's mouth drops open.

"Y-you could make that happen?!" she asks.

"Of course! Just come find me later, tonight's show probably won't go very late and I know Eula wanted to meet with some of the attendees."

"Oh my God, honey, thank you!" shouts Diamond, wrapping her arms around Bea in a great bear hug.

"Of course, of course," says Bea as she notices Graham Kelly across the way. "Oh, could you excuse me for a few? I see one of my neighbors over there."

Bea makes her way through the crowd over to a couch that Graham Kelly is sharing with his girlfriend.

"Graham!" says Bea.

"Hey there!" he says, standing up to give her a hug. "You remember my girlfriend, Chelle."

"Hello, again," says Bea. "It's so nice to see you."

"You, too!" says Chelle.

"So, wow! I had no idea that Eula was leading this crazy double life," says Graham. "Who knew we had a celebrity in the building this whole time?"

"Well, I did, dear, but I was sworn to secrecy! Eula would have it no other way."

"She is something," says Graham.

"She has an amazing voice!" says Chelle.

A blonde guy with his hair pulled into a ponytail walks up carrying three drinks.

"Oh, Tyler, you remember my neighbor, Bea, from Claythorn Manor?"

Tyler hands Graham and Chelle their respective drinks and turns to Bea.

"Hey there," he says, extending his free hand.

"Great to see you again, cutie!" says Bea, pushing away Tyler's hand and pulling him into a hug. "Alright, I'm going to see who all else is here. I'll see you dears later!"

Bea disappears into the crowd as Tyler sits down with Graham and Chelle.

"She's really good!" says Tyler, nodding toward Eula.

"I know," says Graham. "And it's so crazy that I had no idea she had this whole other life that hardly any of us knew about!"

"And a huge fan base," says Chelle. "Wow!"

"Right?" says Tyler. "I mean, Diamond St. Delicious is even here!"

Chelle takes a drink as Graham sees his neighbor Charlie walk up to the bar.

"I'll be right back," he says, getting up.

Chelle turns to Tyler.

"You okay?" she asks.

"Yeah," he says. "I'll be alright. I just haven't been here since the night you and Graham first met and you may recall who else was with us that night…"

"I know," she says. "Come on, let's go dance."

Graham approaches the bar that Charlie is leaning over.

"Ready to cash in on that drink?" asks Graham.

"Oh! Hi Graham," says Charlie. "If you insist."

Graham catches the attention of one of the bartenders.

"His first drink's on me," says Graham.

Charlie orders a seven and seven and when it is delivered, they clink glasses.

"To the Plaza," says Charlie.

They drink.

"What do you think's going to happen now?"

"I don't know," says Charlie. "I guess we'll have to wait and see. I know this whole thing tonight was part of some plan Eula had cooked up and, well, take a look around. This place is packed! I'm willing to suspend a little disbelief on the hope that she's got things worked out."

Graham nods his head.

"What about you, Graham?"

"How do you mean?"

"A young man like you living in an old place like this... it won't last forever. So, what's next for you?"

"Well," says Graham. "I don't know what's next, really. Another semester and then one more after that and beyond that... who knows."

Charlie nods.

"You're right though."

"About what?"

"This won't last forever," says Graham. "But I'll be having a hell of a time for as long as it does!"

Charlie smiles.

"I'll drink to that," he says. They clink their glasses again.

"Hey, Charlie!" says a voice behind them. Graham and Charlie turn around to see a younger guy standing there holding hands with a girl.

"Well, hello Ravi," says Charlie.

"This is my girlfriend, Alontay," says Ravi, introducing the girl. "She works in the mall with us!"

"Oh, really?," Charlie asks. "What a small world, I own Bezel & Crown! Nice to meet you, Alontay. This is my neighbor, Graham."

"Neighbor?" asks Alontay. "So you live here?"

"Yeah, we both do," says Graham.

"Isn't that funny," says Alontay. "So does my granddad, Felix!"

"I've known Felix for years!" says Charlie.

"Oh my God," says Graham. "It *is* a small world, he and I live on the same floor!"

Ravi steps up and orders two drinks as Graham looks around the room.

"Excuse me, guys," he says. "I'm gonna go find my girlfriend. It was great to meet you both!"

Graham steps away as Ravi and Alontay's drinks are brought over.

"We've gotta go find her granddad," Ravi tells Charlie. "I'll come find you later, man, you gotta hear what went down at the book store two days ago!"

Charlie watches Ravi and Alontay disappear into the crowd.

"What a party," he says.

Alontay finds her granddad standing near the stage, tapping his foot along with the music as Eula sings her heart out.

"Granddad!"

"Hey baby!" he yells, wrapping his arms around her in a firm hug. "Hey there, big man!"

"Hey, Mr. Jackson," says Ravi.

"I keep telling you, boy, call me Felix! Isn't this incredible?"

"This place is wild," Alontay says. "Who knew there was something like this down here?"

"Well, I always did but we couldn't make too big a deal out of it. That's all about to change, though."

Alontay looks at her granddad, confused.

"Eula up there took care of a few things for me and I think we'll actually be able to make this place a bona fide business soon! It's got a name and everything!"

"Well that's a step in the right direction!" says Alontay.

"Oh, I'm so glad you both came out tonight," says Felix. He looks around the room, so thrilled to see so many people. His eyes land on a familiar face and he turns to his granddaughter.

"I'll be right back, baby," he says.

"We'll be here!" she says, smiling at Ravi.

Felix approaches the armchair that Claire Tenyson sits in as she pulls a cigarette out of her bag.

"Hello, Claire," he says. "How many times we gotta do this dance?"

"What are you talking about, Felix?"

"I always tell you, I don't care how you break the rules upstairs, but down here you can't smoke!"

Claire grins a mischievous grin.

"Things have changed a bit, love," she says. The end of her cigarette suddenly glows a bright blue. "And technically, I'm not smoking."

"What's that?"

"Heard of those vapor cigarettes?"

"The expensive ones?"

"That's what I smoke now, more or less."

Felix looks at her, confused.

"I'm trying to quit."

"Oh, good for you, *chére*!" yells Felix. "Can I buy you a drink later to celebrate or did you give that up, too?"

"Come on now, Felix," she says with a wink. "I can't give up all my vices."

"I don't blame you one bit!" He nods toward his drink and gives her a wink before heading off into the crowd. Claire sits along and watches Eula sing.

"She's amazing, isn't she?" asks a man who sits down.

"Mmhmm," says Claire, glancing his way. A woman sits down next to him.

"She's our neighbor, you know," says the man. "We've known her for so long and we never had any idea about this side of her."

"She's your neighbor?" asks Claire. "She's my neighbor, too!"

The woman smiles and extends her hand.

"Hi, I'm Meg and this is my husband," she says.

"John Pershing," he says, with a nod.

"Claire Tenyson," she says. "I think we live on the same floor."

"I thought you looked familiar!" says Meg.

"We've seen you around, but we both work so much we've never had much of a chance to know most of the neighbors," says John. "You've probably seen our kids?"

Claire inhales from her electronic cigarette.

"The twins and their sister? They're yours?"

"Guilty," says Meg.

Claire lets out a chuckle.

"They're not so bad," she says. "And your daughter is very mature for her age. I helped keep an eye on them on the night of the storm."

"Oh," says Meg. "Thank you for that!"

"It's nothing," says Claire.

"We both felt bad that they were by themselves that night," says John. "There was just no way to get out here sooner."

"Understandable," says Claire. "I was happy to do it, make sure they were safe and sound."

"Thank you for that," says Meg. "I know we only really just met, officially, but you should come up for dinner sometime!"

"I-I'd like that," says Claire, smiling. "Very much."

"Well, you're welcome any time," says John. "We're just down the hall from you."

"I'll keep that in mind," says Claire. "Thank you."

They turn toward the stage where Eula continues to sing. She starts the final verse of her song, looking out into the crowd. She is already getting tired, but the energy she feels from the crowd will keep her going through the night.

By 9:30 P.M., she will reach the end of her set, her swan song complete.

Before her final song, she takes the microphone in her hand.

"Friends," she says, the noise of the crowd dwindling so she can speak easily. "I have to tell you, this has been the most incredible night for me."

The crowd gives Eula a standing ovation and she continues when their cheers quiet down.

"I know tonight has probably meant a great many things to each of you, but before we conclude our little show, I just wanted to thank you. All of you. It truly means the world to look out into the crowd and see all of you here to share this moment with me, this celebration.

"And before you leave, make sure to get yourself on the mailing list for The Plaza Speakeasy, because if I have anything to do with it, tonight is just the beginning for this beautiful place!

"Sadly, though, I'm afraid we've come to the part of the evening I like the least, and that is where our show concludes and I leave you. But worry not! The band will play on until around one o'clock, I'm told, and I will be down here for a little while longer to visit with any of you who wish to come and say hello!

"But for now, I think it's time we get to our last song, don't you?"

The crowd roars with applause.

Eula looks behind her as the music starts and catches Felix's eye. She can see his smile from behind the trumpet he's playing.

"Thank you," she mouths silently.

Turning around and blinking away tears, Eula faces the crowd and starts to sing her final song.

* * *

That night, Eula Belle passes away in her sleep, warm and comfortable in her bed.

After spending time visiting with the crowd, Felix escorted her upstairs to her apartment. He noticed how heavy her breathing was and how labored her steps were.

Somehow, he knew the end was near.

"They've got things taken care of downstairs," he'd said. "I'm staying the night."

"Okay," said Eula. "I'd like that."

Felix sat next to her bed as she fell asleep, his hand over hers. Once he was sure that she was sleeping, he went to the living room and made up a bed on the couch.

When he went to check on her in the morning, she was gone.

\* \* \*

Eula's funeral is not a typical funeral, though this comes as no surprise to those who knew her. She left detailed instructions on her final wishes, including what music to play at the funeral and the request that no one wear black.

"This is, after all, a celebration of my life," she had written in her will. "Anybody in black better expect to be thoroughly haunted!"

A week later, several tenants of the Plaza at Garden Park are summoned to the lobby of the building for the reading of Eula's will.

They cannot believe it when they learn that Eula's will creates a trust in the name of the tenants of the Plaza to purchase and restore the building. Their mouths hang open when they see just how much money Eula had amassed in royalties and interest on stocks. When the lawyer leaves, a few of the tenants remain in the lobby.

"If you'd have told me back in January this was how this year was going to play out, I never would have believed you," says Claire.

"I still can't believe she's gone," says Bea.

"That's our Eula, though," says Felix. "Still taking care of us."

"Very true," says Charlie. "Are you still going to be operating The Plaza Speakeasy?"

"You better believe it!" says Felix. "She got all that paperwork in order before she passed, I won't let her work go to waste. There's just a little adjustment I need to make first."

"What's that?" asks Bea.

"I'm changing the name," says Felix. "The Plaza Speakeasy's gonna be known as Eula's from here on out."

Bea's eyes glisten with tears.

"She would have liked that very much," says Claire.

"And if you need any business advice, I'm always available," says Charlie. "I've been running the watch shop for so long, I think it'd be a fun change of pace to help out with a place like that."

"That would be great, Chuck," says Felix.

"I have something I'd like to share with everyone," Claire says.

"What's that?" asks Charlie.

"Well, you all know I worked for Eula. She paid me to help her around her apartment, run errands and such."

The others nod.

"Well, a few weeks ago, she approached me with an idea for a project and I couldn't turn her down. She wanted me to interview her about her life and write a biography. I had an idea she was working on something for all of us, I just, I don't know, I never imagined it would be something like this. I'm only sorry she wasn't able to see it with us.

"She cared for all of us very, very much. She always said we were as much a part of her story as she was of ours. And all of us coming together to save the Plaza... nothing would have made her happier."

# THE HAUNTING OF
# CLAYTHORN MANOR

"Sorry, Chel," says Jade Verrit. "You're on your own for this one."

"Oh, come on, you don't really think it's haunted... Do you?" asks Chelle Mastens.

"I don't know," says Jade. "But I'm not trying to find out."

It is near the end of the day at Caramaya's Bar and Grille in early April and Jade is out back smoking a cigarette near the dumpster. A pop up thunderstorm earlier in the afternoon has given way to a muggy spring evening. Chelle just asked if Jade and her boyfriend, Bobby Glachome, would be interested in joining a group she is assembling to stay the night at Claythorn Manor, an old mansion in Garden Park with a ghostly reputation that now houses a bed and breakfast.

"Tyler and Mack already said they're in."

"Of course they are," says Jade, taking one last drag on her cigarette. She exhales into the heavy air. "Besides, Bobby's actually gonna be free that night. I'll have to live vicariously on this one."

"Oh, alright," says Chelle, sighing.

"Who all else is going?"

"Tyler's bringing Alan – "

"Alan? Really?"

"Yeah, even after you told him about El Scorcho."

"I wish he'd just finish that entry in the little pink book and move on."

"Seriously."

"Bright side?" asks Jade.

"Try me."

"At least he's not still stuck on Pete."

"I'll give you that," Chelle says, shaking her head. "Anyway, he said Phin and Carrie want to go. And then I texted a few other people, Brannon and Kate said thanks but no thanks; Genevieve's down if we have room."

"If you have room?"

"Yeah, they cap each room at two people."

"Oh."

"Yeah, so Gen might end up rooming with Mack that way they can split the cost."

"He'll be down with that, for sure."

"Right?"

"Sounds like a good group. You guys will have fun," says Jade. She flicks her cigarette into the sand bucket near the back door. "We'd better get back inside before anyone says anything about us being out here too long."

\* \* \*

Three weeks later, Tyler Welik pulls into Claythorn Manor's parking lot. He closes his sunroof and gets out of his car, grabbing his overnight bag. There are only a few other vehicles in the lot, among them his brother's SUV and Chelle's car.

*I'm glad I'm not the first one here,* he thinks, feeling a chill as he looks toward the old mansion. He walks around to the front of the house and up the steps to the porch. The plaque next to the door declares the house's status as a place of historical significance as well as hours of operation for tours and a number to call for more information.

*Here we go,* he thinks as he grabs the handle and pushes the door open. He steps over the threshold into Claythorn Manor and almost as soon as the door closes behind him, he starts to feel uneasy.

A dimly lit hallway stretches before him, with stairs leading to the upper levels of the mansion as well as rooms branching off on either side.

"Hello?" he calls. There is no answer.

He walks slowly down the hall, passing what appears to be a dining room on the left and a parlor to the right. A collection of portraits featuring the house's previous residents hang on the walls, seemingly staring at him with unblinking eyes as he passes. A little further down the hall, he starts to hear voices talking and laughing.

"Hello?" he calls again.

"Hello?" comes a reply.

Tyler is relieved to recognize Chelle's voice. A moment later, she peeks around the corner of one of the rooms.

"Hey you, come on in!" she says. "We're just hanging out in the bar until everyone else gets here."

Tyler smiles, relieved to finally be in the company of friends.

"Hey guys," he says, setting his bag down on a couch in the hallway before entering the bar. Tyler is immediately taken aback by the large stained glass windows that flank the old bar showing a man and a woman.

*So creepy,* he thinks.

His brother, Phin, is perched on a stool at the bar next to his girlfriend, Carrie. Chelle's boyfriend Graham gets up from the table in the corner and comes over.

"Hey, Tyler," he says. "This is my neighbor, Bea Olloman."

An older, heavyset woman with glasses perched atop her head comes out from behind the bar and extends her hand.

"Great to meet you, cutie," she says.

Tyler smiles, shaking her hand.

"Isn't this place great?" says Chelle.

"It's something," says Tyler.

"I think we're going to wait a little bit more for the rest of the group to get here and then Bea's going to show us to our rooms."

"Do you want a drink while we wait?" asks Bea, once again behind the bar.

"That would be great," says Tyler. "Bloody Mary?"

"You got it!"

Chelle raises her eyebrows at Tyler.

"Since when do you drink Bloody Marys?"

"Just getting into the spirit of things," says Tyler, grinning.

* * *

A little while later, Genevieve Delphe and Kevin Mackenzie have both arrived and everyone is sitting together in the bar waiting for the eighth and final guest to show up when Tyler gets a text.

"Don't tell me he's canceling," says Chelle.

"No," says Tyler, looking up from his phone. "But he *is* running late. He says to go ahead without him."

Tyler pretends not to notice Chelle rolling her eyes.

"Well, then, let's get you all to your rooms!" says Bea. "I'll collect your check in agreements before we head out." She moves about the room, picking up the agreements that everyone had to sign that went over the house rules, essentially agreeing that they would not trash the place overnight.

"I'll leave one behind for the eighth person to fill out," she says.

"Leave one behind?" asks Carrie from her stool at the bar.

"Oh yes, dear, didn't you know? The rest of the staff and I go home at night, you'll have the place all to yourselves. The whole house is yours to explore, with the exceptions of the kitchen and this room, the bar. There are motion sensor alarms in place that will let us know if you entered either room. And, of course, we leave plenty of contact information in case you need to get a hold of any of us for anything."

"Fucking sweet!" Phin mouths to his brother while putting his arm around Carrie to comfort her.

"Alright then, dears," says Bea, grabbing a clipboard from the counter. "If there's nothing else, you can all follow me into the hall and grab your bags then we'll head upstairs!"

The party takes their drinks out to the hall and collects their things, following the older woman up the stairs.

"These stairs lead solely to the second level of Claythorn Manor," says Bea, once they reach the top. "There's a staircase in the back that spans the entire house, from the basement to the attic. There are four bedrooms on this floor and three more upstairs. You all will be in the four of the rooms on this floor, but you may explore the house by using that back staircase. The rooms that are not yours will be locked, of course.

"You'll find a welcome basket in each room. Feel free to take any leftover treats with you. Oh, and there are vending machines upstairs in case you're looking for anything extra. Now, let's get you into your rooms!"

There are two rooms across from each other and two more down the hall toward the back of the house. Bea produces a ring of old, brass keys and makes her way to the room on the left.

"What's that room?" asks Tyler, looking toward a door to the right of the stairs.

"That? Oh, that's just a storage closet. We keep it locked, nothing too exciting in there." Bea leads the group around the balustrades and toward the front of the house where two large doors face each other on opposite sides of the hall. She opens the door to the left.

"This is the green room, and I do believe Phin and Carrie are going to be staying in here," she says, looking down at her clipboard.

"That's right," says Phin, walking to the front of the group while holding Carrie's hand. He looks around in awe at the room, furnished almost entirely in green, which contains a sitting area and a sleeping area divided by a set of sliding doors that can be used to separate the spaces.

"Isn't it lovely?" asks Bea. "It overlooks the gardens and also gives you a nice view of the gazebo and the carriage house in the back."

"This is incredible," says Phin, setting his bag down on the bed.

"And we've only just begun," says Bea, with a smile. "If you'll all follow me across the hall, we'll get Tyler and Alan settled into the purple room."

"Oh," says Tyler. "Alan's the one who's not here yet."

"That's right," says Bea, snapping her fingers. "Well, you'll all be able to give him the tour when he arrives!"

Across the hall, the group looks around in awe at the lavender suite. A dining room sized table sits in the middle of the seating area, surrounded by chairs, while a gilded statue of a little boy sits in the corner, surrounded by the leaves of a plant behind it.

"This room overlooks the parking lot, but has a great view of the city. The purple room also has a private bathroom," says Bea. She opens a door that most of the group had assumed to be a closet and leads the group into a large, circular bathroom with marble walls.

"Wow," says Genevieve.

"Now, if you'll follow me, this door leads back out to the hallway," says Bea, taking everyone out of a door in the bathroom most had initially overlooked, again assuming it was a closet. Upon exiting, they find themselves in the hallway that leads to the back of the house from the landing at the top of the front stairs.

"You'll come to find there are many different ways to get to the same place in Claythorn Manor. Now, there are two rooms back here," says Bea. "The red room and the blue room... Graham? I believe you and Chelle are in the red room, which is right through this door." She unlocks the door and leads them into the large, rectangular room complete with old, red wallpaper that is starting to peel along the seams.

"Aww, no sitting room?" jokes Graham, winking at Bea.

The group laughs as Graham and Chelle put their things down.

"Alright, we have one room to go," says Bea, walking back out to the hall. She makes her way toward the back of the house, stopping at another locked door.

"This is the blue room," she says. "Genevieve and Mack, you'll be staying in here." The blue room is set up similarly to the red room but instead of old wallpaper, the lower part of the walls are covered in a marbled blue tile, the dark part of which matches the deep blue the rest of the room is painted.

"I'm going to leave you all to get settled in," says Bea. "I'll be downstairs in the bar area for another half an hour or so if you'd care for any more drinks before I head out for the night. Oh, and one last thing – the front door will be locked once I leave. The only way in or out of the house will be the door out of the atrium to the back porch.

"As a reminder, there are no open flames allowed in Claythorn Manor, this includes candles and cigarettes. You are welcome to smoke anywhere outside, although we kindly ask that you dispose of the butts.

"If there're no questions, I'm heading downstairs. I'll be sure to let you know before I leave for the night."

Everyone thanks Bea as she leaves the blue room.

"So what do you guys think?" asks Chelle. "Is this cool, or what?"

"This is awesome!" says Phin, his arm around Carrie.

Tyler checks his phone.

"Any word from Alan?" asks Mack.

"Not yet," answers Tyler.

"Well I don't know about you guys, but I'm about ready for another drink," says Genevieve.

Everyone murmurs in agreement.

"Once Bea leaves, I've got some booze out in Chelle's car," says Graham. "So don't rack up too much of a bill at the bar."

"I brought some too," says Phin.

"Awesome," says Genevieve, smiling.

"Wanna go get some of our stuff out?" Carrie asks Phin.

"Sure," he says. "We'll see you all downstairs in a bit."

Everyone makes their way to their rooms, leaving Genevieve and Mack alone in the blue room.

"So what do you think," he asks. "Is this place haunted?"

"I don't know," says Genevieve. "But I guess we'll find out!"

* * *

Alan Brodecker knocks on Claythorn Manor's front door before pushing it open and stepping into the entrance hallway.

"Nice of you to join us," says Chelle, descending the front staircase with a camera in hand. Everyone else is upstairs in their rooms.

"I got stuck at work," says Alan. "I think Jacie and Imani might stop by later."

"Alright," says Chelle, reaching the ground floor. "Just don't say anything about it in front of Bea."

"Bea?"

"The woman who checked us all in... if she hears there's more people coming, she might try to charge us more."

"I won't say anything."

"Come on, she's gotta check you in and I think she's in the bar," says Chelle. She takes the batteries out of her camera as she walks down the hall.

The two enter the bar to find Bea talking with one of the other staff members, a short girl with dark hair. She signs the top sheet on a clipboard the girl is holding and the girl leaves.

"Oh, hello there," she says. "Can I help you two with anything?"

"This is Alan, the last one of our group."

"Hello, Alan," says Bea. "I left a waiver with Tyler upstairs that you'll need to fill out. If you could leave it behind for me tomorrow, that would be great."

"Sure thing."

"Hey Bea, question for you," says Chelle.

"What can I do for you?"

"Do you have any spare Double A batteries?"

"Oh, what for?"

"It's my camera," says Chelle. "I have rechargeable batteries and I swear I just charged them but they're dead already. So I tried to use the spares I keep in my bag, but they're dead, too."

Alan gives Chelle a confused look when Bea starts to laugh.

"Oh dear," she says. "It's not your batteries, I'm afraid."

"What do you mean?"

"It's the house, or rather, the *energies* in the house. The spirits like it if you ask permission before taking photographs here, as a sign of respect."

Chelle raises an eyebrow.

"You think I'm crazy," says Bea. She pulls a pair of batteries out from a drawer behind the bar and hands them to Chelle. "Give it a try when you get a chance, and preferably before these die out on you, too. I'd advise everyone here do the same with all of their electronics or else you'll spend the whole night recharging all of your devices."

*What the hell,* thinks Chelle. *I have nothing to lose really.*

She smiles at Bea and looks around the room.

"You have a lovely home," she begins. "My friends and I, we don't mean anyone here any harm. Claythorn Manor is beautiful and we'd like to share it in pictures and video with those who couldn't come with us tonight, if that's alright with you.

"Thanks," she says after a pause.

"Excellent," says Bea. "I don't think you'll have any more trouble keeping your electronics charged during your stay."

Alan looks at Chelle and shrugs his shoulders.

"It was nice to meet you," he says to Bea. "I'm gonna go upstairs and see what Tyler's doing."

"Of course," says Bea. "And I'd better be going. My friend Eula is having a few of our neighbors over for dinner tonight and I don't want to be late."

Alan leaves the bar and heads upstairs.

"Thank you for showing us around," says Chelle.

"It was a pleasure, dear," says Bea. "Oh! I almost forgot."

She pulls an old, leather-bound book from under the bar.

"Here's a little history of the house, in case you or your friends are interested. Just leave it on a table in the breakfast room and one of the staff will collect it tomorrow."

Chelle picks up the book.

"Wow," she says. "Thank you!"

"You're very welcome. Alright, I'm setting the alarms and locking up. I hope you all enjoy your stay!"

\* \* \*

"Where do we want to put the cooler?" asks Graham.

"Let's take it up to the purple room," answers Phin. "I think that's where everyone's been hanging out."

Having left Claythorn Manor via the back door, the two are in the parking lot bringing in a cooler of food and drinks that no one felt comfortable bringing in while the staff was still present.

"Tyler and Alan won't mind?"

"Nah, they'll be fine. Besides, their room is really more like two rooms plus they have that bathroom."

"Sounds good to me," says Graham, closing Chelle's trunk. He picks up a cooler as Phin swings a bag over his shoulder. They walk around to the path behind the mansion and up the stairs to the back porch.

When they get to the purple bedroom, Chelle is sitting next to Tyler on a couch looking through the book Bea left them. Alan sits on the bed next to Carrie and Genevieve, all three watching the TV in the armoire opposite the foot of the bed.

"Where's Mack?" asks Graham, setting down the cooler.

"He went to take some pictures," Genevieve calls from the bed.

"Yeah," says Alan. "He wanted us to radio him when you guys got back in."

"Radio him?" asks Phin.

Carrie gets up from the bed and walks toward the sitting room.

"He brought a set of walkie talkies," she says. "There's four of them and they're all on the same frequency. He said it'll be a more reliable way to communicate tonight than cell phones."

"Nice," says Phin, noticing the yellow radio that sits on the table. Carrie picks it up and presses a call button.

"Hey Mack?" she says. The radio blips as she takes her finger off of the call button and she is relieved when he replies almost immediately.

"Yeah?" he replies. The radio blips again as he releases his call button.

"Hey, the guys are back up here with the cooler and stuff." She pauses before adding, "Over."

"Awesome," he says. "I'm on my way back."

She sets the radio down and it blips again.

"Over," Mack says, laughing.

"What's with the 'over' thing?" asks Phin.

Carrie laughs and takes a bottle of wine out of the cooler Graham brought up.

"I don't know," she says. "Isn't that what you're supposed to say when you radio people like this?" She pops it open and pours herself a glass.

Phin rolls his eyes.

"Hey, pour me one," Alan yells from the bed.

Carrie pulls two cups out of Phin's backpack.

Graham sits on the edge of the couch next to Chelle and Tyler.

"What are you reading?" he asks. He pops the top on a can of beer and takes a long drink.

"Just an old scrap book," answers Chelle. "Bea left it behind for us to look through."

"It's really creepy," says Tyler. "There's a bunch of pictures and newspaper clippings about this place."

"Is it real?" asks Graham.

"Why wouldn't it be?" replies Chelle.

"I don't know," says Graham. "Maybe they made it to scare the groups that come to stay here?"

"Maybe," says Chelle. "It's a pretty elaborate prop if it is."

Everyone hears footsteps outside of the room and a few seconds later, Mack walks in.

"We ready to eat?" he asks.

"Almost," says Carrie, taking three sub sandwiches out of the cooler and cutting them into pieces. Chelle closes the book and goes to the table with Tyler and Graham, leaving the book on the couch. Genevieve comes over and opens a bag of chips that is on the table.

"This was a great idea," she says. "Bringing our own dinner, I mean."

"And there's snacks for later," says Chelle.

"When do you guys want to start going out into the house?" asks Alan as he picks up a piece of the sub sandwich.

"We were thinking once it got dark outside," says Graham.

"We're gonna leave the house lit as dimly as we can," says Tyler, grinning. "That'll make it extra creepy."

"Except this room, right?" Carrie asks quickly.

"Right," says Tyler. He grabs a handful of chips and tosses them onto a paper plate. "Think of the purple room as a safe house. We'll leave all the lights on in here and I brought some DVDs we can watch later if we want."

"Okay, good," says Carrie, relieved.

One by one, each of the friends makes themselves a plate of food and grabs a drink out of the cooler. They sit around talking and laughing as the sun starts to set outside. On the surface, eight friends are having a simple dinner in an old mansion, but beneath their lines of conversation, lurks a different feeling entirely.

Each one of them is trying to ignore a growing sense of uneasiness.

\* \* \*

"Okay wait, tell me the thing about the batteries again?" Tyler asks.

An hour has passed and everyone is finished with their dinner. A few of them pass the time by playing cards at the table while others are watching a movie.

"She told me to ask permission from the spirits in the house and I felt so stupid but I did it and haven't had any problems with my camera since."

"That's gotta be bullshit," says Alan. "I mean, I heard you do it but that can't be the reason."

"It's not bullshit," says Mack. "I was having trouble with my camera, too, and when Chelle told me that, I figured I'd give it a try... haven't had any problems since."

"This place is so creepy," says Tyler.

Alan shrugs his shoulders.

"So what do you say, you guys wanna go look around?" asks Tyler.

Genevieve sits at the table with Graham and Carrie. She looks up from her hand of cards.

"I'm game," she says.

"That's just because you're about to lose," says Graham.

Genevieve casually tosses her cards on the table.

"Two pair," she says. "Now can we go?"

"Well played," says Graham. He lays down his cards to reveal a failed attempt at securing a straight. "Who all's going?"

"Would you be okay with staying in here awhile longer?" Carrie asks Phin.

"Yeah, no problem," he replies. "We can hold down the fort in here while you guys head out."

Mack retrieves the case with his walkie talkies and gives one each to Tyler and Chelle, keeping one for himself.

"I wanna leave one in here to charge," he says. "Hey Phin, listen for it in case we call for anything, okay?"

"Sounds good," says Phin. The group slowly files out of the room and into the hall, leaving Carrie and Phin alone on the bed in the purple room watching a movie.

"You okay?" he asks.

"Yeah," she says. "I'm alright. This place is just... I don't know. I didn't expect it to be this creepy."

"It definitely has character."

"I think that's what's freaking me out the most," says Carrie, her voice trailing off as the movie starts.

* * *

"Where do you guys want to go?" asks Genevieve.

"We were thinking the attic," says Graham.

"What about you?" Genevieve asks, turning to Mack who in turn looks down the hall toward the back staircase.

"I don't know you guys," he says. "I'm not really feeling the attic. Gen, you wanna come downstairs with me?"

"Sure," she says. "Anyone else?"

"I really wanna check out the attic," says Alan. Tyler and Chelle murmur in agreement.

"Okay, so that works," says Chelle. "You two go down to the main level and we'll head up. Here, you can have my walkie." She hands her radio to Genevieve. "Just in case."

"Thanks," says Genevieve. She and Mack walk to the main staircase and go down to the ground floor of Claythorn Manor.

Chelle looks around at the three boys she's left with.

"You guys ready?"

"Let's go," says Tyler. They walk toward the back staircase, floorboards creaking beneath their feet.

"I have kind of a stupid question," says Graham once they reach the second floor landing. He looks over the railing and feels a chill come over his body. The stairs flank the walls between each story of the house, leaving an empty space from the attic to the basement.

*I wonder if anyone's ever gone over these rails?* he thinks.

"What's up, babe?" asks Chelle.

"Is anyone else getting a little scared?"

The shadows on the wall dance as the chandelier that hangs from the top of the staircase flickers.

"Kind of," admits Tyler. "But that's part of the fun, right?"

"Right," says Graham. He takes the lead and heads for the attic, pausing momentarily to look out a window toward the parking lot.

"Our means of escape still there?" asks Alan, his dry delivery causing Graham to wonder if he is serious or not.

"Uh, yeah," he says. "All the cars are accounted for."

The group continues to the attic, shining their flashlights around as they gather on the landing. They stand looking around the sitting area at the top of the stairs. Chelle shivers when her beam of light lands on the painted face of a harlequin clown doll.

"Really?" she asks. "Does that thing have to be here?"

Alan walks over and picks up the doll, flipping it over in his hand.

"Just a little doll," he says, setting it back on the table it had been propped up on.

"You say that now, but what about when he comes alive and tries to kill you?" asks Tyler, obviously joking.

*We couldn't be so lucky,* thinks Chelle, rolling her eyes at Alan in the dark.

"What rooms are up here?" asks Tyler. He looks to his left out the locked glass doors that lead to the rooftop terrace and can see the city in the distance.

"This hallway leads to three more bedrooms, all of which are locked since we're staying in the four on the second floor," Graham answers.

"Bedrooms in the attic?" asks Alan.

"Probably used to be servants quarters," says Graham.

"Creepy," says Alan.

The group walks into the dark hallways to the right, passing a heavy looking door on the left.

"That would be the pink bedroom," says Chelle. "I saw it on a floor plan of the house that was in the book Bea left for us."

"What about that?" asks Tyler, tilting his head toward another door.

"That's probably another closet or something," says Chelle. "The other two rooms are down here."

At the end of the hallway there is another sitting area with a skylight over the center of the space. An old vending machine sits in the corner, humming quietly next to a bookshelf. Two doors stand on the opposite side of a worn couch covered in floral print.

"This isn't set up to be creepy at all," Alan says sarcastically.

Tyler playfully elbows him.

"Let's go find those other two," says Alan. "Looks like the attic was a bust."

He starts to walk back toward the landing when Graham stops him.

"Hang on a second, man."

Graham tries the handle of the door on the right only to find that it will not budge.

"Bea said they'd all be locked," says Chelle.

"Well, you never know," he says, walking to the door on the left. He tries the handle and to the horror of the four friends, it turns and the door easily swings inward.

Graham gasps as Chelle screams and jumps back from the door.

"Holy fuck!" yells Tyler, a rush of adrenaline pumping through his body.

"Really?" asks Alan. "You guys are so wound up tonight. How do we know they didn't forget to lock this room or maybe Bea left it open on purpose to scare you all?"

"I don't know," says Graham. "But I'm not going to miss out on looking around! You guys coming in with me?"

Chelle looks at Tyler and can tell he is uneasy.

"I don't know," he says. "I mean, I don't want to get in trouble for going in a room we didn't pay to be in, you know?"

"We won't mess with anything," Graham says. "We just want to look around. Alan? What about you?"

"Well, I'm up here so we might as well try," Alan says. "Come on, Ty."

*I hate when he calls him 'Ty',* thinks Chelle.

The group slowly enters the bedroom, looking around with their flashlights.

"Does something feel a little off about this room?" asks Tyler.

"Yeah," says Alan. "It doesn't really feel like it belongs in the house."

"You know what? I do remember reading something about the construction in the attic in that book," says Chelle. "A lot of the attic was unfinished but they added these two rooms a few years ago in a big renovation project."

"Hey check this out," says Graham. "This room has its own bathroom, too!"

He walks in and shines his flashlight around, looking from the sink up to the mirror and over the shower, down to the floor past the clothes hamper.

When his beam of light lands on a face on the floor, he screams.

"What is it?!" yells Chelle, running to the door.

"Nothing," says Graham, laughing uneasily. "I just freaked myself out. See? Down there, there's some toy cars and the one has a face on it like a jack 'o lantern."

"This attic's really freaking you out, huh?" asks Alan.

"Nah," Graham says. "I'm just, uh, well really, I'm probably my own worst enemy here." He leaves the bathroom and sits on the loveseat in the room; Chelle sits down next to him. Alan sits on the bed as Tyler looks at the paintings in the room.

"What was in there?" he asks, not taking his eyes off of a painting of a ship.

"Just some toy cars," says Chelle.

"Oh."

"Toy cars?" asks Alan.

"Yeah, why?" says Graham.

"It's nothing really," his voice trails off. "I'm remembering an urban legend I heard about this place when I was a kid."

"Oh?" asks Chelle, leaning forward.

"Yeah," says Alan. "I don't really remember the specifics, but it had to do with one of the men of the house fathering a child with one of the servants. Obviously, that shit didn't fly back in the day, so the child had to live out all of its days up here. I want to say the kid was a boy and that he didn't survive to adulthood."

"Did someone kill him?" Tyler asks, turning from the paintings and facing the others.

"I don't think so," says Alan. "I don't really remember that part of it, though it's also likely the kid was just sickly and died from being locked away."

"How are you suddenly an expert on this place?" asks Chelle.

"It's just the stories I've heard here and there from growing up in the city," says Alan. "They said you could see his face from time to time from the street in the windows of the attic. And gauging from where we are in the house…"

"These would be the windows he would have been looking out," says Tyler.

All four sit in silence as each feels a chill shoot through them.

"You're making this up, aren't you," says Graham.

"I swear I'm not," says Alan. "And I'm not saying I'm buying into this place being haunted but when you said there are cars in that bathroom, it just reminded me of the story and it's weird that there's toys in one of the rooms that would fit right in with the urban legend."

Tyler starts to say something but he is cut off by a blip from his walkie talkie. He grabs it and pushes the talk button.

"Hello?" he calls. "Who's there?"

There is no answer and the four sit in an uncomfortable silence.

"We should go downstairs," says Chelle. "I want to make sure everyone's oka-"

Chelle is interrupted by a scream that comes from the floors below them and pierces the silence of Claythorn Manor.

* * *

Chelle and Graham race down the back staircase.

"Where are you guys?!" yells Chelle as soon as they hit the main floor.

"We're in the hall," calls Phin.

Chelle and Graham run to the main hall to find Carrie sitting on a couch next to Genevieve with Phin and Mack standing close by.

"What happened?" asks Graham.

"Something touched me," answers Genevieve.

"What?" asks Chelle.

"I'm not kidding." She looks at the faces of the others in the dim light. "Mack and I were sitting in the parlor seeing if we could make contact with any spirits."

"That room over there," says Mack.

"I'm okay now, but I swear to you something touched me. I was sitting in one of the arm chairs with my palms up and it felt like someone came up and slapped my hand."

"Did you see anything?" Phin asks Mack.

"Nothing," he answers. "I was sitting there with her one minute and then we both got kind of quiet, just listening to see if we heard anything, I guess, and the next thing I know she jumps up screaming her head off."

Genevieve takes off her glasses and rubs her face with her hands.

"Goddamnit, I need a drink," she says. "You guys wanna go back upstairs?"

"Are you okay to walk?" asks Carrie.

"Yeah, I'm fine," Genevieve answers. "I'll *be* fine."

The group walks toward the main staircase and heads back to the purple room. Mack walks next to Chelle and Graham.

"Did you guys find anything cool in the attic?" he asks.

"Actually, get this," starts Chelle. "One of the bedrooms up there is unlocked."

"What?"

"Yeah, and it's not supposed to be."

"You guys went in, I'm assuming?"

"Of course," she says.

"And?"

"And it's a newer room so it feels a little out of place, but Graham found a bunch of toy cars in the bathroom."

"Like, just little cars?"

"Sitting on the floor," says Graham.

"That's creepy."

"No," says Chelle. "What's really creepy is the story it reminded Alan of about a little boy who supposedly died here."

"Alan told you this?" asks Mack.

"Yeah," says Chelle. "Alan, you tell it better… Alan?"

She looks around, quickly realizing that neither Tyler nor Alan accompanied her and Graham down the stairs.

"Oh my God," she says.

"Babe, what's wrong?" asks Graham.

"Where's Tyler?" she asks. "And Alan?"

"I guess they didn't come downstairs with us," says Graham,

shrugging his shoulders.

"No, no, that's not like Tyler," says Chelle. She starts to walk again, this time with a brisk pace. "I know him, he'd want to stay in a group in a place like this."

"I'm sure they're fine," says Graham.

Chelle catches up with the rest of the group.

"Hey, Gen, let me see your walkie a minute," she says.

"Sure," says Genevieve, handing it over.

Chelle pushes the call button and waits for an answer as Phin doubles back.

"What's going on?" asks Phin.

"Take a look around, Phin," says Chelle. "Notice anyone missing?"

"My brother."

Chelle nods.

"Tyler? Hello? Alan? Where are you guys?" she says into the walkie talkie.

\* \* \*

In an upstairs room, a walkie talkie sits on a bed, with the staticky voice of Chelle Mastens calling over and over.

"Is anyone there?" she says.

Alan and Tyler sit facing each other on the floor in the bathroom, lit only by the beam of a flashlight, the toy cars Graham stumbled upon placed between them.

"You should probably answer her before she calls the police," says Alan.

"She's just worried," says Tyler. He stands up and goes to grab the radio.

"She *needs* to butt the hell out," Alan mutters to himself.

Tyler pushes the talk button.

"Hey Chelle, it's Tyler."

"Oh my God! Fucking finally! Are you alright?"

"Yeah, we're fine."

"Why didn't you answer me? What are you guys doing?"

"We're, well… I can't believe I'm saying this, but we're seeing if we can talk to the ghost of the little boy up here or if there even is one at all. Alan thought we might have better luck with fewer people up here."

"Oh," she says.

"Is everyone okay down there?"

"Yeah, Genevieve had a little incident is all."

"Oh God, is she okay?"

"She's fine now, she's having a drink and then I think we're going to head back out. Do you want us to come up to you guys?"

"No," calls Alan from the bathroom. "Too many people up here will kill the energy."

"I think we're okay," Tyler says into the walkie talkie. "I'll call you guys when we're heading back down."

"Okay, let us know if you need anything."

"Will do," says Tyler. "Over."

"Over."

"Turn that fucking thing off," says Alan.

"Alright," says Tyler. He powers off the walkie talkie and rejoins Alan on the bathroom floor.

"Where were we?" asks Alan.

"We were just making small talk, I guess," says Tyler.

"Oh yeah, just trying to put the energy at ease."

"I didn't know you knew anything about any of this stuff? I thought you were like, the ultimate skeptic."

"Just because I'm skeptical doesn't mean I'm ignorant of the other side."

"Hmm?"

"I wouldn't have agreed to come here tonight if I didn't think there was a chance to see something supernatural."

"Is that what you think is going on here?"

"Maybe," says Alan. "Here, take my hands."

The two join hands around the toy cars once again.

"Follow my lead," Alan whispers. "And close your eyes."

Tyler nods.

"Hello," he says. "My name's Alan. And this is Tyler."

"Hi," says Tyler.

"Is there anyone in here with us?"

Tyler listens intently.

"We're just here to talk. We're not here to do you any harm, do you understand that?"

Tyler shakes his head. The tile floor feels cold on his legs.

"Nothing," he whispers.

Alan furrows his eyebrows.

"We know who you are, and we know what they did to you. It's not right, being kept in a place like this, not being able to go outside with the other kids, being shut away from the world. Are these your cars?" He pauses. "Do you want to talk to us?"

The hair on the back of Tyler's neck stands up; his breathing quickens.

"My name is Alan and this is Tyler. We just want to talk to you. We just want to help you."

Tyler starts to feel cold and, inexplicably, alone.

"Alan, I'm not liking this," whispers Tyler, keeping his eyes shut.

"Shh," says Alan. "If you're here, let us know. Move one of your cars or knock two times. Move one of your cars or knock two times to let us know that you're here and you want to talk."

Tyler's arms and legs are covered in goosebumps as he listens to Alan attempt to make contact with the spirit. His palms sweat profusely and all he can think about are his friends in the rooms below while he sits in this dark room. His eyes still shut, he visualizes himself alone in this dark room, the darkness growing around him by the second until he feels the emptiness around him is an expanse as wide as the ocean.

"...knock two times if you want to talk," says Alan, Tyler refocusing on his words.

Tears begin to seep past Tyler's eyelashes as the cold feelings of loneliness continue to escalate until he cannot bear it any more. His hands shaking, he snaps his eyes open and breaks away from Alan's grasp, jumping to his feet.

"Tyler?"

"I'm getting the fuck out of here," he says. "And you should come with me."

* * *

"Over," says Chelle before setting down her walkie talkie.

"So they're still upstairs?" asks Phin.

"I guess, yeah," says Chelle. "We'll check in on them later. What are you guys gonna do now?"

Phin looks over to where Genevieve is pouring a round of drinks.

"Hey, could you pour me one, too?" he asks.

"Sure."

"You sure you wanna drink in a place like this?" asks Carrie.

"Why not?" asks Phin. "I'm not scared at all."

"Lucky you," she says.

"Carrie, you want one?" asks Genevieve. "Might calm your nerves a bit."

"Maybe later," says Carrie.

"Alright," says Genevieve. She picks up her glass and swishes it around before taking a drink.

"I have an idea," says Mack.

"What's up?" asks Graham.

"I want to go back to the parlor."

The other five members of the group stare at him in disbelief.

"You wanna go *where?*" asks Carrie.

"The parlor," says Mack. "Genevieve just experienced something down there and, yeah, we were freaked out at first but now that we know something might actually happen, I want to go back down."

Carrie shakes her head.

"I'll go," says Genevieve.

"I'd be interested to see what happens," says Graham, looking at Chelle.

"I don't know," says Chelle. "I think I might sit this one out."

"Carrie?" asks Phin.

"No way," she says.

"Okay, well, what if you and Chelle stayed up here and I went down with the group, would that be alright? I'd just be a floor below you."

"Just make sure you keep a walkie close by," says Carrie.

"Of course," says Phin. "What about my brother and Alan?"

"They're doing their thing upstairs," says Chelle. "They can meet up with us whenever they're done doing whatever it is they're doing."

"Okay," says Phin.

"You guys ready?" asks Mack. He tosses his backpack over his shoulder and picks up a walkie talkie before going to stand by the door.

"Let's go," says Genevieve.

"Please don't do anything stupid," says Carrie.

Phin winks and gives her a kiss on the cheek before following the others out into the hall. He follows Mack, Genevieve and Graham back down the main staircase to the parlor on the first floor. The dim lights in the hallway continue to flicker causing the shadows to shift around the portraits hanging on the walls. They can hear music coming from somewhere in the house.

"Was that playing before?" asks Phin.

"Yeah," says Genevieve. "I think there's a timer on the stereo in the bar."

Phin nods his head as the group enters the parlor.

"So what do we do now that we're in here?" asks Graham.

"I don't know," says Genevieve. "We were just kind of looking around earlier, moving slowly and staying aware of things that were going on."

Mack shines his flashlight around the ceiling and down to the paintings on the wall as Phin walks over to examine a hutch.

"What's in here?" he asks.

"We looked at that earlier," says Mack. "It was just old plates and stuff."

"Oh," says Phin. He gets on his knees and looks at a cabinet near the bottom, the beam of his flashlight highlighting the old brass fixture.

"Did you find something?" asks Genevieve, walking over.

"Maybe," says Phin. "I don't know." The latch on the cabinet feels old and heavy; it refuses to budge. Phin jiggles it until a small noise brings a hushed silence over the room.

*Click.*

"Did you get it open?" asks Mack.

"I think so," says Phin, carefully pulling the old door open on hinges that creak in the process. All of the attention in the room is focused on him.

"Is anything in there?" asks Graham.

No one can see the color fall from Phin's face in the darkness of the parlor.

"Y-yeah," he says slowly. "You guys aren't going to believe this."

He stands and turns around, a large object in his hands.

"What is that?" asks Genevieve.

Graham's mouth hangs open.

"No fucking way," he says.

Phin looks around at the faces of his friends.

"You guys," he says. "It's a spirit board."

\* \* \*

"Hey," Alan calls after Tyler. "Are you okay?"

"Yeah," Tyler replies. "I'm fine."

When Tyler jumps up from the bathroom floor, Alan follows him, putting a piece of chalk in his pocket before he grabs the powered off walkie from the bed. He closes the door to the suite that was supposed to have been locked in the first place.

"What happened back there?" asks Alan, catching up with Tyler on the top landing to the back stairs. The harlequin clown on the table stares at them through the darkness, its marble eyes reflecting a light from the terrace.

Tyler stands at the top of the stairs and slowly turns around.

"What are you talking about?"

"You can't tell me you didn't feel something in that bathroom."

Tyler shrugs his shoulders.

"Are you sure you're okay?"

"Fine," says Tyler. "Let's go downstairs."

"Lead the way," says Alan.

Tyler starts to walk down the stairs, slowly at first as though his feet are on pins and needles.

*He's not acting right,* thinks Alan.

The two descend the stairs from the attic and Tyler continues walking past the second floor landing.

"Hey, you passed our floor," says Alan.

"Down here," mumbles Tyler. "The others came down here."

He pauses when he reaches the landing for the first floor of the house. Shooting a grin toward Alan, he walks toward the front of the house and the parlor where four of his friends are attempting to hold a séance.

\* \* \*

"If there's anyone here that would like to communicate, now's the time," says Genevieve. She sits next to Phin and across from Graham who is next to Mack. Each touches the pointer in the middle of the spirit board which is set up on a table in the parlor. Mack had pulled two candles from his bag and lit them, adding an eerie glow to the thick atmosphere in the room.

"You know my momma always said don't mess with shit like this?" says Mack.

"Says the guy who carries candles around in his bag," says Phin.

"Oh, shut up. We're only here for one night, you know?"

Phin rolls his eyes.

"I still can't believe we found this thing."

"Shh," says Genevieve. "Do you want it to work or not?"

"Sorry," whispers Phin. The wax drips down one of the candles, hardening as it cools.

"We have to concentrate," says Genevieve. "Think about the house and the spirits who are here with us tonight."

They sit in silence for a moment, the faint music from the bar being the only sound they hear.

"We're not here to hurt you," says Mack. The pendulum in the grandfather clock in the hallways swings back and forth, the clock ticking in rhythm.

"Are you here to hurt us?" asks Phin.

"Don't ask it shit like that!" snaps Graham. "What's wrong with you?"

"Sorry, sorry, it was the first thing I thought of." The shadows on the wall sway as the flames on the candles flicker in the uncomfortable silence.

All four of them gasp as the pointer moves slightly.

"Oh, fuck off," says Graham.

"Someone's pushing it," says Phin.

"It's not me," Genevieve says breathlessly.

"Me neither," whispers Mack.

The pointer moves slowly in a circle, not pointing at anything in particular.

"A-are you the spirit who touched my hand earlier?" asks Genevieve.

The pointer stops moving.

"Did you touch my hand earlier?" asks Genevieve, this time with a commanding presence. From somewhere above the parlor, they hear the creaking of a floorboard.

The pointer starts to slide over the board, finally stopping as it points toward a word printed in the corner.

"Yes," says Genevieve. An uneasy feeling rises from the pit of her stomach, bringing a sour taste to the back of her throat. "Holy shit."

"Ask something else," says Phin, his fingers trembling on the pointer.

"You ask it something," says Genevieve.

Phin shakes his head.

"Can you tell us your name?" asks Mack. All four sit with fingers on the pointer, their breaths catching in their chests as they await any sign of movement.

Nothing happens.

"Who are you?" asks Mack. "Do you want to talk to us? If you're still here, give us a sign. Give us a sign if you're still in the room."

"I-I don't think it – " Genevieve is interrupted by a distinct sound that catches them all by surprise.

*Knock, knock.*

They all scream and jump up from the board, knocking the pointer aside in the process.

"What the fuck was that?!" screams Phin.

"Was that you?" Mack asks aloud. "If you're still with us, show yourself."

"We just want to talk to you," says Graham. He shines his flashlight around the room, looking from the paintings on the wall to the crown moldings on the ceiling, turning around to look behind him before the beam finally rests on the relaxed face of Tyler Welik.

\* \* \*

"You've got to be shitting me," says Alan, raising a cigarette to his lips. "A fucking spirit board?"

"Yeah," says Genevieve. She is on the back porch smoking with Alan, while Tyler stands facing the carriage house behind the mansion. "I should have known it was a bad idea, now everyone is all riled up. Kind of reminds me of that night on the Southside Pier when we were kids, huh Ty?"

Alan looks at her, confused.

"It's a long story," she says.

Alan's phone goes off and he pulls it out to read a text.

"Oh, looks like my friends aren't gonna make it," he says, exhaling a cloud of smoke. "That's probably for the best. Everyone's already buying too much into this haunted house crap."

"It's not crap," whispers Tyler.

"Hmm?" asks Alan.

"Nothing," says Tyler, his voice barely audible.

Alan and Genevieve take another drag off of their cigarettes.

"Is he okay?" she whispers to Alan.

"I don't know," says Alan defensively. "We were up in the attic and ever since we came down he's been acting weird."

"So wait," says Genevieve, putting her cigarette into a bucket of sand. "Are you telling me *you're* buying into 'this haunted house crap' now?"

Alan sighs.

"I don't know. I don't think so, but I ... I don't know."

"Let's go inside," says Genevieve. "Come on, Tyler."

Tyler continues to stare toward the carriage house, lost in thought.

"Tyler? Come on," she says.

He doesn't move.

"Tyler, let's go in the house," says Alan.

Tyler jolts to attention and slowly looks toward Alan.

"Sorry," he says.

When the three of them are inside, Genevieve pulls Alan aside.

"Look," she says. "I don't know what you're trying to pull…"

"What are you talking about?" asks Alan.

"Tyler acting all weird, what's going on? What happened in the attic?"

"Nothing, we... we tried to contact a ghost and he got scared so we came downstairs. That's it."

Genevieve raises an eyebrow.

"Seriously! I don't know why he's acting like that."

"Well we better make sure someone stays with him until he snaps out of whatever's going on. Things are really getting weird."

"Alright," says Alan. He walks around the corner and jumps when he sees Graham standing in the hall.

"What are you two doing here?" Graham asks.

"Me and Alan were outside smoking," says Genevieve. "Have you seen Tyler?"

"Yeah, he walked by a minute ago," says Graham. "I think he was heading toward the back staircase. Oh! And he said something about the attic. I asked if he wanted me to go with him but I guess he didn't hear me. He dropped his flashlight, too, I heard it fall and saw the light rolling around."

Genevieve looks at Alan.

"I don't like this," she says.

\* \* \*

"Hey Phin, can you come here for a minute?" Genevieve asks from the doorway to the purple room. Phin is on the bed with Carrie and Chelle.

"Sure. I'll be right back," he says to Carrie.

Once Phin is in the hallway, Genevieve and Alan tell him what is going on with Tyler.

"And he just wandered off?" asks Phin.

"Yeah," says Alan. "Graham was the last one to see him."

"That's really not like him," says Phin. "Especially if he went to the attic alone. We were talking about this the other night and he mentioned how much he didn't want to be by himself in here at all."

"So you'll come with us?"

"Of course," says Phin. "Don't tell the others what's going on."

"Are you kidding? They'd probably ask if we're high or something," says Alan.

"I was more worried about not freaking anyone out," says Phin. He goes back into the purple room to grab a walkie talkie and a flashlight.

"Where are you going?" asks Carrie.

"Oh, Alan and Genevieve want me to go look at something with them," Phin says. "Nothing major, just something they saw in the attic."

"Where's everyone else?" asks Chelle.

"I think Graham was taking Mack to have a look at the carriage house."

"What about your brother?"

"He's with them," Phin lies.

"Okay, have fun," says Chelle. "Give us a call if you need anything."

"We'll be right back," says Phin.

After he leaves Chelle looks over to Carrie. They are alone in the purple room watching a movie; the lights in the room are turned as bright as they can go, providing a false sense of security.

"Did you buy that?" she asks.

"Not really," says Carrie. "It must not be serious or they would have told us. And if something supernatural is going on, I'm sure we'll hear about it before too long."

\* \* \*

Alan leads Genevieve and Phin up the back staircase to the attic. He doesn't have very much to say.

"Where do you think he's going to be?" asks Phin.

"I'm not sure," says Genevieve. "But Graham said he heard him talking to himself about going to the attic, so I figure we start looking there."

"And what is it you want me to do?"

"Talk to him, see if you can get through to him. You've just gotta snap him out of whatever daze he's in."

"Alright."

"Come on," says Alan. "I bet I know where he is." He leads the other two down the hallway to the side-by-side rooms and opens the door to the one of the left.

"Tyler?" he calls softly and waits for a response that does not come.

"So this is the room you guys were talking about," says Genevieve.

"How did you guys get in here, again?" asks Phin.

"I don't know," says Alan. "We were up here earlier. Graham tried the doors and this one was unlocked." He goes to look in the bathroom he and Tyler had sat in only a short time ago, but no one is there.

"And the cars haven't moved."

"What?" asks Phin.

"There's toy cars in the bathroom that urban legends say the ghost of a little boy who haunts this part of the house likes to play with."

Phin's mouth hangs open slightly.

"Come again?"

"Just go with it," Alan says sharply.

"Alright," says Genevieve. "He's not in here… any other ideas?"

"There's a closet out in the hall we could try," says Alan.

"But he came out of the closet years ago," says Phin. "Why would he go back in now?"

"Hilarious," Alan says, shooting Phin a dirty look.

They leave the room and head toward the closet in the hall. Alan reaches his hand toward the handle and stops suddenly.

"What's wrong?" asks Genevieve.

"I, uh… I don't know," says Alan. "I just realized I have no idea what's on the other side of this door."

"You decide to think of that now?" asks Phin. "It's just a closet and we've got to find my brother!"

"Alright," says Alan. His hand shaking, he takes hold of the old handle and slowly turns. The door clicks and he pulls it open, nerves racing. Phin shines a flashlight into the space to find that it isn't a closet at all.

"What the hell is this?" he asks.

"It looks like a crawl space," says Genevieve.

"But you can stand in it," says Phin. His flashlight reveals cobwebs hanging from the slatted walls, dust particles shimmering in the ray of light. Various relics of Claythorn Manor's past are stored in the room, all of them covered with dusty sheets.

"I bet the whole attic used to look like this," says Alan.

"Tyler's not in here," says Phin. "Let's keep looking."

"There's nowhere else up here that he could be," says Alan.

"Then we go back to where we last saw him," says Genevieve. "The main floor."

Alan shuts the door to the crawl space, not noticing the rocking chair in the distance that has slowly started to rock back and forth. The three quickly descend the back staircase to the landing on the main floor.

"Tyler?" calls Genevieve.

Again, there is no answer.

"What's that?" asks Phin.

"What?" asks Alan.

"The shadow on the ceiling there," he says, pointing to a shape next to a dim chandelier. "This was the last place you guys saw him?"

"Yeah," says Alan. "We came in from the porch and he walked off while Genevieve and I were talking."

Phin rounds a corner and sees the light source for the shadow. Tyler's discarded flashlight sits propped up, casting a ghostly glow over most of the main hallway onto the ceiling. And there, next to the flashlight, sits Tyler, intently drawing on a notepad.

\* \* \*

"I'm getting the fuck out of here," Tyler says. "And you should come with me."

As he stands outside of the unlocked bedroom waiting for Alan to close it up, he starts to feel lightheaded.

*What's going on?* he thinks. *It's probably the drinks from earlier.*

"What happened back there?" asks Alan.

"What are you talking about?" Tyler asks.

*Damnit my mouth feels heavy.*

"You can't tell me you didn't feel something in that bathroom."

Tyler shrugs his shoulders.

*The parlor,* he thinks. *I need to get down to the parlor.*

"Are you sure you're okay?"

*No.*

"Fine. Let's go downstairs."

"Lead the way."

The next thing he knows, Tyler is standing in the parlor, staring into the faces of his friends.

*They found a spirit board,* he thinks. *That's not good.*

Ten minutes later, he is standing outside facing the carriage house.

"A fucking spirit board?" Alan says to Genevieve as he takes a drag from his cigarette.

"Yeah, I should have known it was a bad idea, now everyone is all riled up."

*I'm starting to think coming here tonight was a bad idea,* Tyler thinks, temporarily tuning out the conversation between the others.

"I think everyone's buying too much into this haunted house crap," says Alan.

"Not crap," Tyler says slowly.

*Why did I say that?* thinks Tyler. *God, my head's fuzzy... I need to go inside and lay down or something.*

"Tyler, let's go in the house," says Alan.

*Oh crap, he's talking to me,* thinks Tyler.

"Sorry," he says. He goes back into the house, moving slowly.

*It's like I'm sleepwalking or something, but I'm awake... what's going on?!*

"Hey Tyler," says Graham.

Tyler looks him up and down.

"The attic," he whispers. "I have to get to the attic, upstairs to the attic."

Graham looks at him, confused.

Tyler walks away toward the back staircase, dropping his flashlight as he walks. He takes the stairs two at a time and soon finds himself back in the attic, his eyes fully adjusted to the darkness; he stands in the hall for several minutes deciding what to do.

He suddenly walks over toward what he had previously believed to be a closet door and flings it open to find a crawl space full of old items. Hearing footsteps coming up the stairs, he pulls the door closed to avoid the others.

"And what is it you want me to do?"

*Phin,* thinks Tyler. *My brother.*

"Talk to him, see if you can get through to him. You've just gotta snap him out of whatever daze he's in."

*And that's Genevieve.*

As their voices grow distant, he grabs a pad of paper and a marker off of a shelf and sneaks back down to the main floor.

*The center of the house,* he thinks. *I need to be in the center of the house.*

Back on the main floor, he picks up his dropped flashlight and sets it up to have some light. He sits down on the floor and starts to draw.

Suddenly, he hears a voice.

"Tyler?"

He looks up.

*Who are you?* he thinks.

"What are you doing?"

Tyler looks down at the mess of papers scattered about. He looks up and sees three people staring at him.

*Who are they?* he thinks.

"Do you know who you are?"

Tyler nods slowly.

"Do you know who I am?"

Tyler looks at him.

"I'm Phin," he says. "Your brother?"

*My brother? I don't have a brother.*

Tyler looks at him, confused.

*Wait, yes I do. What am I thinking? I have two brothers. Phin and Cody. And our parents, Tom and Meredith. And I'm in this creepy old house with a bunch of my friends and Alan, the guy I...*

Tyler shakes his head quickly and sits upright. He looks at the faces of the three people staring at him.

"Why are you guys looking at me like that?" he asks. "What's going on?"

"Are you back?" asks Alan.

"What?"

"Are you you?"

"Well yeah, who else would I be?"

"You tell us," says Genevieve carefully.

Phin stands and offers Tyler a hand.

"You had us a little freaked out, bro."

"I think I need some air," says Tyler.

* * *

Chelle and Carrie lay on the bed in the purple room watching a movie on TV. Other than an occasional creaking floorboard, they are unaware of what is happening elsewhere in Claythorn Manor. When the movie goes to a commercial break, Carrie turns to look at Chelle.

"Hey, I have a question."

"What's up?"

"D-do you think I'm boring for wanting to stay in here all night?"

"What?"

"Do you think I'm boring?"

"Not at all," says Chelle. "I mean, you're here, aren't you?"

"Well, yeah, it's just... I don't know. I feel bad that Phin paid for both of us to come here tonight and I haven't even left the safe room."

"You can change that, you know."

Carrie raises her eyebrows.

"I'm serious," says Chelle. "It's not really that scary out there. I mean, you'll probably let your imagination get the best of you, I know I did, but really, this is just an old house. Nothing more."

"You're right," says Carrie. She rolls over and stares at the ceiling. "It's a beautiful house, too."

"Have you seen any of it at all?"

"Just the bar and the parts that Bea showed us."

Chelle sits up.

"Come on," she says. "Let's go for a walk."

"Where do you want to go?"

"I don't care, I just don't want you to feel like you wasted your night here."

"Alright," says Carrie. She gets off the bed and walks over to the table. "I'm gonna bring one of the walkies with us. Do you think we should tell anyone we're heading out?"

"Nah," says Chelle, slipping on a pair of flip flops. "They'll figure it out. Besides, we're all in the same house."

"True," says Carrie, fixing her ponytail, a streak of pink hair falling loose from the back. "Where do you wanna go?"

"I was gonna leave that up to you," says Chelle.

Carrie thinks for a moment.

"Would you be opposed to checking out the basement?"

"Seriously? You haven't left the room all night and you want to check out the basement?"

"Sure, I mean, why not? It's just an old house, right?"

"I can't argue with that," says Chelle. "You know what? Let's do it. Let's go down to the basement."

\* \* \*

Down the hall, Graham sits on the bed in the darkened blue room while Mack goes through his suitcase.

"I know I had spare batteries for my flashlight in here somewhere," he says.

"That sucks the carriage house was all locked up," says Graham.

"I know. I would have liked to have gone in. Aha!" says Mack, holding out a small package. "Found them!"

"I wonder where everyone else is?"

"Probably scattered throughout the house," says Mack, putting the batteries into his flashlight. "Did you see or hear anyone when we were on our way up?"

"No," says Graham. "This room is really creepy in the dark."

"Agreed. I mean, the whole house is, really."

Suddenly, they hear a bang followed by a crash.

"Oh, God!" shouts Graham, jumping up from the bed.

"What was that?"

"It came from that wall!"

"Let's go back to the purple room and regroup with everyone."

\* \* \*

While Mack is looking through his bag upstairs, Tyler leads Alan, Phin and Genevieve out through the atrium to the back porch. Once outside, Alan pulls out two cigarettes and lights them simultaneously before handing one to Tyler. Genevieve lights up, as well.

"So, I'm gonna ask this point blank," says Phin. "What the hell happened back there?"

Tyler shakes his head.

"I have no idea."

"It was fucking weird," says Genevieve, the lights from the carriage house reflecting in her glasses.

They stand in silence a moment.

"What was it like for you?" she asks Tyler.

"It was like watching a movie," he answers. "I could see and hear everything, but I couldn't react. It was like being strapped into a ride and having no choice but to just… go."

"Do you remember all of it?" asks Phin.

"I think so," says Tyler. "Parts of it are fuzzy, but for the most part I can. I just wish I had a better idea of what happened."

"I might have an idea," says Alan slowly.

The others turn to face him.

"What?" asks Tyler.

"When we were in the attic trying to contact the spirit, I wasn't just talking out loud."

"What do you mean?" asks Phin.

"I was talking in my head, too. Out loud, I was trying to talk to the spirit, coax it into interacting with us. But in my mind, I was telling it that if it needed to use a medium, to use Tyler. If it needed a voice, to use Tyler. The nearest I can figure is that it somehow worked." He takes a drag from his cigarette.

"Are you fucking serious?" asks Tyler.

Alan nods.

"Wow," says Genevieve.

"That's kind of a dick move," says Phin.

"I'm sorry," Alan says to Tyler. "I didn't think anything would actually happen."

"Well it did," says Tyler. "But I guess I'm alright now, so… what?"

He looks at Genevieve whose eyes are suddenly very wide, her mouth hanging slightly open as the cigarette between two of her fingers is held in midair.

"B-b-behind you," she manages to say.

Tyler, Phin and Alan all turn to look at the window Tyler was standing in front of to see a curtain on the inside whipping back and forth.

\* \* \*

Just as Genevieve closes the door to the porch upstairs, Chelle and Carrie reach the bottom of the back staircase.

"So I guess this is the basement," says Carrie.

"Yup."

"It's not as bad as I thought," says Carrie. To her right, she sees a door that leads to a large kitchen while several other rooms are to her left.

"We can't go in there," says Chelle. "Bea said there's some kind of motion alarms."

"Alright," says Carrie. "What's back there?" She shines her flashlight through a door that opens up behind the stairs.

"I don't know," says Chelle. "That looks like a freezer though, so it's probably food storage or something."

"Oh, well, we'd better leave that alone then."

Chelle leads Carrie through the doorway to the left to start exploring the other rooms in the basement. Neither notices the light that suddenly illuminates the bottom of the door to the walk-in freezer from the inside.

* * *

Upstairs, Phin is getting ready to open the door and jump inside to catch whoever is messing with the curtain. Alan and Genevieve are finishing their cigarettes, hearts racing from the adrenaline rush. Tyler has put his cigarette out and is taking pictures of the window as quickly as he can. The curtain is still moving slightly.

Phin silently counts down.

"Three... two... one..."

In one quick motion, he flings open the door, jumps inside and whips around the corner through the atrium to the back room where the curtain had been moving.

He slowly appears in the doorway, his face pale.

"What is it?" asks Tyler.

"Yeah, who was there?" asks Alan.

"No one," says Phin.

"What?!" yells Genevieve.

"No one was there," Phin says again. "And even better? There's a table in front of that window, so if there *was* anyone there, they wouldn't have been able to run away quickly or hide. I would have seen them."

"Then it must have been a vent or something," says Genevieve.

"That made it thrash about like that?" asks Tyler.

"You never know," she says weakly.

"No, I thought of that, too," says Phin. "So I looked and there's no vent near that window."

Alan puts his cigarette into the urn next to the door.

"Then what was that?" he asks.

"Oh my God!" shouts Tyler, looking at the screen on the back of his camera. "You guys, come look at this!"

"What is it?"

"I-I, well, I noticed something off about this picture," he says, showing the others a picture of the window. "So I zoomed in and found... this."

Tyler zooms in on the image and scrolls over a little.

"No fucking way," says Alan quietly as Genevieve gasps. Phin is speechless.

"I mean, you guys are seeing what I'm seeing, aren't you?" asks Tyler.

The others nod as Tyler looks down at the image, the unmistakable face of a translucent dog staring out the window.

* * *

Upstairs, Mack and Graham stand in the empty purple room, the only sound coming from the television that Chelle and Carrie left on.

"Where did everyone go?" Mack says aloud.

"I don't know," says Graham. "But I can't get anyone to answer on the walkies."

"That's weird," says Mack. "What was the noise we heard?"

"I have no idea, but everything seems to be okay in here..."

"...except that there's no one here."

"Well yeah, there's that."

"Let's check the other rooms."

"Alright," says Graham.

They head across the hall to the green room and while they are relieved to find everything in order, they grow increasingly anxious when they are unable to find any of their friends. The same thing happens in the red room – everything's in order, but there's no one to be found.

"If there's no one up here, then where did that noise come from?" asks Mack. They stand in the hall near the top of the main staircase.

"You know, there's a room we haven't checked yet," says Graham. He looks over toward the door of the room that Bea had told them was storage.

"Do you think they'd be hiding in there?"

"Maybe," says Graham. "Couldn't hurt to check."

The two walk over to the door.

"It's probably locked anyway," says Graham as he reaches for the handle.

His heart sinks when it turns and the door swings open.

"Not again," says Graham, groaning.

"That's two rooms now that were supposed to be locked," says Mack.

"I know."

They enter the storage room and start to look around, the only light coming from their flashlights. The items in the room are mostly covered by sheets, though a few old mirrors and paintings are stacked against the far wall.

"Do you notice anything about this room?" asks Mack.

"Like what?"

"It's circular."

"Like the atrium! We must be directly above it," says Graham.

"Right," Mack says as he continues to look around the room. Walking toward the center, he finds himself looking at an old doctor's chair.

"This is some creepy shit," he mutters to himself.

"Hey Mack," calls Graham. He stands in front of a dusty shelf filled with various items. "Come check this out."

Mack walks over to Graham.

"I think I found the source of our noise," says Graham. He shines his flashlight down to the floor where a dusty bowling ball leans against an old rocking horse. He follows the trail the ball left in the dust back toward their feet next to the shelf.

"Look here," says Graham. "You can see where it was on the shelf because of the outline in the dust. It must have fallen off and rolled over there."

"Interesting," says Mack. "But what made it fall?"

"That I don't know," says Graham.

The walkie at his side suddenly blips followed by a scream of pure terror.

* * *

"Who was that?!" Tyler shouts as the four from the porch rush into the house.

"Hello?!" Graham shouts as he and Mack race down the main staircase.

They meet with Tyler, Alan, Phin and Genevieve in the front hall.

"Was that any of you?" asks Mack.

"No," says Phin. "And it wasn't either of you?"

"Negative," says Graham. "Wait, Chelle's not with you guys?"

"No, she's up in the purple room with Carrie," says Phin.

"No she's not!" says Mack. "We were just up there and they're both gone!"

"What?!" shouts Tyler.

"Yeah, it was empty! There's no one in any of the bedrooms."

"Oh, shit," says Alan.

"Alright, we split up," says Tyler. "They have to be in either the basement or the attic. I've had enough of the attic for one night, so I'll go to the basement with Phin and Mack. Graham, you wanna take Alan and Genevieve and check the attic? They're probably together, so let us know if you find them."

"Alright," says Graham.

"Let's go," says Phin. They make their way to the back staircase and part ways, with Phin leading the group into the basement.

"Have either of you guys been down here yet?" asks Phin.

"I have," says Mack.

"What's the layout?" asks Tyler.

"Pretty basic, just a bunch of rooms. At the bottom of the stairs, the kitchen is to the right and there's a series of rooms to the left that span most of the house. They're set up as dining rooms, probably for when they have private parties."

"I think Graham said they do dinner theaters here, too," Tyler says.

"That's not surprising," says Mack. The three reach the bottom of the stairs and look around.

"That's weird," says Tyler.

"What?" asks Phin.

"There's a light at the bottom of the door there. Isn't that a freezer?"

"Yeah," says Mack. "And it's padlocked."

"The staff probably left it on," says Phin.

*I don't remember that light being on earlier,* Mack thinks.

"Hello?" calls Tyler.

When they don't receive an answer, they head through the door to the left into the first of the basement dining rooms.

"I don't think there's anyone in here," says Tyler, the beam of his flashlight moving from table to table.

"Let's keep looking," says Mack. He walks toward the front of the house into another room full of tables, looks around and continues on.

"Carrie?" calls Phin. Tyler can hear the rising panic in his brother's voice.

"We'll find them," says Tyler.

"Hey you guys," calls Mack. "In here!"

Tyler and Phin rush through another room to where Mack in standing to find Carrie and Chelle seated at a table, their walkie in between them.

Phin rushes to his girlfriend's side.

"Oh my God, baby, are you okay?"

"Yeah," she says. "I'm fine, we just… I don't know, we panicked a little."

"I don't know how much more I can take of this place," says Chelle. "Remind me again why I thought this would be a good idea?"

Tyler rushes over to his best friend and gives her a hug.

"I'm going to let the others know we found you," he says. He steps away and radios the group in the attic.

"So what happened?" asks Phin.

"Well, we came down here because – "

"– because I didn't want to stay in the room all night."

"Baby, you could have come with us any time you wanted!"

"I know, I know, I just … I don't know, I wanted you to think I was brave."

"Carrie," says Phin. "You came to the basement of Claythorn Manor alone with Chelle! That takes some serious balls!"

She smiles.

"So, why were you screaming on the walkie?" asks Mack.

"We were in the middle room there and we both started to feel like something wasn't right. Both of our legs started to tingle like, oh God this sounds so crazy, almost like a dog was brushing against us," says Chelle.

Tyler snaps his head to look at her.

"A dog?"

"Yeah, I know…"

"I don't think you're crazy," he says. "So then what happened?"

"I started to get really dizzy," says Carrie. "It started with my hearing, I couldn't hear out of my left ear. It was like someone was holding their hand over it. I would have fallen, actually, if Chelle hadn't been there to help me catch my balance."

"Thank you," Phin says to Chelle.

She nods.

"So then we came back here to sit for a few minutes," says Carrie. "And while I was sitting here, we were just talking and Chelle picked up the walkie to try and get ahold of you guys when I saw it."

"Saw what?" asks Phin.

"It was like an arm," says Carrie. "It looked like someone swinging their arm through the air and I thought someone was coming back here and I didn't recognize them, so, I uhh…"

"She screamed her head off," says Chelle. "Right as I hit the call button. And then I couldn't get any of you guys to reply when I tried to call after that."

"We've been having trouble with the stupid walkies all night," says Mack.

"Well, hey, let's get back upstairs," says Tyler. They stand and walk toward the back staircase and as they reach it, Carrie lets out a gasp.

"What is it?" asks Phin.

"That light there," she says. "Chelle, do you remember that light being on?"

Chelle looks at the light on the bottom of the freezer door.

"N-no, I don't," she says. "And look, it's locked. I didn't notice that earlier, either." A chill runs through her body.

"Let's get out of this basement," says Mack.

The group heads back upstairs to the purple room and when everyone is situated, Tyler stands up.

"I'm gonna radio the others, see where they're at," he says, stepping out into the hall.

"Hey, you guys there?" he says, pushing the call button.

"Hey Tyler, it's Gen," comes the reply, a few seconds later. "Where are you guys at?"

"We brought the girls back to the purple room, just wanted to see where you three are at."

"We're still looking around up here, Alan wanted to see something."

"Anything interesting?"

"Well… kind of."

"What do you mean?"

"You know those cars in the bathroom?"

"Yeah."

"Alan apparently drew little chalk lines around them earlier tonight when you guys were up here."

"Okay."

"Was anyone up here at any point other than what we all know about already?"

"I don't think so, we've all been with each other all night. Why?"

"The cars have moved."

"What?"

"Yeah, they've been scattered around the bathroom. I didn't know if one of you had been up here or not."

"No… we haven't."

"Damn," says Genevieve. "Alright, we'll be heading back down in a few."

"Alright, see you then."

Tyler leans against the wall and quietly reflects on the night's events. He pulls out his phone to check the time and see that it is almost 3:30 A.M.

"I think that's enough for one night," he says to himself.

* * *

A half an hour later, the group has decided to all sleep in the lavender suite. They have brought blankets and pillows from the other rooms and lay strewn about, the door to the hallway tightly locked.

One by one they fall asleep, exhausted from the evenings events until only Tyler lays awake, washed in the blue light from the TV. With his night in Claythorn Manor nearing its conclusion, he starts thinking about things in his life outside of the house, specifically something Jade had told him about Alan. He rolls over on the bed to face him, working up the courage to have the conversation he's had in the back of his mind over the past few days.

"Hey," he whispers. "Are you awake?"

Alan stirs.

"Mmm," he groans. "Kind of, what's up?"

"Did you have a good time tonight?"

"It was interesting," Alan whispers.

"Yeah."

"Are you okay?"

"Yeah, I'm alright," says Tyler. "I have a question."

"What's up?"

Tyler's heart starts beating quickly.

*Here's hoping Jade was telling the truth,* he thinks.

"You know I try to avoid rumors and gossip, he-said-she-said bullshit, right?"

"Yeah," says Alan.

"Well, I wanted to ask you about this directly because I'd heard through the grapevine that you went to dinner with another guy."

Alan props himself up. Across the way, Carrie rolls over on the pullout couch she is sharing with Phin.

"At El Scorcho?"

"Yeah."

"I figured that was going to get back to you," Alan says with a sigh. "That was an old friend of mine from the last time I was in school. He was just passing through town and wanted to catch up."

"Oh, I mean, it's not a big deal at all, I was just, you know... I wanted to ask you about it directly," says Tyler, feeling like an ass for even bringing it up.

"You're fine," says Alan. "And in case you're wondering, the answer is no. He and I never dated or did anything sexual at all, for that matter."

*I hope that was convincing enough,* thinks Alan.

"Oh," says Tyler. "Okay."

*Wait, if he wasn't on a date that night...* Tyler's thoughts trail off.

"Hey, I had something else I want to ask you."

"Go for it," says Alan.

"Well, okay," starts Tyler. "We've been off and on since what, October?"

"I guess, yeah."

"So, I was just wondering if, you know, if you were ready... I'd like to be your boyfriend."

The silence that follows is broken only by the sounds of the television and the clock on the nightstand. Mack snores softly from where he is asleep on the floor.

"What, like see each other exclusively?" Alan finally responds

"Yeah, I mean, we hang out all the time, we're practically together already..."

"Can I think about it?"

*What's there to think about?* Tyler thinks.

"Yeah, sure, of course," he says.

"I just want you to be sure this is what you really want," says Alan. "And I'm still waiting to hear about that study abroad program. I don't want you to jump into anything that would just get ripped away a short time later."

"No, I totally get it," says Tyler.

*You've more or less been my damn boyfriend for the last six months, I'm*

*pretty sure I know I'd like to exclusively see you at this point,* thinks Tyler. *And even if it ends soon after, I'd rather have that little bit than nothing at all.*

"Well hey, I'm beat," says Tyler. "I think I'm gonna fall asleep now."

"Okay," says Alan. "Good night, Ty."

Alan gives Tyler a kiss goodnight before he rolls over. It's not long before Alan's steady breathing lets Tyler know he has fallen asleep, though he will lie awake for at least another half an hour.

\* \* \*

Sunlight streams through the windows of the lavender bedroom in Claythorn Manor, gradually rousing the eight guests who are fast asleep. The daylight creates a different atmosphere throughout the entire house, so much so that when they finally leave the room to go down to breakfast, each one has a hard time believing this is the same house that had spooked them all so badly the night before.

At breakfast, they recount the various incidents from their stay in Claythorn Manor, debating whether or not their experiences were truly brushes with the paranormal or simply the products of overactive imaginations in just the right set of circumstances.

Ultimately, each forms their own opinion on whether or not Claythorn Manor is truly haunted, though the staff overhears their conversations and are not at all surprised to hear of the things that had happened during their stay. They pack their bags and depart, leaving as a group through the front door. A few final pictures are taken of the outside of the house during the day before the cars are packed and they leave Claythorn Manor.

The next few days are spent sharing the pictures and stories from the night in Claythorn Manor with various friends and family. These are met with a range of responses, from skepticism to belief. One thing remains constant, though: For each of the eight, for one reason or another, the night spent in Claythorn Manor is one that will not soon be forgotten.

# GRADUATION

"Sarah Bethany Aaron," Mr. Leonard MacClayton reads off of an index card. The girl at the front of the line smiles as she walks up the stairs and across the stage. She shakes hands with the various administrators before receiving the padded case that will hold her diploma and posing for a photo with Mr. Marvin Hirsch. She continues the walk across the stage, descending the stairs at the opposite side and walking back to her seat.

Sarah Aaron is the first person in her class to graduate.

Mr. MacClayton continues taking index cards from the students in line and reading their names as they walk across the stage.

"Dawn Christine Bailey."

After successfully completing this year's yearbook, with the exception of a few pages dedicated to the end of year celebrations that are only waiting for pictures to be dropped into templates, Dawn set her sights on the internship program at *Cityzine*, the city's premier life and style magazine. She assembled a portfolio of her best work and submitted her application. Dawn knew it was a longshot, particularly since she had not even started college yet. She was disappointed when she received a rejection letter from *Cityzine*, but not surprised.

But two weeks after graduation comes the phone call that will change everything.

One of the interns *Cityzine* selected has decided to take another internship and Dawn is the first alternate for the program. She happily accepts the position and a month after she graduates, Dawn starts her career in publishing as an intern at *Cityzine*.

She poses for a photo with Mr. Hirsch, feeling a little awkward to be in front of the camera instead of behind it. The flash goes off, she shakes his hand again and finishes her walk across the stage.

"Alexa Eileen din Tei."

As she climbs the stairs to the stage, Lexie din Tei cannot hide her grin at the turn of events over the past few weeks since prom.

*Has it already been a few weeks?* she thinks. *Wow...*

Chaos had erupted after she heard the crash in the men's room at prom. She ran to tell Mr. Verrit and Miss McKee and after they took over, she thought about just going home. She didn't really have anyone she felt like being around; it seemed like everyone was running around and Dana was preoccupied with Tim.

But suddenly there she was, Dana Peterson, standing in front of her.

"Hey," she'd said.

"Hi," Lexie replied.

"Is everything okay?"

"No," said Lexie. "Not really."

They stood there for what felt like hours, each studying the other, until Dana finally broke the silence.

"Do you want to dance?"

"What?"

"Do you want to dance?" repeated Dana. "With me?"

"Sure," said Lexie. "That'd be nice."

She smiled as Dana held out her hand, taking Lexie's in her own and leading her to the dance floor.

Lexie pauses for a photo with Mr. Hirsch, though she looks beyond the camera into the audience of her classmates. Had anyone told her a month ago that only a few short weeks later she would feel like she belonged with her classmates, that her piece would finally fit in the puzzle with her peers, she would have laughed in their face. But here she is: graduating, happy and, for the first time in recent memory, excited about what's to come.

"Timothy James Foster."

Six months after he graduates, Tim will run into his old girlfriend, Dana, while he is out shopping. The Christmas shopping season is in full swing and he's walking through an electronics store when he sees her looking at two different sets of earbuds. He walks up behind her; she doesn't notice him.

"You should go with the purple ones," he says.

She spins around and smiles.

"Tim!"

She throws her arms around him.

"Hey, Dana," he says.

"How have you been?"

"Good, good," he says. "Just finishing up my first semester. You?"

"Same here," she says.

"How's Lexie?"

"She's good," says Dana, carefully.

"That's great," says Tim. "I'm glad to hear it."

"Hey, you're not still... you know I... ugh... let me start over," says Dana. She takes a breath. "I hope you're not too upset with me for how things played out between us."

"Oh, no! I mean, I never thought my girlfriend would leave me at our senior prom, least of all for another girl, but hey – it's a hell of a story."

He laughs, attempting to reassure her that he harbors no negative sentiments towards their relationship and the way it ended.

"You're welcome?" she says, laughing. "Seriously though, I'm sorry if it dragged things out for you. I had some things I just didn't want to face, I guess."

"What, the part about you being a lesbian? I hate to break it to you, but it was kind of obvious, especially in retrospect."

"Really?" Dana asks, laughing.

"Little bit," says Tim. "I mean, you checked out the cheerleaders at the hockey games more than I did!"

Dana and Tim both laugh.

"And, if I'm being honest, you always lit up when Lexie was around. Eventually, I just put two and two together."

Dana smiles.

His phone vibrates and he looks down. "Oh hey, I'd better get going."

"Okay," says Dana. "It was good to see you."

"You, too," he says, giving her a hug. "Tell Lexie I said hey."

"I will," says Dana. "And give your nephew a hug for me, will you?"

"Of course."

The camera flashes in Tim's face and he walks back to his seat. He can't believe he just graduated. He can't believe all the years of hard work have finally paid off. He can't believe his girlfriend left him for another girl.

But then, upon further reflection, it all starts to make sense.

"Evan Jacob Gallagher."

Evan climbs the stairs and begins his walk across the stage. While part of him is excited to get this ceremony over with, he's anxious for what he knows he has to do later.

He knows he has to end his relationship with Annika.

This is it; this is graduation, the end of high school. She's going back to Europe and he's going to boot camp in August.

*It's not going to work,* he thinks. *And I think we both know it.*

The conversation that happens between Evan and Annika a few days later goes well enough. They end their relationship amicably and agree to stay in touch. It turns out that she knew as well as he did that their breakup was inevitable. They hug each other goodbye and that's the last he sees of her before she flies home.

August comes and Evan leaves for boot camp, thus beginning an entirely new chapter of his life, though he will never forget the time he spent with Annika.

"Garrett Franklin Harmon."

Garrett takes the stairs slowly, his knees shake and he feels as though he could fall or vomit at any moment. Just before getting in line for the entrance processional, his girlfriend, Holly Rogers, pulled him aside.

"We need to talk," she said.

"Now? Okay, is everything alright?"

"No," she said. "I'm pregnant."

Garrett's mouth hangs open in shock as Holly starts to cry.

"I've been so scared, Garrett, and I'm sorry but I couldn't wait any longer to tell you."

"I-I… oh my God. Wow…"

Miss Kim McKee walked by and noticed Holly crying.

"You okay, Holly?"

"I'm fine," she said, wiping her eyes. "Just a little emotional about graduating."

"I get it," said Miss McKee. "This is a big night for you guys and I know it can be scary and overwhelming, but this is *your* night – try to enjoy it as best you can, okay? You guys have earned it."

"Thanks, Miss McKee," said Garrett, his arm around Holly.

"I think we're going to be walking in shortly, so get back in line, okay?"

"You got it," said Garrett.

Miss McKee walked on and Garrett turned to Holly.

"Hey," he said. "Take a deep breath. It'll be alright. We'll get through this together, you and me."

He pulled her in close.

"I love you," she whispered into his ear.

"I love you, too," he said.

Garrett's palms sweat as he shakes Mr. Hirsch's hand on stage.

*Oh my God,* he thinks. *A baby… I'm going to be a father. I don't know what to do. I was finally starting to figure things out, figure myself out… Now what am I going to do?*

He smiles weakly at the camera, utterly terrified of the life that awaits him on the other side of the stage.

"Annika Rose Heighesser."

Annika walks up the stairs to the stage for the second time this evening. Earlier in the ceremony, she and the other exchange students had been presented with American flags to commemorate the year they have spent studying in the states. She thinks of the friends she's made, particularly Evan, the boyfriend she knows she has to break up with, and Cody, the boy who was fated to only ever be a friend.

She accepts the diploma holder and shakes Mr. Hirsch's hand, smiling for the camera. Annika has very much enjoyed her year as an exchange student, but she's ready to go home. Her host family and friends have been wonderful, but she misses the comforts of home, the little things that, try as anyone might, cannot be replicated. Her father's laugh, her mother's cooking, kisses from her dog… these are the things she can't wait to get back to.

But there are a few things she needs to wrap up before leaving. Annika knows that she will have to break up with Evan; she just hopes that they will still be friends. She liked being Evan's girlfriend and hopes that he won't be too upset with her.

*He has to know,* she thinks. *We're both leaving and I don't know when I'll see him next. Who knows? We may never again live on the same continent…*

And then there's Cody. Annika had gotten her prom pictures back and made a duplicate of the picture of her and Cody that his friend Colleen had taken. She's going to the store tomorrow with her host mom to look for a nice photo frame to put the picture in as a parting gift for Cody, a memento to remember her by until she returns to the states.

Before she descends the stairs on the other side of the stage,

Annika pauses to look out over the crowd of students. She remembers how scared she was on her first day as their classmate. And now, though she is about to move half a world away from them, she knows that most of them will never be far from her heart.

"Hunter Randell Jamison."

Silence quickly falls across the arena after Hunter's name is read.

Everyone knows that he was in a terrible car accident after prom. Rumors ran rampantly through the school, ranging from what substances may or may not have been involved to the fatality that occurred as a result. Hunter returned to school a week ago to finish his senior year. The lacerations on his face are healing well enough, though his broken leg will take a good deal longer. He uses a wheelchair to get from place to place, though he is able to walk short distances with crutches.

Hunter puts on a brave face, but he's scared. He's healing, but he's still weak and he's struggling to understand why this happened to him.

*Is it something I did? Something I didn't do?* he asks himself on a daily basis. *Am I being punished? Is this fate? How did I survive?* Why *did I survive?*

In this moment, however, Hunter is mostly nervous about having to walk across the stage by himself under the gaze of the thousands of people in attendance, most of whom know all about his accident.

He is relieved to have planned ahead and looks to his two teammates, Evan and Blake, who are standing on either side of him, ready to help him up the stairs and across the stage. Each takes one of his arms, helping him out of his chair and up the stairs. When he reaches the top, everyone in the arena stands to their feet with thunderous applause.

Hunter quickly looks to where he knows his family is in the seats, smiling at his mother who in turn waves at him, smiling through tears of joy.

Mr. Hirsch comes over to help him across the stage, letting Hunter prop himself up against his shoulder as they stop for the photographer. The applause from everyone in attendance continues until well after Hunter's teammates have helped him down the stairs on the opposite side of the stage. There isn't a dry eye in the arena.

Hunter knows he has a long way to go with his recovery, that this is just the first step. He will be walking on his own by July and, after a few short months in physical therapy, he will be able to play football again.

"Jazmine Taleah Lloyd."

Jazmine looks back to her twin sister, Janelle, gives her a wink and starts toward the stage. She pauses every few seconds as she approaches Mr. Hirsch, waving to several of her friends as well as various people in the seats.

*Yes, girl – work this crowd!* she thinks jubilantly.

This skill will help her later this summer when she is approached at a club about a job opportunity as a brand ambassador for an energy drink. She happily takes the job and starts getting paid to do what she does best – interacting with people.

As she poses for the picture with Mr. Hirsch, Jazmine feels a twinge of pain in her back.

*Damnit,* she thinks. *Not now… please not now.*

Luckily for her, the pain quickly passes and she continues her walk across the stage. It won't be until October that she decides to finally go to a doctor for the various symptoms that have developed along with the pain, including frequent headaches and feeling tired all of the time. The visit leads to another with a series of tests and follow up visits. Finally, she gets the call that her doctor has a diagnosis.

Her sister Janelle will be with her when her doctor tells her that she has lupus.

Though she is scared, Jazmine faces the disease head on, determined to keep her symptoms under control. By Christmas, she will be feeling much better, and will stay proactive with managing her health.

*Remember my name, folks,* she thinks as she gets to the bottom of the stairs. *This is just the beginning…*

Jazmine turns around to watch her sister graduate.

"Janelle Yvette Lloyd."

Janelle walks across the stage, proud of her sister for graduating just before her and excited to graduate herself. She looks out to the crowd, looking for her boyfriend, T.J. Trovato.

It had not been an easy few weeks for T.J. since his best friend had been taken away by the paramedics from their senior prom. Janelle did her best to be there for him as a friend, despite hoping he saw the potential for a relationship with her as she did with him.

Two nights ago, she was reading a book in her room when her sister came in and sat down on her bed.

"Hey sis," she said.

"What's up?"

"You have a visitor," said Jazmine, smiling.

"I do?"

"Yup, he's downstairs."

Janelle jumped up from her bed and ran downstairs to find T.J. standing in their living room.

"T.J.!"

"Hey, Janie," he said, smiling.

"What's up? I thought we were going out tomorrow night?"

"Oh, we are," he assured her. "There was something I wanted to do before that, though."

Janelle raised an eyebrow; Jazmine listened intently from the landing upstairs.

"Well, okay. I know it hasn't been easy to hang out with me since everything happened with Erik and all."

*Where is he going with this?* thought Janelle.

"So I wanted to say thank you for that, first of all. And then, well, I don't know. I like you… a lot. And I feel like I can talk about things with you I can't talk about with anyone else and it's scary but it's, like, the good kind of scary, if that makes sense? And I don't know what you were thinking of this thing between us was or wasn't or anything, but – "

*Oh, come on already!* Jazmine thought upstairs. *Out with it!*

"I was wondering if you wanted to make this official between you and me. I know we're graduating the day after tomorrow, so I wanted to ask you beforehand."

A grin spread across Janelle's face.

"Will you be my girlfriend?"

"Of course!" she practically screamed, jumping into his arms.

*Get it girl!* thought Jazmine.

Janelle winks at T.J., who smiles back at her. She poses for a photo with Mr. Hirsch and walks the rest of the way across the stage, hugging her sister at the bottom of the stairs before they both walk back to their seats.

"Heather Nicole Matthews."

After prom, Mike the DJ took Heather to his beat-up car and they had sex in the backseat. She only told a few of her friends, but the story of course made its way around school. What Heather successfully kept under wraps, though, was that Mike the DJ gave her crabs after their encounter in the parking garage. She knew something was wrong a few days later and a quick internet search left her resolved to take a covert trip to a clinic downtown.

*I'm leaving all of that behind me,* she thinks as she accepts the diploma case from Mr. Hirsch. *I'm turning my life around, starting today.*

The trip Heather took to the clinic after prom wasn't the first time she had made the trek, as a pregnancy scare last fall also found her on a bus heading straight downtown. It's true she enjoys sex, but thinking back, she only started drinking, smoking and having sex because that's what her friends were doing.

*I'm not giving a third trip to the clinic the chance to be the charm,* she thought as she returned home a few weeks ago, special shampoo in hand.

Heather will spend all summer shying away from the hard partying friends she has surrounded herself with for the last few years. Three months from now, she will be at her college's involvement fair when she happens upon a table for Campus Ministries. She gets into a conversation with one of the guys behind the table. He's attractive, he's intelligent and he doesn't judge her for her past. Before she knows it, she's agreed to go to their next meeting.

For the first time, Heather will feel like she actually fits in with the people she's surrounded by. But right now, as she exits the stage, Heather has nothing much to go on other than the great deal of hope for the new life she is beginning.

Maxwell David Noire's name is skipped.

Max Noire is currently sitting at home playing a video game. He was informed last week that he would not be graduating as a result of his failing grades and that he would have to return to Central High in the fall to finish his credits.

*I don't give a fuck,* he thinks at the thought of the ceremony he is missing. *That shit sounds boring anyway.*

What Max doesn't know is that in a few short weeks, two detectives will arrive at his home to question his connection to the fire that destroyed the Southside Pier. He thinks he has evaded law officials, but unfortunately his time has run out. After months of investigation, they finally have the evidence they need to link him with the fireworks that caught the pier on fire back in October.

His lawyer will ensure he doesn't go to jail, but he will have to complete five hundred hours of community service and will spend the next five years on probation.

Max pauses his game and lights a cigarette. He takes a drag and goes to the kitchen, his father's snores emanating from his room. He pops open a beer and takes a drink.

*What difference will a stupid piece of paper make?* he thinks.

"Dana Joanna Peterson."

Dana Peterson is nervous to walk across the stage.

*If I can get through prom, I can get through this,* she thinks.

When she saw Lexie din Tei walking to the bathroom by herself at prom, something finally clicked in Dana's mind and she knew she had made a mistake in shutting Lexie out of her life.

*I have to make this right,* she thought, her head resting on her boyfriend's shoulder.

"Hey, Tim?" she said.

"What's up?"

"I'm really, really sorry," she said, lifting her head and looking him straight in the eye. "I can't do this."

"Do what?"

"You're a really great guy, but I can't keep this up," she said.

"Dana, what's wrong?" he said, concerned about his girlfriend.

"I know this is like, the worst timing in the world," she said. "But I couldn't live with myself if I didn't do this tonight."

"Okay…"

"I'm pretty sure I'm a lesbian, Tim."

"Oh."

"Like, borderline positive," said Dana. "A hundred percent."

He looked at her and let out a sigh.

"Don't take this the wrong way, but… I kind of figured," he said.

"Really?"

"Yeah."

*Oh God, what did I just do? I think I'm gonna throw up… Is he pissed? I just ruined his prom, I'm such a terrible pers –*

"Go!" Tim said, giving her hands one last squeeze before letting his arms fall to his side.

"What?"

"Go after her," he said, smiling. "There's a girl here you want to go to, am I right? I want you to be happy, Dana, even if it's not with me. Or any guy, really. So go! Don't waste any more time."

"What about you?"

"Me?" he asked. "I'll be fine, don't worry about me."

She gave him a kiss on the cheek before running away into the crowd.

"Thank you," she whispered.

*Yeah, this was nothing compared to prom,* she thinks as she finishes her walk across the stage. *Hard to believe it's over, really.*

"Blake Stephen Pines."

After helping his friend Hunter down the stage stairs, Blake returned to his seat until it was his time for his row to approach the stage. While his friends would be going away to school or joining the army, Blake had other plans in mind. He had played football all four years of high school, but his true passion had always been music, specifically creating remixes and beats. A few weeks ago, he had even approached one of the DJ's at prom as the night was winding down.

"Hey man, you got a minute?" he asked.

"Sure," said the DJ named Philip. "I gotta tell you though, we're not taking any more requests."

"Oh no, it's not that."

"Alright then, what can I do for you?"

"Hi, I'm Blake," he said, extending his hand.

"Philip," said the DJ, shaking Blake's hand.

"This might sound kind of stupid but, how did you get to where you are?"

Philip looked at him, confused.

"I mean, how did you get a job as a DJ?"

"Oh!" said Philip. "Well, to be honest, I knew some people. But really, DJ jobs like this are pretty common. You've just gotta keep an eye out for ads online and stuff. You into music?"

"Yeah," said Blake. "I have a couple programs on my computer at home I've been playing with, mixing songs and stuff. There's just so much I feel like I want to do, I'm just not really sure where to start."

"Well a job like this would be a good place."

Blake could feel the DJ sizing him up.

"Tell you what," said Philip, handing him a card and a pen. "Write down your name and number, I'll pass your info along to my boss. We're heading into summer, I'm sure we could use some extra help. I can't promise anything though."

"Really?! Oh my God, that's awesome! Thank you!"

"Don't mention it, kid – just don't ever give up on your dream."

Blake wrote his name and number on the card, thanked Philip again and took off to find his friends, hopeful that things would pan out with the DJ company. A week later, Blake got a phone call from the owner of the DJ company who wanted to meet with him about coming on as a part time DJ for parties and events throughout the summer. They decided that Blake would start shadowing another one of the company's DJ's the following week.

*It's all up from here,* Blake thinks as the camera flashes and he shakes Mr. Hirsch's hand. He points to his family in the crowd as he walks across the stage.

*Here we go!*

"Holly Carol Rogers."

Four months after graduation, Holly is six months pregnant with Garrett's son and the distance between them continues to grow. They had told their parents about the pregnancy together and while the reactions were decidedly mixed, everyone came around in their own time and began making preparations for the arrival of Holly and Garrett's little boy.

Holly opted to stay home and go to the community college with Garrett, though she was only taking a few classes to keep a light workload during the pregnancy. Garrett had picked up a second retail job to help with money alongside his school schedule. They're both determined to make the situation work, if not for themselves but for their son.

One night, Garrett will take Holly to dinner, knowing that he is about to have an important and particularly difficult conversation.

"I-I think I'm gay, Holly."

She sits with her mouth hanging open, fork in midair.

"You're... w-what?"

"Gay."

She blinks.

"Well, I'm glad you decided to figure this out when I'm six months pregnant."

"I didn't decide it, Holly. I'm just so... I have so much back and forth in my head, so much going on – "

"And I don't?!" she screams, dropping her fork and catching the attention of other diners.

"I'm sorry, but I wanted to tell you because, well, because I know you've felt like things haven't been right between us and I've felt it too and it's something I've been fighting in my head and to be honest," Garrett's voice cracks and he pauses. "I can't fight it anymore. And I'm sorry."

"I don't know what to say," she says, her voice barely audible. "After all the time we've spent together... was it all a lie?"

"No, not at all!" says Garrett. "Everything I felt for you, everything between us was real. It's just... you work so hard to be like other guys, be what people consider 'normal'. But deep down, you know you're different, *I* knew I was different. I've known it my whole life but I didn't realize what that meant until recently.

"And it scares the hell out of me, the possibility of losing everything in my life I've worked so hard for. But I know in my heart… this is what I have to do."

"Are you breaking up with me?"

"I guess in so many words, yeah. But I'm not going anywhere, I'm still going to be there for our son because he's *our* son. We're not going to be together but I'm still going to be there, I'm going to be a part of his life and yours."

A week after Thanksgiving, Holly will give birth to a healthy baby boy. It will take time, but she will eventually come to terms with Garrett's sexuality. Garrett will be there for his son's birth and remain a constant part of his life, the epitome of a father figure.

And in the spring, Holly will be excited to meet the boy Garrett has started dating.

"Amanda Kathryn Seton."

Mandy Seton had cried alongside most of the student body when Hunter Jamison graduated, walking across the stage as best as he could. He has made sure everyone knows she saved his life, but what they don't know is how scared she was throughout the whole ordeal, how that night will stay with her for some time to come.

The image of Hunter's bloody face, unconscious in his car, has haunted her dreams ever since the night of prom.

"No! No, no, no," she'd screamed as she ran up to Hunter's car, realizing it was his. She could see the other car, flipped upside down and smoking in the ditch; glass sprinkled the road like freshly fallen snow.

Mandy whipped out her phone and called 911, telling the dispatcher that there had been an accident and her location and when she hung up, she knew she had nothing to do but wait for the police and paramedics to arrive. She could see Hunter's chest rising and falling slightly, despite the blood that was oozing from the cuts on his face. Mandy didn't want to leave his side, but knew she had to check on the other driver.

She quickly ran to the side of the road, but didn't see anyone in the other car. A quick look around the area didn't show anyone, either, though the night was dark and the other driver had to be there somewhere.

*I'll let the cops deal with that,* she thought as she ran back to Hunter's car. She could hear sirens screaming in the distance over the sound of the night bugs.

"Hunter!" she yelled as she approached the car.

He moaned in response.

"It's okay, Hunter, you don't have to talk," she said, opening his car door. She knelt beside his wrecked car and gently took his hand in her own. "Just know that I'm here and please be okay, Hunter. Please be okay…"

Everyone at graduation applauds Mandy as they did Hunter, knowing how she had saved a life only a few weeks ago.

*I hope they never have to experience anything like that,* she thinks as she smiles out to her classmates. She catches Hunter's eye and he winks at her.

He already knows he wants to ask her on a date, but he won't work up the courage to do it until a barbeque they both attend for the Fourth of July.

"Paul Joseph Christopher St. John."

From an early age, Paul St. John knew that he had been called to the priesthood. He had always felt at home in a church and was happiest when worshipping. While he is excited to be graduating high school, he is even more excited to be entering the seminary in the fall.

As he walks across the stage, he cannot help but feel lucky – lucky to have such a supportive family and group of friends. He often feels anxious about sharing his life plans with his peers, worried they'll judge him for following what he feels in his heart or won't understand his points of view. Paul is pleasantly surprised almost every time.

Many people even come to Paul for advice, which he is all too happy to give. That's how Cody Welik wound up sitting with Paul toward the end of prom – he needed some advice and he knew he could trust Paul's blunt honesty.

"So what was the eye roll for?"

"What do you mean?" asked Paul, cleaning his glasses.

"The eye roll when Annika and I were taking pictures."

"Come on, Cody, do you really have to ask what that was about?"

Cody raised an eyebrow.

"I don't know what this thing is between the two of you, but you know she's Evan's girlfriend."

"Okay."

"And she's about to fly back to Europe, on top of that."

"Yeah, there's that," Cody said. "So what should I do?"

"About what?"

"About Annika? And my feelings for her? You can't expect me to just ignore them."

"Well, no, I wouldn't go that far. But, if I'm being honest – "

"I'd expect nothing less," Cody interrupted.

"If I'm being honest, then I'd say just enjoy her company but don't have any preconceived ideas about your relationship with her. Whatever you think you two are, you're just friends."

Cody looked down.

"Unless there's more, which I don't need any sordid details about."

Cody laughed.

"Nah, nothing like that."

Paul nodded.

"Besides, you'd have been one of the first to know," added Cody.

Paul put his palm to his face.

"You always have to go a step farther, don't you."

"You get a kick out of it, Paul, that's why we're friends."

"I get no such thing."

"You're gonna be a shitty priest, you know that? Telling people the things they don't want to hear."

Paul gave Cody a dirty look.

"Come on, you know I'm just giving you trouble," said Cody, laughing. "That's what's gonna make you a great priest. Hell, maybe I'll even go back to church if you're giving the service!"

"Well, I'll be there every Sunday."

Cody laughed.

"And some weekdays!"

"Don't be crazy," said Cody.

"Wouldn't dream of it," said Paul, smiling. "Heathen."

Paul crosses himself as he steps off the stage, a high school graduate excited to take the next steps to grow in his faith.

"Thomas Jerome Trovato."

Three days after prom, T.J. went to see Erik in the hospital. The story of what happened to Erik at prom had already made its way through the entire school and T.J. had spent most of the day talking with the crisis counselor.

"Hey man," T.J. said softly, entering the dim room.

Erik stirred on his bed.

"Oh, hey, Teej," said Erik. He sat up slowly. "They letting me have visitors now?"

"I don't think so," said T.J. "Your mom told me I could come by but that I had to come alone, I couldn't bring anyone else."

"Gotcha," said Erik.

T.J. sat down in the chair by Erik's bed, the leather creaking as he settled in.

"How are you feeling?" asked T.J.

Erik sighed.

"I'm in some deep shit, man," he said.

"Yeah."

"I feel like crap. I'm embarrassed… and I'm guessing everyone at school knows."

"I mean this in the best way possible, but they call you 'Stoner Erik'… they're not too surprised."

Erik turned his head, looking out the window.

"I hate that."

"I know, man. I do, too."

They sat in silence for a few minutes.

"So what's next?" asked T.J.

"I think I'm getting out of here in a day or two and then rehab, probably," said Erik. "I'm pretty sure I'm getting expelled from school for bringing that shit to prom. There's gonna be a hearing with the school board, I heard my mom talking about it."

"That sucks, man."

"I know, but I did it to myself. I can't blame anyone else."

T.J. looked sadly at his best friend, struggling to process everything that has happened over the past few days.

"The worst part is that I really just wanted to change on my own, you know? I didn't want to drag you through this, I didn't want to drag my mom through this. I know what everyone says about me at school and I don't give a flying fuck what they think about me. I just… I guess I feel bad that they associate you with me."

"Oh God, Erik, don't even think like that!" said T.J. "Trust me, if I hear anyone say a fucking word against you, I will fuck them up."

"Thanks, Teej."

"You fucked up, it's true," said T.J. "But you're doing what you need to do to change now. Right?"

"Right."

Shortly after that, T.J. left Erik to head for home. He made it four blocks before pulled over his car and started to cry. Burying his face in his hands, he sobbed, his breath coming in gasps as his shoulders shook.

*I don't want him to die,* he thought over and over.

After a few minutes, he calmed down and pulled out his cell

phone. Scrolling through his contacts, he landed on Janelle Lloyd and hit the call button.

"Hey Janie, it's T.J.," he said. "Can I come over?"

The flash of the camera leaves spots in T.J.'s vision as he finishes his walk across the stage. For the first time in weeks, he feels a sense of peace. About Erik, about Janelle... for the first time in weeks, he actually thinks things will be okay.

"Cody Louis Welik."

Cody Welik can feel the stress and pressures of high school leaving him with every step he takes across the stage.

*I wonder if anyone else felt like this when they were up here?* he thinks. *All the work, all the drama, all the highs and lows, they've all lead to this moment and once I'm across this stage, none of it matters anymore.*

He looks out to the audience and sees the faces of his friends. From Annika, his unrequited crush, to Paul, his saintly confidant, he is filled with memories of the years spent with these people who are now about to go their separate ways.

Cody reaches Mr. Hirsch and shakes his hand.

"Congratulations, Cody," Mr. Hirsch says to him.

"Thank you, sir," he replies. They look to the photographer and smile for the camera. Cody can hear his brothers, Tyler and Phin, cheering him on from the seats. He waves to his family, only slightly embarrassed over how loud they can be. Laughing, he walks on.

When he reaches the other side of the stage, he pauses to look back. The line of students left to graduate is dwindling and Mr. MacClayton is getting ready to read the next name. For a moment, Cody can visualize himself on his first day of school so many years ago, a little kid with a backpack that's a few sizes too big and a brightly colored lunchbox, his mom taking a picture of him and his brothers.

He smiles to himself, thinking of how far he's come since that day, playing it out in his mind as if it happened just last week. He turns around and continues walking. When he reaches the bottom of the steps, a high school graduate, he has only one thought.

*Now what?*

By the time he has returned to his seat, he has answered his own question.

*Anything,* he thinks. *Anything at all.*

As the line of students grows smaller and smaller, Leonard MacClayton looks down at the class list he keeps on the podium to get an idea of how many students are left to go. He pauses over a name that has a red line through it.

*Erik Charles Winters,* he thinks to himself. *Poor kid.*

Erik Winters was right when he told his friend T.J. that he was likely to be expelled from school for having cocaine at prom. He may have brought it, he may have bought it off of one of the DJ's, he doesn't remember and he knows it doesn't matter anyway. When you're the guy who left prom on a gurney, the details of how you got there don't matter so much as the simple fact that the administrators had to call an ambulance to take you away.

When he's released from the hospital, Erik's life becomes a mess of meetings and hearings. He heads to a drug rehabilitation facility and is home by the end of summer, though his mother barely lets him out of her sight. When he is able to see what's left of his friends, he knows that they look at him differently, even T.J.

*I never wanted it to be like this,* he thinks.

Having been expelled from school, he resolves to get his GED, though his plans are sidelined by a relapse in the fall that lands him back in rehab for most of the winter. It is during this second stint in rehab that he meets a girl named Ashley who has faced many of the same struggles as he has. They form a close bond, determined to stay clean together.

A year after his senior prom, Erik Winters will be well into his journey of recovery. He will be five months sober, living in a group home with Ashley and studying to earn his GED. His road will not always be easy, but he is determined to do what he needs to in order to survive.

After the last of the students return to their seats, Marvin Hirsch walks over to the podium on the stage.

"Would the graduates please stand," Marvin says. He looks into the crowd, into the faces of the young men and women he is about to release into the world, feeling a great swell of pride. What he's about to say has always been his favorite part of these ceremonies.

"Graduates, you may turn your tassels!"

# A LITTLE BIT OF
# MAGIC IN OLD TOWN

Adrienne Maschera came to town when the leaves turned orange. An artisan in her mid-thirties from another part of the world, she had made a life traveling from place to place, selling her pieces for whatever interested customers could afford to pay. Never staying in one place for too long, Adrienne set her sights on the city and arrived by train a month later.

Within a week, she had secured a small storefront in Old Town which included a two bedroom apartment on the floor above. Shortly after, she was officially open for business as an array of handmade trinkets, jewelry pieces and masks arrived in crates from all over the world just in time for Halloween.

* * *

*The Palm Reader*

Five months later, Adrienne sits at a small, iron table just outside of her shop with Vera Sugarbaker, another shop owner. Vera's store, The Old Town Herb & Gift Co., features items handmade with herbs she grows herself, ranging from candles and soaps to teas and spices. There are two glasses of iced tea on the table next to a plate with lavender shortbread cookies. It is late in the morning on one of the first warm days they have had this spring.

"Don't you just love this weather?" asks Vera, her cat eye reading glasses perched atop her messy hair.

"Oh yes, especially after such a bitterly cold winter!" replies

Adrienne. She takes a drink of tea; the scent of fresh mint lingers in the air from the leaves that float in her glass.

"I was starting to doubt if it would ever warm up," Vera says as she tucks a few strands of hair that have fallen from her barrette behind her ear.

"Me, too," says Adrienne. "So how's it going in the Plaza?"

"Hm?"

"Your neighbors, have you made any progress with getting to know them?"

"Well, I, uh... no. I haven't."

"Why not, Vera? I'm sure they've all come out of hibernation, what with the improvement in weather and all."

"Most of them have," says Vera. "They're an odd bunch, though."

"That's rich coming from you, you know," Adrienne says with a laugh.

"I know, I know... or rather, I suppose I *don't* know. They all seem like a family and I don't really... I don't feel like I fit in their family portrait."

"I understand the feeling, but you can't fault them exclusively if you haven't made an effort yourself."

Vera takes another sip of her tea.

"Why are you so anxious about getting to know your neighbors?"

"Good fences, my dear," says Vera.

"Clever," Adrienne says, nodding her head. "But Frost wasn't talking about an apartment building."

"I guess you're right," says Vera. She pauses. "But just because we live in the same building doesn't mean we have to be friends."

"But that's something you all have in common that no one else in the world would understand! Wouldn't you prefer to feel a connection to the people around you rather than..." Adrienne trails off.

"Come on, Adrienne, you've been pushing me to get to know them practically since the day we met!"

"Not since the *first* day we met," Adrienne says. "Gosh, that feels like it was so long ago."

"It was only back in November."

"It was the day I bought my first bar of soap from you!" Adrienne says, rubbing her hands together to smell the enduring scent of the oatmeal and goats milk soap she buys from Vera.

"What brought you to my shop that day?"

"Well, if I'm being honest, I'd been here almost a month and other than my landlord and my customers, I hadn't really had any other human interaction." She pauses. "Really, I was just looking for a friend."

Vera picks up a cookie and takes a bite.

"No offense, but why me? I wasn't exactly welcoming to you at first."

"There was something about you, Vera. I could tell that maybe you were in need of a friend, too." Adrienne pauses. "And besides, you think I'm the kind of person to find out there's an herb shop down the street from me that offers palm readings in the back room and I'm *not* going to try to befriend the owner?" Adrienne says with a grin.

Vera smiles.

"Point blank, you were far too interesting to let pass by."

"Wow," says Vera. "Interesting? I don't think I've ever been called interesting before in my life."

"So you see? I was right. You needed my friendship just as much as I needed yours!"

Both women laugh.

"And, of course, your selection of products didn't hurt anything, either."

"You did make a beeline for the teas once you were in the door," says Vera. "And your palate is quite sophisticated."

Adrienne smiles.

"I appreciate you buttering up my taste, but don't think you've gotten me off on too far of a tangent," she says. "Your neighbors in the Plaza… are you worried they'll be afraid of you?"

"Some of them already are," Vera says, with a cynical snort.

"The twins?"

"The terrors," says Vera. "I'd rather they stayed afraid of me."

"Oh, Vera – they're children. You had to be young once!"

"I was never *that* young."

"That I doubt, very much," says Adrienne.

Vera looks out into the street as a car passes by and sighs.

"You'd be surprised," Vera says slowly.

"Oh?"

"Well, growing up it was just my mother and me; my father died in the war. She was always a frail woman and I had to learn at an early age that the roles of parent and child aren't always so clearly defined."

Adrienne puts her hand on Vera's and gives it a squeeze before picking up another cookie.

"When my mother passed, I had nothing left out in the country where we lived, so I packed up and moved here. I didn't have much, but I was able to get an apartment and a job, my job at The Herb & Gift Co., actually.

"I made a decent living, met some interesting people... told some fascinating fortunes along the way. When the couple that opened the shop starting thinking about retirement, they came to me and asked if I'd be interested in taking over the business. So I did! Expanded the selection to sell more of the things I'd learned to make with the herbs I grow and, well, here I am."

Adrienne sits back in her chair.

"I've always been kind of a loner, even when I was a kid. Maybe it's because I had to grow up earlier than my classmates or maybe it's because the daydreams I had about them had a tendency of coming to pass a few days later, I don't know... I was just always content to be by myself." She pauses.

"I had no idea about any of that," Adrienne says quietly.

"I've never really talked about it before," says Vera.

"Thank you for sharing that with me. Really, thank you."

Adrienne smiles at Vera, who picks up a cookie.

"I guess you're right, though," she says.

"About what?" asks Adrienne.

"I guess part of me is nervous that they'll reject me if they find out about... you know..."

"How would they know about your gifts unless you told them?"

"Well how did you know?"

"Intuition."

"Exactly," says Vera. "You don't have to tell people that you have precognitive talents with a knack for accuracy for them to figure out you're the lady who reads palms in the back room of the herb shop in Old Town. It's bad enough most people think I just tinker around in the greenhouse all day."

"Why is that bad?"

"It's not what people would consider a 'normal' job, I guess."

"You could always get an office job?"

Vera looks at Adrienne over the rim of her glasses.

"Just putting things in perspective, *mon ami*," Adrienne says with a grin.

"I'm being serious though," says Vera. "Keeping myself a safe distance from people has helped me get this far in life, why stop now?"

"Was that a rhetorical question?"

"Well, I meant it as one, I guess, but if you have an answer…"

"You should stop now because shutting yourself off from everyone else will only take you so far."

"I've always been a loner with very few exceptions, present company included."

"I'm glad to be on such an exclusive list," says Adrienne. She finishes her tea. "Give it a try, Vera. Just get to know one of them, the woman with the pink curtains maybe? You've mentioned her a few times. Take her something from the store; see where the conversation goes from there. You never know when people will surprise you."

"I guess there's no harm in taking her a candle," Vera says. "And I did just make a fresh set of vanilla jars yesterday."

Adrienne smiles.

"You know, I was thinking about something the other day," she says. "And you might be able to help me."

"What's that?"

"Well, you've worked in Old Town for quite some time, right?"

"Yeah, almost since I first moved to the city."

"Right," says Adrienne. "Do you know if there's anything for the people who we see day in and day out?"

"I don't know that I follow you."

"Are there ever any celebrations? You know, a chance to get the people of Old Town together? Festivals? Fairs? All this talk about connecting with people got me thinking about our own little community."

"We used to have things like that a couple of times a year, street festivals and such, but they haven't been put on in quite some time."

"Hmm," says Adrienne, staring off down the street.

"I know that look," says Vera.

Adrienne looks to her and grins.

"I have an idea that might be worth a second thought or two."

"Intriguing…" Vera picks up her glass and finishes her tea.

The door to Adrienne's shop opens and a girl sticks her head out, her dark hair pulled into a messy bun on top of her head.

"Sorry to interrupt," she says. "Adrienne, the delivery guy is out back."

"Oh! Not a problem, Tara," says Adrienne. "Vera, have you met

Tara?"

"Y-you look familiar," Vera says to Tara.

"Tara Ellis," she says with a smile. "I give a few walking tours of Old Town a week when the weather is nice."

"I brought Tara on to help with the shop during the winter months," says Adrienne. "Tara, this is Vera who owns The Old Town Herb & Gift Co. down the way."

"Oh, yeah," says Tara. "I've seen you around! It's great to finally meet you."

Vera nods nervously as Tara goes back into the store.

"Well, I'd better get back inside," says Adrienne. "Should we try to do this again? Same time in a few days?"

"I'd like that," says Vera. The two women stand and hug good bye.

"Have a great afternoon!"

"You, too," says Vera. She waits a moment. "Adrienne?"

"Yes?"

"Thank you for being my friend. It's been so long since I've had one, I'd almost forgotten how nice it can be."

Adrienne smiles warmly.

"Don't forget what I said... you never know when people will surprise you."

* * *

*The Tour Guide*

"So tell me a little about yourself," says Adrienne. Though it is only the afternoon, the darkness outside gives the illusion that it is later in the day, the lingering snowflakes from a snowstorm that morning swirling through the cold, wintry air.

Adrienne sits in her shop, wrapped warmly in a heavy cloak, interviewing one of the final applicants to be her assistant. Though she had initially set out to run Maschera on her own, she realized after a while that if she was going to find continued success, she was going to need some help.

"My name's Tara Ellis," says the girl sitting opposite Adrienne. "I'm twenty three and I've lived in the city all my life. In the warmer months, I work as a tour guide down here, leading walking tours through Old Town for historical groups, tourists and such."

"Very interesting," says Adrienne. "How did you find yourself in that position?"

"Oh, well, I grew up coming out to Old Town with my mom and granny. Old Town's always been a special place for me and when the opportunity to work down here and show it off to people came my way, I knew I couldn't turn it down!"

"So you'd do that year round if you could?"

"Definitely," says Tara. "I even tried to convince my boss at the tour company to let us continue past October. We usually stop giving regular tours by the end of October and only do specially scheduled ones in the winter. He said it wasn't feasible but that it was an idea worth holding onto."

"Interesting," Adrienne says again. "So what else do you do? Are you in school?"

"I was," says Tara. "I graduated last year with a degree in history, but I'm still trying to figure out just where I want to go with my career."

"I think a lot of people find themselves in that boat, these days," says Adrienne. She looks down at Tara's resume in front of her. "So I see on here that you have some retail experience... that's good... you'll be comfortable working in my shop?"

"Oh, yes, definitely!"

"Excellent," says Adrienne. "Part of the position will be looking after the store when I'm away, and I'll give you plenty of notice for when I need you to do that. The rest of the time, I just need someone to help run errands and take care of little things for me, nothing too strenuous but I'm only one woman, you know?"

Tara nods.

"What kind of schedule are you looking for?" asks Adrienne.

"I have open availability right now," says Tara. "So, I'd be able to work anything you needed, really."

"With my last assistant, we set up the work schedule usually a few weeks in advance. There may be times I'll need you on nights and weekends, but it won't ever be more than thirty hours a week or so."

"That sounds great!"

Adrienne smiles.

"So, I want to talk a little more about your job as a tour guide in Old Town," says Adrienne.

"Yes?"

"What kinds of things do you cover on the tour?"

"Oh, all kinds of things, from stories straight out of the history books to local legends... a ghost story or two. We talk about all the places, shops and restaurants, the gardens and squares and about how it all makes Old Town such a unique part of town.

"Doing it for as long as I have, I started when I was fifteen, you get to know a lot of people along the way, the store owners and street performers as well as the tourists."

"Street performers?"

"Oh, yes," says Tara. "When the weather's nice, there are street performers all over Old Town. There're artists selling their work or drawing pictures for people, people that dress up and stand like statues posing for pictures with the tourists. There's this magician who comes a few times a week to put on a big show that pretty much stops traffic in the square down the street. It's incredible."

"So you're very passionate about Old Town?"

"Very much so," says Tara.

"Why? What about Old Town speaks to for you?"

"Well…" Tara starts, her voice trailing off. She thinks for a moment. "Honestly, it goes back to when I would come here with my mom and granny as a little girl. Old Town was just so magical, it felt like stepping into a place from a fairy tale. The opportunity to be a part of that story has been a driving force in my life the last few years, especially since… well, since my granny passed away."

"Oh, I'm so sorry to hear that," says Adrienne.

Tara smiles.

"So if you're hired for this position, what sets you apart from the other applicants?"

Tara thinks for a moment and takes a breath.

"You could talk to every person in this city, but not one of them would put as much of themselves into the position as I would. I can tell you're looking for someone with passion, and not one of them is as passionate as I am… about anything, really. Old Town, this job, the future… and I also bring a retail background to help you run your shop. In short, I believe myself to be exactly the candidate you're looking for."

Adrienne sits back in her chair.

"I have one more question," she says.

"Okay."

"Can you start next week?"

"Oh my God, are you serious?!" Tara almost shouts. "Yes!"

Adrienne smiles.

"I've interviewed several other candidates for this position, and not one of them had the heart to back up their ambition. I see great potential in you, Tara, and I'm very much looking forward to having you work with me. I'll give you a call in the next day or so so we can set your schedule."

"Thank you so much!"

"You're a passionate young woman," Adrienne says. "Passion makes life worth living, don't ever lose that."

\* \* \*

*The Magician*

"So you're the famous magician."

"'Famous' is kind of a lofty term to describe myself," the magician says before flipping his card table to its side. He kicks the legs in before swinging the table in on itself. Locking it closed, he leans it against the wrought iron fence that lines the square in Old Town. It is late in the afternoon and he is packing up from a day of performances.

"You're not really like the other street performers, are you?" asks Adrienne.

"What makes you say that?"

"I haven't been hearing all about them for the past few weeks from my customers."

"What can I say?" the magician says with a shrug. "People like a good show."

"I'm serious, I've been hearing all about the Old Town street performers who would be coming back when the weather warmed, but none so much as you."

Adrienne holds out her hand.

"Adrienne Maschera," she says. "I own a shop just outside of the square, up the street a ways."

"Yorick," says the magician, shaking her hand firmly. "Yorick Dalton."

"It's a pleasure to meet you."

Yorick looks up from packing his props into his rolling suitcase.

"Well hey, thanks for checking out my show," he says.

Adrienne laughs.

"You must be a busy man," she says. "I won't keep you; I just wanted to give you something, a token for good luck, if you will."

Yorick stops what he's doing and stands up, pushing his hair out of his face.

"Really?"

"Just a little something from one Old Town resident to another."

She hands him a silver medallion.

"Wow," he says, turning the aged metal over in his hand. "Thank you. Seriously, I get little things from people all the time but this is really cool."

Adrienne smiles.

"I might even be able to work it into one of my tricks."

"Oh?"

"Not that I could tell you how, you know… a magician never tells his secrets."

"Never?"

"Almost never," says Yorick. "It's funny, I never meant to become a magician, but here we are."

"Does anyone ever mean to become what they are?"

"I'd like to think so, but lately I'm not so sure."

A car drives past.

"So you never meant to become a street magician?" asks Adrienne.

Yorick smiles.

"Fell into it completely by accident," he says, zipping his suitcase closed.

Adrienne raises an eyebrow.

"How does one 'fall into' becoming a magician?"

"It literally happened by accident two summers ago," says Yorick. "I was down here visiting a friend of mine who works at the winery. A couple glasses of wine too many and the next thing I know, I'm tripping over my own two feet right into one of the guys who used to work down here."

"Another magician?"

"No," says Yorick. "An artist with little wire sculptures. I knocked into his table and sent a lot of them flying. I'd learned how to juggle as a kid so I'm trying to catch as many as I can. The next thing I know, I'm juggling four of them and the artist is freaking out because I'm screwing around with his work. Finally I get them all back onto his table and that's when I realize there's a few people who've gathered around to watch what I was doing.

"Naturally, my obnoxious ass decides to bow and that's when it happened."

"What?"

"Two of them tossed dollar bills my way and walked away. That's when it clicked – I could come out to Old Town, dick around on the street and get paid for it!"

"What were you doing at the time? For work, I mean."

"Retail… really putting my marketing degree to good use."

Adrienne nods.

"It's kind of funny, you know? You do everything you think

you're supposed to do. You work hard, you study hard, you get the good grades and then the degree and you have everything in the world going for you but when the time comes, there's always someone else, someone just a little bit better. Maybe they know someone you don't or had an extra string to pull, who knows.

"But you keep doing what you think you're supposed to, what everyone tells you, and you still wind up at square one, folding t-shirts or answering phones for a living while you wait for a call that you can only hope will come someday.

"And one day, I guess I just got tired of waiting."

"I can't say I blame you at all," says Adrienne. "So you just decided to become a street performer and that was that?"

"Not exactly," says Yorick. "It took a little while to figure out what worked and what didn't. Genevieve, my friend who worked at the winery, couldn't believe that it actually became a thing. Really though, I just had to get a permit and that took care of the paperwork side of things. I started as a juggler, mainly. Later on, I brushed up on a few tricks and developed a whole show, invested some of the initial income in a small P.A. system and a microphone and it all kind of took off from there. I'm still in retail, too, for the winter months and the steadier income."

"Your street shows are quite profitable, though?"

"Think about it," says Yorick. "There was minimal startup costs and with all the people that come through Old Town when the weather's nice, even just getting pocket change or a buck or two... all the pennies in my bucket add up after a while."

"That's incredible."

"I even got to use my marketing background a little to help get my name out there. Word of mouth spread, I did a few interviews for local media and the next thing I know, people are making a point to come to my show."

He pauses.

"It's been a fun ride," Yorick admits.

"But?"

"But I'm not sure how much longer I want to do it."

"Why?"

"I don't know, I look around and I only ever see the same people out here, day in and day out entertaining the crowd but never really getting anywhere with what they do. And when one leaves or moves away, there's always more just waiting to take their spot. Waiting... seems like that's all anyone does around here. And here I thought I was through with waiting."

"Are you still waiting for something?"

Yorick looks out toward the street.

"I shouldn't be," he says.

"Is it some*one* you're waiting for?"

He turns to face Adrienne.

"Is it that obvious?"

"I just had a hunch," says Adrienne.

Yorick sighs.

"It's this girl. Kate. We grew up together and we were always close and, I don't know, I guess she never saw me the way I saw her."

"Have you talked to her about it?"

"That's where it gets complicated," says Yorick. "You see, all the time I was waiting for her, she was waiting for someone else... and now he's back in the picture. Has been since Christmas, actually. And they've been inseparable ever since."

"I'm sorry," Adrienne says quietly.

"Don't be... I should have seen it coming, really."

"Do you still talk to either of them?"

"Oh, yes," says Yorick. "Some days are easier than others."

"Maybe you should distance yourself from them more?"

"It's not that easy, I mean, we *are* friends, you know? And I'd rather they stay in my life, since we've all known each other so long. I just... once again, I'm tired of waiting for things to happen."

"Can't you change it?"

"What do you mean?"

"You just told me how you became a magician, how you were tired of waiting around and you decided to do something about it. What if you did that again?"

Yorick thinks for a moment.

"What would I do?"

"Nothing immediately, just start thinking of new things to do, new paths to happiness. It could lead you back to school or maybe to a new calling. Do you still like doing the magic shows?"

"Well, yeah, I guess I do."

"So keep doing that for now, but start preparing for your next big adventure. That's how I've tried to live my life." She pauses. "You never know what you'll find."

"Hmm," says Yorick.

"What?"

"You've just given me a lot to think about, is all."

Adrienne smiles at him.

"If you don't mind my saying, an enterprising young man such as yourself is meant for things far greater than performing magic shows in Old Town, as popular as they are."

"I appreciate that, Adrienne."

"It's the truth."

Yorick smiles.

"I have a proposition," Adrienne says.

"Yeah?"

"It sounds like there's a close bond between all the street performers…"

"Most of them," Yorick says.

"Well, I've had an idea I've been working on the last few weeks and I thought you'd be an excellent person to talk to."

"Oh?"

"Yes, you see, I've gotten to know a few people in Old Town and I was talking the other day with a friend of mine who owns The Old Town Herb & Gift Co. – "

"You *talk* to that lady?" he asks, surprised.

"Oh, yes," says Adrienne. "Vera's actually become quite a close friend."

"Wow," says Yorick. "I didn't think she *had* friends! I mean, wow, I didn't mean for that to sound so… *mean*, but… well, she's not the easiest person to interact with."

"It was a challenge at first," Adrienne admits. "But good things take time."

Yorick nods.

"Anyway, I'd had an idea to host an event, a party kind of, to get the community of Old Town together sometime this summer. Vera told me of the street festivals they used to have in the area and I started thinking from there."

"I remember those!" Yorick says. "I used to come to those with my friends when we were kids."

Adrienne nods her head eagerly.

"So you'll help?"

"Well, what did you have in mind?"

Adrienne takes a deep breath.

"A masquerade ball."

"A masquerade ball in Old Town?" asks Yorick.

"Do you think people would even come to it?"

"I think it's kind of crazy no one has thought of that yet!"

"Really?"

"Oh, yeah!" says Yorick. "The people around here would love something like that!"

"Really!" says Adrienne, a wide smile on her face. "That's great to hear! So, would you have any interest in helping me put it on?"

"Of course," says Yorick. "I'll take any chance I can get to dust off that marketing degree."

"Excellent," says Adrienne. She looks at her watch. "Come to my shop sometime tomorrow or the day after and we can chat more about it."

"Sure!"

"I'm so excited! I love doing things like this."

"Me, too," says Yorick.

Adrienne turns toward the street.

"I really must be getting back to my shop," she says.

"Thank you," Yorick says, standing.

"For what?"

"Listening to me... reigniting my fire... making me feel like I'm not crazy."

"You're not crazy at all," says Adrienne. "Just promise me one thing."

"What?"

"Don't spend too much of your life waiting on things to happen," she says. "You're the kind of person to make them happen for yourself and if no one else has that faith in you, please remember that I do."

\* \* \*

*The Portrait Artist*

"Come on over, have a seat," says the portrait artist, gesturing toward Adrienne. He stands leaning over the back of his chair, an unbuttoned shirt hanging loosely over the tank top underneath. Though the day has only just begun, the temperature is nearing ninety degrees and he can already feel his armpits sweating.

"How much for a picture?" asks Adrienne. She is wearing a bright sundress to keep cool; a scarf holds her hair out of her face as it falls onto her bare shoulders.

"My rates are flexible," the artist says as Adrienne takes a seat opposite his drawing desk. He sits down and smiles. "By which I mean my pictures are free."

"Oh?"

"Yeah, see, I'm actually in an art class at the university downtown and this is one of the immersion projects we can do throughout the term. The school has an agreement with the business office down here that we can come out here and do this, but we can't charge anything."

"What an incredible opportunity!" says Adrienne. "I was thinking that you didn't look familiar, and I know quite a few people down here."

"Yeah, this is only my second day in Old Town. I'll be here two or three times a week, weather permitting, over the next six weeks."

"Excellent! I'm Adrienne Maschera, I own a store two blocks over."

"Pete Rangle, nice to meet you," says the artist with a smile. "So, are you still interested in a picture?"

"Of course!"

"Cool! Well, uhh, okay, sit however you feel most comfortable," says Pete as he pulls out his sketching pencil. "You get to keep it, of course, I just have to take a picture for my class portfolio."

"Not a problem," says Adrienne. "What media do you use?"

"I start with pencils to get a basic sketch," he says. "Then I just kind of go from there. I have some oil pastels, a few pieces of charcoal for shadowing. Kind of a mixed bag."

"I can't wait to see how it turns out," says Adrienne, smiling at the couple who have stopped to watch Pete start his sketch. "I'm sure it will be a masterpiece!"

Pete laughs.

"I don't know that I'd go *that* far," he says. "But I'll do my best."

Adrienne sits in silence for a few minutes as Pete works intently on sketching out the shapes that will become her facial features. His eyes dart from the paper to her face as he tries to commit her proportions to memory. He wipes sweat from his brow, his other hand moving gracefully across the page.

"It's gonna be a hot one today," says Adrienne.

"I know," says Pete. "Really makes me glad I decided to take this class during summer session!"

"Are you studying art?"

"No, but I'm minoring in art history."

"What are you majoring in?"

"Communications, at the moment," he says. "Started out as a public relations major but then switched... who knows, though, I may end up going back to that."

"Well, you have time to figure everything out," says Adrienne.

"Yeah, it's the tuition that's the problem."

"Are you working? Other than this, I mean."

"I wait tables a few nights a week at a restaurant downtown. It can be hit or miss depending on the night." He pauses. "I'm on scholarship, but that doesn't cover everything."

Adrienne nods.

After a few more minutes of sketching, Pete looks up.

"Could you shake your head a little bit for me?" he asks. "I want to see how your hair falls, I want to make sure I get it right."

"Like this?" Adrienne pulls her fingers through her hair, shaking her head gently.

"Excellent," says Pete, sketching furiously. "Thanks."

"So what else do you do?" asks Adrienne. "Besides school and work and drawing people."

Pete laughs.

"Well, on the rare occasion that the boyfriend and I have a night off together, we'll go to a movie or something." He pauses. "That doesn't happen a lot, though."

"What's his name?"

"Dillon."

"How long have you two been together?"

"A little over a year," says Pete. "We got together after my ex and I…. well, we got back together after my ex and I split."

"I see," says Adrienne. "You got *back* together?"

"Yeah," says Pete. "I don't really talk about it much."

"Oh, I'm sorry."

"You're alright, it's not like *I* have a problem with it. Dillon just doesn't like when I talk about Tyler."

"Was it a nasty breakup?"

"Yeah, I mean, it was a complicated situation."

"How so, if you don't mind my asking?"

"Long story short, I was kind of talking to Dillon before I met Tyler and then that became pretty serious pretty quickly. It didn't last, though, and when Tyler and I broke up, Dillon gave me a second chance. We've been together ever since, but Tyler's still a part of my life and Dillon isn't always happy about that."

"Understandable," says Adrienne. "But why is he still a part of your life?"

"He and I were going to the same school, so we'd keep running into each other. It turns out we actually make pretty good friends, despite a few bumps in the road along the way."

Adrienne raises an eyebrow and Pete sighs.

"He had a habit of writing me letters for a while. Tyler, I mean."

"What kind of letters?"

"He said he realized too late the mistake he made in letting me go. The letters were sweet at first, I could tell he was sorry things ended between us the way that they did. He blamed himself, but our relationship just wasn't working; I don't think either of us was ready for the other.

"The letters were flattering, really, but after a while they got old. And to be honest, they didn't change anything. I'd moved on and he needed to do the same."

"Did you tell him that?"

"No, I probably should have, but... I don't know, I guess I was just trying to ignore them and hope the whole thing would go away." He smirks. "That was always the problem when we were together, really. I think we both knew we were done before we actually ended things, but neither of us wanted to face the reality so we ignored it and hoped things would just magically work out.

"Neither of us was perfect, but I think we were both doing the best we could at the time, I really do."

"But that's all you *can* do, though, you know? Do your best and let the rest sort itself out?"

"I guess so," says Pete. "Tyler's not a bad guy. I hope he finds someone the way I found Dillon. He deserves to be happy."

Adrienne smiles.

"Like I said, I'm sure things will sort themselves out."

Pete nods as he continues to work on Adrienne's portrait. After a few more minutes of silence between the two, he leans back and looks from his portrait to Adrienne's face.

"Alright," he says. "I think it's finished!"

"Hooray!" Adrienne yells, clapping her hands a few times. "May I see it?"

Pete takes a picture of the drawing with his phone. He unclips the paper from his desk and turns it around so Adrienne can see. She gingerly takes it from him, studying the image closely.

"This is amazing," she says quietly. She looks up at Pete. "Thank you! Your work is incredible!"

Though Pete's cheeks are already tinged with redness from the heat, they turn a deeper shade of scarlet.

"You're welcome," he says humbly.

"I have to give you something for this! Talent like yours deserves to be compensated," she says, holding out a twenty dollar bill.

"Oh! I can't accept that much," says Pete.

"Go on," Adrienne says, holding the bill in midair. "Take it, you've earned it."

Pete slowly takes Adrienne's tip and slips it into his pocket. Adrienne sits mesmerized by Pete's portrait as he tidies his desk.

"Pete, do you ever do commission work?"

He looks up.

"Sometimes," he answers. "It depends on the project and what else I have going on at the time. Why, do you have something you need help with?"

"I do, actually. I'm organizing a Masquerade Ball later this summer, just an event to get everyone in the community together and celebrate Old Town. Would you have any interest in helping me with the artwork for the posters? Maybe a few flyers?"

"Oh yeah!" says Pete. "I could totally do stuff like that for you! What did you have in mind?"

Adrienne notices a man and a woman looking at the sign by Pete's desk and can sense they are debating whether or not they want to sit for a portrait.

"I think you're about to have your next subjects," says Adrienne. "I won't keep you, but maybe if you have some time later, you could come by my shop? I'm just two blocks over, my store is called Maschera. Come in when you're finished and I'll show you some of the ideas I have."

"Sounds like a plan," Pete says, smiling. "I'll see you later today!"

"I look forward to it," Adrienne says, standing. She and Pete shake hands and before she leaves, she leans in and quietly says, "Remember, do your best and keep your head held high, everything that's supposed to happen will sort itself out."

\* \* \*

*The Historian*

"What do you think?" asks Adrienne. She has just opened a parcel containing fifty copies of a poster that Pete designed advertising the upcoming Masquerade Ball.

"I like them!" Tara says enthusiastically. The poster features an array of stylized masks as well as the information about the event, which will be held in Adrienne's store.

"The colors printed out very true to Pete's original," says Adrienne.

"Oh yeah," says Tara. "I really like the purple one toward the bottom there."

Adrienne looks at the mask Tara is pointing toward.

"You know I have one similar to that with the other masks toward the back? It just came in last week," says Adrienne.

"Really!" says Tara. "I hadn't seen the new masks yet; I'll take a look at it later this afternoon."

The door to Maschera opens, the attached bell jingling, as a burst of the heat from outside rushes into the store. An older couple enters and closes the door quickly to keep any more of the cool air from escaping. They smile at both Adrienne and Tara.

"Hello," says Adrienne. "Welcome to Maschera!"

The couple nod their heads and murmur their hello's.

"Alright, I'm gonna go get these put up," Tara tells Adrienne.

"Perfect, let me know if you need anything while you're out," says Adrienne. "And take a bottle of water – it's hot out there, sweetie, you need to stay hydrated."

"Will do!" says Tara, picking up the box of posters. She ducks through the curtain to the back room of the store and grabs a bottle from the refrigerator before slipping out the back door.

With Tara gone, Adrienne turns her full attention to the two customers presently browsing her collection of handmade jewelry.

"Hello again," she says, approaching them.

"Hi there," says the woman.

"Is there anything I can help you find?" she asks.

"Oh, no thank you," says the woman. "We're just browsing."

"Alright, well please don't hesitate if you have any questions. My name is Adrienne, by the way."

"Nice to meet you; I'm Marilyn," says the woman. "This is my husband, Leonard."

Leonard nods at Adrienne.

"Pleasure to meet you both," says Adrienne. Marilyn moves on to look at a shelf featuring sculptures of various creatures, including trolls, mermaids and dragons. Adrienne turns to walk back to the counter when Leonard stops her.

"You have quite a selection of merchandise," he says.

"Thank you!" Adrienne says, turning around. "I create a lot of the things you see in here based on materials I find or inspirations I've had on my travels. The rest I order from the various artists I've met from around the world."

"There's really no shop quite like yours down here," he says. "In

Old Town, I mean."

"I appreciate that," says Adrienne. "I try to provide one-of-a-kind pieces so anyone who buys something from me feels like they've made a special purchase. Are you very familiar with Old Town?"

"Marilyn and I think of ourselves as Old Town aficionados," he says with a laugh. "We both enjoy eating at all the little restaurants and cafés down here and she can't get enough of the shops."

"How have I not seen either of you in here before, then?" Adrienne jokes.

"Well, we tend to frequent the restaurants more than the stores," Leonard admits. "And there are so many, it's hard to hit them all!"

Adrienne laughs.

"Just giving you a bit of trouble," she says, grinning. "I have the impression that the shops aren't your favorite part of the area?"

Leonard seems to think for a moment.

"She enjoys the shops as much as I enjoy the history of Old Town."

"Ahh, a history buff."

"You could say that," he says. "I'm a high school history teacher. Or, well, I *was*… I just retired last month."

"Well, congratulations!" says Adrienne.

"Thank you," Leonard says. "I taught at Central High for forty one years."

"Wow!"

"It didn't seem like that long while I was still doing it, but now that I'm on the other side, I can't believe I was there for so long! Somedays it feels like I just found out I'd be going to work there… until I look in the mirror of course," he says.

"Forty one years devoted to educating young people is an incredible accomplishment and something to be very, very proud of," Adrienne says.

Leonard smiles as a shadow of sadness passes over his face.

"It was a time," he says.

Adrienne can sense that something is wrong.

"And after all that time, leaving it behind must be difficult."

Leonard nods.

"I must admit, it's becoming more difficult than I thought it would be."

"How so, if you don't mind my asking."

"Well, I don't know… I just, I had such a routine with teaching and the school year and my time off and now that I don't have that, I feel like I'm facing an endless summer. Of course, I'll be going back to Central to sub from time to time, but that will only be a few times each semester and the students won't be *mine* anymore... I'll just have them for a day or two and then hand them back over to their regular teacher."

Leonard sighs.

"It's incredibly freeing, but to be honest, there's so much possibility that I'm finding it to be overwhelming. To look forward to it is one thing, but to actually be living through it is a different experience entirely."

Adrienne nods.

"That's understandable."

"I guess I just don't know where to start, what to do first."

Adrienne thinks for a moment.

"If I were in your shoes, I would start by thinking about what I enjoy doing the most. I'd say it's pretty clear you were passionate about history, having taught it for over four decades."

Leonard nods.

"And you said you and Marilyn very much enjoy being down in Old Town?"

"Oh yes," says Leonard. "We're down here two to three times a week, at least."

"What if you were to do something that brought those two interests together?"

Leonard raises an eyebrow.

"How do you mean?"

"Well, you may have seen Tara, my assistant, earlier when you walked in? When she's not working for me, she gives walking tours of Old Town."

"I thought she looked familiar!"

Adrienne smiles.

"I could talk to her about that if you like?"

"I don't know," says Leonard. "My knees aren't what they used to be and I had an episode of heat exhaustion last year... As much as I would love that, I don't know that I could handle the physical side of it."

"True, Tara's told me that the job *can* be physically demanding."

Leonard thinks for a moment.

"You know what though," Leonard says slowly. "I think there *might* be something I could do that would involve both of those things..."

"Oh?"

"Old Town is very rich in culture and history," he says. "And just because I may not be able to guide people in person, that doesn't mean I can't share the stories of Old Town with them in another way!"

Marilyn walks up.

"Did you find anything that caught your eye?" Adrienne asks.

"Oh, all of it," Marilyn says quickly. "You have so many fascinating things in here!"

"Mare, I was telling Adrienne here about how much we enjoy Old Town and she got me thinking…"

"Oh, don't bring up the idea of moving down here again! You know I would in a heartbeat but I like being so close to the grandkids!"

"No, no," says Leonard. "Not that – she got me thinking about how I could put my knowledge and experience with Old Town to use and I thought *What if I wrote a book about Old Town?* It would be a bit of history, a bit of a walking guide – you could even add some anecdotes of your own!"

Marilyn stares at her husband for a moment.

"I think that's a great idea!" she finally says.

A wide grin spreads across Adrienne's face.

"Well, I for one can't wait to read this book!" Adrienne says before turning to Marilyn. "Are you ready to check out?"

"I am," says Marilyn, placing a small mermaid statue on the counter. "I just can't pass her up!"

"An excellent choice," Adrienne says, ringing Marilyn out.

"What's this?" Leonard asks, gesturing toward one of the posters for the Masquerade Ball.

"Oh! I should have thought of that earlier," says Adrienne. "I'm hosting a Masquerade Ball in a few weeks for the shop owners and some of the street performers, basically anyone who wants to connect with the community in Old Town."

Leonard and Marilyn glance at each other.

"I would be honored if the two of you could make it!"

"We'd love to!" says Leonard.

"Excellent," Adrienne says, clapping her hands. She carefully wraps the mermaid, placing her in a bag and handing it to Marilyn. "Here you go."

"Thank you, dear."

"Anytime," says Adrienne. "I hope to see you both again soon!"

"Oh, we'll be back," says Leonard. "I'm going to get cracking on the book when we get home! I'll bring you some writing samples as soon as I have them ready."

"Excellent," says Adrienne. "And remember – don't be too overwhelmed by the possibilities that lay before you. Find what you're truly passionate about and run with it! So long as you're doing something you love, you can't go wrong."

* * *

*The Pickpocket*

On a balmy summer's eve, Adrienne weaves through the guests at the masquerade ball, mingling and talking with everyone in attendance. Her dress swirls around her ankles as she dances through the crowd, an ornate pink mask affixed to her face.

The simple marketing campaign Yorick put together proved to be quite effective, as the turnout far exceeded what Adrienne had hoped for; the crowd spills out onto the sidewalk in front of her store. The various business owners and performers relished the idea of the masquerade ball and the question of when the next event would be was already a topic of conversation throughout Maschera.

Adrienne takes a step back to look at the crowd. Music pulses through the room, wine glasses clink. Shop owners mingle with customers while trays of food are walked around; there is a constant sound of laughter. Adrienne smiles to herself.

She is talking with Yorick and his date, Rachel, when her eyes first land on a dark figure standing in the corner.

He stands ominously alone, dressed in all black from his shoes to his jacket. His black hair is spiked straight up; he wears no masquerade mask. His eyes dart from person to person in the room.

Adrienne excuses herself and takes a deep breath as she walks toward him.

"Hello, Max," she says.

He shoots her a dirty look.

"How do you know my name?" he finally says.

"I've gotten to know a lot about Old Town in the time I've lived here," she says. "That, of course, includes you."

He stares at her, her grey eyes piercing through the pink plaster of her mask.

"Oh?"

"Oh, yes," says Adrienne. "You think people don't see you, that they don't notice you hanging around Old Town like a shadow, lifting this and that. You think people don't notice when the little things go missing, a few dollars from a pocket or a keychain from a counter. But all those little things add up, Max."

"I don't know what you're talking about."

"I think you do. I'll give you an example," Adrienne says slowly, looking around the room before finally spotting the person she was looking for. "See that girl over there in the feathered mask? Her name is Genevieve. She works at the winery down in the square."

"So?"

"So, back in November, she was visited by an old friend and he had some pocket money go missing. He didn't think anything of it, figured it fell out of his coat somewhere along the way, causing him to get a smaller coffee than he'd wanted. No *serious* harm done there, but you and I both know where that money went."

"Are you accusing me of stealing?"

"We both know that money helped pay for a pack of cigarettes later that night."

"You're full of shit, you crazy bitch," says Max.

Adrienne shakes her head.

"Am I? Right until I walked up to you, were you not trying to figure out how best to get your hands inside the purse of my dear friend Vera, which, incidentally, is a very, *very* bad idea?" She pauses. "The truth hurts when you hear it from someone else, doesn't it, Max?"

"Are you fucking threatening me?"

"No," says Adrienne. "I'm giving you an opportunity to see yourself from the outside in, to fully realize where you fit in the puzzle of life. You think people don't notice you, but they do.

"People know you're a thief, Max. You tried to steal from your classmates at your prom; you steal from strangers in Old Town. People warn their friends about you. Is that how you want to be known? To be remembered?"

Max looks to his shoes and back to Adrienne's face, his lips pursed.

"You think I give a fuck what anyone else thinks?"

"I think you do. You'll deny it before God, but deep, deep down, you do."

Max rolls his eyes.

"Max, you're already under investigation for the fire that destroyed the South Side Pier, I thi – "

"How the fuck do you know about that?!" he shouts. A few people spin around to see what's going on, turning away only when

Adrienne nods in their directions.

"I told you, Max, you think people don't see you, but they do. You're only eighteen years old... what's next? All the booze, the drugs... sex... how are you going to pay for everything once the pockets around you dry up? With your body? Your life? You're on a slippery slope, and only you can make the choice to change."

Max looks away from Adrienne.

"You could start that change tonight, Max... what do you think?"

"I think..." he says before trailing off, his eyes going out of focus for a moment. He shakes his head a little and looks back to Adrienne straight in the face.

"I think you're a crazy, stupid bitch," he says defiantly. "And I'm getting the fuck out of this place. This party's fucking lame anyway!"

Max storms through the crowd in Maschera toward the exit, cursing under his breath as he passes the unblinking eyes of a ventriloquist dummy propped up on a shelf.

Adrienne looks after him sadly.

"That was your chance, Max," she says to herself. She sighs. "Can't win them all, I guess."

\* \* \*

*The Artisan*

On the night of the storm, Adrienne Maschera sits alone on the chaise lounge in her apartment, sipping a cup of jasmine tea. She wears a thin nightgown to keep cool on the summer night, her legs nestled under a chenille blanket. The shadows on the wall dance in the flickering light of a candle; the storm has knocked out most of the power in Old Town.

She sees lightning in the distance through the rain drops that remain on her bedroom window.

*That was some storm,* she thinks, raising her cup to her lips. *I'm glad Old Town made it through without any major damage.*

She sets her cup on the stand next to her and leans back, staring at the ceiling.

*Have I really been here for almost a year?* she thinks. *In a few months, yes, I guess so...*

Adrienne remembers the first day she came to the city, alone except for her own suitcase. Despite knowing no one around her, she set out on her journey, determined to make the best of her time in the city.

That time would, of course, be coming to an end soon. She will tell Tara first that within the next few weeks, she will be packing up and moving on to her next destination.

*Sweet Tara*, thinks Adrienne. *She's such a good hearted girl. I couldn't have done any of this without her. I'll have to leave her a letter of recommendation that she can use in my absence…*

*I'll have to tell Vera soon, too*, she thinks. *That won't be easy, but she'll be alright…* Adrienne thinks of her friend Vera, the palm reader, and how far she's come from being the stuttering owner of the herb shop down the way.

*Even now, she's with her neighbors*, thinks Adrienne, picturing Vera in a darkened apartment with the other tenants of the Plaza at Garden Park.

*Six months ago, there's not a chance that would be happening. I'm so proud of her*. Adrienne thinks of the dummy downstairs and the liking Vera has taken to it; she decides to leave him with Vera as a parting gift. She will take what she can pack with her and have the rest shipped to wherever she ends up next.

*Where should I go?* she wonders, looking at the map she has hung on her wall. Next to it hangs the portrait that Pete Rangle drew for her at the beginning of the summer. She picks up her cup of tea and takes another sip.

*Pete really did an incredible job with the posters for the ball*, she thinks. *I hope they continue to have events like that down here after I'm gone… I'm sure they will, everyone had such a great time at the Masquerade Ball.*

Lightning flashes again followed by a low rumble of thunder a few seconds later.

*They would be smart to keep Yorick on hand, too*, she thinks. *It was his plan that got the word out for the ball, which made sure everyone knew it was happening and that people would attend. He's another one that's going places.*

*And of course the MacClaytons, dear Leonard and darling Marilyn… it's a shame I won't be able to read their book*, she thinks. *Maybe I'll track down a copy someday.*

*But then there's Max… I hope he gets himself sorted out before it's too late. It's never too late to change, I guess, but* he's *going to have to want to change his ways, no one else can do it for him.* She pauses in her thinking for another drink of tea.

*You can't dwell on him*, she tells herself. *You came here to help those who needed it, Adrienne. But you can't help anyone who doesn't want it.*

Adrienne pulls the blanket that's covering her legs up to her shoulders, folding her arms across her breasts as she thinks of all the people she has met during her time in the city, the way she's seen them grow in such a short time.

*I will miss them all,* she thinks. *Very much.*

Another flash of lightning gives way to thunder as Adrienne picks up her cup of tea, finishing her drink with drowsy movements.

*But it's time to move on,* she thinks to herself. *Time for my next big adventure... I still have time to figure out the details. It's been awhile since I've seen my sisters... maybe I'll pay them a visit. We'll see.*

Pushing the blanket aside, she stands and stretches, walking over to the stand where the flame on the wick stands tall as wax drips onto the candlestick.

*For now, it's time to sleep.*

Adrienne puckers her lips and blows out the candle, plunging the room into a darkness that is pierced only by the distant lightning that still flashes over the city.

# THE STORM

She stands on the balcony overlooking the yard, her elbows on the railing and a cigarette casually perched between her fingers. She brings it to her lips and draws a breath, exhaling a cloud of smoke into the air only a few moments later.

Lightning flashes in the distance followed quickly by a long rumble of thunder.

The door behind her slides open, allowing the sounds of the party to escape, a mix of idle chatter and jazz music. A man steps out, quickly closing the door behind him. He approaches her cautiously.

"Hello," she says without turning around.

"Hello."

She takes another drag of her cigarette.

"Can I have a light?" he asks, pulling a cigarette out from behind his ear.

"Sure," she says turning around, the rhinestones around the bust of her white dress sparkling under the terrace lights. She lights his cigarette from the cherry of her own. He holds it between the forefinger and thumb of his left hand, inhaling sharply.

"Thanks," he says.

"Don't mention it," she replies, turning away to look across the yard again. Another streak of lightning races across the sky, this one followed by a louder crack of thunder.

"Looks like this could be a pretty bad storm, don't you think?" he asks. She turns her head to face him, noting how the deep green of his shirt brings out the color of his eyes. He puts his cigarette to his lips once again.

"Quite," she says curtly.

They stand in silence for a moment.

"Don't you find it odd that there are so many – "

He is interrupted by a loud pop from inside followed by a thunderous crash.

"What the…" he says, trailing off.

The door suddenly flings open; another young woman stands there panting. Screams can be heard from inside as her eyes dart from the woman to the man, her orange earrings swinging wildly with the movements.

"Come quickly," she says.

"What's going on?" asks the man.

"What was that noise?" asks the woman.

The woman in the doorway takes a deep breath before speaking.

"There's been a murder!"

* * *

Two weeks earlier, Chelle Mastens walks out the back door of Caramaya's Bar and Grille to find Jade Verrit leaning against the brick wall of the building. She is looking down at her phone, tapping the screen quickly as a wisp of smoke escapes the cigarette between her lips.

"Mack said you were looking for me?"

Jade looks up from her phone and takes the cigarette from her mouth.

"Hey," she says. "I was! Guess who I just heard from."

"Bobby?"

Jade raises an eyebrow.

"Cute," she says.

"Oh yeah, sorry," Chelle says quickly, looking down.

"It's okay," says Jade. "Lizzy finally texted me back and she's going to be in town in a few weeks!"

"Oh, that's awesome!"

"She's coming in for four days. She's got some modeling audition, but wants to spend the rest of her trip catching up with Tara and me."

"That'll be fun," says Chelle. "I know you've missed her."

"Yeah," says Jade. "I figure we can show her around, hit up the bars and stuff while she's here."

"Oh! You know what else we could do?"

"Hmm?"

"A murder mystery dinner!"

Jade looks at her and blinks, flicking some ash off the end of her cigarette.

"Like go to a dinner theater?"

"No, no," says Chelle. "Not exactly... I saw this thing online about these party games that they sell now, it was this big fad a while ago and they're coming back. You invite a group of people over and everyone has a character to play for the evening. There's different stories you can get to play out but the basic gist is that there's a murder and everyone works to solve it."

Jade thinks for a moment.

"That could actually be kind of fun," she says. "Can I nominate someone to play the victim?"

Chelle smirks.

"That bad, huh?"

"He's just been distant lately," says Jade. "And when I try to bring it up to him, he acts like nothing's wrong."

"Kind of sounds like where I was at with Simon right before we..."

"I know, I know," says Jade.

"But that was me and Simon! We're talking about you and Bobby, totally different scenario."

"True."

"So what do you think, you want me to pick up one of those games?"

"You know what? Do it. It'll be something new for the group and Lizzy won't feel weird about being thrown into a group of strangers because everyone will be playing someone else."

"Great!" she says. "I'll have it at my place."

"Sounds good to me," says Jade.

Chelle looks at the watch on her wrist and groans.

"Do you think I can blame going over on my break on a broken watch?" she asks.

"It's worth a shot," says Jade.

Chelle smiles.

"I'm heading back in, you coming?"

"I'll be in in a minute."

* * *

Two days later, Jade uncorks a bottle of wine in Chelle's apartment. Chelle sits on the couch, looking through the paperwork that came with the mystery party game she purchased, "Murder at Minuit Mansion". Music plays softly from Chelle's stereo, masking the sounds of the air conditioner and a dog barking outside.

"Hey Jade, check this out! It comes with a suggested menu and everything," she says, looking from one paper to the next.

"That's cool," says Jade. "Do you wanna do that or still have people bring stuff?"

"Let's still do potluck," Chelle says, reading through a recipe.

Jade walks over with the open bottle of wine and two glasses, both of which she fills with a hearty pour.

"Alright," she says, picking up a page with character descriptions. "Let's figure out who will be playing who!"

Chelle takes her glass of wine and picks up a notepad, the top page of which has ten names scribbled in a list.

"Okay, who do you want to do first?" she asks.

Jade takes the pad from Chelle and skims the list.

"Let's pick our characters," she says. "Have you read through any of them?"

"A few," says Chelle. "There was one I thought of you might like, let me see..."

Jade swishes the wine around the bottom of her glass before taking a drink.

"Oh, here we go! Miss Snow."

"Miss Snow?"

"Yeah," says Chelle, looking at the paper. "Listen to this: 'A fresh faced student, Miss Snow has spent the last four months interning for Senator Minuit. How far will she go to ensure a long, successful career?' How does that sound?"

"It sounds like I'm a naughty intern," says Jade. "What other characters are there to choose from?"

"Miss Pumpkin, Madame Crimson, Justice Thistle and Priestess Rose... it says here that Justice Thistle, Captain Cobalt and Dr. Umber can be played by either a man or a woman."

"Tell me about Priestess Rose."

"'With glimpses into the future and messages from the afterlife, Priestess Rose has been Senator Minuit's spiritual advisor for years. But what secrets from the other side does she keep from him?'"

"Oh, let's give that one to Lizzy!" says Jade.

"Alright," Chelle says, writing "Priestess Rose" next to Lizzy's name. "What about you?"

"If you're alright with it, I'll be Miss Snow."

"Okay," says Chelle, adding notes to the paper.

"Who are you gonna be?" asks Jade.

"I was leaning toward Miss Pumpkin," says Chelle.

"What's her deal?"

"'Miss Pumpkin is Senator Minuit's cherished goddaughter, the daughter of a close friend. With no apparent heir, is she alone named in the senator's will?'"

"I feel like we're casting a play!" Jade says, laughing. "So you're going to be Miss Pumpkin... who all else are we working with?"

"Let's see... if you and me and Lizzy are taken care of, that leaves Graham and Bobby, Tyler, Mack, Tara... and Brannon and Kate," says Chelle. "I'm glad we invited those two, by the way!"

"Me too," says Jade. "We'll just keep it between us that they only got an invite because Phin and Carrie already had plans."

"Uhh, yeah," says Chelle, winking at Jade. "I was thinking Bobby could be Sir Emerald?"

"Let me see that paper," says Jade. She picks up the page with the character descriptions on it and reads softly to herself, "'Sir Emerald and Senator Minuit were roommates at a European boarding school in their teens. Is their friendship strong enough to keep the ghosts of the past buried?'"

"Well?"

"Yeah, he'll like that one. Oh, hey, what about Dr. Umber for Graham? Says here he's 'a world renown psychiatrist'... weren't you just telling me you how much you like it when Graham talks nerdy to you?" Jade asks, giggling.

"Oh shut up!" Chelle says, laughing. "That's fine, I'll put Graham down for Dr. Umber. What about Tara?"

Jade looks up and down the paper in her hand while Chelle finishes the wine in her glass.

"How about Justice Thistle? It says the character can be played by a man or woman but it sounds like the part was written more for a woman. 'A celebrated judge, Justice Thistle oversaw a scandalous case Senator Minuit was implicated in many years ago. Why have the two remained in such close contact over the years?' Wanna bet she's a booty call?"

"Oh crap, mystery solved," Chelle says, giggling. "I'll put Tara down for Justice Thistle. That leaves Tyler, Mack, Brannon and Kate."

"Well, it looks like Madame Crimson is the only female part left, so that's who Kate will have to be."

"And it has nothing to do with her red hair!"

Both girls laugh.

"So what does it say about Madame Crimson?"

"'The mysterious Madame Crimson is an ambassador from a foreign country that Senator Minuit has encountered many times. Is their relationship strictly professional?' Oh my God, Chel, are they hooking up, too? Is this us accidentally hosting a key party?!"

Both girls dissolve into a fit of giggles and refill their wine glasses.

"Okay," says Chelle. "Let's get back on track... I'm thinking Tyler for Mr. Mist, the personal assistant. And what about Mack for Captain Cobalt?"

"The army friend?" asks Jade. "Nah, I was seeing Brannon as more of the army friend, and having Mack play the accountant."

Chelle thinks for a moment.

"You know what," she says. "I like that better. So we'll have Mack play Mr. Gold and Brannon will be Captain Cobalt."

"And is that all of them?"

"I think so," Chelle says, looking at the guest list on her pad of paper and making sure each person has an assigned character. "Yup, everyone's accounted for."

"So, wait, no one plays the senator?"

"No, I don't think so," says Chelle. "The host instructions said that the host could play the senator or any additional guests, but since we had a list of ten, I figured we'd leave it at that. Besides, there aren't any extra missions or anything for the senator to play, so it would be kind of a useless part."

"Missions?"

"Oh, yeah! Check this out," says Chelle. She pulls a stack of passport-sized documents out of the party box. "Each guest gets one of these and you aren't supposed to open them until the night of the party. Each one contains information about the character you're playing and some clues for you to use as well as a page of notes and three additional missions to uncover additional clues."

"Well that's... thorough," says Jade. She takes a sip from her glass and looks back toward Chelle. "Wanna read them all now?"

Chelle snorts.

"I kind of do," admits Chelle. "But we'll play fair... besides, everyone would know if we'd read them beforehand."

"Alright, alright," says Jade.

"Oh, look! The game comes with a CD, too! It says to start it about ten minutes after the last guest arrives. I guess it's timed based on that or something because it says the CD will go over instructions for the game with everyone."

"That's cool," says Jade, smiling. "I'm excited!"

"I know," Chelle says. "I'm glad we decided to do this!" She tops off the wine glasses on the coffee table with the remaining wine in the bottle. It makes a hollow clink as she sets it back down.

"Good thing I brought two," Jade says.

"Oh, thank God!" says Chelle, her cheeks rosy. "We've got a party to plan!"

* * *

The day before the party, Jade finds Chelle in the kitchen at Caramaya's.

"Hey," she says. "Lizzy just landed! She's on her way to baggage claim."

"Awesome! Is she heading straight to your place?"

"No, she's gonna come get my key first."

"Oh, yay!" says Chelle. "I can't wait to see her!"

"I know she's excited to see everyone again," Jade says, smiling. "So did Tyler find you yet?"

"No, why?"

"Well, you didn't hear this from me, but apparently Alan's been accepted into that yearlong study abroad program so he's trying to spend time with Tyler before he leaves, and Tyler's wanting to know if he can bring him tomorrow night."

"Oh, damnit," says Chelle. "Seriously?"

"Yeah," says Jade. "He asked me but I told him he had to double check with you because it's at your place."

"I – uh… shit. Shit!" Chelle yells. "What can we do? We can't say no!"

"Yeah we can."

"But then he probably won't come… and if he does still come, he'll probably be pissy all night."

Jade shrugs.

"Fucking Alan," says Chelle. "At least he'll be out of the picture once he leaves."

One of the line cooks comes to the counter with two plates of food.

"Order's up, Chel," she says.

"Thanks," says Chelle, loading the plates onto a tray.

"He's at the bar," says Jade.

"Alright, I'll stop by after I drop off this order," Chelle says.

"Thanks for the heads up."

"No problem," Jade says as Chelle walks off.

*Goddamn Alan, showing up whenever he feels like and screwing with him,* she thinks as she walks to the dining room. *And damn Tyler for not putting a stop to it!*

She delivers the food and walks over to the bar where Tyler is drying wine glasses.

"Hey," says Chelle. "Jade said you were looking for me?"

Chelle's exasperated tone is all Tyler needs to hear to know that Jade told her why he wanted to talk to her.

"Oh hey," he says, trying to be extra cheerful. "Yeah, I was... um, so I know the mystery dinner is tomorrow night and all and I was just wondering if Alan could come? I mean, he's getting ready to go abroad for a year and I didn't want to just show up with him because I know we have assigned parts and all, so I wanted to ask befo–"

"Yeah," Chelle interrupts. "That's fine."

"Really?" Tyler asks. "It won't be a problem with the game or anything?"

"Not really," Chelle says slowly, an idea coming to her. "Actually, there's an eleventh character he could play."

"Yeah?"

"Yeah," says Chelle. "He can be the senator."

"Okay," says Tyler.

"To be clear, the senator is the one who gets murdered, so there won't be a whole lot for him to do, but that way he'll at least have a character."

"Hey, something's better than nothing, right?"

Chelle forces a smile.

"I've gotta check on my tables," she says and turns to walk away.

"Hey wait," says Tyler.

Chelle stops.

"Thank you," he says. "I know Alan's not your favorite person... hell, I barely know where I stand with him, myself. But I appreciate you letting him come."

As Chelle tries to decide on a response, the pause in conversation becomes an awkward silence.

"Don't mention it," she finally says. "I'll stop back by later."

Tyler smiles at Chelle then looks at the television behind the bar, where meteorologist Rex Benford is talking with one of the news anchors.

" …with the heat wave we've been having and this unseasonable cool front moving through the low pressure system, we're expecting a severe weather outbreak that could be the worst we've seen in the last ten years," he says. "The highest risk being, of course, tomorrow evening."

Tyler notices a customer walk up to the bar and turns away from the television.

*Tomorrow's going to be interesting, that's for sure,* he thinks.

\* \* \*

"Come on, Graham! Everyone's gonna be here soon," Chelle says as her boyfriend wraps arms wrapped around her waist from behind.

"Who says *that's* what I'm after?" he asks.

Chelle laughs.

"Maybe I'm the killer," Graham whispers into her ear.

Chelle snorts and continues slicing peppers.

"What if *I'm* the killer?" she asks, holding her knife up.

"Well, you're killing this veggie tray," he says, grabbing a carrot and backing away from his girlfriend. She spins around to face him.

"Smooth."

"You look great, by the way."

"Thanks," she says, swiveling her hips in her orange dress, her orange earrings swinging with the movement. "Do you think everyone will wear their colors?"

"Probably," says Graham. "You and Jade may have stressed the importance of it to everyone a few… hundred… times."

Chelle rolls her eyes and grins.

"Seriously though, you two have planned a hell of a party. Try to enjoy it?"

"Okay," says Chelle. She gives Graham a kiss on the cheek and turns back to finish preparing the tray of vegetables. "I hope the weather holds out."

"It rained earlier today," says Graham. "Maybe it's done?"

There is a knock at the door.

"I'll get it!" Graham says.

Chelle smiles as she rinses her cutting board in the sink.

*Tonight's going to be fun,* she thinks. *Even if Alan's coming.*

"Hey Chel!" Jade says, her heels clanking on the floor as she walks into the kitchen and sets down two paper bags loaded with food. She is followed by a curly haired blonde in a floral dress. "You remember Lizzy? Or, well, Priestess Rose?"

"Hey!" says Chelle, quickly drying her hands on a towel before she hugs Lizzy.

"Great to see you again," says Lizzy. "And thank you for planning this! You guys really didn't have to go to all of this trouble."

"Oh, it's no trouble at all!"

"Yeah," says Jade. "I told you we'd show you a good time while you're here!"

"And you're just here for a few days?" asks Chelle.

"Just a few days," Lizzy answers, looking around the kitchen. "I had an audition for a modeling gig, so we'll see what happens with that."

"Hey, that's cool," says Graham, walking into the kitchen. "Where at?"

"Oh, a studio downtown," Lizzy says quickly. "I was there earlier today, so we'll see if I get a callback or anything."

"Well good luck or break a leg, whichever it is," Graham says, dipping a carrot into the small bowl of ranch dip.

"Hey, hey," Chelle says to him. "Could you put those out on the table?"

"You got it," he says, grabbing the bowl in one hand and the tray of vegetables in the other.

Chelle turns to Jade.

"Did Bobby come with you guys?"

Jade rolls her eyes while she puts a six pack of beer bottles into the refrigerator.

"Negative," she says. "He got tied up at work, but said he wouldn't be too late."

"Oh," says Chelle.

"I'm excited to meet him," says Lizzy.

"You haven't met him yet?" asks Chelle.

"No," answers Jade. "He was working last night, so it was just the two of us."

"Did you guys go out?"

"Nah," says Lizzy. "Tara couldn't make it out, either, so we stayed in and played catch up over a few bottles of wine."

"The best way to play catch up!" says Chelle.

Jade smiles as she continues to unpack her bags.

"Hey, can you pop this chili cheese dip into the oven for a few?" she asks.

"Of course," says Chelle. "Need help with anything else?"

"I think I'm good," says Jade, grabbing two bags of chips. "I'm gonna put these out on the table."

"Perfect," says Chelle.

There is another knock at the door and Jade turns back to Chelle, smiling.

"Here we go!" she says, leaving the kitchen.

As Chelle finishes washing the remaining dishes in the sink, she hears Graham open the door to greet Tyler and Alan.

*Yup,* she thinks. *Here we go.*

Jade calls Lizzy to the living room where she is introduced to both Tyler and Alan. A few moments later, Chelle finishes drying the last pan when Alan enters her kitchen holding two bottles of wine.

"Hello Chelle," he says.

"Hey."

"Is there room in the fridge for these?" he asks.

"Oh yeah," she says. "There should be plenty, just put them wherever."

Alan opens the refrigerator and puts the wine bottles next to a two liter of soda.

"Hey, thanks for letting me come," he says.

"It's no problem."

"I went to one of these things awhile back and they're a lot of fun."

"Yeah," says Chelle. "I'm excited."

There is another knock at the door.

"I know I'm the victim, so I'll try to stay out of everyone's way."

Chelle fights the urge to roll her eyes.

"Okay," she says.

"So how are you and Graham?"

"Oh, we're good."

"Good," says Alan. "I still think about that night we met him in Garden Park. That was a fun time – we should go to the speakeasy again before I leave, if we can."

Chelle forces a smile, hoping it looks natural.

"That'd be fun," she says.

Tara Ellis walks into the kitchen wearing a shimmering purple dress with a black blazer and carrying a plate of cookies.

The same thought runs through both Chelle and Alan's minds.

*Thank God.*

"Hey girlie!" Tara says.

"Hey! Those look great!"

"Thanks," says Tara. "They're lavender sugar cookies; it's a recipe my boss taught me."

"Sounds delicious," Chelle says.

"So the good judge can cook," Alan says, reaching to shake Tara's hand. "I'm assuming you're playing the judge?"

"Justice Thistle, at your service," Tara says, shaking his hand with a smile. She pulls her hand away, tucking her dark hair behind her ear. "Maybe in more ways than one, but we'll see what the night holds!"

Alan smiles uncomfortably.

"I'm gonna go find Tyler."

"Ahh, Mr. Mist!" Tara says, pointing at Alan. "I saw him perusing the shelves in the library…"

"You have a library?" Alan asks Chelle.

"If by library you mean my bookshelf, singular, then yup, sure do!"

Tara looks between the two.

"He's in the spare room," she says.

"Thanks," says Alan, leaving the kitchen.

Tara whips around to face Chelle.

"What's he doing here? He hasn't been at karaoke in weeks."

"I don't know," says Chelle. "All I know is that he's getting ready to be out of the country for a year and Tyler wanted to bring him tonight and *after* tonight I will hopefully not have to deal with him or his bullshit for a very long time."

"Oh," says Tara. "Gotcha. Well he better lighten up, because I'm here to have some fun and solve a murder!"

"Preach," says Chelle. "Let's get those cookies out on the table."

She leads Tara out of the kitchen and to the dining area where all the food for the evening has been set out.

"I'm gonna go outside while it's still nice out," says Tara. "Wanna come with?"

There is a knock at the door.

"Go on ahead," says Chelle. "I'll be right behind you."

Tara goes to join Graham, Jade and Lizzy on the patio as Chelle answers the door.

"Hey guys!" she says, opening the door for Brannon and Kate. "I'm so glad you could make it!"

"Thanks for inviting us," says Brannon as he steps inside, a bright blue shirt visible beneath his blazer.

"Yeah, I've never been to one of these," says Kate. "Plus it gave me an excuse to wear my red dress!"

Chelle grins, closing the door behind the two of them.

"Jade and I were worried no one would want to dress up for the party."

"Really?" asks Kate.

"Yeah, ask Kate, I was all about dressing the part for this. I even had her cut my hair for tonight," says Brannon, running his hand over his freshly buzzed head. "It's all part of the fun!"

"Exactly," says Chelle. "Alright, put any food on the table over there, drinks can go in the fridge. We're kind of just hanging around while people are still showing up."

"Oh good, we're not the last ones here," says Kate.

"Where is everyone?"

"Tyler and Alan are in the spare room, I think, and everyone else is outside."

"Probably not for much longer," says Brannon.

"How do you mean?" asks Chelle.

"It's really starting to get dark out west," Brannon answers.

"Yeah," says Kate. "I was hearing thunder when we were walking in."

"Oh yeah," says Chelle. "I heard it was supposed to get bad tonight. We were hoping it would hold out though so we weren't stuck just inside."

"They said on the radio it might go north, but the whole city is supposed to get more rain tonight."

"Fantastic," says Chelle. "We'll keep an eye on it. For now, make yourselves at home! I'm gonna go find Tyler; let me know if you need anything, okay?"

"Thanks, Chelle," says Kate.

Chelle leaves Brannon and Kate sitting on the sectional in the living room as she walks down the hall to the apartment's second bedroom that she uses as both an office and guest room. She walks in through the open door to find Tyler sitting on the couch opposite her desk, his blonde hair pulled into a knot on the back of his head. Alan browses her bookshelf.

"Hey guys," she says.

Tyler gets up and gives her a hug.

"Sorry it's delayed, but you were busy when we get here," he says.

"All good, boo," Chelle says. "We're just waiting on Bobby and Mack and then we'll get started."

"Oh, the party hasn't started yet?" asks Alan.

Chelle again resists the urge to roll her eyes.

"Well, yeah," she says slowly. "But there's a CD that narrates the beginning of the game we're supposed to start once everyone's here and cards with missions and stuff to help progress the story."

"Do I get one?" asks Alan. "I mean, I'd figure not since I'm getting killed, but I didn't know…"

"No, there isn't one for the senator."

"Maybe we can share?" offers Tyler. "I mean, like the missions."

"We'll see how it goes," says Alan.

Chelle can see dark clouds gathering outside through the blinds.

"I'm gonna go check on the others," says Chelle. "I'll get you two when we start the game."

"Sounds good," says Tyler.

On her way back to the living room, Chelle finds Jade in the kitchen, pulling the chili cheese dip from the oven.

"Who are we still waiting on?" she asks.

"I just got a text from Bobby," says Jade, setting the pan on the counter. "He's on his way but he said don't wait for him to start."

"You sure?"

"I guess," says Jade. "So we're just waiting for Mack?"

As if on cue, there is a knock at the door.

"And that's probably him," says Chelle, leaving the kitchen to answer the door. Jade slams her phone on the counter and shakes her head. She follows Chelle with the chili cheese dip in hand, putting it on the food table as Chelle opens the door.

"Hey Mack!" she says.

"Mack?" he asks. "I'm sorry, I don't know any Mack… my name is Mr. Gold and you must be Miss Pumpkin."

Chelle smiles.

"That would be correct," she says. "Welcome to Minuit Mansion… or the closest we can get to it!"

Mack laughs, giving Chelle a hug.

"I'm digging the yellow, Ma… Mr. Gold," says Jade.

"Oh, this?" Mack asks, looking down at his bright shirt. "Just something I had lying around the office… I'm the senator's accountant you know."

"And you did your homework," says Jade. "Good job."

Chelle looks at Jade.

"Should we get started?"

Jade shrugs.

"He said not to wait for him."

"Alright then, you wanna go grab Tyler and Alan? I'll bring everyone in from the porch. Get everyone together in here in… two minutes?"

"Sounds good to me."

"Well, I'm getting a good seat!" says Mack, plopping down next to Brannon and Kate on the couch. "Hey, I'm Mr. Gold, but sometimes I work under the name 'Mack' at Caramaya's with Miss Pumpkin and… Jade and Tyler."

Brannon and Kate laugh.

"Brannon, er, Captain Cobalt," says Brannon, shaking Mack's hand.

"Madame Crimson," says Kate, dramatically tossing her hair as she introduces herself. "Foreign diplomat."

"Pleased to meet you," says Mack, kissing her extended hand.

The sliding door opens as Chelle leads Lizzy, Tara and Graham in from the patio. Shortly after, Jade enters the room, followed by Tyler and Alan from down the hall.

"Let's turn on a light," says Jade. "It's getting dark in here."

Graham clicks on the lamp on the end table as everyone gets situated around the living room.

"Much better," says Kate.

"Thanks, babe," says Chelle.

"That's everyone?" asks Lizzy.

"What about Bobby?" asks Tyler.

"He's on his way," Jade says.

"Alright! Awesome," says Chelle, holding a stereo remote. "So let's get started! First of all, thank you everyone for coming. I'm super excited to play out this mystery and I hope you guys are, too! Okay, I think now is when we start… oh, there we go!"

The sound of jazz music starts as soon as Chelle pushes play. Everyone looks around at each other, waiting for something to happen.

"It said to push play as soon as – "

"Greetings everyone," comes a booming voice with a British accent over the jazz music. "And welcome to Minuit Mansion, the home of Senator Minuit."

Alan waves around the room at the mention of Senator Minuit.

"My name is Worthington and I am the head of staff for the estate. I will be guiding you through the evening with assistance from your host or hostess. At this time, please distribute the guests name tags so that we can all begin to get acquainted."

"Oh!" says Chelle.

"I have them," says Jade, running to the counter to grab a stack of name badges, each badge color coded for the specific guest with their name and relation to the senator. She distributes them as the voice on the track continues.

"Though each of you, of course, has your given names, you may find it beneficial to begin calling each other by your designated pseudonyms. Now, help yourselves to food and drink. Talk to and get to know the senator's other guests. Something tells me we're in for a memorable evening…"

As Worthington's voice trails off, the jazz music comes back up, filling the room with a lively ambiance.

"Now what?" asks Graham.

"The directions said to start the track when the last guest arrived and that the game would be guided from there," says Chelle. "So…"

"So, let's help ourselves to some food and drink!" says Mack, hopping up from the couch. Everyone murmurs in agreement and the majority of the party moves to the dining room table where the food has been laid out.

Jade pulls out her phone to check the time.

"He'll be here," says Chelle, walking up behind her.

"I know," says Jade. "Hey, get yourself a plate, I'm gonna go smoke a cig."

"Alright."

Jade pulls open the sliding door and steps out to the patio.

Chelle stands behind Mack and Tara, who are eagerly creating backstories for their characters, Mr. Gold and Justice Thistle. After getting herself some food, she goes to stand by Graham when she hears someone knock on the door.

"Bet I know who that is," she says, setting her plate down before going to open the door.

"Hey, Chelle," says Bobby.

"Hey there," she replies.

"Sorry I'm late," he says. "I got stuck at work and then the weather and everything…"

"Is it getting bad?"

"Not yet, but it's looking like it could. It's really starting to lightning outside."

Bobby looks around the room, waving to the guests he recognizes.

"Where's Jade?" he asks.

"She's outside," says Chelle.

"She okay?"

"She's alright; she's just smoking."

"Okay," says Bobby. "I'm gonna go say hello."

"Alright," says Chelle. "Don't forget to get your name badge!"

"Of course not," says Bobby, smiling.

"Hey man, nice jacket," Brannon calls as Bobby walks through the group.

"What?" asks Bobby. He looks over to see that he and Brannon are wearing the same blazer. "You've got great taste, my friend!"

Brannon laughs and takes a drink of his beer.

Lizzy turns around from the conversation she's having with Tara when she hears the exchange between Bobby and Brannon. Her eyes go wide when she sees Bobby; she tries to turn away before he notices her but she is too late.

"Hello," he says, his eyebrow raised.

"Hi," she says. "Bobby?"

"That's me, and you must be Lizzy," Bobby says slowly. "It's nice to finally meet you."

"You, too," she says. "I'm gonna top this drink off."

Lizzy quickly walks around him to the kitchen. Bobby smiles to himself before stepping out to the porch, closing off the sounds of the party as he slides the door shut.

Jade stands on the balcony overlooking the yard, her elbows on the railing and a cigarette casually perched between her fingers. She brings it to her lips and draws a breath, exhaling a cloud of smoke into the air only a few moments later.

Lightning flashes in the distance followed quickly by a long rumble of thunder.

"Hello," she says without turning around.

"Hello."

She takes another drag of her cigarette.

"Can I have a light?" Bobby asks, pulling a cigarette out from behind his ear.

"Sure," she says turning around, the rhinestones around the bust of her white dress sparkling under the terrace lights. She lights his cigarette from the cherry of her own. He holds it between the forefinger and thumb of his left hand, inhaling sharply.

"Thanks," he says.

"Don't mention it," she replies, turning away to look across the yard again. Another streak of lightning races across the sky, this one followed by a louder crack of thunder.

"Looks like this could be a pretty bad storm, don't you think?" he asks. She turns her head to face him, noting how the deep green of his shirt brings out the color of his eyes. He puts his cigarette to his lips once again.

"Quite," she says curtly.

They stand in silence for a moment.

"Don't you find it odd that there are so many – "

He is interrupted by a loud pop from inside followed by a thunderous crash.

"What the…" he says, trailing off.

The door suddenly flings open and Chelle stands there panting. Screams can be heard from inside as her eyes dart from Jade to Bobby, her orange earrings swinging wildly with the movements.

"Come quickly," she says.

"What's going on?" asks Bobby.

"What was that noise?" asks Jade.

Chelle takes a deep breath before speaking.

"There's been a murder!"

"What?" asks Jade.

"It's the CD! It was playing the jazz music and then suddenly there was a bunch of crazy loud noises and the voice came back on and instructed everyone to gather around. Senator Minuit has been killed and the game's starting!"

Jade puts her cigarette out in the ash tray.

"Well then let's get this party started."

\* \* \*

"Ladies and gentlemen, Senator Minuit is dead… and there is a murderer among us," says Worthington the fictitious butler.

"Oh, shit!" Mack yells.

Everyone laughs, offsetting the air of mystery that the CD is trying to establish.

"If the host or hostess could begin distributing your player dossiers, I will go over the rules for the evening," Worthington continues.

"Here you go," Chelle says to Kate as she begins to distribute small, passport-like booklets to each guest except Alan.

"You will each receive a player dossier that will help guide you through the evening. Your dossier contains all the information you will need to begin your task of unmasking the murderer, their weapon and their motive, including a brief biography of your character as well as two pages on which to keep notes.

"There are clues hidden around the mansion that will help you solve the mystery, though your host or hostess may designate certain areas to be off limits and out of the game. Additionally, each dossier contains three secret missions which, once completed, will unlock additional clues that you may keep to yourself or barter for more information, the choice is yours.

"Be warned – each dossier also contains information about one other player, information that that particular guest would prefer remain hidden. How you use this information is your decision, but remember that no action is without consequence. Just ask the dearly departed senator…"

"I'll plead the fifth," says Alan, sending giggles throughout the room.

"When you believe that you have solved the mystery of Senator Minuit's murder, notify your host or hostess that you have reached a conclusion and you would like to pose it to the group. Your host or hostess will then allow you to read the sealed solution booklet. If you are correct, insert disc two into the player and I will gather everyone together. If you are incorrect, however, you are no longer eligible to win the game. Though you may still interact with other guests, you are not permitted to share any of the information you learned from reading the sealed solution booklet."

Everyone looks around the room at one another as they take in the rules for the evening and begin to formulate strategies on how to proceed.

"Please direct any further questions to your host or hostess," says Worthington. "Now, without any further ado, let the game begin. Good luck to all of you and may the best sleuth solve… *The Murder at Minuit Mansion!*"

As if on cue, a crack of thunder from outside fires through the room as soon as Worthington is finished talking.

"You guys picked a hell of a night to do this," says Mack.

"Yeah, sorry," says Chelle.

"Oh, no," says Mack. "I love it! The storm adds to the mystery…"

"Yeah, don't be sorry!" says Tara. "This is awesome!"

The next track on the CD, a slower jazz tune, starts to play, creating an intimate atmosphere in the room.

"I'm gonna step back outside for a minute," says Jade, heading for the door.

"I'll come with you," Tara says quickly, following her friend outside.

"Hey and just so everyone knows, there's nowhere off limits except the closet in my bedroom," says Chelle. "And not for any reason other than just that I shoved a lot of shit in there before tonight and there's too much to look through for clues."

Everyone laughs as they slowly start to move about the room, some heading off in pairs, others heading off to refill their drinks, each with their dossiers in hand.

Graham looks at Chelle.

"Alright, Miss Pumpkin," he says. "Let's get to work!"

\* \* \*

Tara sits in one of the chairs on the porch, a plate of chips and chili cheese dip on her lap, as Jade paces by the railing. Raindrops start to hit the pavement below as more lightning flashes in the sky.

"You okay?" she asks.

"Not really," Jade replies.

"What's going on?"

"I don't know, I just... I'm so mad!"

"Why?"

"The way Bobby just fucking strolls in here late like nothing's wrong."

"But I thought he got caught up at work?"

"That's the thing though, Tara, he's *always* getting caught up at work and he *never* makes any apologies for it."

"What is it he does again?"

"He works for a media production company downtown."

The wind picks up as the rain starts to come down harder.

"That sounds like a job that could require time outside of a normal business day."

"But it's always about the job," says Jade. "I know I'm going to sound like a whiny bitch by saying this, but I want it to be about *me* for a change!"

"You don't sound like a whiny bitch."

"I'm tired of playing second fiddle to a paycheck."

Tara nods sympathetically.

"Ahh!" shouts Jade. "And now I'm in a shitty mood and everyone's here and trying to have a good time and I just... ugh."

"Don't let it bring you down," says Tara. "Try to focus on the game and having a good time and, I don't know, tell Bobby you want to have a talk with him tomorrow or something."

"Yeah, you're right," says Jade. "Besides, I don't want to ruin tonight for Lizzy, she's only here for a short time."

"See! There you go… do it for Lizzy," says Tara. "Feel better?"

"A little," says Jade.

"Want to try some of this chili cheese dip?"

"Maybe later."

"Boom!" yells Tara, standing up with her plate in hand.

"What?"

"First secret mission is done!"

"What are you talking about?"

"One of the secret missions in the back of my dossier," Tara says, flipping to the back page. "Says right here, 'Offer Miss Snow an appetizer.' My first mission is done!"

Jade smiles.

"What do you win?" she asks.

"Let's find out," says Tara, pulling back the first pull tab on the inside of the back cover of her dossier.

The steady wind starts to blow the rain onto the porch.

"Interesting," she says. "I think I'll keep this one to myself for now."

"Whatever," says Jade. "Hey, it's really coming down out here, we'd better head back inside."

\* \* \*

While Jade and Tara are talking on the porch, everyone inside is dispersing around the apartment. Tyler and Kate head to the kitchen as Graham hangs a few coats in the closet. Bobby catches up to Lizzy in the hall.

"Hi," he says.

She turns around to face him.

"Hello," she says.

"Priestess Rose, right?"

"That would be me," she says.

"Would you, uh… care to read my palm?"

Bobby holds out his hand, palm facing upright.

"Not particularly," she says. "But I can try."

Lizzy takes his outstretched hand into her own and looks down at it, tracing the lines with a finger. Finally, she looks up.

"I see trouble in your future, Sir Emerald," she says.

A rumble of thunder shakes the walls.

"Really?" he asks.

"Yeah," she says. "Jade doesn't know what you really do for a living, does she?"

"No," Bobby admits quietly. "And I'd like it to stay that way for now. It's… it's something I need to talk about with her at a more appropriate time."

"A more appropriate time?" Lizzy asks. "You've known her for what, almost ten months now? There's hasn't been an *appropriate* time before now?"

"It's complicated," says Bobby.

The bathroom door opens and Alan walks out.

"Don't mind me," he says, walking past. "I'm dead."

When he's far enough away, Lizzy turns back to Bobby.

"Look, Jade and I have been friends for years. I care about her. And if you did, too, you'd at least have the decency to be open and honest with her."

"I do care about her!"

"Then don't you think she deserves to know what you do?"

Bobby sighs as a crack of thunder echoes through the apartment.

"That's what I thought," says Lizzy. "I'm not going to say anything tonight, but you'd better have that talk with her soon."

"Are you threatening me?"

"I'm just letting you know," says Lizzy before she turns and walks away.

"You're getting a callback," Bobby says after her.

Lizzy stops.

"I'll pass," she says without turning around, continuing to walk away.

Bobby shakes his head.

*At least I finished one of these missions,* he thinks, pulling out his dossier and opening the tab under the mission that instructed him to have Priestess Rose read his palm. *Even if I didn't like what she had to say.*

\* \* \*

Kate leans against the kitchen counter as Tyler mixes drinks for them both.

"Here," he says. "Try this. I think you'll like it."

"You're not trying to poison me, are you?" she asks, grinning.

"I wouldn't dream of it, Katey."

Tyler and Kate clink their glasses and take a drink.

"Oh, I *do* like that!" she says. "What's in it?"

"Cucumber vodka with lemonade," says Tyler. "Refreshing, no?"

"And not flavors I would have thought to put together," answers Kate, nodding.

Lizzy walks by the entrance to the kitchen just as the two of them hear Bobby greeting someone in the office.

"I wonder what they were up to?" says Tyler.

"Probably one of these missions," Kate says, studying the last page of her dossier.

"Oh, right."

"Who are you again?"

"Mr. Mist," says Tyler. "I don't have any missions with Madame Crimson, I already checked."

"Well, crap," says Kate. "None of my missions are with you, either."

They look around the kitchen.

"Do you think there's any clues in here?" asks Kate.

"Could be," says Tyler. "It wouldn't hurt to look, you know, especially while everyone else is occupied."

"Good point."

"I'll look through the cabinets real quick," says Tyler. "Watch the door."

Kate goes to stand by the entrance to the kitchen, casually leaning against the wall while sipping her drink. Tyler crouches to start looking through the cabinet beneath the sink. He sets a bottle of dish soap aside and looks behind two flower vases before moving on to another cabinet with pots and pans.

"Hard to believe it's been almost a year since Brannon moved back."

"I know," says Kate. "It's gone fast!"

"I always kind of wondered if you two would end up together."

"Really?"

"Come on, Katey," says Tyler. "The only thing less surprising than you two getting together was my coming out of the closet."

"Hey, Gen was surprised!"

They laugh, remembering a period in high school when their friend Genevieve had admitted to having a crush on Tyler and the months of awkwardness that ensued.

Tyler sits back onto the floor and reaches up to the counter for his drink.

"Damn," he says. "Nothing."

"I feel so sneaky!"

"It's all part of the game," says Tyler. "Although I'd better stand up because I'm really not sure how I'd explain just chilling on the floor."

Kate smiles.

271

"Hey, check the pantry."

"Oh, good idea!"

Tyler stands and walks toward the pantry.

"So things are good with Brannon, yeah?" he asks, looking through Chelle's canned goods.

"Oh, yeah," says Kate. "Things are great!"

Tyler smiles.

"Really, *really* great," she says. The tone in her voice causes Tyler to stop looking through the cereal boxes in the pantry. He faces her slowly.

"Like, start-planning-the-wedding great?"

Kate takes a sip of her drink, blinking emphatically.

"Maybe."

Tyler's mouth falls open.

"Oh my God, Katey, really?!"

Kate laughs.

"Not yet, but soon," she says. "We've been talking about it."

Tyler runs over and gives his friend a hug and a kiss on the cheek.

"I'm so happy for you two," he says, clinking his glass with hers.

"Thanks, Ty," she says, finishing her drink. "Wanna whip up two more of these? I think our search is a bust."

"Yeah, probably," says Tyler. "At least you're in the kitchen with the bartender!"

They laugh as a buzz from the drinks they've already consumed sets in.

"Hey, grab me the sugar from the pantry," says Tyler. "I'm gonna rim these glasses for round two."

"Fancy!" says Kate, walking to the pantry. She reaches in and grabs the sugar, walking back toward Tyler. "Do you need a plate or something to dip them in?"

"Yeah, probably," he says, looking around.

"Here you go," she says, handing him a paper plate.

"Perfect."

Tyler lifts the sugar to pour a little on the plate when Kate sees the note taped to the bottom of the bag.

"Oh my God!" she says, struggling to keep her voice low.

"What?!" says Tyler, almost dropping the bag.

"On the bottom of the bag," says Kate. "There's something there!"

Tyler grins as he feels the note on the bottom of the bag of sugar. He pulls it off to find a small envelope marked *Murder at Minuit*

*Mansion – Clue #8'.*

"I guess this wasn't a bust after all," Tyler says, grinning.

\* \* \*

Lizzy walks into the living room as Jade and Tara come back in from the porch.

"There you guys are!" she says.

"Hey, sorry," says Jade. "Just needed some fresh air before I started the game."

"Yeah," adds Tara. "And it's really starting to storm outside."

"Badly?"

"I don't know," says Tara.

"I was gonna ask Chelle if she wanted to turn the weather on the TV, just to keep an eye on things."

"That's not a bad idea," says Lizzy. "Where's the remote?"

"I'll find Chelle and see if she knows," says Jade.

"Wait, hang on," says Tara, looking from Jade to Lizzy. "Before anyone else notices… you guys wanna do a secret shot?"

"Is that even a question?" asks Lizzy.

"Of course," says Jade.

Tara smiles, pulling a small flask from the inside pocket of her blazer. She twists the cap off and takes a drink, the whiskey inside warming her throat as she swallows. Jade and Lizzy each take a swig before handing it back to Lizzy, who quickly tucks the flask back into her jacket.

"Love you bitches," she says, smiling.

"Love you both," says Jade.

Lizzy throws her hands up and brings her two friends in for a hug, though once the three embrace, she cannot ignore the nervous feeling in the pit of her stomach about her connection to Bobby and the inevitability of Jade finding out.

"Alright, I have a mystery to solve," Tara says. She steps away from her two friends, heading toward the food table where Mack stands alone looking through his dossier. The sound of the rain hitting the roof almost overpowers the slow jazz emanating from the speakers in the room.

"Hello, Mr. Gold," she says, approaching the table.

"Good evening, Justice Thistle," he replies.

"How's your investigation going?" she asks.

"Not bad, not bad," he says. "Yours?"

"It's going well. I finished one of my missions."

"So did I – I had to tell Mr. Mist a dirty joke, but it was worth the payout," says Mack, patting his dossier.

"Oh! Can I hear it?"

"The joke or the clue?"

"Well, I was referring to the joke, but if you're willing to share the clue…"

"Maybe we could arrange something," says Mack. "On both accounts."

Tara smirks, thinking of the biography she'd read for her character and the sordid details she'd added for herself.

*I love this!* she thinks. *It's like we're acting out our own movie!*

"You'd be surprised what this lady gets away with," she says, mysteriously.

"Very intriguing," says Mack.

"Tell you what," says Tara. "How about you go grab me a drink and then we'll go look for some clues together? There *is* strength in numbers, after all."

"Sounds like a plan," Mack says, smiling. "I'll be right back!"

\* \* \*

After Lizzy walks away from Bobby in the hall, he ducks into Chelle's spare room hoping to regroup for a few minutes before socializing with the rest of the group.

*What are the fucking odds?!* he thinks to himself. *That's it… she's gonna know now. This is going to change everything.*

"Oh, hey Bobby," says Brannon.

*Shit!* Bobby thinks, startled to discover that he isn't alone.

Brannon sits playing with his phone on the love seat to the left of the door; Alan stands looking out the window with a drink in hand.

"Hello," he says.

"Hey, sorry," Bobby says. "I didn't think anyone was in here."

"Oh, sorry man," says Brannon.

"It's all good," says Bobby. "Mind if I join you?"

"Not at all."

"I didn't mean to interrupt you and the priestess in the hall," says Alan.

"Lizzy? Oh, it's alright," says Bobby. "We were just talking."

"And I was actually just getting ready to find Tyler," says Alan. "I'll see you guys in a little bit." He leaves the room, closing the door behind himself. Bobby and Brannon sit in silence for a few minutes.

"So, have you come to kill me, Sir Emerald?" Brannon finally asks.

Bobby sits in the plush arm chair opposite the couch, laughing.

"I'm not the killer," he says. "At least, I don't think I am… I haven't really started working to solve the mystery yet."

"Neither have I."

"For all I know, it's you," says Bobby.

Brannon shakes his head.

"This whole mystery party thing not your bag?" asks Bobby.

"Not really," admits Brannon. "In case you're wondering though, the senator was sleeping with Madame Crimson who, ironically enough, is the character my girlfriend is playing. Or at least that's what I read in my little pamphlet."

"Awkward," says Bobby, pulling out his dossier. "While we're at it, just in case *you* were wondering, the accountant was cheating the senator out of a shitload of money."

"Big surprise there," says Brannon, laughing. "But yeah, this whole mystery thing sounded fun and Kate really wanted to come, she hadn't seen everyone in a while. But now with this storm – I just had a tornado watch come through my phone, by the way – I don't know, I've got a lot on my mind, I guess."

*Who are you telling?* Bobby thinks to himself.

"What's going on?" he asks.

Brannon sits for a moment.

"Keep a secret?" he finally says.

"Yeah, sure."

"Okay, well, between you and me… Kate and I are taking the next step in our relationship."

"Hold on," says Bobby. "Not to be rude, but you mean to tell me you guys have never had sex?"

"Oh!" says Brannon. "No, wait, crap… I didn't mean it like that. I mean, yes we have, but what I meant was, well, we're getting married."

"Really?"

"Yup," says Brannon. "I don't know when, I mean, I haven't even proposed yet, but we've been talking about it and, well, it's happening."

*Well isn't this some shit,* thinks Bobby. *These two are getting married and I can hardly get Jade to look at me.*

"Congratulations."

"Thanks."

"Shouldn't you be more excited?"

"I am," says Brannon. "I don't know, I guess I'm nervous."

"About what? You know she's gonna say yes."

"Changing, if that makes sense," says Brannon. "Right now, she's my girlfriend and our relationship is what it is. But after this, she'll be my *wife* and who knows how things are gonna change."

Bobby thinks for a moment.

"Yeah, that makes sense," says Bobby. "Everyone's afraid of change to some degree. But she's still Kate, you're both still the same people, you know? Haven't you guys known each other for most of your lives?"

Brannon nods.

"Then I don't think you really have anything to worry about. And it's good you guys talked about it, you're on the same page about the future you both want."

Bobby pauses, taking in the irony of the situation.

*Seriously dude, I'm the last person you should be talking about your relationship with... You'd probably be better off doing the exact opposite of what I'd tell you to do,* he thinks.

"Have you thought about when you're gonna do it? Pop the question, I mean."

"A little," says Brannon. "I have the ring, at least."

"Oh yeah?"

"Yeah, I keep it with me pretty much all the time these days in case the right moment presents itself."

Bobby thinks of all the times he could have told Jade the truth about his job over the many months they have been together, each time talking himself out of it because it didn't feel like the right moment.

"Just be careful not to let it pass you by," he says.

Brannon nods.

"It'll be soon," he says.

They sit in silence for a moment, listening to the sounds of the rain beating against the window.

"We'd better get back out there," says Bobby. He leans over the side of the chair, stretching before he gets up, when something on the back of Chelle's computer monitor grabs his attention.

"Hang on," he says, standing. "What's this?"

Brannon stands and joins Bobby, who is carefully reaching behind the computer monitor on the desk.

Bobby pulls out an envelope marked *Murder at Minuit Mansion – Clue #2'.*

"Hmm," he says, looking at Brannon. "I guess we're back in the game."

\* \* \*

Chelle is walking down the hall as Alan steps out of her spare room.

"Oh good," she says. "I was just looking for you."

"Well, here I am."

"Can I talk to you for a minute?" she asks.

"Sure," he says. "Out here?"

"Come on," she says, leading him to her bedroom.

"Alright," he says, following her.

*This outta be good,* he thinks.

Once they are in her room, Chelle closes the door.

"You can sit down if you want," she says, gesturing toward her bed.

"I'm fine."

"Okay," she says, sitting on the edge of her bed.

"What's up?"

Chelle takes a deep breath.

"What are you doing?" she asks.

"Trying to stay out of everyone's way since I'm not *really* part of this game."

"I mean with Tyler," she says. "I guess I'm just… I'm trying to understand why. Why you keep coming around, why you keep dangling yourself in front of him when you have no intention of making the relationship anything serious."

"Is that what I'm doing?"

"Sure seems like it to me," Chelle says.

They sit in silence, the pouring rain outside the only noise between them.

"I get it," Alan finally says. "I get that you're trying to look out for him, but you don't really know me."

"You're right," she says. "I've known you for months, but I don't *really* know you. Hell, I don't even know if Simon really knew you when we were trying to set the two of you up.

"But I know that shortly after you two met, you told me you were crazy about Tyler. And I know that you have this weird hold over him. I know that he feels like shit every time you disappear. And I know that for whatever reason, whenever you decide to show up again, he runs back to you. Every single time. What I don't know is why."

In the dim light of her room, Chelle can't figure out if the expression on Alan's face relays sadness or anger. Rumbling thunder shakes the walls.

"I don't know what to tell you," Alan says quietly. "And I don't know what you want to hear."

"I want to hear the truth, I don't care about anything else," says Chelle. "Why are you doing this to him?"

"The truth?" asks Alan. "Well, alright. The truth is... Tyler's great. More than great, really, and I *am* crazy about him. I could see myself with him for a long, long time."

*Where is he going with this?* Chelle thinks.

"But the thing is... I've felt like that about guys before. One in particular, actually. We were together for almost five years; we had a condo, a dog. Did Tyler ever tell you any of that?"

Chelle says nothing.

"And almost five years in, I find out he'd been cheating on me for at least the last three. Almost five years I'd wasted, giving everything of myself to someone who couldn't give two fucks about me. He didn't just break my heart... he broke my spirit.

"And that's when I gave up," says Alan. "I decided I had to make myself my main priority, as selfish as that sounds. I packed my shit and moved back home to the city, started over with pretty much nothing to my name. Not even the dog.

"So I might seem heartless, and I'm sure to you I'm the bad guy and that's fine, I get it. But to be honest with you, Chelle, I never intended to hurt Tyler like you say I have. I just... I can't do it. I get to a point with him where I feel comfortable and it freaks me the fuck out."

"Why don't you take a chance on him?"

"I can't get hurt like that again," says Alan.

"Do you really think Tyler would do that to you?" asks Chelle. "That's not really living it's just..."

"Surviving," Alan finishes. "I'm doing what I need to do for myself right now. I've got a decent enough job, I'm focusing on my education... I'm rebuilding my life."

"Then you shouldn't be bringing in anyone new, especially when you're about to leave. I understand not wanting to get hurt again, really I do, but in the process you're screwing with him as bad as that guy who screwed with you."

Alan takes a deep breath and sighs.

"Look, I don't think you're a *bad* guy," says Chelle. "And I'm not going to tell either of you what to do, but you're going away for a year, maybe more, and I think you already know how this story's going to end. But unless you give him some kind of definite answer about where you two stand, he will wait for you.

"Think about all the time you wasted with that guy," says Chelle. "I'm not saying you and Tyler are wasting time on each other, but the longer this goes, the more it's gonna hurt you both except he's not guarding himself the way you are. Just... just think about that."

Alan nods slowly.

Chelle's bedroom door bursts open and Jade walks in.

"There you are!" she says. "We're looking for the remote."

"For the TV?" asks Chelle. "It should be out in the living room, is it not?"

"We didn't see it."

"I'll come find it," says Chelle. "Is everything okay?"

"It's getting kind of bad outside," says Jade. "We just wanted to check the weather."

"Alright," Chelle says, standing up.

"You guys okay?" asks Jade.

"Yeah," says Alan. "We're fine."

He leaves the room.

"What was that about?" Jade asks.

"I'll tell you later," says Chelle.

\* \* \*

Five minutes later, Chelle is standing in the living room with Jade, Graham and Lizzy watching meteorologist Rex Benford report on the severe weather in the area. Tara and Mack stand in the dining area, going over the notes in their dossiers.

"Looks like we're under severe thunderstorm and tornado watches til 11:00 P.M.," says Graham, reading the scrolling ticker at the bottom of the screen. "And there's a severe thunderstorm warning for another half hour."

"I'd say it's already here," says Lizzy, nodding toward Chelle's sliding door and the rain that is beating against it. A flash of lightning outside is followed immediately by booming thunder and a buzzer from the TV, causing a few of them to jump.

Jade sighs.

"Should we pause the game?" she asks Chelle.

"I don't know," she answers. "Maybe we should get everyone together until it passes?"

"I think it's gonna be raining for a while, babe," Graham says, looking at the radar on the screen.

"Yeah, but look at that," Chelle says, pointing toward a bright red line moving across the area. "I think that's the worst of it and it's gonna be here pretty soon."

"I'm gonna grab my phone charger," Jade says. She steps away from the group and heads for the closet, passing Tyler and Alan who are talking in the kitchen.

"Hey guys," she says. "You may wanna head out there."

"What's going on?" asks Tyler.

*He seems frustrated*, thinks Jade.

"Is it the weather?" asks Alan.

"Yeah," says Jade. "There's a line that's going to be moving through in a few minutes, I think it might be a good idea to get everyone together."

"Alright," says Tyler, leading Alan to the living room.

In the hall, Jade can hear Bobby talking with Brannon and Kate in the spare room.

*I wonder what they're talking about,* she thinks, though she is unable to hear their words over the sound of the storm outside. *Oh well.*

She opens the closet door, pushes a few jackets aside and upon finding her purse, grabs her phone charger. She is about to close the door when she notices Bobby's blazer. She looks around and, satisfied no one is around, reaches into the pockets.

*What am I doing?* she thinks. *I don't even know what I'm looking for…*

She moves quickly through the various pockets of the jacket, finding nothing of interest until her fingers grasp a small, cardboard box tucked neatly into the interior chest pocket. Her eyes go wide and her mouth falls open.

*Oh my God,* she thinks. *This, oh my God, this is a ring box… oh shit, he's going to propose!*

She pulls her hand from the pocket, quickly closing the door.

*What am I going to do?* she thinks. *I can't marry him…*

Jade stands in the hallway, lost in thought, until Chelle's apartment is plunged into darkness, the electricity knocked out by the storm.

"Is everyone okay?" Graham shouts from the living room.

"Yeah, we're alright," Brannon shouts back from the spare room. "We're heading toward you!"

"Alright, go slow," shouts Graham. "Chelle's looking for flashlights!"

Jade stands paralyzed in the hallway, petrified that Bobby is about to realize she has been through his pockets.

*Unless he doesn't see me in the dark!* she thinks, standing against the far wall and hoping Bobby, Brannon and Kate pass by without noticing her. *I'll tell them I was in the bathroom, it's perfect.*

But before they can pass by and Jade can enact her plan, the sound of the storm outside intensifies and is joined by another noise that no one wants hear.

*Great,* thinks Jade. *Tornado sirens.*

\* \* \*

"Hey, can I talk to you?" Bobby quietly asks Jade. All eleven guests are standing in the hallway of Chelle's apartment as the tornado sirens continue to blare outside. Chelle has found three flashlights as well as an old, battery operated radio on which they are attempting to listen to updates on the weather on an AM news station.

"Right now?" asks Jade.

Bobby sighs.

"I mean, it's kind of crowded in here is all," says Jade. "Can it wait?"

"Yeah, I guess," he says. "I just had something to ask you."

*Oh, shit,* thinks Jade. *He wants to ask me right now?!*

"Are you okay?" he asks.

"Yeah," she lies. "I'm fine."

"I don't think you're fine," he says.

"Look, I don't want to do this here."

"Do what?"

"Argue."

"I'm not trying to fight with you, Jade," Bobby says. "I'm just trying to talk."

"I don't want to talk right now."

"Why?"

"Because it's not going to fix us!" she shouts, catching the attention of everyone in the crowded hall.

Bobby looks at her, confused, as the radio Graham is holding goes to static.

"Getting married is not going to fix what's wrong with our relationship," Jade says slowly. "I can't marry you, Bobby."

Everyone stands in silence.

"I, uhh... I wasn't going to ask you to, Jade."

The tornado sirens continue to wail outside over the sounds of the storm.

"What?" she asks. "But I... I found a ring in your coat?"

"Oh, shit," says Brannon.

"What?!" Jade says, spinning around to face Brannon.

"Bobby and I have the same coat, Jade," Brannon says. "You didn't find that ring in his... you found it in mine."

A few gasps escape the mouths of the guests, though the darkness hides their shocked faces. Outside, the tornado sirens begin to power down.

"Oh, my God," Jade says before running from the hall and out the front door, her hand over her mouth.

The remaining ten guests stand awkwardly in the hall, no one sure of what to say to each other.

"I'd better go after her," Bobby finally says.

"No," says Lizzy. "I'll go."

"I'll come with you," says Chelle, the two of them running after their friend.

When everyone disperses through the dark apartment, Bobby steps into the spare room and sits down on the love seat, his fingers massaging his temples as he shakes his head.

"What a mess," he says.

* * *

"I know about your talk with Alan," Tyler says to Chelle, approaching her as she cleans up the food table.

Soon after she ran after Jade with Lizzy, Chelle found her on the steps leading down from her apartment, her head in her hands as the rain continued to fall. She came back inside twenty minutes later at which point the power came back on just as the group decided to postpone solving the murder of Senator Minuit.

There had been enough excitement for one party.

"I'm not gonna deny it," Chelle says, scooping the remaining chili cheese dip into a plastic container. "I understand if you're pissed, but I'm just trying to look out for you."

"I don't need you to look out for me, Chelle."

Chelle looks up.

"You're right," she says. "You don't. But I'm going to anyway because I care about you. It may not seem like it right now, but I do and I said what needed to be said to him."

Tyler shakes his head and turns to walk away.

"Where are you going?" she asks.

"Home."

"With him?"

Tyler turns around.

"As a matter of fact, yes," he says. "Alan's coming home with me."

Chelle doesn't say anything.

"I'm just trying to be happy, Chel. Please don't take that away from me."

"Believe me when I tell you that no one wishes for your happiness more than me, Ty," says Chelle. "But Alan? He's leaving. You yourself told me that and a few days from now, he'll be gone. Who knows when you're gonna see him again."

Tyler starts to say something and hesitates, blinking away tears as he looks sadly at his friend.

"Don't you think I know?" he asks.

\* \* \*

Jade and Bobby sit quietly on the stairs outside of Chelle's apartment.

"I don't know what else to say," he says.

"I don't think there's much left to say," she says.

The rain continues to fall and thunder from the storm that has passed rumbles in the distance.

"Are we over?" asks Bobby.

Jade sighs.

"I think we've been over for a while now, Bobby, it's just… neither of us wanted to admit it."

"So that's it?" he asks. "Almost ten months and we're done just like that?"

"I don't know," admits Jade. "I still really care about you. I just… I have things I need to sort out and I think we need some time apart."

Bobby looks down.

"I'd agree with that," he says.

Jade puts her hand on his and he doesn't pull away.

"I think I'm gonna go home with Lizzy," she says.

"Isn't she staying with you?"

"Not to my apartment, I mean," says Jade. "When Lizzy goes home in a few days, I think I'm going to go with her. Get out of the city for a while… clear my head."

"Alright."

He gives Jade's hand a squeeze and pulls his own away before standing up.

"Give me a call when you're back in town, okay? We'll see where things go from there," he says.

"Okay," she says.

He leans down to give her a hug.

"No matter what happens, I will always love you," he whispers into her ear.

She smiles and wipes away tears.

"Thank you," she says. "I love you, too."

Bobby walks down the stairs and out of sight, leaving Jade alone with her thoughts and the remnants of the storm that has wreaked havoc across the city.

Lizzy steps out of Chelle's apartment and sits down by Jade, putting her head on her shoulder.

"How you doing, boo?" she asks.

"I-I'm ready to go home," Jade says softly.

"I figured," says Lizzy.

"Bobby told me everything," says Jade.

Lizzy stops.

"What do you mean?"

"About his job," she says. "And how you two met before tonight."

"Oh," says Lizzy. "That."

"Yeah."

"Are you mad?"

"At you?" asks Jade. "Of course not! I just wish he would have told me, you know? I mean, he lied to pretty much everyone... my friends, my brother..."

"Yeah, I about died when he walked in earlier," says Lizzy.

"So you only just met him?"

"At the audition today, yeah."

"So, wait," says Jade. "Are you trying to get into porn now?"

"No," says Lizzy. "What his company does, it's not *porn*, really, it's just like boudoir modeling photos and videos and stuff. They sell subscriptions, yeah, but nothing is x-rated."

"But people get off to it, don't they?"

"Probably," admits Lizzy. "But that's on them. I was just trying to expand my portfolio."

"Gotcha," says Jade. She sighs. "I don't even feel like going back inside."

"I brought your stuff," says Lizzy. "We can leave right now if you want?"

"Yeah," says Jade. "Let's go, I'll text Chelle later."

"Okay," says Lizzy.

"I'm sorry tonight had to end like this," Jade says.

"Oh, don't be," says Lizzy. "I'm just glad I could be here for you, not that you aren't in capable hands with the rest of your friends here."

"Yeah," says Jade, smiling.

"Come on," says Lizzy, standing. "Let's go home."

\* \* \*

In the parking lot next to Chelle's apartment building, Brannon and Kate sit in Brannon's car listening to the sound of the rain on the roof.

"Some party, huh?" asks Kate.

"Yeah," says Brannon. "They'll be talking about this one for some time."

Kate smiles, tucking her hair behind her ear.

"So, about that ring Jade found…"

Brannon smiles, his cheeks turning red.

"That was yours, huh?"

"Yup," says Brannon, nodding sheepishly.

They sit in silence for a moment.

"Hey Kate," Brannon finally says.

She turns to him, grinning.

"Yes?"

He pulls the small box from the inside pocket of his jacket and opens it to reveal a solitaire, princess cut diamond ring.

"Will you marry me?"

Kate gasps before grabbing Brannon's hands in her own.

"Yes!"

He puts the ring on her finger and she holds out her hand, admiring the diamond.

"Yes, yes, a thousand times yes!" she says, smiling wide.

"I love you," he says.

"I love you, too!"

And there, sitting in the car outside of Chelle's apartment, they kiss, excited about the life that lay ahead of them as husband and wife.

\* \* \*

"Hey Tara, wait up!" calls Mack. He had been helping Graham clean up the living room as the other guests had started to leave, but ran to follow Tara out the front door when he noticed she was leaving.

"Hey Mr. Gold," she says when he catches up to her.

"Justice Thistle," he says, nodding his head.

They both laugh.

"This was fun, wasn't it?" he asks.

"It was," she says. "I just wish we figured out who did it!"

"I'll talk to Chelle, maybe get her to just open the solution booklet for us."

"That sounds like a plan," Tara says, smiling.

"So, um... I had a great time hanging out with you tonight at the party and was wondering if, you know, sometime you'd maybe want to..."

"Just ask," she says, smiling.

"You wanna go out sometime? Just you and me?"

"Sure," says Tara. "I mean, did you have any plans right now?"

"Right now? Oh, no," says Mack. "I was just gonna help inside for a little bit and take off... why, did you?"

"Not really," says Tara. "But now that the storm's passed, I was thinking maybe I'm not ready to go home yet?"

"I could go out for a awhile," says Mack.

Tara smiles.

"You wanna go to Sugar's? I'm sure they're open," she says.

"Wait, the diner?" says Mack. "Hell yeah! Let me run inside and grab my stuff!"

"Awesome!" says Tara. "I'll wait here."

When Mack gets back outside with his things, he and Tara walk side by side down the stairs to their cars.

Three hours later, it is still raining as they run to their cars outside of Sugar's 24 Hour Diner. They had spent their time in the diner recounting the events of the party, theories on the solution to the murder mystery and, of course, getting to know each other. They end their evening with an exchange of phone numbers and a kiss goodnight.

* * *

Chelle leans against the doorway to the kitchen where Graham is drying a mixing bowl with a dish towel. She has changed out of her party dress and into her pajamas, her hair pulled into a loose bun on top of her head.

"Hey baby," she says. "You coming to bed soon?"

"Yeah," he says. "I was just finishing these up so we didn't have to worry about them tomorrow."

"Thanks," she says, smiling.

A distant rumble of thunder reminds them of the storm that had moved through earlier.

"It's supposed to do that off and on all night, you know," says Graham.

"Yeah, I saw that on TV," says Chelle. "Half of the city doesn't have power, from Old Town to Garden Park."

"Oh, yeah," says Graham. "I got a text from Bea that our building's electricity finally came back on."

"That's good; they're working on it at least."

"I'm still gonna stay the night though. They said one of the bridges is out and traffic sounds like a mess everywhere."

"Okay," says Chelle. "Hey… was tonight a bad idea?"

Graham sets down the bowl and looks at her.

"Why do you ask that?"

"I don't know," says Chelle. "I just… with the weather getting bad and everything that happened between Jade and Bobby and then Tyler left upset… I'm just wondering if it was even worth having this party tonight at all. I mean, we didn't even finish the game."

"Tonight was fine, Chel," says Graham. "You guys had no way of predicting the weather when you planned this party. And I know there were some rough spots and all, but do you know what people will remember about tonight?"

Chelle shakes her head.

"They'll remember the experience as a whole," says Graham. "They won't get bogged down in the 'he said this' and 'she did that'."

"I guess."

"And people had fun with the game! Several of them told me they'd never even heard of parties like that and they loved it, even if we didn't finish."

Chelle laughs.

"I'm half tempted to just open the solution and see who did it, myself."

"No, don't do that!" says Graham. "I told everyone we'd try to get together sometime to finish the game out."

"Alright," Chelle says.

Graham walks over and puts his arm around Chelle, letting her rest her head on his chest.

"It was a great evening, don't worry so much about it," he says. "Even if the senator was your dad."

Chelle picks her head up.

"What?!"

"Oh yeah," says Graham, giggling. "The secret that my character knew? Was that your character was the secret daughter of the senator."

"Which means…"

"Alan was playing your dad."

"Oh, God," says Chelle. "That's… I have no words."

"I knew you'd get a kick out of that," says Graham.

Chelle shakes her head, laughing.

"I'll use that as a reason to call Tyler tomorrow."

"He's not gonna stay mad at you forever, you know."

"I know," says Chelle, yawning. "Alright, let's go to bed."

"After you," says Graham, flipping the switch on the wall as he walks past, turning the lights out in Chelle's apartment.

* * *

Tyler bolts upright in bed, the rain outside streaming down the windows of his loft. The first thing he realizes is that he is alone in his bed, covered only by a sheet. A flash of lightning is not followed by thunder for almost a minute. He looks over at his night stand and sees that it's a few minutes after 4:00 A.M.

"Alan?" he calls. He knows there will be no answer, that Alan slipped out quietly after he fell asleep. He knows that Alan will be leaving in a few days to study abroad and he will likely not see him again for at least a year, maybe more.

Tyler lies on his back, staring at the ceiling. He knows Chelle was right all along about Alan, that she had just been trying to look out for him.

*I'll call her in the morning,* he thinks.

He rolls to his side and watches the rain run down the window. He thinks of the party, his friends and the things that had happened between them, how so many things would be different now. A break up, an engagement… a lot happened over the course of one night.

And then he thinks about Pete.

*Pete would have had a fun time at that party,* he thinks. *Pete Rangle… what are you doing right now? Hopefully you're sleeping, probably next to Dillon… I wonder if I'll see him again next Tuesday? Maybe, maybe not, who knows… It doesn't matter, I guess. I can't think about him right now.*

Another flash of lightning jars Tyler from his thoughts followed by another rumble of thunder.

He sighs.

In a few hours, it will be daytime and the sun will be shining. He has to work tomorrow; he'll see everyone, be surrounded by people again. But for now, Tyler is alone, curled up under a sheet watching the rain as it falls just outside his window from the safety of his bed.

# TUESDAY NIGHT KARAOKE

*Fall*

At 8:30 P.M. on the Tuesday after Jade and Tyler met Bobby and Alan respectively, Ian Santiago rushes into the El Scorcho on Canal Street clutching his laptop, his curly hair hidden beneath a backward ball cap.

"Hey Rachel," he calls to the bartender, barely stopping before continuing on to the side room. "Sorry I'm late!"

"It's all good," she says. "I don't think anyone's here for karaoke yet anyway."

"Awesome!" he yells over his shoulder, stepping into the empty side room where one of the waitresses, Peggy Sue Ogden, is wiping down one of the tables.

"Damn campers wouldn't get out of here," she says, looking up to greet Ian. "How are you?"

"Good," he says. "Running behind though… Can you put my laptop up on the table for me? I'm gonna go grab the speakers."

"Sure thing," says Peggy Sue. "Anything else?"

"Nah," says Ian. "I'll be set… maybe grab me a whiskey and cola when you get a minute?"

"You got it!" says Peggy Sue.

"You're awesome," Ian says on his way out of the side room.

An hour later, the first of the regulars for Tuesday Night Karaoke at El Scorcho walks in and heads straight for the side room where Ian is chatting with two girls who had happened in from the bar next

289

door.

"Here comes trouble," he says into the microphone upon seeing them enter.

"Hello, Ian," says Chelle Mastens, laughing as she sits down next to her boyfriend, Simon Dawes. They are joined by Simon's co-worker, Dominic Thorton, who immediately begins paging through the binder of song choices on the table.

"Hey guys!" says Peggy Sue, walking up to the table. "The usual?"

"Of course," says Chelle. "I love the new look!"

"Thanks," says Peggy Sue, running a finger through her cropped hair. "And it's freshly bleached!"

"It looks good!" says Chelle.

"You're so sweet!" says Peggy Sue before turning to Simon. "And for you?"

"I'll take a pitcher of the dark ale," says Simon.

"I'll take a glass to go with his pitcher," Dominic says.

"You got it," says Peggy Sue, winking at him.

Ian calls one of the two girls sitting at the table opposite the group to come to the stage as another group of four people walk in the side room. By the time the girl hits the chorus of her song, Peggy Sue has returned with their drinks.

"Hey, come here," says Chelle, taking a drink of her cocktail. "We're gonna have newbies with us tonight!"

"Oh yeah?"

"Yup," says Chelle. "Tyler and Jade are *both* bringing guys!"

"Shut up!"

"No, seriously!" says Chelle, taking another drink. "Make sure they introduce you!"

"Oh, you know I'll be all over that!" Peggy Sue says before walking over to the group of four to take their orders.

Twenty minutes later, Chelle, Simon and Dominic have been joined by Jade Verrit and Bobby Glachome as well as Tyler Welik and Alan Brodecker.

"Are Phin and Carrie coming tonight?" Chelle asks Tyler after Peggy Sue introduces herself to both Alan and Bobby.

"I don't think so," answers Tyler. "Phin has an early shift tomorrow so they're sitting this week out."

"Hey Chelle," Ian says from the stage. "Get up here and sing!"

Chelle grabs her drink and heads for the stage. While she is singing, Genevieve Delphe arrives and comes to sit with the group after greeting both Rachel and Peggy Sue. Shortly after, Peggy Sue arrives at the table with Genevieve's beer as Jade and Bobby are recounting the story of how they met the Friday before.

"If I ignore the parts that involve Mike, that *almost* sounds like a fairy tale beginning!" Genevieve says, winking at Jade over the black rim of her glasses.

Jade rolls her eyes.

After Chelle finishes her song, Ian calls Tyler up to sing next.

"So what do you think?" Chelle asks Alan, nodding toward Tyler.

Alan looks to the stage.

"I'm crazy about him," he says. "I know I only just met him but seriously... I really, really like him!"

"I knew you two would hit it off," says Simon, pouring the last of the beer from the pitcher into his cup.

As if on cue, Peggy Sue walks up.

"Ready for another?" she asks.

"Uh... sure," says Simon, shifting in his seat.

"Chelle?" asks Peggy Sue.

Chelle looks from her empty glass to the waitress.

"Yeah," she says. "Can we make this one a double?"

"Thatta girl!" says Peggy Sue, walking away.

Tyler returns to the table from the stage and sits next to Alan.

"That was great," says Alan, beaming.

"Really? Thank you!" says Tyler, finishing his vodka cranberry.

Chelle leans in to talk to Jade, grinning.

"I love Tuesday nights!" she says.

* * *

A few weeks later, on the first Tuesday of November, Peggy Sue walks up to the table where Jade is sitting with Bobby, Tyler and her friend, Tara Ellis. Tyler's brother Phin and his girlfriend Carrie Candelario are on stage singing a duet.

"Here you go," says Peggy Sue, handing Bobby another rum and cola.

"Thanks," Bobby says with a smile.

"No Chelle this week?" Peggy Sue asks.

"I don't know," says Jade. "She was going out with Simon and then they were supposed to be coming here."

"Alright," says Peggy Sue. "Just making sure I wasn't missing anyone!" She heads off to check on another of the tables in El Scorcho's side room.

"Seriously though, should we be worried they're not here?" Bobby asks, sipping his drink.

"Nah," says Jade. "They're probably on their way."

Fifteen minutes later, Chelle walks in and shouts a hello to Rachel and Peggy Sue behind the bar before heading to the side room where she is greeted warmly by her friends. Simon shuffles in behind her, his hands in his pockets.

"Where'd you guys go?" asks Tyler.

"We had dinner at Aria," answers Chelle. "You know, the Italian place? The service was slow but the food was really, really good!"

Simon nods.

"Oh, nice," says Tyler. "I've been thinking about taking Alan there."

"Is he coming tonight?"

"I don't know," says Tyler. "He didn't respond to my texts."

"That's weird," says Chelle before turning to Simon. "Have you talked to him today?"

"No," says Simon. "He was off today."

"It's alright," says Tyler. "I'll call him later or something."

"Bobby! Come on up here," calls Ian. Everyone at the table claps as Bobby gets up, drink in hand, and heads for the stage.

Carrie leans in to talk to Simon.

"Did your store manager get a chance to look at my application yet?"

"Ivy?" asks Simon. "I know Alan gave her your stuff, she said she was gonna give you a call."

"Okay, cool! I was getting nervous that maybe my hair was too much?" Carrie says, pointing out the pale pink streaks in her platinum blonde hair. "I don't know, I'm probably obsessing."

"Oh, no, you're fine," says Simon. "I know there's a thing about extreme colors, but I think that's subtle enough."

"Awesome!" says Carrie, sitting back and giving Phin a kiss on the cheek.

While Carrie is talking with Simon, Jade catches Chelle's attention.

"You okay?" she mouths.

Chelle rolls her eyes.

"What?" asks Jade.

"I'll tell you later," Chelle mouths.

Jade nods.

*That can't be good,* she thinks.

An hour later, karaoke is drawing to a close and Ian has only a few songs and singers left on his list for this Tuesday.

"Up next, we've got… Chelle and Simon!" he announces.

Simon jerks his head to look at Chelle.

"What?"

"Come on," she says, standing up. "We'll go up there together."

"I don't want to."

"Seriously, come on, Simon," says Chelle. "There's only a few people in here and you haven't come up there with me in weeks!"

"Well maybe I don't want to," Simon snaps.

Chelle stands, staring at him with her lips pursed.

"You guys coming?" Ian asks from the stage.

"Skip us, Ian," Chelle says. "I'll go next week."

"Alright," says Ian, going back to his list.

"I'll be right back," Chelle says. She walks off to pay her tab at the bar and while Rachel is running her credit card, she realizes that Jade has followed her.

"What's going on?"

"I can't do this, Jade."

"What do you mean?"

"This whole thing with Simon," says Chelle. "It's just not working, I can't do it. He never wants to do *anything*, I barely even feel like his girlfriend anymore. Just getting him to go to Aria tonight was like pulling teeth and even then we barely talked at dinner! It's like… we're just two people who hang out a lot and kiss each other goodbye. He won't even hold my hand, anymore."

Jade puts her arm around her friend.

"I'll support whatever you do," she says into her ear. "You know I love you."

Chelle sighs.

"Thanks," she says. "Love you, too."

Twenty minutes later, Chelle and Simon are standing outside of El Scorcho.

"I can't do this anymore, Simon," she says.

"Do what?"

"This," she says. "You and me. Us."

Simon says nothing.

"I'm done," Chelle says quietly.

Simon looks to the ground.

"Are you going to say anything?" she asks.

He looks up from the ground, his eyes sad.

"I'm sorry."

"That's it? That's all you've got?"

"I'm sorry it didn't work out," he says. "I'm sorry I didn't want to sing tonight and I'm sorry I couldn't be the boyfriend you wanted me to be."

Chelle shakes her head and steps to the curb.

"It's not just about the singing," she says, raising her hand. Within seconds, a cab pulls over and she opens the door.

"Good bye, Simon," she says, climbing into the back seat.

She closes the door and the cab drives away.

* * *

On the Tuesday after their visit with the company owner goes well, Alan Brodecker brings a group of his co-workers from The C³ to El Scorcho for karaoke, including Jacinda Hall, Dominic Thorton and Imani Tahan.

Simon Dawes quietly declined the invitation.

Alan leads the other three into the side room and smiles at Peggy Sue, who is talking with Jade and Bobby. Jacinda, Dominic and Imani sit down at a table in the corner while Alan goes to greet them.

"Hey there," he says.

"Hey stranger!" says Jade as Bobby nods hello behind her.

"Hope you guys don't mind, I brought a group from work," says Alan. "It's been a crazy week with the visit and a chaotic weekend, we could all use a good unwinding."

"Is Simon coming?"

"No," says Alan. "He didn't say why but I'm sure it's because Chelle's going to be here."

"She's not, actually," says Jade. "She wasn't feeling so great earlier, so she left work early. She's probably passed out about now."

"Well, isn't it ironic?" says Alan.

"Don't you think?" says Jade, smiling. "Tyler will be here soon."

"Oh yeah," says Alan. "I talked to him earlier today. I've been so busy with work and my classes... I'm glad you guys do this every Tuesday, gives me something to look forward to when I can make it!"

"I know," says Jade. "Sometimes it's all that gets me through the week, too."

Alan nods and notices Peggy Sue walk back into the room and approach the table where Jacinda, Dominic and Imani are paging through the binder of song choices.

"I'm gonna go sit with them, if you guys don't mind?"

"Not at all," says Jade. "Feel free to come back over any time!"

"Will do," Alan says before walking to sit with his other friends.

Jade looks at Bobby.

"I don't know what to make of that guy," she says.

An hour later, Imani and Jacinda are on stage butchering a popular song when Alan comes to the table where Tyler sits with Jade, Bobby, Tara and Genevieve.

"Hey poodle," he says, sitting down.

"Hey," Tyler says coolly.

"Sorry about the last few weeks," he says. "I know it was kind of a dick move of me to vanish on you."

"No, no, you're fine," Tyler says before taking a long drink of his double vodka cranberry. "I've been busy with stuff, too."

"It's just been nuts at work and then I've been applying for that study abroad program," says Alan.

"Oh yeah," says Tyler. "How's that going?"

"I had to write like five different essays and get three letters of recommendation," Alan says. "So it's been a pain in the ass, but it'll be worth it if I get picked."

"That's awesome," says Tyler.

"But anyway, I wanted to make it up to you," says Alan, putting his hand on Tyler's leg. "Are you free on Friday night for dinner and a movie?"

"Oh yeah," says Tyler. "Well, wait, my friend Brannon is having a few people over on Friday night, but, small world, he moved into my building so I could probably just stop by before heading out or something."

"Alright, just let me know," says Alan, sliding his hand up his thigh. He winks at Tyler before going back to sit with another co-worker who has arrived, Kirby Cochrane.

Tyler leans over to Genevieve.

"Hey, Gen, are you still going to Brannon's on Friday?"

"Oh, yeah!" she says. "Isn't the whole group?"

"I don't know if anyone's heard from Kate," says Tyler. "Anyway, I don't know if I'm gonna be able to make it. Do you think Brannon will be upset?"

"I don't think so," says Genevieve, taking a drink of her beer. "Besides, it was kind of short notice."

"True," says Tyler. "He needs to come here with us sometime!"

Genevieve nods enthusiastically as Peggy Sue walks up; Tyler orders another drink. Shortly afterward, his brother's girlfriend Carrie walks in and, after greeting everyone at Tyler's table, sits with Alan.

"Come on up here, Tara," Ian says into the microphone. Tara

heads to the stage while Bobby heads to the bathroom. Jade catches Tyler's attention and nods toward Carrie at the other table.

"She got that job, didn't she?" she asks.

"Yeah," he says. "I'm guessing that's why she's over there."

"Does she like it?"

"She told Phin there's a lot of politics and their manager plays favorites, but so far it's alright."

"I wonder if it's weird for her to be working with Simon."

"I don't think it's too bad," says Tyler. "She's not really close with Chelle and I don't think she works with him much. I mean, Phin said he saw him last week when he dropped her off and it was only mildly awkward."

"I just wouldn't know what to say, I guess," says Jade.

"Yeah, I know," says Tyler. "I'm kind of annoyed with Carrie right now, actually. She hasn't been much help with the Alan situation over the last few weeks."

"You can't blame her for that though," says Jade. "I wouldn't want to get mixed up in that either, especially since she's dating your brother."

"Yeah, I guess you're right," says Tyler, glancing across the room at Alan who is laughing with his arm around Kirby's shoulder.

Bobby returns from the bathroom with Phin in tow, who delivers Carrie's drink to her before sitting with his brother. Before they know it, Peggy Sue calls last call, their tabs are paid and everyone is parting ways outside of El Scorcho while Ian wraps his cords inside and Rachel wipes down the bar, another Tuesday night coming to an end. And though a feeling in the pit of his stomach warns him not to, Tyler lets Alan kiss him goodnight.

\* \* \*

*Winter*

After a two week break in karaoke nights because of the holidays, everyone is excited for the first Tuesday Night Karaoke of the year, from the El Scorcho staff to the regulars. Despite the snow that flurries through the dark, wintry sky, they know that the drinks will still flow, the music will play on and they will be surrounded by friends.

Jade steps inside and shakes the snow off of her coat, followed by her brother Luke, who unravels a scarf from his neck.

"So this is El Scorcho," she tells him.

"Nice," he says, looking around the main room. "Do they still serve food during karaoke?"

"Little bit of bar food but the regular menu cuts off at 9:00."

"Gotcha," he says.

"Come on, you gotta meet the staff!"

Jade leads her brother to the bar where Rachel is stocking glasses.

"Jade!" she says, waving.

"Hey Rach!" says Jade. "This is my brother, Luke."

"Nice to meet you," Rachel says, holding out her hand.

"You, too," he says, shaking it. "So you guys do this every Tuesday?"

"Yup," says Rachel. "Every Tuesday! Your sister and her friends are some of our best customers."

Jade smiles.

"And I think everyone's coming tonight!" says Jade.

A couple walks in from outside, bringing a burst of cold air with them through the open door.

"Awesome," Rachel says to Jade and Luke as the couple walks up to the bar. "Excuse me just a sec." She greets the couple who proceed to order their drinks.

"Let's go get a table," Jade says to Luke before leading him to the side room. Peggy Sue is talking with Ian, who sits behind his laptop. Jade introduces her brother to the both of them.

"So what do you do?" Ian asks after Peggy Sue heads to the bar with their drink order.

"I'm an English teacher at Central High," Luke answers. "We're still on winter break so I told Jade I'd tag along for tonight."

"Very cool," says Ian. "The DJ company I work for does their prom, I think."

"Oh, really? I think I'm chaperoning prom this year, actually," says Luke.

"I'll look for you if I get put on that one," says Ian. "You gonna sing tonight?"

"Oh, sure," says Luke. "So long as my little sis does, too!"

"Well, that's a given," says Ian. "This girl's a rockstar!"

Jade blushes.

"Seriously," says Ian. "You and Tyler and Chelle and the crew make Tuesday night so much fun."

"We try," Jade says, smiling. Peggy Sue walks up with a pitcher of beer and two glasses.

"Here you go!" she says.

"Thank you, Peggy Sue," says Jade.

"Where's Bobby?" she asks.

"He's working late," says Jade. "He'll be here, though!"

"Yeah, I'm excited to meet him," says Luke.

"Oh," says Peggy Sue, looking between the two. "You didn't run into him over the holidays?"

"No," says Jade. "Bobby went out of town, actually."

"Gotcha," says Peggy Sue. The couple from the bar wanders into the side room followed by a group of three girls.

"Duty calls!" says Peggy Sue. Ian cranks up the music and Tuesday Night Karaoke is underway.

An hour later, Tyler is at a table with Chelle and their coworker Kevin Mackenzie, checking his phone for a text from Alan. Bobby and Luke sit at another table talking while Jade sings on stage.

"Jade told me you're in media?"

"Oh yeah," says Bobby, grabbing his beer. "Media production and sales."

"That sounds exciting," says Luke.

"It can be," says Bobby, finishing his beer. "I, uh, I don't do a lot of hands on stuff there, mostly technical. We do a lot of stuff with corporate training, nothing mainstream really. Video, social media, little bit of marketing… stuff like that."

"Gotcha," says Luke. "You want another one?"

"Actually, I think I'm good for now," says Bobby, looking at his empty glass. "Thank you though!"

"No problem," says Luke. "So you and my sister, huh?"

Bobby smiles.

"She's awesome," Bobby says stiffly.

"Relax," says Luke. "I'm not here to be the intimidating big brother."

"That's good," says Bobby, laughing.

"Besides, she can handle herself," says Luke. "She was always the tougher of the two of us."

Bobby smiles.

Tyler walks over and sits down.

"Hey, Luke!" he says. "Sorry I haven't gotten over here yet. I haven't seen you in forever! How've you been?"

"Great, great," says Luke.

"I'll be right back," Bobby says, deciding now is an opportune time to head to the bathroom, if only to let Luke and Tyler catch up. When he leaves the bathroom, Jade is standing against the wall holding a full beer bottle.

"Hey," she says, grinning.

"Hello," he replies.

"I saw my brother chatting you up from the stage," she says. "Sorry if it was awkward."

"Not at all!" Bobby says. "He's really nice."

"Good," says Jade. "Because I told him I like you a lot and he'd better be nice to you."

"He was fine," says Bobby. "And I think he knows I like you a lot, too."

"Yeah?"

"Yeah," Bobby says. "I like you so much, I'd really, really like to call you my girlfriend."

Jade's eyes go wide; a grin spreads across her face.

"Wow," she says coyly. "You must like me a *lot*..."

"Well?" asks Bobby, raising his eyebrows.

"I think we can arrange something," says Jade, wrapping her arms around him as they kiss.

\* \* \*

Three weeks later, on what could go down as the coldest night of the year, Rachel Avery stands behind the bar in El Scorcho watching the door. The forecast called for snow, but so far the weather has held out. There is one couple finishing their dinner at a table on the far side of the main dining room. Ian is in the next room playing music for the three people that are seated there; Peggy Sue is back in the kitchen, folding towels. Rachel pulls out her phone to check the time, hoping that the snow will hold out until the end of her shift.

The door opens and Tara Ellis walks in.

"Hi Rachel!" she says.

"Hey!" says Rachel. "Keeping warm?"

"Trying to," says Tara. "No snow yet, though, so that's good!"

"Oh, good" says Rachel. "I really, really don't want to have to go home in it later."

"I know," says Tara. "I might cut out early if it starts."

"I don't blame you," says Rachel. "Can I get you a drink? I can have Peggy Sue bring it over if you wanna go grab a table."

"Oh, sure," says Tara. "Could I actually have a glass of moscato to start? Don't you guys keep a few bottles of that around?"

"We do!" says Rachel, reaching into the cooler to pull out a bottle of wine. "Fancy this week, huh?"

"For now," says Tara, laughing. "I have a job interview tomorrow afternoon, so I'm treating myself tonight."

"Nothing wrong with it! Where are you interviewing?"

"Down in Old Town," says Tara. "I'd be like an assistant for this artist and also help work in her shop."

"That's awesome," says Rachel, pulling the cork out of the bottle. "Anyone I might have heard of?"

"I don't think so," says Tara. "Her name's Adrienne Maschera? She's only been in town for a few months... she was really sweet on the phone. I'm just excited to be back down in Old Town before tour season starts."

Rachel sets down a glass and fills it with wine.

"Well, good luck," she says. "I know you'll do great!"

"Thanks," says Tara. "Can I start a tab?"

"Of course," says Rachel. "I'll let Peggy Sue know."

Tara smiles and heads to the side room. Not long after, Jade and Chelle arrive followed by Tyler and Alan and a small assortment of random people, including a couple they had seen there a few weeks ago.

"I'm telling you guys, you'll love it," says Alan.

"And it's out in Garden Park?" asks Chelle.

"Yeah," he says. "It's in the basement of an old apartment building. I think it used to be an actual speakeasy!"

"That sounds cool," says Tyler.

"Yeah, one of the tenants that lives in the building runs it, so it's a little sketch but one of my friends was telling me about it and I wanna check it out sometime soon."

"I'm in if you guys are?" says Jade.

"Yeah," says Tara. "Just let me know!"

"For sure," says Chelle. She turns to Jade. "Bobby's invited too!"

Jade smiles.

"Hopefully he won't have to work late the night we decide to go."

Chelle and Tara nod.

Peggy Sue walks by with a tray of drinks for another table.

"Oh, hey guys?" she says, pausing for a moment. "Just wanted to let you know it's started to snow outside. I just ran outside for a smoke and it's really coming down."

"Oh, crap," Chelle says to Jade. "We should probably head out soon, then."

"Yeah, that might not be a bad idea," Jade says, nodding. "Can we go ahead and pay our tabs?"

"Sure," says Peggy Sue. "I'll go get them from you!"

"Thanks," says Chelle.

"Do you wanna go, too?" Tyler asks Alan.

"Nah," he says. "We'll stay here a little bit longer."

"Okay."

"I think I'll tag along with you guys, if that's alright?" Tara says to Jade and Chelle. "I want to get home before it gets too bad."

"Yeah, no problem," says Jade.

After they've paid, the three girls say their goodbyes and head out into the wintry night. A few of the other people in El Scorcho have filtered out, as well.

Alan picks up the binder with karaoke songs in it.

"One song and then hit the road?" he asks Tyler.

"Sure," Tyler says, smiling. "You wanna come over? Get snowed in with me?"

Alan looks at him and smiles softly.

"We'll see how bad it looks when we leave," he says.

"Okay," says Tyler.

Ten minutes later, they are singing a classic rock song on stage. Fifteen minutes after that, they have paid their tabs and leave, heading for Tyler's loft. By the time Rachel is locking the front door of El Scorcho, Alan has his arm around Tyler, both of them naked in Tyler's bed as the snow continues to fall outside. Once he is sure Tyler is asleep, Alan sees himself out, locking the door behind him as he goes.

* * *

A month later, it is Mardi Gras and the staff of El Scorcho has filled the restaurant with an array of decorations and enough purple, green and gold beads to blanket a parade route. The weather has started to warm up and they are expecting a large turnout for this particular Tuesday night of karaoke. Rachel stirs a jug of hurricane mix made especially for tonight's drink special while Ian plays zydeco music in the next room.

At quarter after ten, Graham Kelly opens the door and holds it for the group he is arriving with, including Chelle, Jade, Bobby and Mack. Tyler steadies himself against the building outside while Alan finishes a cigarette.

"Oh my God," says Tyler. "Didn't I tell you Mama Gumbo's had the best Cajun food? Didn't I tell you that?"

Alan nods, taking a final drag on his cigarette.

"That you did," he says. "And the hurricanes didn't hurt either, am I right?"

Tyler giggles.

"Come on, Drunky," Alan says, stepping out the flame at the end of his cigarette butt. "Let's get inside."

By the time they get to El Scorcho's side room, Peggy Sue has taken everyone's drink orders and Jade has already given Ian two slips of songs she'd like to sing: one solo, one duet with Chelle.

Tyler flops down into the seat next to Graham.

"You picked a great firs'night to come with us," he says, his words slurring together. "Mardi Gras's one of my favorite holidays!"

Graham laughs.

"You gotta sing though," says Tyler. "You're gonna sing, right?"

"Of course," says Graham. "You gonna sing with me?"

"Me?" Tyler asks, laughing. "If you want me to!"

Peggy Sue returns to the table with a bucket of beer bottles, two hurricanes and a cranberry vodka for Tyler.

"For me? But I didn't even order yet!" he says when she sets it in front of him.

"I know what you like, sugar," she says with a wink.

"You're so sweet to me," says Tyler. "Come here, give me a hug!"

Chelle looks at Mack while Tyler gives Peggy Sue a hug.

"Don't worry," says Mack. "He's off tomorrow."

"And Alan's taking him home, right?" Chelle asks.

"Oh yeah," says Mack, laughing.

"Did you meet Graham yet?" Tyler asks Peggy Sue.

"I did," she says. "He's here with Chelle, right?"

"Yup," says Tyler. "That's right! Aren't they cute?"

Peggy Sue laughs.

"I'll be back to check on you guys in a bit," she says, patting Tyler's shoulder.

"She's so sweet," Tyler says after Peggy Sue walks away.

A half hour later, Tyler finally finishes his drink and Alan pays their tab. They leave karaoke early, Tyler assuring everyone he is fine but just a little tired. Mack has moved to another table where he is flirting with a group of three girls, determined to get at least one phone number tonight.

"Jade… Chelle… you guys are up!" Ian calls from the stage.

"What did we even put in for again?" Chelle asks Jade as they walk to the stage.

"Guess we're about to find out," Jade says, laughing.

While the two girls are singing, Bobby turns to Graham.

"You ready for another?" he asks, gesturing toward Graham's beer bottle.

"Sure," says Graham.

Bobby grabs two bottles from the bucket on the table and hands one to Graham.

"Thanks," he says.

"No problem," says Bobby. "So what do you make of the Scorcho?"

"I like it," says Graham. "Honestly, I haven't been out much since moving here, so it's nice to get out and explore."

"Why not?"

"I've been busy with schoolwork and stuff," says Graham. "And I don't know if they told you, but I live out in Garden Park so getting down here takes a while and with the weather being so cold…"

"Yeah, I don't blame you," says Bobby. "It's been so cold, it makes me really glad I get to travel."

"Oh, yeah?"

"Oh," says Bobby. "Yeah… I, uh, I travel for work from time to time. Check in on the satellite offices and stuff."

"Oh, cool," says Graham. "Where do you work?"

"Just a little media production studio," Bobby says quickly. "Hey, I was gonna ask you, how often does that speakeasy open in your building? Chelle was telling Jade about it."

"You know, I'm not totally sure," says Graham. "My neighbor runs it and I think he just opens it up whenever he and his friends feel like it."

"Gotcha," says Bobby. "Yeah, I was out of town when they went… the night they met you, I guess? Anyway, I know Jade wants to go sometime and I'd like to check it out, myself."

"Sure," says Graham. "I can ask Felix and I'll let you guys know!"

"That would be awesome."

"No problem," says Graham. "So how long have you and Jade been together?"

"Officially, almost two months," says Bobby. "But we met back in October."

"Very cool."

"Yeah, she's great," says Bobby. "Sometimes I wonder why she's with me, I feel like she could do so much better…"

"Don't sell yourself short, man," says Graham. "You seem like a pretty legit guy, everyone in the group likes you."

"Thanks," says Bobby, taking a drink of his beer.

*I need to talk to Jade later,* he thinks. *I gotta tell her the truth.*

The girls get back to the table, giggling from the rush of singing on stage.

"You guys miss us?" asks Chelle.

"Of course," says Graham, putting his arm around her shoulder.

"Hey," Bobby says to Jade. "Wanna run to the bar with me?"

*Here goes nothing,* he thinks, his heart starting to beat faster.

"Sure," she says. "Everything okay?"

"Yeah," says Bobby. "Just wanna stretch my legs, thought you might wanna come with."

*And I have to tell you the truth about my job,* he mentally adds.

"Hey Jade," Mack yells from the other table. "Come here real quick, you gotta hear this!"

"Can I meet you over at the bar in a few minutes?" she asks Bobby.

*Crap,* he thinks.

"Sure, yeah," he says. Jade heads over to talk with Mack and the three girls he is sitting with as Bobby heads to the bar.

And despite all of his intentions, the night ends before he has a chance to have a private conversation with Jade about his job and the company he works for.

*I'll tell her soon,* he thinks to himself as he drives home.

* * *

*Spring*

On the third Tuesday of March, it starts raining during the afternoon and continues through the night as Tyler rides to El Scorcho in the back of a cab with Phin and Carrie. Though the side room is crowded when they arrive, they immediately spot Jade and Bobby sitting at their usual table.

"The owner ran an ad in *Cityzine,*" explains Peggy Sue. "I guess the new issue came out, so we've been packed!"

Carrie and Tyler nod in acknowledgement.

"Well, that's gotta be good for business, right?" asks Bobby.

"Oh yeah," says Peggy Sue. "And don't you guys worry about drink service, you know I'll have you covered!" She winks and heads off to check on another table; Ian calls a woman named Cathy to the stage.

"So this is new," says Jade, looking around the busy room while pouring herself a beer. "We'd better get our song requests in so Ian doesn't lose us in the lineup."

"He'll get us in," Carrie says, sipping a gin and tonic. "I'm sure we'll be fine."

Jade continues looking through the song binder.

"Is anyone else coming tonight?" asks Phin.

"Brannon and Kate said they're gonna try to come out," says Tyler, swirling a straw through his vodka cranberry. "He texted me a little while ago and said they're on their way."

"Cool," says Jade. "Is Alan coming?"

"Oh, uh, no," says Tyler, quickly taking a drink. "He's working on his speech for his study abroad thing… he moved on to the next round, did I tell you guys that?"

Jade rolls her eyes while Carrie shifts uncomfortably in her seat.

"Once or twice," Jade mutters to herself.

"Oh, hey!" Phin says, standing to greet Brannon and Kate, both of whom are soaked with rain.

"Hey guys," Kate says, smiling as she pulls her matted red hair out of her face. "It's really coming down out there!"

Brannon pulls out a chair for Kate to sit down.

"Such a gentleman," Carrie says, playfully elbowing Phin.

"Quit making the rest of us look bad, would ya?" Phin yells over the crowd.

"That's your own fault, punk," Brannon says, sitting down.

"Good to see you, man," says Phin, holding out his hand.

"It's kind of weird to be drinking with you," says Brannon. "I can still remember you running around, Tyler's annoying kid brother."

"Well this little brat's gonna buy you a drink, old man," says Phin, waving to Peggy Sue, who is finishing dropping off a bucket at another table. Ian calls a trio of girls to the stage to sing an old pop song.

"I've got his first drink," Phin tells Peggy Sue when she walks up, pointing to Brannon.

"Alright," she says. "Hello! So many new faces tonight!"

"This is Brannon and Kate," says Tyler. "Chelle and I grew up with them out in the suburbs."

"Gotcha," says Peggy Sue. "Well, welcome to El Scorcho! If you're hanging with this crew, then I know you guys are a good time. What are you drinking?"

"What beers do you have on tap?" Brannon asks. While Peggy Sue goes over the selection with him, Kate grabs Carrie's attention.

"What do you have?" she asks.

"Amaretto sours," says Carrie. "Want to try it?"

Kate takes a drink of Carrie's cocktail and orders one from Peggy Sue, who heads off to the bar.

"So you guys come here every week?" Kate asks.

"Pretty much," says Jade. "We miss a few here and there, but it's fun and the staff knows us by now."

"That's cool," says Kate. "Is the food good?"

"You know…" Jade starts to say, trailing off.

"I don't think we've ever actually eaten here," Tyler finishes, slightly amazed at the realization. "I mean, we've had appetizers here and there but yeah, we've never eaten here."

"We need to try it sometime," Jade says.

A few minutes later, Peggy Sue arrives with their drinks.

"You know what we just realized?" Tyler asks her.

"What's that, babe?"

"We come here almost every week for karaoke but we've never actually been here for dinner or anything!"

"Yeah, you have," she says.

"None of *us* have," says Jade.

"No wait, last week, I thought I saw – " Peggy Sue stops suddenly. "You know what, nevermind, you guys are right!"

*I wonder what she's talking about,* Jade thinks to herself.

"You'll have to come in early some night, the food's almost as good as Rachel's drinks," Peggy Sue says quickly over the noise of the people in the room. "I'll be back to check on you guys."

She walks off.

Jade looks at Bobby, an eyebrow raised.

"I'm gonna run to the bathroom, I'll be right back," she says, taking her drink with her.

"Up next we have… the brothers Welik!" Ian announces from the stage. "Phin, Tyler… get your asses up here!"

Phin and Tyler head for the stage to sing a standard karaoke crowd pleaser receiving thunderous applause.

Over in the other side of El Scorcho, Jade leans against the bar waiting for Peggy Sue to walk by. When she passes, Jade grabs her attention.

"Hey Peggy Sue, I wanted to ask you something."

"Hey Jade, what's up?"

"Just out of curiosity, and of course it will stay between us… how come you clammed up back there? Is everything okay?"

"Oh," she says quickly. "It was nothing, I'm fine."

"Okay," says Jade. "Just wanted to make sure you were alright, you ran off kind of quickly."

Peggy Sue sighs.

"You swear my name won't be brought up?"

"Of course."

"Alright… that guy who comes in here with Tyler sometimes, Alan, right?"

"Yes."

"He had dinner here last week," says Peggy Sue. "With some guy I didn't recognize."

"What?"

"I wasn't their server so I don't know really what was going on between them," says Peggy Sue. "They did seem *pretty* friendly with each other, though."

"Interesting."

. "If you want to say something to Tyler, that's fine but you didn't hear it from me. I care about you guys, but I'm just here to work, make sure everyone has a good time," says Peggy Sue. "I'm not trying to start any trouble."

\* \* \*

The Tuesday before the group has reservations to stay the night in Claythorn Manor, they sit in El Scorcho passing around a book on the mansion's dark past. Ian is playing music during a break in karaoke and the smell of nachos hangs in the air from three tables over.

"Yeah, I'm not sorry I'm missing this," Jade says, paging through the book.

Peggy Sue walks up to check on the table.

"Kinda slow tonight?" Chelle asks, looking around.

"Yeah," says Peggy Sue. "The special from *Cityzine* ended in March and it's died down a little bit since then."

"Gotcha."

"Hey, what's that?" Peggy Sue asks, pointing toward the book in Jade's hands.

"It's a book about Claythorn Manor," Chelle says. "The history and stuff."

"Oh, God," says Peggy Sue. "The haunted mansion in Garden Park?"

"That's the one!" says Genevieve.

"You've heard of it?" asks Graham.

"Dude, yeah," says Peggy Sue. "I grew up hearing about that place."

"These fools are going to stay the night there," says Jade, looking around the table.

"Seriously?"

307

"Yup," says Tyler. "You ever been?"

"No, sir," says Peggy Sue. "I will happily steer clear of that place."

"Do you believe in ghosts?" asks Phin. "Or are you just scared of the urban legends?"

"I'm honestly not sure about any of that," says Peggy Sue. "But I'm not keen on taking any chances, either."

"Amen, sister," Jade says, holding her hand up for a high five from Peggy Sue.

"So you're not going with them?" she asks.

"Negative," says Jade. "I'm sitting this one out."

"Smart girl," says Peggy Sue, winking before she walks away.

"People are really freaked out about this place," Carrie says to Phin. "I'm kind of nervous about going."

"You'll be fine," Phin says. "Besides, you'll be with me and you won't have to go anywhere or do anything you don't want to do."

"Promise?"

"Yes," says Phin. "And if it gets to be too much, we can always go home."

Carrie smiles.

"I'm excited we're going," says Chelle, grabbing her drink.

"Me, too," says Genevieve. "I feel like I've been cooped up all winter, so what better activity to do with everyone than spend the night in an old, potentially haunted mansion?"

"I'll cheers to that," says Phin.

Everyone at the table clinks their glasses.

"Who all's going, again?"

"All of us," says Chelle. "Except Jade, unless she changes her mind…"

"Not happening," says Jade, taking a drink of her beer.

"Don't forget Alan," Tyler says quietly. "He's coming, too."

Jade gives Chelle a look.

"Oh yeah," says Chelle, looking away.

"And Mack's in my room, right?" asks Genevieve.

"Yup," says Chelle.

"I haven't seen him in so long!" says Genevieve. "I'm excited to catch up."

"I talked to Bea the other day, by the way," says Graham. "She's excited for us to come!"

"I can't wait," says Chelle, smiling as she gives Graham a quick kiss.

"Excuse me, love birds," Ian says to Chelle and Graham from the stage. "You guys wanna come up and sing or do you need to just get yourselves a room?"

Chelle laughs.

"Here we come," she says.

As Chelle and Graham take the stage, Jade grabs Tyler's attention.

"Hey, I'm gonna go outside for a smoke," she says. "Wanna keep me company?"

"Sure," he says.

They head outside as Carrie picks up the book about Claythorn Manor and starts paging through it with Genevieve.

Outside of El Scorcho, Jade pulls a cigarette out of her pack.

"Got an extra?" asks Tyler.

"Sure," she says, handing him one before lighting it with her lighter. Moments later, they exhale smoke into the night sky.

"Hey, I've gotta tell you something," says Jade. "And you can't be mad at me or upset, okay?"

"I can't guarantee an exact reaction without knowing what it is you're about to tell me, but I'll do my best," Tyler says, resting the cigarette between his fingers. "What's up?"

"I don't know the context, so it might not be anything at all, but I wanted you to know that Alan had dinner here a few weeks ago," says Jade. "With another guy."

Tyler swallows the saliva that pools in his mouth.

"Oh, yeah?" he finally asks, taking a drag on the cigarette.

"Yeah," says Jade. "Please don't be upset with me, I didn't know whether or not I should tell you and finally, I don't know, I figured if the situation was reversed, I'd want you to tell me."

Tyler nods.

"How did you find that out?"

"Someone told me they saw him," says Jade. "A third party."

Tyler exhales.

"What are you gonna do?"

"Well, I'm gonna ask him about it," says Tyler. "I just have to figure out how without sounding crazy or like I've got people stalking him."

"Yeah," says Jade, finishing her cigarette. "I know you'll do what's right for you. I just wanted to tell you before you guys had your night in Claythorn Manor, I know you two are supposed to be sharing a room. Let me know if you need anything, okay?"

"Sure," says Tyler. "Hey, you can go back in if you want, I'm gonna be a minute."

"Okay," says Jade. She pulls open the door and heads back to the table, leaving Tyler alone outside of El Scorcho.

He leans against the building lost in thought, the cigarette between his fingers burning to ash. Finally, he pulls out his phone and scrolls to Alan's number. He hesitates a moment before pushing the button to dial.

The phone rings twice and half-way through the third ring, the call goes straight to Alan's voicemail.

\* \* \*

A month later, Chelle texts Peggy Sue to let her know that the group is taking a week off from karaoke for various reasons, but that they will be back the following week and to have the music cued and the drinks ready. Peggy Sue gets the message while sitting on a stool at the bar talking with Rachel. She replies to Chelle that she'll miss everyone this week and that she hopes all is well.

"So none of them are coming?" asks Rachel, breaking up the freshly produced sheets of ice in the cooler.

"I guess not, they're all either working or staying in."

"Oh, well," says Rachel. "I figured this was going to happen sooner or later."

"What do you mean?"

"Just because they come in every week doesn't mean they'll be here *every* week, you know?"

"Yeah, I guess you're right," says Peggy Sue.

"It will be weird not seeing any of them this week," admits Rachel. "Hopefully this isn't the beginning of the end."

Ian walks in carrying his laptop followed by a young guy in a red baseball cap carrying a speaker, a bag with speaker stands slung over his shoulder.

"Hey ladies," he says, walking up. The kid puts down the speaker and pulls off his cap, readjusting the dreadlocks underneath.

"Who's this?" asks Rachel.

"This is Blake," says Ian. "He's shadowing me tonight."

"Oh, cool," says Rachel. "How old is he?"

Ian looks around.

"Eighteen."

"He's not supposed to be in here after 9:00 P.M."

Ian looks at Peggy Sue then back to Rachel.

"He's not on your payroll and he's not going to be drinking."

Rachel doesn't say anything.

"It's just for tonight," says Ian. "The boss wants him to see how I run a karaoke night for a few parties we've got coming up later this summer."

When Rachel hesitates, Ian walks closer to her and lowers his voice.

"I got the kid a fake I.D.," he says. "So on the off chance tonight is the first night a cop wanders in here, he's legit. I made sure he's got everything on there memorized, middle name, zip code, hell, even the guy's zodiac sign. I mean, come on, look at him. He looks older than I do."

Rachel looks from Blake back to Ian and sighs.

"Alright," she says as Blake smiles at her. "He stays mostly out of sight and we don't talk about it. Deal?"

"Sounds good to me," Ian says before turning to Blake. "Blake Pines? This is Rachel and that's Peggy Sue."

"Hello," Blake says.

"Nice to meet you," says Rachel. "Don't get us in trouble, okay?"

"Okay."

Peggy Sue gets off her stool and walks over to shake his hand.

"You're gonna have a blast tonight," she says. "And don't worry too much about Rachel, she's always worrying about stuff. Let me know if there's anything I can get for you, okay?"

"You got it," says Blake, smiling. He picks up the speaker and follows Ian into the side room. The two work quickly to set up the stage and are ready long before the first guests arrive for karaoke.

An hour and a half later, Blake looks up from Ian's laptop during a break from singers and is caught off guard by the flashy trio of drag queens he sees walking into El Scorcho's side room.

"What's the matter?" asks Ian. "Haven't you ever seen drag queens before?"

"Not in person," says Blake.

The lead queen spots Ian and waves to him. Her two friends grab seats at an empty table as she heads to the front of the room, her dress sparkling and her hair teased to a height that Blake only previously thought possible in comics.

"Honey, it's great to see you!" she says.

"Oh, Diamond," says Ian. "The pleasure is all mine."

"I wasn't talking to you, you nincompoop... I was talking to Blake here!"

"Oh, uh, hi," Blake manages to stammer. "I'm sorry, have we met somewhere before?"

"Come on, Ian... where's my introduction?" the drag queen says.

311

Ian shakes his head.

"Blake, allow me to introduce Miss Diamond St. Delicious," he says as Diamond takes a bow. "Or as you may also know *him*... Philip Warner."

"What?!" says Blake, not believing that the extravagant woman in front of him is the DJ from his prom he asked for career advice, ultimately leading him to this moment in El Scorcho.

"That's right, boobah," says Diamond. "Just had to swing by and see how your first bar gig's going!"

"Let's not call a whole lot of attention to him being in a bar," Ian says in a singsong voice.

"Oh! Right, right," says Diamond. "Well, I was just gonna pop in for a little song and dance and then be on my way! The girls and I are heading to Underland, you know. Care to cue something up for me, Blake?"

"You, uhh... you got it, Diamond!"

"That's my boy," she says, beaming. Diamond St. Delicious takes to the stage and has the crowd on their feet as she sings her way through a classic crowd pleaser. Rachel even comes out from behind the bar to stand by Peggy Sue in the doorway, watching the performance.

"The regulars are gonna be sorry they missed this," she says as she claps along with Peggy Sue.

\* \* \*

*Summer*

"I'm sure she'll be fine with it," says Genevieve Delphe. She is sitting in the side room of El Scorcho talking with her old friend, Yorick Dalton. Peggy Sue is across the room serving drinks to a group celebrating one of their friends' twenty first birthday; Ian plays music on his computer as he compiles the initial list of singers for the evening. The air conditioner works overtime to keep the restaurant cool, but pockets of warm air from the open front door waft through the restaurant.

"I mean, they already have a bulletin board, so I figured it'd be alright, but I don't know, I want to ask before I just put it up," he says.

"Just go ask Rachel behind the bar," says Genevieve.

"Alright," says Yorick, grabbing his satchel, posters sticking out of the open top. He walks to the bar side of El Scorcho just as Tyler and Chelle arrive.

"Hey, Yorick!" Chelle says, running up and hugging him. "I didn't know you were coming tonight!"

"Hey, yeah," he says. "I hadn't been in a while, thought I'd tag along with Genevieve."

"Does she have a table already?" asks Tyler.

"Yeah," says Yorick. "We're on the other side if you guys wanna go sit down. I have to go talk to Rachel for a minute."

"Okay," says Tyler. "See you in a few!"

Tyler and Chelle head off to sit with Genevieve; Yorick makes his way to the bar.

"Hey there," Rachel says as he walks up. "I'll be right with ya!"

"Okay."

Rachel finishes pouring a margarita for a girl on the other side of the bar and adds it to her tab before walking over.

"What can I get you?" she asks.

"Oh, well, I'm actually sitting with friends on the other side," he answers. "I had a question for you though."

"What's up?"

"So, I know you guys have a community board here, would it be cool if I put something up?"

"What is it?"

"I'm helping organize a Masquerade Ball in Old Town and I just have a few posters for it, if that's alright?"

He pulls one out of his bag to show her.

"Oh, yeah," says Rachel. "I saw a thing about that in *Cityzine*."

"I bought that ad!"

"Really?" says Rachel.

"Well, okay," he admits. "Maybe *I* didn't buy it... but it was my idea to take one out."

Rachel laughs.

"No, I get it," she says. "I had the owner here put an ad in an issue this past spring and our business blew up for a while. Hopefully it does the same thing for you guys."

"We'll see," says Yorick. "It would be awesome though, it could really kickstart things down in Old Town."

"Do you work down there?"

"I, uhh... I'm a street magician."

"You know, I think I've heard of you, actually," says Rachel. "You do a few shows a week, pretty much shut down one of the squares every show?"

"I don't know if I'd go *that* far..."

"I've been meaning to come down and see one sometime."

"Really? You should!" says Yorick. "I mean, you know, sometime when you're free."

"I'll see what I can do," says Rachel, smiling.

Yorick smiles back at her.

"Hey," he says. "This may be a little presumptuous, but... would you want to come with me to the Masquerade Ball? It's not for about a month."

As Rachel considers his offer, Peggy Sue walks up with a list of orders from the side room.

"You know, that sounds like fun," she says. "I've gotta get these drinks out, but get me your number and we'll set plans, okay?"

"Alright," he says, a grin on his face.

He walks over to the community board with a stapler and positions the poster advertising the upcoming Masquerade Ball.

*I'd say that went exceptionally well,* he thinks.

\* \* \*

On the Tuesday before the storm, Tyler sits alone at a table in the side room of El Scorcho, reading and rereading a series of texts on his phone from Alan, apologizing for his absence over the last several weeks and announcing his acceptance into the academic program that will keep him out of the country for at least the next year.

Needing some time alone before being surrounded by friends, Tyler arrived early and had Peggy Sue bring him a pitcher to mull his thoughts over with.

*I don't know how to take any of this,* thinks Tyler, watching the bubbles in his beer float to the surface. *I'd all but written him out and now... here he is again and this time I know he's going to be going away. It doesn't change how I feel and I know it's going to piss everyone off, but what do I do?*

Not long after, Chelle and Graham walk in.

*Showtime,* Tyler thinks, smiling wide so as to hide the conflicting emotions he is grappling with internally.

"Hey, guys!" he calls to them.

They wave and walk to the table.

"You're here early," Chelle says, sitting down.

"Yeah," says Tyler. "I didn't have much else going on, so I figured I'd get here a little early to make sure we had our table."

"Aww," says Chelle. "You should have called me! We were just watching a movie."

"It's all good," Tyler says, smiling.

An hour later, Peggy Sue is taking drink orders from Jade, Phin and Carrie.

"Hey, sorry again we can't make it to the party," Carrie says.

"Oh, it's okay!" says Chelle.

"Yeah," says Jade. "You'll just have to come out with us another night that Lizzy's here."

"Sounds good to me," Carrie says.

"Jade... Tyler... get up here, you guys!" Ian calls from the stage.

"We're up!" says Jade.

Tyler takes a gulp of his beer before standing. They take the stage and sing their song, receiving a warm reaction from the crowd. Before leaving the stage, Tyler catches Jade's attention.

"Grab a shot?" he asks.

"Sure," she says. They head to the bar where Rachel is pouring a series of lemon drops.

"Want anything in particular?"

"Those lemon drops look pretty good," says Jade.

"Lemon drops it is!" Tyler says. "And can I get another beer?"

"Sure thing, babe," says Rachel.

While she's mixing their shots, Tyler looks over at Jade.

"No Bobby tonight?" he asks.

"Nope," says Jade. "He's working. Big shocker there."

Tyler nods.

"So, I'm not gonna beat around the bush," he says. "Alan texted me today. He got accepted into that program. He'll be leaving soon and wants to hang out and I was wondering if I might be able to bring him to the party this week?"

*Seriously?* thinks Jade.

"Oh," Jade says. "Well, good for him. The party though... I mean, it's a mystery game so there won't be a character for him to play..."

"I figured," says Tyler. "I just thought it might be nice if he could come with me, you know?"

"Ask Chelle," says Jade. "It's fine with me if it's alright with her."

"Okay," says Tyler. "I'll try to ask her at work tomorrow or something. I don't wanna mess with it tonight."

"Two lemon drops and a beer," says Rachel, walking over with their shots and one that she poured for herself. They clink their shot glasses and take them in one swallow.

"Excellent as always," Tyler says, smiling.

"From one bartender to another, that means a lot," says Rachel. "Thank you!"

Rachel walks away and Jade grabs Tyler's arm.

"Hey," she says, her tone dramatically shifting to a sense of urgency. "Don't turn around, but I think Pete just walked in."

Tyler's heart starts racing.

"What?"

"Yeah," says Jade. "I think Pete just walked in with some friends. I don't see Dillon, but I'm pretty sure that's him. Oh shit, oh shit…"

"What?!"

"He saw you."

"What do I do?"

"I don't know," Jade says quietly. "Talk to him or don't, I guess… Either way, he's walking over here."

Tyler turns around as Pete approaches. He is wearing a white shirt, not unlike the one Tyler has seen so many times from behind in his recurring dream. Only now, there is no crowd between them, no sea of conversation to shout over.

"Hi," he says.

"Hey Ty," says Pete.

"What brings you out?"

"The legendary karaoke night, what else?"

Tyler smiles and looks over his shoulder to see that Jade is halfway back to the other room, no doubt to tell everyone who has just arrived.

"I always forget that you're twenty one now. I mean, you could have come here any time, really, but now it's legit."

"Yeah," Pete says, laughing. "It's weird for me, too."

"No Dillon tonight?"

"Nope, he's still underage," Pete says before turning to introduce his friends. "This is Sam, Nic and Mary."

"Hey, I'm Tyler."

They smile and nod as Rachel walks over to take their orders.

"So are you here with a bunch of people?"

"Most of the group you know is here," says Tyler. "They're all on the other side. I think I hear Chelle singing, actually."

"I thought that voice sounded familiar," Pete says, laughing.

"Yeah," Tyler says, shuffling his feet.

"Well hey, I'd better order," says Pete. "I'm glad you're here, though! Maybe I'll get to hear you sing tonight?"

"Oh, maybe," says Tyler. "We'll see how the night goes."

"Awesome," says Pete. "Hopefully *my* voice isn't too rusty."

"I'm sure it's fine," says Tyler.

Rachel comes back over to take Pete's order.

"Hey, I'll see you in a bit," Tyler says. He grabs his beer and walks off toward the side room. He stops momentarily, leaning against the wall in the hallway connecting the rooms as he runs his fingers through his hair, trying to make sense of the conversation he just had with his ex-boyfriend.

*Don't read too much into it,* Tyler thinks. *You're just two guys in a bar.*

His phone vibrates in his pocket and he pulls it out to see another text from Alan. He shakes his head as he walks back into the side room.

\* \* \*

A week later, Jade Verrit walks into El Scorcho for Tuesday Night Karaoke. She is alone and not sure of the reaction she is about to get from her friends after the disastrous party she had thrown with Chelle on the night of the storm only a few days prior.

"Hey Jade," Rachel says from behind the bar.

Jade waves as she heads to the side room. Ian is on the stage while some guy she does not know is slurring his way through an old rock song. The place is not particularly crowded and she quickly spots her friends. Tara sits next to Mack, laughing with Carrie and Phin. Tyler and Chelle pore over the binder with song selections. As Jade walks over, Tyler looks up from the book and smiles.

"Hey you," he says as she sits next to Chelle.

"Hey," she says.

"How you doing?" he asks.

"I'm good," she says. "Just about packed, ready to go."

He nods.

"I was wondering if we were going to see you tonight," Phin says.

"I don't leave til tomorrow and I figured since I didn't have much left to do, I might as well come by," says Jade.

"How long are you gonna be gone?" asks Carrie.

"I don't know," says Jade. "Caramaya's gave me the extended request I asked for but I may not take the whole time. Just need to get out of the city for a while, clear my head, you know? Lizzy wanted me to come home with her, but I couldn't get a flight, so I'm gonna start driving tomorrow morning."

"I get it, the whole 'head clearing' thing, I mean," says Tara. "Adrienne told me today that she's moving to a new city, so I'm thinking about taking a few weeks to myself before really starting to job hunt again."

"Oh, God, I'm sorry," says Jade. "I know you loved working for her!"

"Thanks," says Tara. "It's alright, though. I'm still giving tours and I'm sure something will come along."

Jade smiles.

The next hour goes by in a flash of jokes, drinks and karaoke songs. Peggy Sue, who has started training as a bartender under Rachel, even makes her a special shot after hearing that Jade will be leaving town for a while.

*I needed this,* Jade thinks, looking around at the faces of her friends. *God, I needed this.*

All too soon, another Tuesday night of karaoke at El Scorcho has come to an end. Carrie and Phin had left earlier; Tara and Mack had just said their good byes. Jade stands outside of the restaurant with Tyler and Chelle.

"You *are* coming back, right?" Chelle asks, half kidding, half serious.

"Well, yeah," says Jade. "I just… after the Bobby thing, I just want to take some time for myself."

Tyler nods.

"Hey," Jade says, turning toward Tyler. "I didn't want to bring this up earlier in front of everyone, but I've been meaning to ask — what happened with Alan after the party?"

"He came over and left after I'd fallen asleep," Tyler says. "Nothing really out of the ordinary."

"Did you talk to him before he left town?"

"Over text, yeah."

"Oh."

"Yup," says Tyler. "Short and sweet, that's how we left it."

Chelle looks at the ground.

"I'm sorry," says Jade.

"Don't be," says Tyler. "I'm starting to see the whole Alan thing for what it really was… just a long game of cat and mouse."

"He's not a bad guy," Chelle says. "He just needed to figure out what he wanted, you know?"

Tyler nods.

"What about Pete?" asks Jade.

Tyler shakes his head.

"I think I've actually figured out what *I* need right now," says Tyler. "I need to focus on myself for a little while, not with anyone in particular, just, I don't know, trying to be a better *me*. Kind of like what you're doing, only I'm staying in town to do it."

They laugh.

"I'm gonna miss you while you're gone," Chelle says to Jade.

"Same here," says Tyler. "Who's gonna keep us in line at work?"

Jade smiles.

"You guys'll manage," she says. "Besides, I'll be back before you know it. And if anything *really* good happens, I'm only a text away."

The lights inside El Scorcho turn off.

"Damn," says Jade. "It must really be getting late."

"Yeah, we should probably head out," says Tyler.

"Come here," says Chelle, holding out her arms. She pulls Jade in for a hug and Tyler wraps his arms around both of them.

"Be careful on your drive," Tyler says.

"Keep us updated, okay?" adds Chelle.

"Of course," says Jade. She rests her head on her two friends. "You know I love you guys."

"Love you too," Tyler and Chelle say in unison. After one last squeeze in the group hug, they separate.

"You sure you don't want a ride home?" asks Tyler.

"No thanks," says Jade. "I appreciate it though. All of it, actually. I don't know what I would do without you guys."

"That's what we're here for," says Chelle, smiling.

"Thank you," says Jade.

Soon enough, Tyler and Chelle head off to where Tyler's car is parked while Jade heads in the opposite direction toward the railway station. She turns around for one last look at her two closest friends before she leaves town in the morning. They walk down the street hand in hand, Chelle's other arm swinging by her side, Tyler laughing at something she said.

Jade smiles to herself, wiping away the tears that threaten to spill from her eyes. She blows them an unseen kiss before turning around and walking away into the night.

# ABOUT THE AUTHOR

Born and raised in St. Louis, MO, Andrew Noles has been a storyteller since before he could even write, dictating stories to his parents when he was just a few years old.

Over the years, he followed this passion for storytelling across various media and industries before launching the Halloween blog *Your Best Halloween Ever* with his partner, Devin, in 2018. Featuring daily posts in the fall with tips, tricks, and treats for your best Halloween ever, the blog is viewable year-round at yourbesthalloweenever.com.

Andrew continues to reside in the suburbs of St. Louis where he is often to be found working on projects of the writing, baking, or crafting variety.

His first novel, *Cityscape*, was released in 2014, with his short story collection *Thirteen Tales for Halloween* following in October 2021.